SLAVES OF LOVE
AND OTHER NORWEGIAN SHORT STORIES

Slaves of Love

and other Norwegian short stories

SELECTED AND EDITED BY
James McFarlane

TRANSLATED BY
James McFarlane and Janet Garton

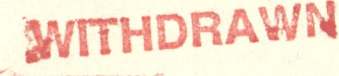

PT
8721
S54
1982

Oxford   New York
OXFORD UNIVERSITY PRESS
1982

Oxford University Press, Walton Street, Oxford OX2 6DP
London Glasgow New York Toronto
Delhi Bombay Calcutta Madras Karachi
Kuala Lumpur Singapore Hong Kong Tokyo
Nairobi Dar es Salaam Cape Town
Melbourne Auckland
and associates in
Beirut Berlin Ibadan Mexico City Nicosia

Copyright in editorial matter and selection
© James McFarlane 1982
English translations
© James McFarlane and Janet Garton 1982
First published 1982

All rights reserved. No part of this publication may be reproduced,
stored in a retrieval system, or transmitted, in any form or by any means,
electronic, mechanical, photocopying, recording, or otherwise, without
the prior permission of Oxford University Press

British Library Cataloguing in Publication Data
Slaves of love and other Norwegian short stories.
1. Short stories, Norwegian – Translations
into English. 2. Short stories, English –
Translations from Norwegian
I. McFarlane, James   II. Garton, Janet
839.8'2301'08   PT8722
ISBN 0-19-212601-6

Library of Congress Cataloging in Publication Data
Main entry under title:
Slaves of love and other Norwegian short stories.
1. Short stories, Norwegian – Translations into
English. 2. Short stories, English – Translations
from Norwegian. I. McFarlane, James Walter.
PT8721.S54   839.8'2301'08   82-2269
ISBN 0-19-212601-6   AACR2

Printed in Great Britain by
The Thetford Press Ltd.
Thetford, Norfolk

Contents

INTRODUCTION ix

BJØRNSTJERNE BJØRNSON (1832–1910)
The Father 1

JONAS LIE (1833–1908)
Isaac and the priest of Brönö 4

AMALIE SKRAM (1846–1905)
Karen's Christmas 9

ALEXANDER KIELLAND (1849–1906)
At the ball 16

ARNE GARBORG (1851–1924)
Dying 22

KNUT HAMSUN (1859–1952)
Slaves of love 30

HANS KINCK (1865–1926)
White anemones 37

SIGBJØRN OBSTFELDER (1866–1900)
The Plain 43

TRYGGVE ANDERSEN (1866–1920)
Gilded revenge   54

RAGNHILD JØLSEN (1875–1908)
Hanna Valmoen   75

OLAV DUUN (1876–1939)
The Chapel   84

KRISTOFER UPPDAL (1878–1961)
By Akerselva   91

JOHAN FALKBERGET (1879–1967)
Approaching death   101

CORA SANDEL (1880–1974)
Cousin Thea   106

OSKAR BRAATEN (1881–1939)
Going home   115

ARTHUR OMRE (1887–1967)
Curried eel   123

ARNULF ØVERLAND (1889–1968)
Missing, presumed dead   131

SIGURD HOEL (1890–1960)
The Murderer   136

TARJEI VESAAS (1897–1970)
It snows and snows   144

AKSEL SANDEMOSE (1899–1965)
The Rat   149

JOHAN BORGEN (1902–79)
In the grass — 157

TORBORG NEDREAAS (1906–)
Red reflections — 163

NILS JOHAN RUD (1908–)
You are no older than you were — 174

TOROLF ELSTER (1911–)
In a small room — 184

AGNAR MYKLE (1915–)
Raisins of degradation — 196

SOLVEIG CHRISTOV (1918–)
The Glory of Mankind — 208

JENS BJØRNEBOE (1920–76)
Life and the youth — 219

KJELL ASKILDSEN (1929–)
Encounter — 226

BJØRG VIK (1935–)
Liv — 236

DAG SOLSTAD (1941–)
At the theatre — 247

BRIEF BIOGRAPHIES — 255

Publisher's Note

The publishers gratefully acknowledge the financial assistance and other help given by Norsk Kulturråd in connection with the publication of this volume.

Introduction

Two co-ordinates help to plot the Norwegian short story in modern times. One axis is represented by those preoccupations of theme and style which are essentially national, by qualities that were (and still are) felt to lend a distinctive Norwegian-ness to the genre. The other is the international axis, the thrust of change and innovation in culture and literature which over the years has become progressively less tied to purely national endeavour: the successive waves of Modernism and its constituent sub-movements, the oscillations of the cosmopolitan modern spirit as it responded to the cultural shocks and spiritual assaults of a world grown rapidly smaller. Together, these co-ordinates provide a framework of reference for collating the rich and varied detail of this literary form in Norway and for making identifiable a pattern of advance within which many varied and disparate talents have made their individual contribution.

Bjørnstjerne Bjørnson, whose story 'The Father' appropriately – many would even say 'inevitably' – stands first in this anthology, was in no doubt himself where on this graph the real starting point was to be found. When, near the end of his life, he looked back over his own career and on the almost incredible achievements within Norwegian literature during the second half of the nineteenth century, he saw one supreme source of inspiration: 'We came to understand', he said of the 1850s and 1860s, 'that the language of the sagas lived on in our peasants, and that this peasant life was close to that of the sagas. The life of the people was to be built upon our history, and the peasants were to provide the foundation.'

These were years that were witnessing a powerful and still growing national consciousness, something which had been gathering strength ever since the age of Napoleon: a conviction that the destiny of modern Norway – 'a new country but an ancient kingdom', people assured themselves – was intimately yet subtly related to its great and heroic past, and that its culture and its standing in the community of nations had an inherent distinctiveness which it was the duty of all to foster. The key figure in this national self-awareness, the custodian of those traditional values – spiritual, moral, existential – was then the Norwegian peasant, the *bonde*. He was seen as the living embodiment of an exemplary way of life upon which a glorious future could be built. It was from a faith of this kind that Bjørnson's 'peasant tales' of the late 1850s and early 1860s sprang. The emphasis in them on what the nationally romantic mind of the day considered to be characteristically Viking virtues – powerful but undemonstrative feeling, strength of will and purpose, loyalty to kinsman and friend, ruthlessness in a just cause – together with the attempt to echo something of the laconic but doom-laden directness of saga language was wholly deliberate.

Clearly, then, it was not mere chance that led Bjørnson at this time to adopt the short story as one of the main vehicles for his cultural campaign; in its economy of form he found an excellent match for the terseness of his didactic intent. He was of course by no means the only writer in Europe in this age writing within the tradition of the 'village story': inside Scandinavia itself, two or three decades earlier, there had been the earthily regional tales of Steen Steensen Blicher, firmly rooted in his native Jutland; Bertold Auerbach had given a picture of Black Forest peasant life in his *Dorfgeschichten*; and Jeremias Gotthelf had had didactic designs (not wholly dissimilar from Bjørnson's) in writing his Novellen of Swiss peasant life. Within Scandinavia, and doubtless contributing significantly to the build-up of factors within which Bjørnson fashioned his narrative style, there were also two other different but complementary literary influences: the collections of Norwegian folktales by Asbjørnsen and Moe which reconstructed with startling liveliness of expression and freshness of vision tales which had lived on only in oral tradition; and the often seemingly ingenuous but essentially highly sophisticated tales of Denmark's Hans Andersen, the significance of which for the art of the short story in modern times has been uniquely great.

It was from such conditions of life and literature that Bjørnson set himself the task of creating the new genre. In their more immediate objective, these tales were in large measure successful; by the sheer popularity of their appeal they undoubtedly made a considerable social impact, affecting the lives and attitudes of the people in a very real way. More relevant to our present purposes, however, is also the fact that time can be seen to have augmented rather than diminished their specifically literary significance: they take their rightful place at the start of a distinguished tradition of short-story writing of impressive variety and quality, and have continued to exert an enduring influence on the genre right down to the present age.

Alongside the intrinsic appeal of the individual stories in this anthology, there is therefore the additional fascination of being able to follow the tradition of the Norwegian short story as a genre over a hundred and more years of organic development, of observing how the two main constituent elements – the national and the international – respond and react to each other, combining and compounding and fusing to produce a body of literature which has its own inner coherence, a shared national identity of distinctive quality, which yet gives impressive evidence of wide variety.

Sometimes an individual work will reveal its Norwegian antecedents boldly and directly: as does, for example, Jonas Lie's folktale-inspired story, 'Isaac and the priest of Brönö', conceived unambiguously in the tradition of the *folkeeventyr* and given a highly localized and recognizable Norwegian setting, which also exults in introducing those mysteriously irrational forces which, in the folktale tradition, fill the lives of those who wrest a living from the sea. Against this can then be set those other stories, still overwhelmingly Norwegian in atmosphere, in which above all it is the sense of locality which is most powerfully at work, as in the stories of Johan Falkberget, Olav Duun, Hans Kinck and others. In their case, however, it is not simply a defined topography of setting – the looming presence of mountain and sea, the menace and delight of sun and seemingly endless snow, the trials of wind and weather, the sights and sounds and smells of landing stage and summer pasture – which proclaim them as unmistakably Norwegian. The merely outward signals of geography and occupation are of only secondary significance here. Rather it is something to do with the deeper response to these externalities, a shared intuitive sense engendered by long centuries of exposure to them, a collective familiarity with the way these things are able to invade and impose themselves on the fabric of life as it is lived at these latitudes, a strong dark knowledge of the joys and fears inseparable from them.

At the other end of the scale are those pieces in which an internationalism of both content and style seem wholly to predominate, particularly since the Norwegian-ness of the language and its idioms has been filtered out through translation. The story by which Alexander Kielland is here represented is not only Parisian in setting, but also strives for an elegance of style which its author would himself have been delighted to hear called French. Knut Hamsun suggests an equally cosmopolitan setting (Munich?), and emphasizes the *allgemein menschlich* nature of its insights rather than anything particularly Norwegian. Sigbjørn Obstfelder gave his allegiance perhaps more to a period than to a country, and proclaimed with every hushed and self-consciously vibrant sentence his affinity with the ideals of the European nineties. And as we approach nearer the present day, it is evident even from this present limited selection that the impact of the American short story – tough, taut, urgent – became ever more potently felt.

Finally, in the middle ground between the explicitly national and the assertively international, many other preoccupations obtrude: the moral courage of Arne Garborg in the face of the social and religious conflicts of his day; the disciplined honesty of Tryggve Andersen in anything to do with the art of the writer; the sensitive exploration of female psychology in the work of Cora Sandel, Torborg Nedreaas, and Bjørg Vik; the social commitment of Amalie Skram, Arnulf Øverland, Sigurd Hoel, and latterly Dag Solstad; the deft yet unrelenting examination of the dimensions of modern terror by Tarjei Vesaas; the pursuit of the problem of identity in Johan Borgen; and Jens Bjørneboe's sustained and anguished assault on the problem of evil.

No ponderous theory of the short story underlies the choice of items in this anthology. The intention was simple: to try to bring together a reasonably representative selection of the country's shorter fiction written since the middle of the last century, allowing no author more than one piece. The Contents pages reveal at once that a number of Norway's most distinguished writers during this period are not represented at all: notably Henrik Ibsen (who wrote no fiction) and Sigrid Undset (who, though a major fiction writer, was never very impressive in the shorter form). Some of those who do figure are better known in another field: Hamsun in the novel, for instance; and Obstfelder in the lyric. Pressure of space has led in one or two cases to an author being represented by a piece shorter than one would ideally have chosen, if quality had been the only criterion. As one moved nearer the present day, the choice inevitably became more difficult; and here again, many who would otherwise have qualified on grounds of quality had perforce to be excluded for reasons of space. In the end, just about a quarter of those represented in these pages are living authors. They provide an eloquent index – though, alas, in their restricted numbers, not exactly a fully documented case – for the continuing vitality of the art form in Norway today.

J. W. McF.

BJØRNSTJERNE BJØRNSON

The Father

The most powerful man in the parish, of whom this story tells, was called Thord Överaas. One day he stood in the priest's study, tall and serious.
'I have got a son,' he said. 'And I want him baptized.'
'What is he to be called?'
'Finn, after my father.'
'And the godparents?'
Their names were named; they were the best men and women of the village belonging to the man's family.
'Is there anything else?' asked the priest. He looked up.
The peasant stood for a while. 'I would like to have him baptized on his own,' he said.
'That means on a weekday?'
'On Saturday next, 12 noon.'
'Is there anything else?' asked the priest.
'There is nothing else.' The peasant twisted his cap as though about to go.
Then the priest rose. 'Just this,' he said and went over to Thord, took his hand and looked him straight in the eyes. 'May God grant that the child will be a blessing to you!'
Sixteen years after that day Thord stood in the room of the priest.
'You are looking well, Thord,' said the priest. He saw no change in him.
'I have no worries,' answered Thord.
To this the priest was silent; but a moment later he asked: 'What is your errand this evening?'
'I come this evening about my son who is to be confirmed tomorrow.'
'He is a clever lad.'
'I did not want to pay the priest until I'd heard what place he had been given in the ceremony.'
'He is in first place.'

'I am glad to hear it – and here is ten daler for the priest.'
'Is there anything else?' asked the priest. He looked at Thord.
'There is nothing else.' Thord left.

A further eight years passed, and then a commotion was heard outside the priest's study. For many men had come, with Thord at the head. The priest looked up and recognized him.

'You come with many men this evening.'

'I want to ask for the banns to be called for my son. He is to marry Karen Storliden, daughter of Gudmund, who is standing here.'

'She is the richest girl in the parish.'

'What you say is right,' answered the peasant. He brushed his hair back with one hand. The priest sat a while as though in thought. He said nothing, but entered the names in his books, and the men signed. Thord place three daler on the table.

'I only want one,' said the priest.

'I know. But he is my only child. I wanted to do well by him.'

The priest accepted the money. 'This is the third time you stand here on your son's behalf, Thord.'

'But this marks the finish,' said Thord. He folded his pocket-book, said farewell and left. The men followed slowly.

Fourteen days after that day, father and son were rowing across the water in calm weather to Storliden to discuss the wedding.

'This boat seat is not very secure under me,' the son said, and he stood up to put it right. That same moment the floorboard he was standing on gave way; he threw up his arms, uttered a cry and fell into the water.

'Catch hold of the oar!' shouted the father. He stood up and held it out. But after the son had swum a few strokes, he got cramp.

'Wait!' cried the father, and began rowing. But then the son rolled over on his back, looked long at his father, and sank.

Thord could not rightly believe it. He held the boat steady and stared at the spot where his son had gone down, as though he might come up again. A few bubbles rose, then more, then one single big one which burst – then the lake lay once again as smooth as a mirror.

For three days and three nights people watched the father row round that spot without food and without sleep. He was dragging for his son. And on the morning of the third day he found him; and he went and carried him up the hill to his homestead.

A year or so might have passed following that day. Then late one autumn evening the priest heard a rattling at the door in the entrance, a cautious fumbling at the latch. The priest opened the door and in stepped a tall bent man, lean and white of hair. The priest looked long at him before he recognized him. It was Thord.

'You come late,' said the priest and stood quietly before him.

'Ah, yes! I come late,' said Thord. He sat down. The priest also sat down, as though waiting. There was a long silence.

Then Thord said: 'I have something here I would like to give to the poor.' He rose, placed money on the table, and sat down again. The priest counted it.

'This is a lot of money,' he said.

'It is half of my farm. I sold it today.'

The priest remained sitting a long time in silence. At length he asked gently: 'What will you do now?'

'Some better thing.'

They sat there a while, Thord with his eyes on the floor, the priest with his eyes on him. Then the priest said, slowly and quietly: 'Now I think your son has finally been a blessing to you.'

'Yes, now I think so too,' said Thord. He looked up, and two tears ran sadly down his face.

[Original title: *Fadren*. Translated by James McFarlane]

JONAS LIE

Isaac and the priest of Brönö

In Helgeland there was once a fisherman called Isaac.
One day when he was out fishing for halibut he felt something heavy on the hook. He hauled in his line, and there was a sea-boot.
'That's strange,' he said.
He sat for a long time looking at it. It looked as though it might well have been his brother's who had gone down in the great storm last winter as he was on his way home from fishing. There seemed to be something still inside the boot, but he didn't dare look. And he didn't really know what to do with the sea-boot either. He didn't want to take it home with him and frighten his mother, nor did he feel like throwing it back in the sea again. Then it occurred to him that he might look in on the priest at Brönö and ask him to bury it in Christian fashion.
'Can't bury a sea-boot,' said the priest.
'Suppose not,' said the man.
But then he wanted to know how much of a person there had to be before it could enjoy Christian burial.
'I can't really answer that,' said the priest. 'A tooth or a finger or a lock of hair won't do. There has to be at least enough left for one to feel that the soul has been present there. And there can be no question of using holy scripture over some toe in a sea-boot.'
But Isaac managed on the sly to get it buried in the churchyard all the same. Then he went home. He felt he'd done the best he could. It was better that something of his brother should lie close to God's house than that he should have flung the boot back again into the black sea.
But then, later in the autumn as he lay off the skerries hunting seals, when the current carried along tangled masses of seaweed, it so happened that he brought up on his oar a knife-belt and an empty sheath. He recognized them at once as his brother's. The tarred thonging had come undone and was bleached by the sea. And he well

remembered how, as his brother had sat cobbling away at this sheath, he had talked with him about the leather for the belt which he had taken from the old horse they had slaughtered. Together they had bought the buckle over at the store that Saturday when Mother sold the cloudberries and the wood-grouse and those three pounds of wool. They had got a little drunk and had had fun with the old crone over on the headland who used a bast-mat for a sail. He took the belt and said nothing about it. There was no point in causing sorrow unnecessarily, he thought.

But the longer winter dragged on, the more he found himself wondering about what the priest had said. And he didn't know what he ought to do if he came across another boot, or something else that a squid or a fish or a crab had been at work on, or a Greenland shark had bitten off. He grew quite terrified of rowing the stretch of sea out by the skerries. And yet it was as if he was constantly drawn there by the thought that he might come across some remains substantial enough to convince the priest that the soul had been in them, and that he should give them Christian burial.

The thought weighed heavily upon him as he went about his work. And in addition he began to have bad dreams. The door burst open in the middle of the night with a blast of cold sea-air, and it seemed to him as if his brother went stumping about the room shouting that he had to have his foot back – the banshees were driving and working him so hard. He stood long hours over his work without doing a hand's turn, staring at some unseen wall. Finally, he felt he must be going completely out of his mind because of the great responsibility he had taken upon himself of burying the foot in the churchyard. He didn't want to throw it back in the sea again, but neither could it lie where it was. It was clearly borne in on him that his brother could not achieve salvation; and he began thinking of all the things that might be lying and drifting and tossing out there among the skerries.

So he took to dredging there, and lay out by the sea's edge with ropes and dragging tackle. But all he brought up was seaweed and seawrack and starfish and other unedifying things.

One evening as he sat out there by the skerries trying his luck at fishing, he cast out his line with its weight and all its hooks on it and the last of the hooks caught in one of his eyes. And down to the bottom went the eye. There was no point in searching for it; he rowed home without it.

That night, kept awake by the pain, he lay with a bandage over his eye, thinking, thinking till everything seemed utterly black. Surely nobody in the world could be in such a bad way as he. Suddenly everything went very strange. He seemed to be looking about him in the depths of the sea as the fishes went flitting and darting round the fishing line in the darkness among the seaweed. They bit at the bait, and twisted and tried to work themselves free – first a cod, then a ling, then a coalfish. Then came a haddock which quietly mouthed the water as though pondering before swallowing. And he saw what he couldn't take his eyes off: the back of a man, as it might be, in leather clothes with one sleeve caught under a boat's grappling hook. Then came a huge white halibut and swallowed the hook, and then it became pitch dark.

A voice said: 'You must throw the big halibut back again when you catch it tomorrow. The hook tears my mouth so. It's no use searching except in the evening when the tide in the sound is on the turn.'

Next day he went and took a piece of gravestone from the churchyard to weight his line; and in the evening, when the tide was on the turn, he lay out in the sound again to dredge. Immediately he hauled up a boat's grappling hook, the prongs of which had hooked in a leather jerkin with the remains of an arm in it. The fishes had been at work on it as far as they could get inside the jacket.

He rowed off to the priest.

'You're asking me to read the service over an old waterlogged leather jacket?' said the priest of Brönö.

'I'll throw in the sea-boot as well,' Isaac replied.

'Lost property and salvaged goods should be announced on the church notice-board,' thundered the priest.

Then Isaac looked the priest straight in the eyes. 'The sea-boot has been a heavy enough burden, without my having to cope with the leather jacket as well,' he said.

'I don't just throw the church's consecrated earth to the winds,' said the priest. He was getting angry.

'Suppose not,' said Isaac.

And with that he had to go home. But Isaac found neither peace nor rest. Such a great weight lay upon him. At nights he again saw the great white halibut. It swam sadly and slowly round and round in the same circle in the depths of the sea. It was as if some invisible net surrounded it, and all the time it was trying to slip through the mesh.

He lay there, looking, looking, till his blind eye caused him pain.

No sooner was he out dredging again and had paid out the rope than some great ugly squid would come along and and squirt the sea all black. But one evening he let the boat drift as the current took it, beyond the skerries but within the islands. Finally it came to rest at one spot as though anchored; and it grew strangely quiet, not a bird in the air, no life in the sea. All at once a big bubble rose up close by the rowlock, and he heard a deep, heavy sigh as it burst.

But Isaac saw what he saw. 'And now it's the priest at Brönö who will see to the funeral,' he said. Ever since that day, the word got about that he had second sight, and saw many things around him which were hidden from others. He could say where the fish were to be found out at sea on the fishing banks, and where they were not. And when they questioned him, he would say: 'If I don't know, my brother does.'

Then one day it happened that the priest of Brönö was called out to a place along the coast, and Isaac was one of those helping to row the boat. They set off with a brisk favourable wind. The priest arrived safely and quickly finished his business, for he had to hold church service the following day.

'The fjord looks a bit rough to me, and it's getting on towards evening,' he said. 'But since we got here all right, I suppose we can get back again.'

They hadn't got very far on their way home before a storm blew up, and all they could do was take four reefs in the sail. And away they went, with the spray and the blizzard swirling about their ears, and the waves as big as houses. The priest of Brönö had never been out in such weather before. They sailed into the storm, they ran before the storm. It became black night. The sea shone like a glacier, and the gusts increased rather than diminished in force. Isaac had just taken in the fifth reef when one of the planks amidships stove in and the sea came pouring in, and the priest and the crew jumped up on the gunwale shouting that the boat was sinking.

'I don't think there's anything to worry about,' said Isaac; he remained sitting where he was by the helm.

But, as the moon shone fitfully through the hail shower, they saw a strange boatman standing in the scuppers bailing the water out of the boat as fast as it poured in.

'I didn't know I'd hired that man for the trip,' said the priest. 'He looks to me to be bailing with a sea-boot. Nor does he seem to have either trousers or skin on his legs, and up above there's only an empty, flapping leather jacket.'

'I rather think the priest has seen him before,' said Isaac.

Then the priest became angry. 'By the authority of my holy office,' he said, 'I call upon him to remove himself from amidships.'

'Ah yes,' said Isaac, 'but can the priest also plug where the plank has sprung a leak?'

Whereupon the priest, remembering the danger, thought again.

'The man looks mortal strong to me, and we have great need of him,' he said. 'Nor is it any sin to help one of God's servants over the sea. But I want to know what he asks for his hire,' he shouted.

The surf foamed, and the wind whistled about him.

'Only three shovelfuls of earth on a rotten sea-boot and a mouldy leather jacket,' said Isaac.

'If you're able to come back and haunt people, you're also capable of entering into blessedness,' shouted the priest. 'You shall have your sprinkling of earth.'

And the moment he said this, the water within the skerries at once became smooth, and the priest's boat ran high and dry on to the sandy beach, snapping its mast.

[Original title: *Isak og Brønøpræsten*. Translated by James McFarlane]

AMALIE SKRAM

Karen's Christmas

On one of the steamship quays in Christiania some years ago there used to stand a grey-painted wooden hut with a flat roof and no chimney, about two and a half metres in length and a little less in breadth. In both end walls there was a little window, the one exactly opposite the other. The door was on the seaward side and could be fastened both from the inside and from the outside with iron hooks, which fitted into slots of the same metal.

The hut was originally built for the ferrymen, so that they could have a roof over their heads in rainy weather or in the winter cold while they were sitting around waiting for someone to come and ask for a boat. Later on, as the small steamers absorbed more and more of the traffic, the ferrymen departed for elsewhere. After that the hut was only used occasionally by people who found it convenient. The last people to use it had been some stoneworkers, who had eaten their meals there two at a time while they were repairing part of the quay in the vicinity one summer.

Since then no one had paid any attention to the little old shack. It remained standing where it was, since it did not occur to the port authorities to have it removed and since no one filed any complaints about it being in the way of anyone or anything.

Then came a winter's night in December, just before Christmas. There was a little snow in the air, but it melted as it fell and made the sticky slush on the cobblestones of the quay progressively wetter and thicker. On the gaslights and the steamships' cranes the snow lay like a greyish-white, finely fringed cover, and if you went down close to the ships you could make out through the darkness that it was hanging from the rigging like garlands between the masts. In the dark grey, misty air, the flames of gas in the lights took on a dirty yellowy-orange hue, while the ships' lanterns gleamed with a cloudy red glow. Every now and then the clanging noise of the ships' bells pierced the damp atmosphere with a strident harshness, when the bells for the change of watch on board were rung.

The police constable who was patrolling the quay stopped by the gaslight outside the former ferrymen's hut. He pulled out his watch in order to see what time of night it was, but as he held it up towards the light he heard something which sounded like a child crying. He lowered his hand, looked around and listened. No, there was nothing. Up with the watch again. There was the sound again, this time mingled with the sound of gentle hushing. Again he lowered his hand, and again all was quiet. What tomfoolery was this, in the devil's name? He had a look round near where he was but could not find anything. For the third time he raised his watch to the light of the gas lamp, and this time he was left in peace to observe that the time was nearly four o'clock.

He walked slowly along past the hut, wondered a little, but decided in the end that it must have been his imagination, or something like that.

A little later, as he was coming back the same way and drawing near to the hut, he glanced at it. What was that? Couldn't he see something moving in there? The gas lights on both sides threw their light in through the windows, so that it looked as if it was lit up inside.

He went over and looked in. Quite right. There was a figure sitting on the bench just under the window, a little hunched-up form, which was leaning forward, busy with something he could not see. A step round the corner and he was at the door, trying to get in. It was fastened.

'Open up!' he shouted, and knocked with his knuckles.

He heard someone jump up with a start, and a sound like a stifled, frightened exclamation, and then all was quite still.

He knocked again with his clenched fist and repeated: 'Open up, in there! Open up at once!'

'What is it? Oh dear, there's no one here,' said a fearful voice from just beside the door.

'Open up. It's the police!'

'Oh lord, the police! – Oh please, sir, it's only me, I'm not doing anything, just sitting here, honestly.'

'Just get this door open and quick about it, or there'll be trouble. Will you . . .'

He did not get any further, for at that moment the door opened, and the next moment he made his way stooping through the doorway into the low-roofed room, where he could just stand upright.

'Are you mad? Not open the door for the police! What are you thinking of?'

'I'm sorry, Mr Policeman – I did open the door for you, didn't I?'

'That was just as well,' he muttered. 'What sort of girl are you, and who said that you could take up lodgings here?'

'It's just me, Karen,' she whispered. 'I'm sitting here with my baby.' The police constable looked more closely at the speaker. She was a skinny little girl with a thin, pale face and a deep, scrofular scar down one cheek, straight up and down like a lath, and she was obviously hardly fully grown. She was wearing a light brown top, a sort of jacket or jerkin which – you could tell by the cut – had seen better days, and a darker coloured skirt, which hung down in shreds at the front and reached to her ankles. Her feet were pushed into a pair of army boots with holes in and without any laces in the front openings.

In one arm she had a bundle of rags which she held across the front of her body. Out of the top end of the bundle protruded something white. It was the head of a baby which was suckling her thin breast. Around her head she had a tattered piece of scarf, which was knotted under her chin, and wisps of hair stuck out of it round the back of her neck. She was shaking with cold from top to toe, and when she moved her boots made a squelchy, squeaky noise, as if she were treading in some mushy substance. 'I didn't think anyone would mind,' she went on in a whining voice, 'it's just standing here, this shed.'

The policeman was aware of an oppressive feeling. For the first few moments he had thought of driving her out with a few well-chosen words and letting her off with a warning. But when he saw the wretched child standing there holding the little brat in her arms and cowering back against the bench, not daring to sit down for fear and meekness, he felt suddenly moved.

'But in Christ's name – what are you doing here, my lass?'

She registered the milder tone of his voice. Her fear receded a little, and she began to cry. The constable pushed the door to and shut it.

'Sit down a bit,' he said. 'It must be heavy, standing holding that child.' She slid down quietly on to the bench.

'Now then,' said the policeman encouragingly, and sat down on the bench opposite.

'Oh God, Mr Policeman, let me stay here,' she lisped through her tears. 'I shan't be any trouble, not the least little bit – I'll keep the place clean – you can see for yourself – there's no mess here – that over there, that's crusts.' She pointed to a bundle of rags down on the floor. 'I go round and beg in the daytime. There's a drop of water in the bottle. Let me stay here at nights, just till I get my place back – just till the missus comes –' She stopped and blew her nose in her fingers, which she wiped on her skirt.

'The missus, who's she then?' asked the constable.

'It was her I was in service with. I had such a good post with four kroner a month and breakfast, but then I got into trouble, so I had to leave, of course. Mrs Olsen went herself and got me a place at the hostel, she's nice to me she is, Mrs Olsen, and I kept my place right up to when I went to the hostel for lying-in, 'cos she's on her own, Mrs Olsen, and she said she'd keep me right till I couldn't do any more. But then it happened that Mrs Olsen had to go away, 'cos she's a midwife, is Mrs Olsen, and then she got sick out there in the country and stayed there, and now they say she'll not be back till Christmas.'

'But for heaven's sake, fancy wandering round humping that kid with you while you're waiting for your missus. What on earth are you doing that for?' The constable shook his head.

'I've nowhere to go,' she whimpered. 'Since my dad died, there's no one to stand up for me when my stepmother throws me out.'

'But what about the child's father?'

'Oh, him,' she said and gave a little toss of her head. 'It's no good trying to get anything out of him.'

'But you know you can go to court and make him pay for the child.'

'Yes, that's what people say,' she replied. 'But how can I do that, when I can't get hold of him?'

'Just you tell me his name,' returned the policeman, '– we'll soon track him down.'

'I would if I could,' she said quietly.

'What! Don't you know the name of your own child's father?'

Karen put her finger into her mouth and sucked it. Her head tipped forward. Her face took on a helpless, half-witted grin. 'No – o – o,' she whispered, with long-drawn-out emphasis and without removing her finger.

'Well, I've never heard anything like it in all my born days,' exclaimed the constable. 'In heaven's name, how did you get together with him, then?'

'I met him in the evenings in the street, when it was dark,' she said, 'but it didn't last long before he disappeared, and since then I've never seen him.'

'Haven't you asked around?'

'Oh yes, I did that all right, but no one knows what's happened to him. I should think he's taken a job on a farm, he must have had something to do with horses or cows, I could tell by the smell of him.'

'This is a fine mess, and no mistake,' muttered the constable. 'You'd better go and report to the Poor Office,' he said out loud, 'so we can get all this sorted out.'

'No, I won't,' she answered, suddenly stubborn.

'It'd be better to go to the Poor House and get food and shelter, rather than what you're doing now,' said the constable.

'Yes, but as soon as Mrs Olsen comes – she's so kind, Mrs Olsen – she'll take me on as a daily, I know she will, 'cos she promised – and I know a woman who'll give us a room for three kroner a month. She'll look after the baby while I'm at Mrs Olsen's, and then I'll do her work when I come back from the missus. It'll be all right, just as soon as Mrs Olsen comes, and she's coming at Christmas, they say.'

'Well, my girl, you're grown up so you can suit yourself, but you've no right to stay here.'

'If I just sit here at night – what harm is there in that? Oh, dear God, please let me, I'll not let the baby cry. Just till the missus comes – please, Mr Policeman, just till the missus comes.'

'But you're freezing to death, you and the baby.' He looked at her pitiful clothes.

'But it's better here than out in the street, anyway. Oh, Mr Policeman – just till the missus comes.'

'I ought really to take you down to the station, you know,' said the constable, scratching behind his ear as he thought it over.

She jumped up and came over to him. 'Don't do that, don't do that,' she moaned, as she caught hold of his sleeve with her frozen fingers. 'I beg of you – in God's name – just till the missus comes.'

The constable thought it over. Three days to Christmas, he reckoned.

'Well, all right then,' he said out loud, as he got up. 'You can stay here till Christmas, but not a day longer. And mind – no one must know.'

'Oh, God bless you, God bless you, and thank you,' she burst out.

'But make sure you're out of here by six o'clock sharp in the morning, that's when people start moving about,' he added, as he was half-way out of the door.

The next night, when he passed the hut, he stopped and looked in. She was sitting sideways, leaning back against the window frame. Her profile, with the scarf knotted round her head, could be faintly seen against the window-pane. The child was at her breast, suckling. She did not move, and seemed to be sleeping.

The next morning a frost set in. During the course of the day the thermometer dropped to twelve degrees below zero. It was bitterly cold, the air clear and still. The windows of the little ferrymen's hut were covered with a thick layer of white frost, which made it impossible to see through the glass.

On Christmas Eve the weather changed again. It thawed and dripped everywhere. You almost needed an umbrella, even though it was not raining.

Down on the quay the windows of all the warehouses had become clear of ice again, and the slush on the ground had grown worse than ever.

In the afternoon, around two o'clock, the policeman came that way. He had been off work the last two nights with a feverish cold, for which he had had a doctor's certificate. Now he was on his way over to see a man on one of the steamers.

His way led past the hut. Although it was already growing dusk, he saw, quite a few paces before he reached it, something which made him stop short with a strangely uneasy feeling. She was sitting there in exactly the same position as she had done on that night two days ago. The same piece of profile showed through the window. He did not really think about what it meant, just felt a sensation of dread at this petrified sameness. He shuddered involuntarily. Could something have happened?

He reached the door quickly; it was fastened. So he broke a window-pane, found an iron bar and reached in through the opening with it until he managed to lift the hook from the slot. Then he went in, quietly and cautiously.

They were stone dead, the pair of them. The baby was lying close up against its mother, and even in death it still held her breast in its mouth. From the nipple a few drops of blood had run down over its cheek and dried on its chin. She was horribly emaciated, but her face looked almost as if she were smiling quietly.

'Poor lass, what a Christmas she had,' muttered the constable, as he wiped his eyes. 'But perhaps it's the best thing for both of them. Our Lord must have had his reasons for it.'

He went out again, pulled the door to and fastened the hook. Then he hurried off down to the station to report the incident.

The first working day after the Christmas holidays the port authorities saw to it that the old ferrymen's hut was pulled down and carted away. It couldn't be left standing there providing a shelter for all kinds of vagabonds.

[Original title: *Karens jul*. Translated by Janet Garton]

ALEXANDER KIELLAND

At the ball

She had climbed the smooth marble staircase without disaster, without effort, sustained only by her great beauty and her good nature. She had taken her place in the halls of the rich and the powerful without having had to pay for her entry with her honour or her reputation. And yet there was nobody who could say whence she had come; but it was whispered that it was from the lower depths.

She had grown up as an orphan child in one of the outlying districts of Paris, living and starving among vice and poverty – a life such as only those who know it from experience have any conception of. The rest of us who have our knowledge only from books and other accounts must seek help from the imagination if we are to form any idea of the heritage of misery to be found in a big city – and even then perhaps the most terrifying images we paint for ourselves are pale when compared with reality.

Clearly it was only a matter of time before vice could be expected to seize hold of her – as a cog-wheel seizes somebody who ventures too close to a machine – and then, after whirling her round in a brief life of shame and degradation, to deposit her with the pitiless precision of a machine in some corner where, unrecognized and unrecognizable, she would end that travesty of a human life.

It was then, as sometimes happens, she was 'discovered', at the age of fourteen, by a rich and high-placed gentleman as she ran across one of the city's better streets. She was on her way to a dingy back-room in the Rue des quatre vents where she worked for a woman who specialized in providing flowers for dances.

It was not merely her extraordinary beauty that captivated the rich man, but also her movements, her whole being, the expression in her still immature features – all seemed to indicate that here a conflict was being fought out between an originally good character and an incipient shamelessness. And as he could afford the unpredictable whims that go with extreme wealth, he decided to make an attempt to rescue the poor child.

It was not difficult to take her into his possession since she belonged to nobody. She was given a name and installed in one of the best convent schools; and her benefactor observed with pleasure how all the emergent signs of evil died away and disappeared. She developed an agreeable if somewhat indolent character, a serene and blameless nature, and a rare beauty.

When she grew up, he married her. They enjoyed a very good and peaceful married life. Despite the great disparity in age, he had boundless confidence in her, and this she merited.

Married people do not live at such close quarters in France as they do with us; their demands are therefore not so great and their disappointments less.

She was not happy, but she was content. Her character was attuned to gratitude. She was not bored by wealth. Just the reverse: it sometimes gave her a quite childish pleasure. But nobody suspected it; for her demeanour was always one of confidence and dignity. It was only that people sensed that there was something not quite proper about her origins. But since nobody answered their questions, they stopped asking. There were so many other things to think about in Paris.

She had forgotten her past. She had forgotten it in the same way as we forget the roses, the silken ribbons and the faded letters of our youth because we never call them to mind. They lie locked in some drawer which we never open. And yet if we should some time happen to cast a glance in that secret drawer, we would notice at once if but even one of those roses or even the smallest of ribbons were missing. For we remember it all down to the last detail. The memories lie there just as fresh – just as sweet and just as bitter.

This was the way she had forgotten her past: locked it up and thrown away the key.

But occasionally at night she dreamt terrible things. She felt anew how the old harridan with whom she had lived had shaken her by the shoulder and sent her off on freezing mornings to the woman who did the flowers.

Then she would sit up in bed with a start and stare into the blackness in deathly fear. But then she would feel the silken coverlet and the soft pillows; her fingers would touch the rich embellishments on the magnificent bed; and as little sleepy cherubims slowly drew aside the heavy curtains of dream, she enjoyed in full measure that strange and inexpressible sense of well-being that we feel when we discover that a nasty nightmare was indeed only a dream.

Leaning back in the soft cushions, she drove to the great ball given by the Russian ambassador. The closer one came to one's destination, the slower became the pace; until the carriage reached the final queue where progress was only step by step.

On the square facing the hotel, richly illuminated with torches and gas flames, a large crowd of people had gathered. There were a few strollers who had paused to stare; but for the most part they were labourers, unemployed workers, destitute women and ladies of uncertain character, standing packed together on either side of the row of carriages. Wisecracks and indelicate jokes in the crudest of Parisian speech rained down over the fine gentlefolk.

She heard words she hadn't heard for years, and she blushed at the thought that she was possibly the only one in that long line of carriages who understood these coarse expressions from the dregs of Paris society.

She began to look at the faces around her. It seemed to her she knew them all. She knew what they were thinking, knew what was going on in these heads all so closely packed together; and little by little a swarm of memories came crowding in on her. She resisted as best she could, but she wasn't quite herself that evening.

So she had not lost the key to that secret drawer. Reluctantly she brought it out, and memories overwhelmed her.

She remembered how often – while she was still very much a child – her envious eyes had devoured the smart ladies driving in their finery to the ball or to the theatre; how often she had wept in bitter envy over the flowers she carefully put together for the adornment of others. Here she saw the same greedy eyes, the same unquenchable, hate-filled envy.

And the dark serious men who with half-contemptuous, half-menacing glances eyed the equipages – she knew them all.

Had she not herself as a little girl lain in the corner listening wide-eyed to their talk of life's injustices, of the tyranny of the rich, of the rights of the worker which he needed only to stretch out his hands to take?

She knew that they hated everything – from the well-fed horses and the aloof coachmen to the polished, gleaming coaches. But most of all they hated those who sat in them – these insatiable vampires, these ladies whose jewels and ornaments cost more gold than a whole life's work would bring to any one of them.

And as she contemplated the line of carriages which slowly made its way through the crowd another memory obtruded, a half-forgotten image from her schooldays in the convent.

She was suddenly moved to think of the story of Pharaoh who with his chariots set out to pursue the Jews across the Red Sea. She saw the waves, which she had always imagined as having been as red as blood, standing like a wall on both sides of the Egyptians.

Then Moses raised up his voice; he held out his rod over the waters and the waves of the Red Sea closed and swallowed up Pharaoh and all his chariots.

She knew that the wall that stood on both sides of her was wilder and more savage than the waves of the sea. She knew that it only needed a voice, a Moses, to set in motion that sea of people, to bring it rushing and crashing, inundating the whole glory of that wealth and power beneath its blood-red waves.

Her heart beat violently and, trembling, she drew back into the corner of the carriage. But it was not from fear; it was so that those outside should not see her. For she felt shame in front of them.

For the first time in her life, her good fortune appeared to her to be an injustice, something she felt ashamed of.

Was her place here in this luxurious elegant carriage, among these tyrants and bloodsuckers? Did she not rather belong outside there in the surging mass, among the children of hate?

Half-forgotten thoughts and feelings raised their heads like beasts of prey long confined. She felt a stranger, homeless in this brilliant life of hers; and with a kind of demonic longing she recalled the terrible places whence she had come.

She gripped her expensive lace shawl. There came over her a wild desire to destroy, to rend. Then the carriage turned into the entrance of the hotel.

The servant held open the door; and with her gracious smile and her aristocratic composure she slowly stepped down.

An elegant young man, looking as if he might be an attaché, rushed over to her and was delighted when she took his arm, even more enraptured when he sensed that he detected an unusual warmth in her glance, and in the seventh heaven when he felt her arm trembling.

Full of pride and hope, he led her with exquisite elegance up the smooth marble staircase.

'Tell me, dear lady! What friendly fairy was it who bestowed on you in your cradle this marvellous gift of achieving distinction in everything you do, and in all things that relate to you? Even such a little thing as the flower in your hair has its own special charm, as though it had been moistened by the fresh dew of the morning! And when you dance, the very floor seems to vibrate in obedience to your step.'

The Count was himself quite astonished at this long and successful compliment; for normally he did not find it easy to express himself coherently. And he waited for the lovely lady to express her appreciation.

But he was disappointed. She leant out over the balcony where people were enjoying the cool air of the evening after the dancing; and she stared out over the crowd and over the carriages which were still arriving. She seemed to have caught nothing at all of the Count's fine phrases. Instead he heard her whisper the inexplicable word: Pharaoh.

He was about to protest when she turned round; and, taking a step in the direction of the ballroom, stopped squarely in front of him and regarded him with large, strange eyes – eyes which the Count had never seen before.

'I doubt if there was any friendly fairy there. There wasn't even much of a cradle there when I was born, my dear Count! But what you say about my flowers and my dancing indicates a quickness of perception which has led you to make a great discovery. I shall tell you the secret of the fresh morning dew that moistens the flowers! It is tears, my dear Count! Tears which envy and shame, disappointment and remorse have shed over them. And when it seems to you that the floor vibrates as we dance – that is because it is trembling under the hate of millions.'

She had spoken with her usual composure, and with a friendly nod she vanished into the ballroom.

The Count remained standing quite nonplussed. He cast a glance over the crowd outside. It was a sight he had often seen. He had told many bad and rather fewer good jokes about the multi-headed monster. But it wasn't until that evening that it occurred to him that this monster was essentially the most sinister setting one could imagine for a palace.

Strange and disturbing thoughts went round and round in the Count's brain – where indeed there was plenty of room for them. He felt quite put out, and it lasted a whole polka before he regained his good humour.

[Original title: *Balstemning*. Translated by James McFarlane]

ARNE GARBORG

Dying

'H'm!' My uncle cleared his throat and a smile came to his lips. We were sitting out on the veranda in the warmth of the afternoon sun and looking out over the sea. I had been telling him about my brother who had been lost at sea, and who now lay at rest out there, cold and pale.

'Ugh, Uncle!' I said, trembling. 'It must be awful . . . it must be awful to die!'

'H'm! h'm! So you are afraid of death!'

He looked frail, did Uncle, as he sat there slumped in his rocking-chair, swathed in woollens and furs even though it was high summer. He had been a strapping young man, the most lordly fellow in the locality. But it was said he had lived 'a wild life', as they called it, and now he was only a shadow of his former self. His face was yellow and sunken; his eyes were large and dull as they looked blearily out from under heavy eyebrows; a stubble beard, thick and grey with streaks of yellow and white, covered his cheeks and his chin. He shaved only once a week, every Saturday.

It had been some kind of stroke which had laid him thus low. He had been bedridden the whole winter, more or less. Now the idea was that he should 'spend some time in the country' and try to get better. So he had come to live with us. Here he had relatives and was known; and in any case it was a good thing for him to be living in a doctor's house.

I was endlessly in his company. I had always been fond of Uncle. He for his part did not seem to object to my presence either, I believe. And I persuaded myself that I was helping him to pass the time with my chatter and all the gossip from the stables and from the servants' quarters. I must have been a lad of about fifteen or so.

Mostly he sat there silent, just listening to me. He didn't find it easy to talk. He often struggled for breath; and his speech was slurred and laboured. Now and then he coughed to clear his throat, but that did not seem to help very much. At times it was as if his tongue somehow got tied up; the words came thickly, stickily, as though numbed. He found most difficulty with words that had an 's' in them. Only very occasionally did he liven up; then he found it easier. Then I was happy; for then I thought he'd soon be better.

'Ah, yes. Youth. Then death has . . . an ugly look.'

'Uncle, don't you think it must hurt when you die.'

'No!' He said this so confidently you would have thought he'd tried it. I was curious; I looked at him, enquiringly, quite carried away.

'Death – h'm!' He cleared his throat. 'He comes and salutes us . . . every once in a while. H'm! I . . . know him well. He . . . isn't dangerous.'

'Tell me, tell me! . . . So long as you're not too tired.'

'H'm! Not much to tell. H'm! h'm! I've been . . . in mortal danger many a time. But . . . that's not what I mean. It's . . . h'm . . . when you get so close to Death . . . that you salute him. Then you forget to be afraid.

'H'm! The first time was when I was a child of about four or five. I was lying on a river bank – we lived in the country then – throwing stones in the water. There were masses of trout minnows close in to the bank. Great shoals of them, gasping and gaping in the warm water. I was having fun . . . scaring them. Then – how it happened I don't know – a moment or two later and there I was myself lying down there in the water. And I thought it was so lovely . . . lying there. H'm! I was lying on my back, staring straight up into the sky . . . as if through a blue veil. But it was so brilliant. And blue. And the light up there . . . h'm . . . was so terribly beautiful, I thought.

'Everything around me became lighter and lighter. And . . . brighter. And soft. A white radiance. And light . . . as though I were floating on air, resting on air. Soft, light air . . . gentle, shining, infinitely clear. I wanted nothing else in the world . . . but to lie there and rest. H'm!'

'Oh! How strange that must have been!'

'H'm! I was looking up into infinite space . . . nothing but crystal-blue sky . . . which whitened into sheer light . . . white . . . white. Shimmering, trembling white light, intense, intense . . . so that the whole world turned to a brilliant white haze. An endless sea . . . a sea of cloud . . . of air and light. And in the middle of that sea of cloud . . . I lay at rest. And very good it felt.'

He cleared his throat and took a swig of water from the glass he had standing on the little table beside his chair. And I who sat there tense and pretty near trembling with suspense saw from his eyes that he was beginning to wake to life.

'But didn't it hurt not to be able to breathe?' I asked.

He shook his head.

'It was just fine. Just fine. I didn't feel anything. Just felt so light. H'm. But within this clear white misty light . . . there stretched long wispy shadows of green and brown . . . half-shadows . . . green patches, long brown branches and stalks . . . quite tropical. H'm. A forest of palm trees and creepers . . . and flowers, shadow flowers as big as moons . . . wild, rank, strange. In clumps and folds and long coils. I suppose I must have landed in among the tall water-grass. Among the water-lilies and the rushes and all the other curious things that grow in deep pools.'

He took a long deep breath.

'Were you conscious?'

'H'm. Well, not altogether. They were . . . images that registered on the retina . . . and were reflected in the brain as though through a mist. H'm. That was all I knew until I woke up in the arms of my nanny. She was almost out of her mind. H'm. I was puzzled by that. I was only sorry that I wasn't lying there comfortably any longer. . . . And many's the time since then I've cursed . . . that young man of hers for not keeping her occupied . . . for another three minutes. Then I'd have been finished.'

These last words hurt me, and I tried to comfort him. 'Ah, but you have had lots of good things in your time, Uncle.'

'Have had!' He smiled despondently. His smile couldn't quite make it on one side; it became twisted and looked strangely sick. '*Have had* . . . is nothing compared with *shall get*. . . . H'm. But that's something you don't understand . . . yet.'

Poor Uncle. This was what it was like to be ill.

He drank some water and began again. So long as he didn't talk too much. . . .

'H'm. The second time was when I was about your age. It was a day in early spring. The snow was still lying, but it thawed a little at midday. The rivers rose and broke up the ice . . . in many places. Father let me go with the men to cart hay and straw home from Aurvik . . . that croft of ours, you know. We couldn't drive across the ice any longer. We went by the bridge. But it was the old bridge in those days. Wasn't really a bridge . . . rather a long gangplank without any railings or anything. Planks laid across a support of tree trunks. And it was set high . . . so that the melting ice should not carry it away in the spring. And hardly more than eight feet wide. . . . Only just wide enough to drive across.'

'It was smooth and slippery there at the time of the thaw. The runners used to skid and would sometimes finish up well over the edge. And below, the river ran heavy and swollen. Sending up white spray. In full spate. With a roaring and a rumbling and a booming from the driving ice . . . great huge lumps of it. I would sit on the sledge and scarcely dare look down. It was like looking down into an . . . abyss.'

'Ugh!'

'H'm. On the way home the men drove ahead. Blakken and I followed behind with a load of straw. I didn't dare sit on the load going over the bridge. I walked alongside, leading Blakken. I wasn't afraid. It had gone all right before, so there was no reason why it shouldn't go all right again. Blakken was so clever he could have managed it on his own.

'The first and nastiest part I managed fine. And then I thought I was as good as there. I kept close to Blakken, testing my courage by looking down into the river as I walked across. That was beautiful too, I thought. Extremely. It tossed and swirled, yellow . . . black and deep. And the ice floes tumbled over and over . . . against each other and on top of each other. And just a couple of feet perhaps between me and the edge.

'All at once . . . I don't know how it happened . . . but the load had slid over to my side, and the two feet had narrowed to one. . . .' He drew breath. 'I tried to save myself by moving up alongside Blakken. Then the front end of the load slid . . .'

'Oh, Uncle . . .'

'A little . . . just a little. But the gap had become so narrow that I couldn't get forward any further. Whoa, Blakken! . . . I let go the reins and tried to get clear at the back of the load. Then the back end started slipping.'

'Oh, no!' I gripped his chair.

'Then the whole load slid another inch . . . then stopped.'

He took a long deep breath. I was gripping his chair tensely.

'H'm. Every escape was closed. The gap between the loaded sled and the edge was so narrow that I do believe the toes of my boots projected over it. I had finished up with my back to the sled and I felt a slight pressure on my shoulders. And then I stood leaning forward . . . right over the icy river . . . my arms outstretched . . . hanging poised . . . swaying on the very point of balance, so to speak.'

'Oh, Uncle, don't stop . . . !'

'I couldn't get any grip on the load. I had let go of the reins. If I had so much as raised a hand, moved a muscle . . . I'd have gone straight into the river without mercy.'

He gasped for breath. His fingers twitched. He took a drink of water.

'It was then I looked Death in the eye. H'm. I knew that the next moment I'd be lying down there among the ice. There . . . at *that* point . . . that's where I would fall. Not in the swirling waters, but to one side. There I'd be lying with my very next breath. I was just on the point of losing my balance . . .

'Then a calm came over me. I fixed my eyes on the spot where I would fall . . . familiarized myself with it. . . . And all of a sudden it looked so lovely and soft. It was as if at that moment the river took on the features and the expression of a face. A nice peaceful expression. With its one big dim eye it looked up at me, poor creature that I was, swaying there on the edge of the bridge. . . . And it seemed to be saying to me: "Come! I'm not as cold as I look!" And a silence came over me. The world dissolved in a sigh. I was finished. I was to go. Now I was going. I gave myself up, and it all seemed to be so secure.

'I began to lose my balance . . . when I felt something between the fingers of my left hand . . . A straw!'

'Ah!'

'Yes. I haven't the faintest idea how I'd taken hold of it. Nor do I understand what happened then . . . or how that same moment I got a grip, a real grip . . . and managed to pull myself up and turn round . . . and cling fast to the load. The only thing I remember is the men running up to help me. But by then I was safe.'

I breathed a long sigh. Uncle drained his glass and gave a little smile. His arm twitched, and he stretched himself in his chair.

'H'm. Afterwards I was frightened . . . so frightened that I trembled. But when you look Death in the eye, you feel calm and secure. You're not afraid.'

Again I began thinking that Uncle really shouldn't think so much about such things now; and I tried to turn his mind to other things.

'By the way,' I said, changing the subject, 'have you had a look at father's new bay horse? Don't you think he's great?'

Horses were the one thing he still really cared about; and soon Death was forgotten in favour of the bay horse.

But from that he turned to a horse he had himself had at one time; and before I could put a word in, we were back again on the problem of death.

'Ah, yes! The dun horse! He's old now, poor thing, and good for nothing but the plough. But he was a mettlesome fellow when he was young. H'm. And that was the occasion of my meeting Death yet another time.'

'Ah, yes! That was the time that girl from the theatre met her end, wasn't it? How many years ago was that, now?' I was all too ready to try to get him to tell his stories. And perhaps he wasn't all that frail, after all. . . .

'Ah! H'm. You weren't around then,' Uncle replied. 'I had bought the horse in Denmark. He was a noble beast. H'm. The finest head I've seen on any horse. And such legs! And what a carriage! H'm. You can't judge that – yet. And the ears! So alert and so small. H'm. It still gives me pleasure when I think of that dun horse. Poor creature! He's old now. He's past it, just as I am! Ah, well!

'H'm. So I came home with the horse. Rode him every day. And everyone was fond of Hannibal. There was poor Lizzy . . . she became so fond of the horse she used to come on errands to me, just so that she could be taken out for a drive with him. H'm. But let me tell you this, Hans! Womenfolk often bring disaster. H'm. Strange women . . . be wary of them! In every way! In every way!

'Ah, well! The horse took fright, and unfortunately Lizzy was holding the reins. It all happened so suddenly. Before I could grab the reins and bring the horse under control, one of the wheels landed up in the ditch. H'm. The carriage crashed into the fence and was immediately demolished. Lizzy struck her head on the fence post . . . I was thrown out a little further up, and the impact was not so great. But I too was knocked out. The only difference was that I came round again . . . to this life. H'm. All I have is a faint memory of a run-away flight, a crash, a thud . . . carriage and wheels upside-down in the air. . . . H'm. I didn't feel any pain. Nor did she. That I could see when I saw her afterwards. Her face had only the same excited look which it had when the horse took to its heels. That's how she lay, still holding the reins. A firm set to the mouth

. . . as though to indicate that she could still manage. H'm. Poor thing! I felt sorry for her. But death came easily to her.'

The sun sank lower and lower. I leaned against the balustrade and looked at the clouds. He sat there, staring with dulled eyes out over the sea, or else possibly within himself.

'And then, when I fell ill,' he continued, 'that was also Death again. H'm. I got up that morning as usual. Was about to get dressed, when the floor seemed to give way beneath me . . . I tried to hold on to something, but everything eluded me, slid away . . . and a force which there was no resisting . . . dragged me to the floor. I was more astonished and confused than afraid. H'm. That power which there is no resisting. . . . When you know that's what it is, you become calm.

'When I came to, I was only a heavy . . . h'm . . . weight, lying there and sinking deep . . . deep . . . into something soft and dark. Leaden, leaden, heavy as lead. Weak, weak, miserably weak. . . . It left me aching in every nerve. Oh, so heavy! And my head swimming! The bed seemed to be floating, diving. . . . H'm. I wasn't properly conscious. There was just this great dazed feeling. To open an eye, to move a finger – impossible! Never occurred to me to want to. All I wanted to do was rest. Rest with every drop of my blood, with every cell in my body, every thread, every fibre. . . . Simply sink deeper and deeper into rest, further and further into sleep. To fall asleep, to fall totally asleep. So that all was simply night. H'm. I knew that this night was death, but I longed for it just the same. Longed for it with a quiet, numbed contentment. I knew it would surely come. Merely to remain conscious was in itself such an effort. Ah! To stretch out and die . . . what solace that would be! What comfort! That's the fear one has of death when it comes close enough. H'm.

'It still feels sometimes as though I could quite happily lie back and breathe my last. And that is such a peaceful thought.

'It is foolish of people to picture Death . . . as a skeleton with a scythe. H'm. That is a monkish invention. Those people have never seen Death. It is no skeleton. It is a kind and gentle deity. A man or a woman . . . earnest and pale . . . stern in appearance. But as it approaches, its stern countenance becomes calm and gentle. And the eyes are wide and deep and filled with pity. H'm. Pity.

'H'm. No, it intends no harm. It takes us gently in its arms and carries us off into dream. A bright dream. Then it envelops us deeper and deeper in dream . . . until these dreams swirl and disappear. And light breaks through . . . as when the morning mists lift. That is the other life!'

I leaned out over the balcony and looked at the sky. Stared, stared, until the clouds up there transformed themselves into a countenance, a stern and earnest countenance which gradually became gentler. Gentler and gentler the longer I looked.

[Original title: *Døy*. Translated by James McFarlane]

KNUT HAMSUN

Slaves of love

I

Written by me. Written today to ease my heart. I have lost my job in the café and my happy days. I have lost everything. And the café was the Café Maximilian.

A young gentleman dressed in grey and two of his friends came night after night and sat at one of my tables. So many gentlemen came, and all of them had a friendly word for me – this one said nothing. He was tall and slender, with soft dark hair and blue eyes that sometimes looked at me. A little moustache had begun to grow on his upper lip.

Well, at first he probably had something against me, this man.

He came along every day for a week. I had grown accustomed to him and missed him when he did not come. One evening he wasn't there. I went round the café looking for him; at last I found him near one of the large pillars over beside the other entrance; he was sitting with a lady from the circus. The lady was in a yellow dress and her long gloves reached above her elbows. She was young and had beautiful dark eyes and mine were blue.

I stood for just a moment and heard what they were talking about; she was reproaching him about something; she was tired of him and was asking him to go. I said in my heart: 'Blessed Virgin, why doesn't he come to me?'

The next evening he came with his two friends and sat down at one of my tables; for I have five tables to serve. I did not go to meet him as I used to do; I blushed and pretended not to see him. When he beckoned me I stepped forward.

I said: 'You weren't here yesterday.'

'How lovely and slim she is, our waitress,' he said to his companions.

'Beer?' I asked.

'Yes,' he answered.

And I ran rather than walked to get the three tankards.

II

A couple of days passed.
He gave me a card and said: 'Take it over to . . .'
I took the card before he had finished speaking and took it to the lady in yellow. On the way I read his name, Wladimierz Txxx.
When I returned he looked inquiringly at me.
'Yes, I have taken it,' I said.
'And there was no answer?'
'No.'
He then gave me a mark and said with a smile: 'No answer is also an answer.'
The whole evening he sat staring at the lady and her escorts. At 11 o'clock he rose and went over to her table. She received him coldly; her two companions conversed with him, however, and asked him unkind questions and smiled. He stayed there only a few minutes and when he returned I pointed out that beer had been poured into one of his raincoat pockets. He took his coat off, turned abruptly and looked for a moment back at the circus lady's table. I dried off his coat and he said to me: 'Thank you, slave.'
As I helped him on with his coat again, I ran my hand secretly over his back.
He sat down deep in thought. One of his friends asked for more beer and I took his tankard to fill it. I also made to take Txxx's tankard.
'No,' he said, and laid his hand on mine.
His touch made me drop my arm and he surely noticed it, for he drew back his hand at once.
At night I prayed for him twice on my knees by my bed. And in my happiness I kissed my right hand, the one he had touched.

III

Once he gave me flowers, a mass of flowers. He bought them from the flower girl the moment he came in; they were fresh and red and it was almost the whole of her basket. He let them lie in front of him on the table for a long time. None of his friends was with him. Whenever I could find time, I stood and peeped at him from behind a pillar and I thought: Wladimierz Txxx is his name.
Perhaps an hour passed. He kept on looking at his watch.
I asked him: 'Are you expecting somebody?'

He looked absently at me, then suddenly said: 'No, I am not expecting anybody. Whom should I be expecting?'

'I was only thinking that perhaps you were expecting somebody,' I repeated.

'Come here,' he answered. 'This is for you.'

And he gave me the whole mass of flowers.

I said thanks, but for the moment couldn't get my voice and could only whisper. A blood-red joy swept me away; I found myself standing breathless down at the buffet where I ordered things.

'What do you want?' said the woman in charge.

'What do you think?' I replied.

'What do I think?' said the woman. 'Are you mad?'

'Guess who I got these flowers from,' I said.

The manager went past.

'You haven't taken the gentleman with the wooden leg his beer,' I heard him say.

'I got them from Wladimierz,' I said and rushed off with the beer.

Txxx had not gone. I thanked him again when he got up to go. He hesitated and said: 'Really I bought them for somebody else.'

Well, so perhaps he had bought them for somebody else. But I got them. *I* got them, rather than the person he had bought them for. And he also let me thank him for them. Good night, Wladimierz.

IV

The next morning there was rain. Shall I put on my black or my green dress today, I thought. The green. It's the newest, so I'll take that one. I was very happy.

When I got to the tram-stop, a lady was standing in the rain waiting for the tram. She had no umbrella. I invited her to stand under mine, but she said 'No, thank you.' So I put my umbrella down as well while I waited. Then the lady is not alone in getting wet, I thought.

That evening Wladimierz came to the café.

'Thanks for the flowers yesterday,' I said proudly.

'What flowers?' he asked. 'Don't talk to me about those flowers.'

'I wanted to thank you for them,' I said.

He shrugged his shoulders and answered: 'It is not you I love, slave.'

It was not me he loved – of course not. I hadn't expected it and I wasn't disappointed. But I saw him every night; he sat down at my table, never at anybody else's, and it was I who brought him his beer. Welcome back, Wladimierz.

The next evening he came late. He said: 'Have you very much money, slave?'

'No, I am sorry,' I said. 'I am a poor girl.'

Then he looked at me and said, smiling: 'I think you misunderstand me. I need some money till tomorrow.'

'I have some money. I have a hundred and thirty marks at home.'

'At home, not here?'

I answered: 'Wait a quarter of an hour and come with me when we close, then I'll get them.'

He waited the quarter of an hour and went with me. Only a hundred marks, he said. The whole time he walked by my side and didn't make me walk ahead or behind, as fine gentlemen often do.

'I have only a small room,' I said when we stopped at my front door.

'I won't come up,' he said. 'I'll wait here.'

He waited.

When I came down again he counted the money and said: 'There's more than a hundred marks here. I'll give you ten marks as a tip. Yes, yes, listen to me! I want to give you ten marks as a tip.' And he handed me the money, said good night and left. At the corner I saw him stop and give the lame old beggar-woman a copper.

V

The next evening he immediately said he was sorry but he couldn't pay me back the money. I thanked him because he couldn't. He frankly confessed he'd spent it all.

'What can one say, slave?' he said, smiling. 'You know – the lady in yellow.'

'Why do you call our waitress "slave"?' asked one of his friends. 'You are more of a slave than she is.'

'Beer?' I asked, interrupting them.

Shortly afterwards the lady in yellow came in. Txxx rose and bowed. He bowed so deep that his hair fell over his face. She went past him and sat down at an empty table, but pointedly tipped two chairs up against it. Txxx at once went across to her and sat down on one of the chairs. Two minutes later he got up again and said in a loud voice: 'Very well, I shall go. And I shall never come back again.'

'Thank you,' she answered.

I felt numbed with joy and I ran down to the buffet and said something or other. Doubtless I told them he was never going back to her again. The manager came past; he ticked me off sharply but I didn't care.

When the place shut at twelve o'clock, Txxx accompanied me to my front door.

'Five of the ten marks I gave you yesterday,' he said.

I wanted to give him all ten and he took them, but handed me five back as a tip. Nor would he listen to any of my objections.

'I am so happy tonight,' I said. 'If only I dared ask you up, but I have only a tiny room.'

'I won't come up,' he answered. 'Good night.'

He went. Again he walked past the old beggar-woman but forgot to give her anything although she bobbed to him. I ran across to her and gave her something and said: 'That's from the man who went by – the gentleman in grey.'

'The gentleman in grey?' the woman asked.

'The one with the dark hair, Wladimierz.'

'Are you his wife?'

I answered: 'No, I am his slave.'

VI

For several evenings in succession he said he was sorry he couldn't give me my money back. I begged him not to mention it. He spoke so loud that everybody could hear and many laughed at him.

'I am a villain and a scoundrel,' he said. 'I have borrowed your money and cannot pay it back. I would cut off my right hand for a fifty-mark note.'

It grieved me to hear these words and I wondered how I might get him the money, though I knew I couldn't.

He went on to say to me: 'And if you ask me how things are otherwise, then I can tell you the lady in yellow has moved on with her circus. I have forgotten her. I do not remember her any more.'

'And yet you wrote her another letter today,' said one of his friends.

'It was the last,' Wladimierz answered.

I bought a rose from the flower girl and put it in his left buttonhole. I felt his breath on my hands as I did it and could hardly get the pin through.

'Thanks,' he said.

I asked at the desk for the few marks they still owed me and gave him them. It was a small thing.

'Thank you,' he said again.

I was happy the whole evening until Wladimierz suddenly exclaimed: 'With these marks I shall go away for a week. When I come back you shall have your money.' When he saw I was moved, he said: 'It is you I love!' And he took my hand.

I became confused that he should think of going away without saying where, though I did ask him. Everything, the whole restaurant and the chandeliers and all the guests, swam round; I could not bear it, and grasped both his hands.

'I shall be with you again in a week,' he said, and got up abruptly.

I heard the manager say to me: 'You will have to leave.'

Very well, I thought. What does it matter! In a week Wladimierz will be back with me! I wanted to thank him for it and turned round. He was gone.

VII

A week later I found a letter from him, one night when I got home. He wrote so inconsolably; he told me that he had gone to follow the lady in yellow, that he never could pay me my money, and that he was in deep distress. Then he again accused himself of being a vile soul, and underneath he had written: 'I am the slave of the lady in yellow.'

I grieved night and day and could do nothing. A week later I lost my job and began looking for a new one. During the day I applied at other cafés and hotels and I also rang the bell at a number of private houses and offered my services. To no avail. Late in the evening I bought all the newspapers at half price and read through the advertisements when I got home. I thought: Perhaps I can find something that can save both Wladimierz and me. . . .

Last night I saw his name in the papers and read about him. Straight afterwards I went out, out of the house, round the streets, and I came back this morning. I may have slept somewhere or other, or sat on some steps unable to go on, I don't know now.

I have read it again today. But it was last night when I came home that I first read it. At first I clasped my hands, then I sat down on a chair. Shortly after that I sat down on the floor and leaned against the chair; and as I sat there thinking, I beat the floor with my flat hands. Perhaps I didn't think; but there was a hollow buzzing in my head and I could feel nothing. It was probably then that I got up and went out. Down at the corner I remember I gave the old, old beggar-woman a copper, and said: 'That's from the gentleman in grey, remember?'

'Perhaps you are his fiancée?' she asked.

I answered: 'No. I am his widow. . . .'

And I wandered about the streets until this morning. And now I have read it again.

Wladimierz Txxx was his name.

[Original title: *Kjærlighedens slaver*. Translated by James McFarlane]

HANS KINCK

White anemones

Gertrude sat in church one bright summer's day, her hands clasping her hymn book, leaning slightly forward and pensive. A pale young woman, thirty, with thick golden hair and big blue eyes that stared fixedly from under half-closed lids at the lowest of the chancel steps. She did not wish to look higher, because up by the altar stood the priest's son, strong and broad-shouldered. Today he had come with his father to this remote parish church in the valley to officiate. He had recently come across the mountains, east from Christiania.

She did not catch what he said; as though there were plugs in her ears, and a mist before her eyes. That which had happened a week ago was pursuing her again. It pursued her wherever she was.

. . . Yes, the quiet summer night filled the church. . . . And it was several miles deep into the mountains. Not a glint of the sun among the shining stalks of the grass; no hint of red on the distant peaks. And the white-leaved willows stood sleepily along the banks of the streams. . . . A grey-cool, dew-drenched summer's night.

. . . She could not get to sleep in the barn there on the mountain pasture; she lay hot, tossing, thinking of many things. Also she began to feel afraid, regretting a little after all that she had not gone back with the herd-boy to the village for the evening, Saturday evening.

. . . She lay in the hay, listening. A quiet throbbing had filled all things, a kind of playing, you know, a sort of living . . . a whole herd filling the hillsides, forcing its way over the stone wall, leaping and invading everywhere, tumbling one over the other into the meadow . . . a congress of all kinds of living creatures, so quietly, so gently.

. . . It took possession of her ear, took all her hearing. And the sound drew her over to set her eye to the crack in the barn wall. There in the light-grey mist there were young people, barefoot and light of step, twisting and turning on long supple legs, one group moving from one direction, another from a different one. And at times it seemed as though they rose from the very earth. . . . Meeting among the haystacks, squatting on their haunches, leaping into the air, nestling up to each other, huddling together in larger groups, gathering over by the stream which, spawning and increasing, cut its twisting way down the slope.

. . . And only by the stream did things eventually become thoroughly lively and agitated. Small children whispered and laughed, clung to the white-leaved willows, twining themselves around, then leapt out into the meadow again to dance in circles in sheer abandon, then returned to follow the brook, one group after another, out into the water, out into the grey shining water.

. . . And out there they attached strings, every new arrival who gathered there, so that the yearning bow found sound beneath it, there where it slid lightly and unseen at the river's outlet. But the sound was low and gentle, for fingers pressed upon all the strings.

. . . And so things were played out into long waves. The fiddle drew it out into large assemblies, in the bogs, in the marsh grass, on the smooth water.

. . . And away along the ridge one face stood out . . . a fair-haired man she scarcely recognized, with a high forehead and kind eyes, soft-cheeked and with a smile on his lips. And she lay down in his gaze; and she stroked his cheek.

. . . But it grew darker and darker, and the cheek slid away and the man disappeared.

. . . But the fiddle grew; the whole of the long ridge became the bow, and the broad waters the case. But fingers pressed on all the strings.

. . . No distinct colour, no distinct sound. It merged with the grey night, all the sound of people and beasts . . . with the singing mist-grey night.

. . . But still the fiddle grew, so that the whole expanse of land became fiddle, gently vibrating beneath the barn. And all those impassioned young people took part in drawing the bow, in plucking and stopping the strings. But always there were fingers down there pressing the strings, taking care that the sound was low.

. . . She slid down from the haystack, went over to the door, pushed it quietly open so that the cool of the summer night came flooding over her.

'Oh heigh, oh ho!' she sang as she stood there. All this had taken away her sight, had stolen her voice. She did not know what she sang:

> Oh heigh, oh ho!
> Oh heigh, oh ho!
> Why have you made off with my sleep?
> With the sap rising in the juniper tree!
> And the trout laying its eggs down in the stream!
> Oh heigh, oh ho!
> Oh heigh, oh ho!
> Who has made off with my sleep?

Something within her sang ceaselessly, beginning anew, over and over again. The melody was that of the night itself as it hung over the meadow. It was from it that she got the words.

Then there was a sound of footsteps through the dew-wet grass alongside the barn. A man stopped silently at the entrance. A night-grey man who slipped into the barn, pulled the door shut without a word. She did not know him, did not look at him, did not ask his name. But he must surely be one of those who had been helping to draw the great fiddle bow out there on the meadow. . . .

'God give me comfort!' she sighed as she sat in church clasping her hymn book. She had been sitting there thinking, remembering that summer's night. She had not become aware that the service was already over and people were beginning to leave. She rose and went, glancing at the same time at the pulpit.

She slipped out of the old church and along the grey stone wall where people were sitting closely packed or else lying sunning themselves behind it. Mostly smiling young people who were waiting and listening to the fiddle that sounded on the summer-vibrant air from the cottage on the hillside, where it was the custom for wedding groups from all around to put up. The priest wanted to get his breath back – as he put it – before he married them.

But out here the recollection once again seized her so that the little old fiddle was quite silenced by it. She followed the drifting mist of that summer night past group after group. She felt herself to be like some playful leaf floating in the rippling brook. Only when she was standing far distant under the hill, in among the hazel bushes where no sound of fiddle could reach her, did she come to herself again. She took a few steps in the grass and sat down in the moss behind a hazel bush, her hands in her lap.

... No, she did not know who the man was who had been in the barn that night. Didn't want to know either. She had forced herself to lie there with tight-shut eyes when he left in the morning. . . . But then there was nobody thereabouts, apart from the priest's son, who had a light-grey pack like that. For this she had happened to see just as it was disappearing behind the distant crags down the road to the village. In any case, she had finally rushed over to the door – as soon as she believed he was out of sight – to see whether . . .

She remained sitting lost in thought, listening to the buzzing of a bee, watching the capricious flight of a butterfly.

. . . . The air was like a heavy sea, and on it floated the gentle sounds of summer nights, lapping about the eyes, licking the ears . . . gliding on, rippling through the blades of grass, swirling round the tree-trunks, flooding and flowing everywhere, depositing a light-grey mist over all things.

>Oh heigh, oh ho!
>Oh . . . heigh, oh . . . ho!

said the leaves, said the grass. . . .

All at once it was gone. She heard the voice of the priest's son down on the path below the hill. The young summer-clad lady from the city walked ahead; she was a visitor at the rectory this summer; he walked behind, speaking in a low voice.

They were doubtless taking a walk whilst the priest was conducting the service in the church.

Gertrude rose to her feet and stood listening. She was conscious of him being so far away, yet she felt him strangely close . . . sadness and desire vied within her, halting her breathing. Swooping high and sweeping low like a flock of swallows in flight.

They spoke little . . . breathed only. When he found a flower.

'Oh, how lovely! Oh, how absolutely beau-tiful!' she said.

Then they both smelled it. Stopped and smelled it again, as though they could never have enough of it. Then she was given it.

Gertrude followed them up the hill, flitting softly from one hazel bush to another. Yes, it was the great brow and the gentle eyes of the summer night, it was the soft cheek and the smile on the lips! . . .

'I want one as well, want one from you!' he begged after a while.

'Very well,' she said, seemingly surprised. And she hurried off to find one.

They walked silently, and she looked for the flower.

'But what do you want?' came the question. 'A forget-me-not?' she added, trying to laugh as she plucked a blue forget-me-not from the grass.

'It's *you* I want!' he cried and put his arms about her.

She opened her arms to him, holding him. Gertrude heard whispers, ardent breathing. She moved down closer and closer. Finally she was so close to them that it seemed to her she could feel their warmth. She felt weak at the knees, in her body. She sat down on the grassy bank, finding it difficult to stand.

The couple walked arm in arm further along the path; then they turned and came back.

They let go of each other and grew silent when they became aware of Gertrude. The refined city girl began frantically looking for flowers. Then they walked on slowly again, acting as though they had not seen her on the hillside.

'I won't say anything,' Gertrude said softly after them as they slipped by. She searched the face of the priest's son to see whether this promise made him happy. All she saw was that he looked uncertain and blushed, pretending not to know her, and sniffed a flower.

The city girl turned slightly. 'Oh!' she smiled, quietly and happily, and looked unconcernedly about her at all the hills and mountains, 'people are going to hear about it in any case!'

Gertrude sat watching them go. She wanted to be with them, to know this thing together with them, to help them to keep silent in company with them – just this one thing! . . .

Down there they linked arms again, laughing to each other.

Long after they had disappeared beyond the hazels she remained sitting there, staring down the path.

. . . Yes, that's what people wanted, most of all: to get married! . . . Oh, how sorry you felt for them! . . . Bitter childlike tears in the tremulous sunlit air! . . .

She rose to her feet, swung off on to another path, away from farmstead and church. She was in no mood to watch them getting married over at the church. It hurt so much, hurt so much! She was in no mood to see anybody get married any more. Nothing but bitter childlike tears in the tremulous sunlit air! . . .

She turned off up the valley and into the mountains, the same way she had come that morning to see the priest's son and hear his voice. She did not rest, did not stop to recover her breath. Steadily she continued across the wet bogland, across the mountain knolls and up the steep hillsides. She wasn't aware of walking. It was as if a strongly running stream of silent tears swept her up each hillside.

Only when she reached the mountain pasture did she stop; and only then did a tear well up, one single timorous tear in the corner of each eye. A long time she sat outside, her back to the barn, staring across the flat land.

. . . She couldn't understand how anybody could have the courage for a thing like that . . . to get married and settle down! . . . She, who had believed that a certain man in grey had himself also heard a different fiddle! For what was that feeble wedding march by comparison! It was nothing set against that broad fiddle and that long bow – set against the swelling sea of song which life itself floated on, but which washed high over house and church! . . .

All was quiet within her, quiet around her. Quiet as in a clump of white anemones deep in the forest.

She sat there until the dewy mist began to drift again among the stacks.

And the cool-grey of the summer night spread gently over the meadow with the broad fiddle and the long bow; and from lake and stream, and from the white-leaved sleeping willow came the sound:

> Oh heigh, oh ho!
> Oh heigh, oh ho!
> Here with your sleep I come.

[Original title: *Hvidsymre i utslaatten*. Translated by James McFarlane]

SIGBJØRN OBSTFELDER

The Plain

More and more I love the plain. The fact that the eye can wander, wander for miles and never meet anything to impede it, and where all is light. There is something about this light and about the subdued sounds of the plain which blends with your dreams. In the flow of the stream through the soft greensward there is a kind of human vibrancy; and there is something of the same thing in the song of the church-bell which carries through the air on long undulations that meet with no obstacle, but simply die away in the far distance.

And yet it is not your own self that you find again. If you have lived in a valley with its river and its hillsides, you soon begin to meet memories in each branch and each boulder. They can be bright and beautiful; they can also be heavy and sad. It is different here. It is as if from the distant horizons there comes new hope; and not just hope alone and golden dreams, but fecund thoughts. You see life in a new light; you understand much that you did not understand before.

It is not just the day which is beautiful. When from the dusk the first star comes out like the first wood anemone from the spring earth, it seems so close you think you could walk up to it, if you walked for many days. But when all the other stars come out as well, it looks so different; high, as never before; and yet you see how the sky supports itself upon the earth to north and south and east and west.

All the same, I feel drawn at this time mostly by the darkness itself. It is so great, so limitless. It is a sea in which you always feel that things are happening: roots that creep, life that crawls, destinies that entwine – outwards, unconfined, on towards the next morning.

In this darkness a solitary tree becomes a fable. Walk past it in the light of day and you pay no more attention to it than to any of the others which stand scattered about here and there. But now it rises up powerfully, strangely tall above the earth. You have to extend your path; you have to go near it and let its leaves cool your brow and cheeks.

When I walk these roads where all things are infinite and silent, I feel as though I have been living in a trance. Yes, it is precisely amidst all that turmoil, among all those people, that one lives in a trance. So much of you that has no part in it all. Everything is so fragmented, so trivial.

Oh, when you look back on your life, how little seems to have come of it! Seeking, ever seeking, roving, roaming, in the belief you would find life's loveliness!

Life's loveliness! Perhaps it lies hidden deep within yourself and you are moving away from it, not towards it. And it might be better if, like a tree, you stood in the same place spring and autumn, letting sun and rain bring new leaves, and letting the wind blow them away when they grow old.

Could it possibly be? Could it really be possible that the whole great thing with its wide blue skies of happiness could still come about? I believed that much of what is within me must be dead, killed. And now it is as though something desires to wake, to raise its head. Any moment might see me crying out: 'I have it still! That which I once had lies there still. It has simply been lying waiting!'

Fantasies! This pure rarefied air is causing me to have visions. I am thirty-four. How could it still be possible?

Summer is now breathing its last. Often a warm breath of air sweeps along and makes all life tremble. And me with it. Dreams which I believed forgotten and subdued quicken in my breast. Far away out there I see a pair of cool arms, a tinge of blood that seeks the sun. Is it something that once was? Is it something that is to be? I cannot tell. The vision shimmers so mysteriously. Sometimes it is as if some old and hidden sorrow radiates from it; sometimes some new and strange joy.

And there comes to my mind what I once thought long ago this might be: woman. On a night when the light greets the dark, when every blossom gives off a heavy scent, when the mountain loves the fjord and the fjord the moon and the dewdrop the grass, you encounter it. You walk in fear of life and in fear of death; not daring to tread too heavily for fear of killing the young budding plants, not daring to hum for fear of startling the sleeping butterflies, walking with the fear of death within you, when suddenly a hand rests on your shoulder, and a soul looks out from a pair of eyes. And you do not know whence you know it, but you are filled with glorious strength, for you know; and you are seized by a splendid joy of battle, for now you are able.

Shall I yet encounter this?

I have met a new woman. I remember everything from that evening. I remember how I stood looking at a rose bush while she said farewell to the other people. I remember how all manner of thoughts rushed through my head as I listened to the voices and the laughter: how two roses hung there full on the bush, and a third was pale and withered; how I must make haste and see all things and breathe in all things before the earth's nuptial time was past; how any moment something might come to rob me of my peace.

Then she came, and we walked together down the long silent avenue of maples. The lamps fought a subdued battle with the red of the dying sun which out in the west gave the earth's rim its last kiss before the night. Above us was the hazy blue vault of the late summer night in which the sweet scents of summer collect even as it passes. Within the green darkness of the gardens the lamps often set a halo round something that was still living: a cluster of red currants, an aster, some late wild flowers. Here and there behind a lamp we saw a mother's brooding face, the curly heads of children.

We saw almost nothing, she and I. And yet it was as if the whole time things were happening.

Suddenly it seemed to me that a shudder passed over her body. I looked at her. She was deathly pale.

'I don't know. Don't know what it is,' she whispered.

I remember how still it was as she said that. It, her whisper, sounded like a shriek.

We had come to her door. She looked up at me. Her voice had grown so faint.

'I don't know what it is. There is something about you that . . . that . . .'

And like a flash she was gone.

What was it? Summer was all around us; the glow of daylight had not yet paled; the meadows were steaming; all things sang a glad little song. And *she* was deathly pale. Trembled.

Inside there, she was the liveliest of them. Every moment, every minute of her life she wanted to laugh, she said. Laugh, laugh! And yet when we came out, outside where all things stood smiling, all that was immediately gone, had died away: the red of her cheek, the fire in her eye, the lines of her face.

Who was she? It was as if she walked a different world from the one around us. As if no other being must ever enter the world she walked in.

Why have I forgotten what she looked like? When I think back – I never actually looked at her. Face, hair, arms, waist, these I have never seen. I cannot say what they were like. And yet I think I know how they were.

The voice is the only thing I remember clearly. Constantly it sounds in my ears. 'There is something about you that . . . that . . .'

What did she mean?

I have been a complete fool. I have written to her, asked her to meet me. I have written a long letter.

What will she think? I can picture her as she reads it: smiling faintly, laying it to one side, bursting into laughter: 'God, what dupes men are!' And then she runs to one of her girl friends. Then it is read again, like adding cream to chocolate.

Surely I am too old for such things.

She did not come. That was just as well. Of course it would merely have been a disappointment if I had seen her again. It was the evening that had made me rash.

Much sadness attaches to these days. Summer and autumn continue to whisper to each other, both morning and evening. There is the breath of expiring things and the scent of things in blossom which blend with the smell of decomposition.

I have found a place where summer still lingers. From a distance it looks just like anywhere else; but when you get close, it is in fact a temple. Its pillars are alder trees, and a green light falls through the tiny windows in the vaulting.

It lies just where a brook falls into the river, this temple of mine. The rushing sound of the waterfall is like a quiet mass said for all things transitory: colours, scents, summer, time. The sound is eternal; eternal its church music. Further down, the currents twist and swirl in all manner of mysterious rings. If I knew the world's most profound laws of motion, would I be able to understand them? And could I then guess where the dead leaves which now and then come floating along would find their graves? I always guess wrong. They make the strangest turns against the current, whereupon they glide calmly and majestically into the inlet I had thought least likely.

I do not know what is wrong with me. All at once I am startled. The water bubbles, the grass trembles: 'Don't know . . . don't know what it is.'

I had been out walking. When I arrived back at my door, I saw a pair of galoshes standing there. Quite small galoshes.

The thought went through me: they are *hers*. She is sitting there inside. Inside where the air is heavy with my thoughts. There she sits; she has been sitting there alone before I came.

Why had she come? Why did she not leave me in peace? I had done what I believed she wanted. I had given up the idea of pursuing our acquaintance. So why had she come now?

She drew up her veil. It was she. So this was what she was like! Her face was there before me, white. The eyes regarded me for a second. I only had a feeling of something large, dark, of something I had seen in a dream long ago – a second only, then she looked down. Her head and her eyelashes were lowered as when the sun dazzles one's eyes. As if there was something she was fearful the day might see.

She sat down. I stood behind her. I saw the delicate blue veins on her wrist. I saw the small nails. I sensed the pale blood within.

My window stood open. As in a dream I saw the two tall aspens tremble gently, and on the distant horizon I saw a flock of grey geese flying south. And as one hears a voice in a dream, so I heard hers, so low, so sad: 'I dared not . . . dared not . . . come.'

Then she rose. I followed her out. The small galoshes stood there, so small, so small.

I keep thinking about her. Have I become overwrought? I begin to find myself attaching significance to all manner of things. I keep brooding. *That* was something she used to do. *Thus* it was she held her hand. *This* was the picture she looked at. What does this mean? Why should this happen?

When I am together with her, the silence becomes doubly silent. Then when she speaks, I see before me the entire plain, all the blades of grass, the rivulets. And away over it all go her words; and finally it seems to me that it is from out there, from deep, deep within, that they come.

And all at once I can be reminded of a day long ago, many years ago, a day which will never return. I see her, as I have only now seen her, crossing the plain in the sun, younger than she is now, in a light dress, her hair hanging free. Disquiet overwhelms me: where was I then? Somewhere else, together with other women. Then she dreamed dreams I myself have never dreamed. Why do I not know these dreams? Why do I not know everything that passed through her breast at that time?

I do not believe I shall ever forget those moments she was here. There was such a miraculous silence. It seemed to me that everyone in the district was asleep, that nobody walked the roads; even the cows and the dogs were asleep, and the doves in the dovecotes. We two alone existed in the world. I would not have dared touch a single hair of her head. It would have made too great a noise. I dared not touch her glove lying on the table. I stood looking at it. There was about it something rather like her own self. I dared not touch it.

There is something about her I have not met with in any other woman. I do not know what it is. But on many an occasion when I see the aspens tremble outside and I am aware of a sighing in the air as before rain, she immediately appears clearly before me again.

Finally the grass has begun to turn, innumerable pinpoints reddening towards death. It is as if the leaves sing themselves to death, and each single one of them has its own life's song to sing. No two leaves have the same colour. Maple and lime, aspen and ash, they differ as families differ. But each leaf also has its own melody: purple, violet, lilac, of gold, of blood, of the sleeping cloud and the waking sun. They are all there. And side by side, hand in hand, go the fresh and the light together with the old and the yellowed, just as side by side and hand in hand among human kind go those who are still young and trustful with the weary and the earthbound.

Every night new clouds of leaves have turned; and when day comes they stand there smiling and weeping. And more and more it is as if it is spring. Spring is in all the smiling and all the weeping.

It is as if the world is in some quiet transformation, as if something new is about to arise, an awakening, a totally unexpected germination perhaps of something the shoots of which one always imagined the frost had killed.

And yet these last few nights I have had that terrible fear from the old days, the fear of life. I have felt it stronger than ever before. It is like a long arm reaching in from space through the window, like a heavy black hand that places itself upon one's breast: 'Do you know who you are? Do you know where you are?'

You look round the room for a friendly eye, a human eye. There is none. You dare not look out. For out there stars without number stand and stare: 'I know what you do not know. What do you know, wretch?'

She? I do not know her. It is as if she belonged out there, far far out there.

Only once have I seen her eyes. When I think about it, I feel uneasy and my nerves tremble. This is something I cannot comprehend. I seek and seek; I search far back in my life; I search everywhere I can think of searching, but I cannot find it.

The plain is limitless. So much that is unknown lives out there within those endless horizons. The eye can never come to rest. It runs over grass and rock and ends nowhere; it finds only the imponderable darkness and, high above, the menacing stars and beyond that again the blue profundity, the most terrible thing of all.

I have seen her again. For the first time I saw her in the company of other men. She was radiant. She was as scarlet as a drop of Christ's blood.

All were dressed in white, in bright colours; she alone was in black. I was constantly aware how she stood out against the others, wherever she was in the room.

I stood thinking that she – *she* – had been in my room. It was a delight to stand there hidden and see her dance, laughing and radiant.

Her neck was bare. As she moved past I could see the white down. A comb with four jewels was placed in her hair, and her hair encompassed it as a luxuriant hedge does an iron fence. Into it she had inserted two ivy leaves and a greenish-white flower, the name of which I do not know.

They twisted and turned, waltzing and swaying; there were all kinds of flowers, all manner of crystals – and again and again came that black silk, and again and again those four jewels.

And with the dancing a pain came twisting towards and into me, a pain I cannot explain.

I saw how she showered smiles about her. To me she had never smiled. I saw how her head rested tenderly on some shoulder. She turned her eyes towards me, eyes other than those I had seen, full of a tender happiness which had nothing to do with me. There was nothing in them that named my name.

I went out. Inside I saw nothing, heard nothing any longer. Why had I come here? I did not belong here.

Outside the heavens were so deep. Endless diamonds glittered up there.

I had been a prisoner. I had not been myself. What was it, what was it that had had power over me?

Still a name droned within me, a face confronted me. Like a child's it had been, when it dreams; as when its smile dies away.

So that was how she was: glad, jubilant. I alone caused her face to darken.

I wanted to forget. I never wanted to see her again.

Footsteps sounded, light, restless. Several times they stopped. I seemed to be aware of a head bending and peeping in among the leaves. The steps crept on further; they became swifter. Finally they were quite close; I heard the rustle of silk. Then *she* was there. She sat down facing me. She said nothing. What did she want? Why did she come again to disrupt my peace? Anger fermented within me.

And yet I heard myself softly saying that name I had never uttered to her before.

'Naomi! Naomi, why did you come?'

'I suddenly felt so alone in there. I was so happy, dancing and laughing. Everybody was laughing. All at once there was a strange feeling in my breast. I felt everything was turning and spinning, spinning about itself without aim or purpose. I felt all the faces were distorted, all the words shrieks and howls. The music began ringing in my ears: "In time you will be dead, in time you will be dead, in time you will be dead."

'I had to stop dancing. But it had become so strange in the ballroom. They all seemed like strangers to me. I didn't feel there was anyone I dared talk to.

'Then I had a mad desire to dance myself to death, to dance until everything within me crumpled, until I could remember no more.'

She looked at me with big dark eyes. They had become almost black, unmoving, unblinking. I felt her hot breath, the scent of her soft breast.

She was like a frightened child. She trembled and crept in to me, and my lips touched her mouth.

But her kiss was cold as the dark.

Since then I have not seen her. I asked her to meet me, but she did not come.

The storms have begun. They howl across the bare mountain, lashing all which had at one time been in blossom.

Why had she sat with me under the infinite sky, touching me with her hair and her cheek? Why had she called to life again all those things lying hidden within me, things I believed dead? How can I forget now?

Now I know what it was I saw in her eyes. One night, when I was twenty, I saw it in myself.

I lie awake at night. I seem to see, half-way across the plain, a house with shining eyes. A waltz echoes within the storm. Shadows flit past the windows. Amongst them is a living person. The white down on her neck gleams faintly in the dark. The black silk flickers. A myrtle wreath encircles her temples. But the eyes are closed as on a corpse.

The thought surges through me that I *must* rescue her from that dance of death. Nobody else sees it, knows of it, can do anything. I am the one who must rescue her. All things must come to my aid. I will ask every leaf, beg on bended knee every drop of water, every speck of dust. Outside the storm is howling, howling. Nothing can help me. All things are themselves suffering, are being lashed to death. The leaves fly in terror against the window pane. The trees writhe feverishly.

I shut my eyes in terror. Nearer and nearer it comes. An icy breath passes over my cheek. Lips touch my mouth, cold, cold as the outermost darkness.

I dare not write. Dare not walk past her house. I see her lying outstretched. The eyes are closed. The blood no longer courses through those delicate veins.

The storm had subsided. A few pearly drops still quivered on the tips of the bare branches. The clouds had moved far away towards the edge of the dome of the sky and remained there, resting, waiting.

Dusk began to fall. I was far away, where the pasture ends and the heather grows.

Far beyond I saw somebody coming. It is a peculiar feeling you get seeing something coming towards you on the plain. It changes. With it you are no longer alone.

Tensely you follow the moving thing. First it is merely a black line rising from the limits of vision. Then you see it walking, getting closer. Who can it be? Finally you hear the footsteps. And when it is there you somehow feel you know it, and without being aware of it your head makes a friendly nod. Afterwards you are quite astonished. It is gone, and you will perhaps never see it again in your life.

It was Naomi. She was changed. She had grown so pale.

We stood still. I saw her breast rising and falling. Then she began to speak, breathlessly, without looking at me.

'I cannot go on. I have thought so much. . . . It seems like an eternity since last spring. . . . All was different then. . . . Nothing is as it was before . . . I was so happy. I was fond of everybody. I danced. I took delight in the bright lights and the people and the dresses. . . ⁚ I don't like anything any more, anything. . . . I shut myself in. I weep. I lock the door. It becomes so silent. I draw the curtains. I look into myself, I look. . . . Something has found its way into me, something. . . . No, I daren't say it. . . . The first time I saw you, I ran and locked myself in. . . . It was as if I couldn't breathe. I lay and wept. . . . It was as if the sky had become terrifyingly high. . . . The time you . . . the time you said my name . . . it became so high, so high. . . . It was as if I had never known how puny I was. . . . Everything became so big. . . . I couldn't sleep. . . . Life was so big. . . . There was something I didn't know. . . . There was something terrifying. . . . I felt it coming . . . coming.

'I wanted to flee. . . . I wanted to flee. . . . But it was everywhere. . . . The bushes stood there staring at me. . . . I knew of nowhere I could go, nowhere on earth. . . . I knew of nobody on earth I could any longer turn to. . . . Nobody on earth.

'And so . . . and so. . . .'

She flung her arms fervently around me without looking at me. 'Life's delight' burned on my cheek.

The moon stood between the two aspens. Like the smile of a sleeping woman, its light lay over the earth.

Five months have gone. The first white anemones have already appeared.

She is mine. She has been mine the whole winter. Many many days. Those evenings when the sky turned deep blue for two small creatures who stood and looked out at the horizon. Those mornings when the sun rose red and turned the hoar-frost to diamond dust. Those nights when the plain lulled us to sleep like an ocean. We will never move from here. Nowhere does nature draw such deep calm breath as she does here.

All has become so simple. The things I believed I would never again be close to: the earth, the branches, the tiny buds. These things no longer torment me; I no longer find them strange or incomprehensible.

And yet, as never before, there is a miracle in every drop of water.

And a miracle attaches to her, too. There is something within her I cannot get near. There is a secret within her. Sometimes I seem to see the whole great profundity of the world behind her eyes.

Many is the time, when I have been out in the evening and am returning home to our little house, that I find I am incapable of going in straightaway. I walk up and down. I look for her shadow on the curtain. I look back at the past. I try to understand why all things had to be as they were; and how she, even before I met her, has been woven into all I have lived through. It is so strange to think that all those other people have been together with her throughout her whole life, and yet I am the first to have seen her. No other person on earth has seen Naomi.

It is late now. Outside it is already night. It no longer makes me feel anxious. The night is mine. There is nothing behind it of which I am afraid.

She lies within. I will go and look at her.

She sleeps. Her face swims in billowing hair. Her breast rises and falls in rhythm with life itself, in rhythm with the movement of the planets. I felt something near to dread. It was as though God himself was there within.

[Original title: *Sletten*. Translated by James McFarlane]

TRYGGVE ANDERSEN

Gilded revenge

Under the high, slanting glass lid of the shrine, St. Valerius rests on gold-embroidered velvet cushions. A diadem crowns his skull; precious blue stones glitter in his eye sockets; his nose is a great smoke-coloured crystal; his lips are of heavy silver plate; every single finger on the crossed hands is thickly adorned with rings, and each fingernail is a huge pearl. Numerous golden medallions on golden chains hang about his breast, covering the ribs. Below his loins he is swathed in multi-coloured silks and lace.

St. Valerius glints and glitters and shines. No other saint's image, no other altar in the church is as brilliant with such splendour as his.

But candles are no longer offered at his shrine, and the townsfolk are far from proud of him. They can scarcely bear to hear his name named. If he happens to be mentioned, they will shy away from the subject and make a great to-do of praising the fine, venerable church and telling of the one-time monastery and the wealth and the learning of the monks. The more independent of them will perhaps murmur embarrassedly that his finery is probably not even genuine – nor possibly even the saint himself. If one should press them to be more precise, they will assure you that at one time the monastery did possess the genuine St. Valerius, who *could* perform miracles, and that at that time there were pilgrimages made to him and that the gold *was* gold and the stones *were* precious and the pearls were not imitation – so much was true, of that one could be sure.

But in that terrible, grim Thirty Years War, the so-called Swedish War, the church and the holy shrine were plundered, whereupon . . . whereupon. . . . Well, it isn't all that easy to be sure now what is true and genuine. . . .

The thing was this: the spiritual leaders were always said to have had their doubts about him, and had long since ceased to be zealous on his behalf, when one Whitsuntide it so happened that Resi – the priest's old and doddering kitchen maid – in the last year of her life decided to clean the glass cover; and she was clumsy enough to break it. Whereupon Wastl the carpenter, who was to make good the damage, noticed that some of the ribs were made of whitewashed wood. Wastl had always been a socialist and a gossip, and never could keep his mouth decently shut about anything; and the news reached the doctor just as he was waking from his after-dinner nap. He was a Prussian and a Lutheran; he at once hurried over to the church, looked around, sniffed about, laughed, then rushed across to the postmaster's inn and confirmed the carpenter's assertions, adding that several of the bones failed to match and obviously could not have come from one and the same skeleton.

And the word could not be withheld from the populace that St. Valerius was only a substitute saint.

The priest, poor man, did not dare protest against this, for at night he had secretly measured the bones with the dressmaker's measure belonging to his kitchen maid. The doctor had shortened her life, what there was left of it; and the few days that remained to her she spent whining and lamenting that she had been the cause of this misfortune and profanity.

But before that grim and ugly Swedish War the monastery had possessed the real Valerius, and in those days the gold was gold and the stones and the pearls were genuine.

It was late in the day. Two horsemen came trotting along the dusty road from the south, casting long swaying shadows across the parched fields of the high plateau. The costume of the one had once been fine and expensive, and from the brim of his hat there hung a large crumpled feather. He was a fleshy, fair-haired man, with a ruddy complexion, and he sat confident and indolent on his powerful horse, not bothering to reply to his thin, shabby-looking companion who rode beside him on a dun-coloured nag, talking and shouting volubly, until in time he became bored with his own futile prattle and abruptly stopped. But he found it hard to remain inactive, and as soon as they slackened their pace he turned in his saddle, stretched his neck and stared all round, taking stock. . . .

To the south was a snow-covered mountain range, furrowed by landslides, and with bare patches where the rock fell away most steeply. On the other side were forests; further than the eye could see they stretched to the north-east, imposing a green luxuriance on the open, cleared landscape. To the west, less than a mile away, a narrow cleft valley separated the plain from a series of low ridges. This was filled with yellowish smoke. Gently it followed the course of the river; but occasionally a faint gust of wind caused it to billow up, and an acrid cloud would filter through the pine thicket along the escarpment, and the horsemen could hear the noise of the river and the distant sound of many men shouting, and the roaring of cattle out of control.

The thin man knew the district, knew the names of the mountain peaks. As a lad he had played in these meadows, caught birds in this pine thicket, and he and his father had gone poaching in the woods. . . . Most familiar to him was the township by the monastery. It lay there still, immediately below them, but the great, spreading brick buildings with the spire-less church tower in the middle of them had been blackened by flames and stood roofless – the monks had not succeeded in re-roofing more than a single wing of one building. Little was left of the township; already bushes were growing on the ashes of the open spaces in among the few poverty-stricken cottages.

Five summers ago, one fine day like today, there had been plundering and burning and killing. . . .

He dozed and smiled vacantly, humming and rocking his body in rhythm with the horse's gait, conscious that beneath the shining blue sky there hovered downy-white wisps of cloud – today as on that earlier day. But he felt it was probably hotter today – the sun was burning down quite fiercely – and he licked his lips, sniffed, and quickly smelled the air. Ah ha! That clay-grey streak over the forest – that might betoken something. But it was not rising fast enough and was not black enough and it betokened nothing.

He grimaced at his companion's fat back. Junker Rüdiger swore he was steadfast under fire and against the sword if only he was good and drunk – sober he was pitifully scared even of a miserable little lightning flash. 'Heigh ho!' he intoned, pointing. 'I predict thunder and a good downfall tonight.'

The Junker jerked his reins, turned his head, growled angrily and spurred on his horse. The thin man sneered scornfully, but the sneer faded to a loose grin and his glance became fixed and listless. . . . Five summers since it was burned down. . . . Nine years since he ran away from the body of his father, scared to death, with a stolen crust in his fist. . . .

In the grey light of dawn they had burst out from the edge of the forest, forty horsemen – the whole of Junker Rüdiger's band of deserters, a savage and depraved rabble, the dregs of both Swedish and imperial regiments, of all kinds of religions and sects. With shouts and uproar they had burst across the plain and surrounded the township. But there it was silent and deserted. The people must have had wind of them and saved themselves in time. They just glimpsed the fugitives disappearing into the pine wood. Only one crazed old woman remained behind, sitting on the edge of the well in the monastery, cheering and shouting to them as they approached. 'Sepp! Kind Sepp!' she croaked incessantly at the thin man. 'Have you got my sons with you?' And as they crowded round her, grinning, she went tripping round the circle, staring hard at their faces, began hooting and howling, then flew off, her ragged garments flapping. . . .

Her sons . . . they had run away and joined them five summers ago. . . .

Their stay at the monastery was brief; they succeeded in convincing the common soldiery that there was no point in seeking plunder either in the stripped church or in these miserable cottages. So the band split up into two groups. One was to mount guard on the bridge over the river; the other was to push on a little way up the valley to another township which it was rumoured had so far escaped the ravages of the war. And a strange and merciful destiny so ordered things that this rumour, which had urged them into undertaking this long and dangerous expedition, turned out not to be one of the usual lies that were then current in the district; and that the well-fed peasants allowed themselves to be discovered shamelessly sleeping, so that the poor soldiers after months of painful deprivation were able to stock up with welcome provisions and fodder, and then leisurely make their way with the cattle and the other booty back down the valley to the bridge.

But Junker Rüdiger and his companion had their own errand which they preferred to accomplish alone; and they had therefore once again turned their steps in the direction of the monastery. They had no need to fear its monks or its peasants that day, for terror had driven them into the forest.

The horses were allowed to go at a walking pace. They rode through the flattened parts of the township with a clatter of hooves on the uneven stone paving of the streets. The thin man started up as though waking from sleep, struck his fist hard on his saddle horn, and sat up erect. His eyes glittered, there was a near audible tumult in his breast, though his heart scarce dared to beat for joyful excitement: nine years he had suffered and striven in order to win revenge over St. Valerius and his monks – nine terrible, aching years – and now the hour had come. Now his blissful, golden revenge must not slip out of his fingers! . . . He raised his arms, his fingers extended like claws, and screeched so that the sound echoed back from the walls.

The Junker stiffened fiercely and swore: 'Shut your mouth, Sepp! Shut your mouth, damn you!'

And feebly Sepp shut his mouth; he slumped in his saddle, his limbs slack. Perhaps he had even been made a fool of by that damned fat pig of a monk. . . .

He had not been born here in the district. He could only just remember as a young child being carried one night by his father past burning houses in a narrow street, and that later they led a wandering life as refugees in the north of the country. And at every point the war and the enemy had been at their heels, driving them south until they could see the snowfields. Only then did they find respite from the war. The monks offered them a place to live in the township. His father could make himself useful doing various jobs of work; furthermore, he was not wholly destitute in the matter of valuable possessions.

They were not badly off. The son ate his fill every day, and his pious neighbours taught him to bless his food. He throve, grew older, forgot the world's bloody troubles and became a spirited, open-hearted boy who was a great joy to his father when in the quiet of an evening they would go roaming in the forest in search of something for the pot.

Then one autumn the father fell sick and took to his bed, and that was the end of their good fortune. Week after week he was unable to work for the monks. But he had been a useful servant to them; they did not want to lose him and they treated him with unguents and other medicaments. He became bedridden, without bodily pain but with his mind enfeebled.

As they began to realize that he was hardly likely to be any good to them again and that he and his son might simply become a burden to them, they reminded themselves who the man was – that he was a stranger, an unknown, and that they had neglected to seek reliable evidence of his Christian faith and of his previous conduct. And it had been irresponsible of them to grant him residence on monastery land. They had heavy enough burdens to bear as it was in these godless and expensive times. The township had more than enough paupers already, who so to speak had a hereditary claim on their mercy.

One wondered whether he might not even be a renegade Anabaptist? Certain confused answers he had given one of the brothers with medical knowledge had roused suspicion; and, as the father's condition deteriorated, the abbot had summoned the boy to him to probe and ask questions.

Sepp understood not one iota of what was going on. He recited his creed by heart, and gave a full account of the way he lived. He dared confess quite openly and gave no evidence of heresy. Nevertheless a long-armed, bent-backed, and sour-eyed monk who supervised the distribution of alms announced that henceforth they had not the resources to support immigrant strangers, and that father and son would have to seek a different place to live. And the boy was sent away with an exhortation to call upon the saints, and especially St. Valerius, whose precious relics were in the custody of the monastery – it might well be that with his help they could be saved from their distress.

Back home in their poor little cottage Sepp threw himself on the bench by the stove, sobbing and puzzled. He could not turn for advice to his father who lay there babbling nonsense; and St. Valerius did not grant his favours for nothing, that he knew full well. But the old man had placed his secret possessions in a hollow space beneath a loose tile down by the wall of the hearth: a few silver dollar pieces and a short length of gold chain. He had confided in his son and revealed the treasure to him, while at the same time strictly forbidding him to touch it or to go boasting about it.

In an agony of conscience and fear the boy dug out the silver dollars and took them as a sacrifice to St. Valerius. One by one he carried them along; whereupon his prayers were heard and for some days he did not want for food, in so far as the saint softened the heart of the almoner. That this was not exactly cheap at the price was something beyond Sepp's comprehension of the transaction.

The sacrifice of the length of chain caused the most acute agony. On winter evenings behind locked doors he and his father used to sit by the fire and weigh the smooth, heavy gold links in their fingers, speculating about all the things they could buy for each individual piece; it had in truth become their secret treasure which, hidden deep in its dark hole, brought them a gleam of hope and confidence and faith in the future. Sepp had not tasted any food for forty-eight hours, since the day a widow woman had cheated her own children to give him a few grains of meal. He had begged his way from house to house without reaping anything better than abuse, until finally he dug out the length of chain and ran off with it.

And how St. Valerius showed his appreciation for the sacrifice . . .!

As Sepp was about to leave the church, he was grabbed by the back of his neck by a lay brother and dragged off to the almoner's room. Thence came also the abbot himself, high and mighty and swelling with rage, to interrogate him. Had not the boy or the father found the gold chain and hidden it? Or stolen it? And where was the rest of it?

No, they hadn't . . . they had *not*, he assured them. It had always been rightly theirs and had been kept under a loose tile by the wall of the hearth.

They hadn't robbed some wealthy traveller? It would be better for him if he admitted it at once. It was well known that he and his father used to lurk in the forest at night. . . .

But they weren't after travellers! Only very occasionally after a deer! And the boy fell on his knees, begging 'Mercy! mercy!'

They could not terrify him into saying more. Not a word to suggest that his father had hidden the rest of the chain or other precious things. But he was beaten and thrashed as far as the monks dared go, because he was a poacher and because he had tricked the monastery into giving him Christian alms of mercy which he had no need of.

Finally they bundled him into a corner and ordered him to stay there and not dare leave the monastery until the whole matter had been investigated at the scene of the crime. He sank down and remained lying prostrate, his brow pressed against the flagstones. He heard them leave and lock the door, but didn't dare move. And he sobbed and whimpered as a child will do. His tears dulled the pain, and after a time he fell asleep in his distress.

It was dark when he woke. He got up, brought one last convulsive sob from his breast, and sat there freezing and rubbing his sore eyes. The gnawing pains of hunger brought him fully awake, and at that moment he caught the smell of new-baked bread. He glanced round in the half-dark, sniffing, getting down on all fours and crawling across to the almoner's table. Underneath the table stood a large basket full of warm bread, the steam still rising from it. They must have carried it in while he was asleep.

He put a hand down into the basket, drew it up again, listened for a moment in terror, put one finger in his mouth and licked it. Then he snatched a loaf, opened his mouth wide and sank his teeth into the crust. He chewed and swallowed, crawled quickly back to his corner and remained sitting with the loaf in his lap, thinking.

Quietly he stood up, tiptoed one step at a time along the wall, reached the door and cautiously pressed the latch. It yielded, and the door swung open. For a long time he stood there on tiptoe, holding his breath. In the passage it was nearly dark and empty of people. He slipped through the crack in the doorway and, bent double, in leaps and bounds he ran straight off. The gates were open and on he went. Nobody saw him, nobody stopped him in the town. . . .

At their cottage he crouched down behind the corner and listened. A cold breath of night air whistled across the plain and rustled the roof thatch. The boy was sweating from his run, and now he shivered in his rags. Inside all was silent. The monks must have finished their investigation, and would not be any the wiser for it, he grimaced. . . . He wondered whether his father had cursed them. Every second word was an oath when the old man was delirious; and he wished them joy of all the oaths and all the garbage and the mouse droppings they would have raked about in if they had upturned all the junk there. Just so long as they hadn't turned too vicious, he shuddered to himself; because then they might have beaten his father and he was in no fit state to defend himself and couldn't stand much ill treatment. Oh, surely they wouldn't strike a sick man . . . not somebody who was extremely sick. . . .

But hunger began gnawing at his vitals, and the boy fondled the warm loaf. It was so good to stroke the smooth crust with the back of his hand. It was and remained silent in the cottage. His father was probably sleeping. And Sepp jumped up, confidently crossed the threshold and said proudly: 'Here's something for you to eat, Father!'

There was no reply. He waited, tense, then asked: 'Are you asleep, Father?' The room remained dark and silent; there was no sound of breathing, no groaning. His voice trembling with fear, he again called out: 'Here's something to eat, Father!'

He became aware of the embers smouldering in the hearth, and he made haste to kindle the fire with shavings, blowing on it until it burst into flame. He took his time, picking sticks out of the ashes and causing the meagre flame to flare up; but he was conscious of dawdling so as to put off turning his head. But when he looked to the side, half-blind from staring into the flames, he saw something long and white glimmering on the floor in front of the bed. He gave a start: perhaps his father had rolled out.

Yes, his father was lying naked on the floor. The boy lit a torch and cast light over him. He did not wake. He lay stiff with eyes wide open and had blood on his beard at the corners of his mouth. Sepp realized at once his father was dead.

He bent down and looked closer at the body. It had red weals and patches, the marks of whips and clubs. Across the middle of the breast was a broad rust-brown brand scar to which small pieces of charcoal still attached. Sepp also understood how his father had died, and who it was had tortured him to death.

He straightened his back, fumblingly seized the loaf from the edge of the hearth and rushed into the night, running for his life. . . .

One warm and clear May evening some years later Sepp came slinking through the pine thicket on the edge of the valley and sneaked up to the first house on the outskirts of the town. In it lived a widow and her two sons who had been his childhood friends.

He glanced quickly up the street. He had not been seen; and he pushed his cap at an angle and went boldly in with a greeting. He had grown tall and well-built, was well-dressed and tried to conduct himself like a real soldier. Nevertheless they were able to recognize him when he reminded the widow that she had once given him enough meal for a bowl of porridge while his father lay sick on his deathbed. Apart from that, nothing much was said about his father's death and his own running away; but he talked much about his exploits, about war and battles, and about his being in the service of an imperial colonel whose regiment had encamped at the foot of the valley and who were to defend the country against the Swedes. He had taken a few hours' leave to ride up to the township and look in on some acquaintances, he said. The guards at the bridge were looking after his horse. And he asked many questions about the monks, bore them no grudge and was sorry that he couldn't stay long enough to look in at the monastery.

Sepp remained until late at night. On his departure he presented each of his old friends with a silver coin, at which they were glad. He would very much have liked them to accompany him a little way, but their mother begged them not to – it was too unsafe at that time of night. So he went on his way alone.

The next day the Swedes swooped on the town and the monastery, burning and ravishing. And all those whom flight did not save were killed, and the widow's sons were murdered. But at the head of the Swedish forces rode Sepp. He yelled and bellowed and gave directions; he helped to blow open the church door and immediately rushed to where the shrine of St. Valerius should have stood. It had vanished. Whereupon he screamed like a madman. High and low they searched and rummaged for it; and captured monks were tortured to confess what they had done with it until their shrieks penetrated far across the plains – the Swedes' stern efforts were in vain. The shrine had disappeared. And because of this Sepp, who had led them off on this wild-goose chase into this remote and poverty-stricken district by his stories of the saint's rich splendour, was clapped in irons and delivered up to the provost-marshal. But he was adroit and agile; and before day had dawned he was again free as a bird and deep in the forest.

Years passed, and the stream of war whirled Sepp around the lands of Germany. He was swept right up to the north as far as Pomerania, even though he constantly strove to keep in the south where that deed which had become his life's most burning desire still remained undone. He often changed sides; and what his religion was he would have found it hard to say off-hand, so readily did he change.

One autumn he worked his way south to Bohemia and fell in with Junker Rüdiger and his band. They were the sort of men who mostly practised the trade of war as a form of private enterprise, and never swore allegiance to any marshal's banner if they saw an opportunity to avoid it. But they were exactly the sort he had in mind to join up with. He was received into the band and confided to Junker Rüdiger what he knew about the shrine of St. Valerius which the monks must have buried in some corner of the monastery and which the Swedes must have been too stupid to find.

The Junker wrinkled his brow and sighed thoughtfully. There was no guarantee that the man was telling the truth, and the saint might even have been removed to some safer place; it was quite probable that the sacred bones were now resting within the walls of some fortress town, seeing that the shrine seemed to be so fearfully precious. But he enjoined Sepp to keep silent about the matter; there was no point in sharing out among forty what with luck the two of them could nicely share between themselves. Apart from that, it would be foolish to sharpen the greed of the common soldiery when one couldn't be altogether certain whether it might not be sadly disappointed.

That winter was a bad time for the band. They set up their quarters in a ruined castle and kept body and soul together by foraging in an area which had already long ago been raided and stripped of everything that might serve to feed man or beast. And fear of more powerful leaders kept Junker Rüdiger from venturing out to find a better winter lair. Over Christmas, the situation became so bad that the scraggiest of the horses were slaughtered and eaten; and from about that time on, the wolves began to howl so angrily close to the houses that one might think they envied the humans their miserable fare; and the sentries grew so afraid of them they had to be kept at their posts by threats.

But evening after evening Sepp would sit laughing and joking with the Junker, keeping him in a good humour; and generally he would finish up describing the treasures in St. Valerius's shrine, the glitter of the gold and silver, counting up the pearls and the precious stones and calculating how many thousand ducats they could be sold for and what one could buy with that sort of ready money, and conjured up in the nobleman's poor dull brain visions of the most splendid affluence. He revived the game he and his father had played with the length of chain, and played it in masterly fashion. For eight years he had comforted his vengeful soul with it. He had presented St. Valerius with his chain; and the saint's shrine had become his own precious possession, separated from him only by an as yet unaccomplished act of revenge.

The fields became clear of snow; and Sepp rode off on reconnaissance and was absent several weeks. People began speculating whether the man was dead, or had found better associates; but he did not betray his company. He returned with good news of an unplundered township in the Bavarian mountains, leading behind him on a rope an old bent-backed and sour-eyed monk. It was the almoner whom Sepp had managed to get his claws on; and he had spared neither patience nor cunning to make sure of his quarry.

From sunset to daybreak the Junker and Sepp were closeted with him; and the pious brother raised his voice to such a pitch that not one of the band managed to sleep peacefully that night. When their conversation was finished, they took their leave of a corpse which lay stark naked and blood-spattered on the floor and had a broad brand scar right across the breast. But they now knew what they wanted to know: in the vault below the St. Joseph Chapel there were piles of bones from forgotten graves, and it was there that the saint's shrine was hidden.

The horsemen had arrived. They dismounted in front of the main arched door of the monastery, and Sepp led the horses into the courtyard and tethered them by the well. The Junker trudged behind, stiff-legged and panting, his doublet unbuttoned. They were tired and weary after the ride in the heat of the day, and they took off their hats and stood silent in the cool of the shade, listening to the sound of the horses drinking.

The high walls round the quadrangle were streaked from fire and smoke, and the window openings yawned empty and black. But the place had not been unlived in – quite a few of the monks had reassembled there. Heavily battened doors had been hung at the entrances; the tufts of grass that sprang up among the flagstones in the courtyard showed the signs of a regular tread; near the church wall, right by the door, a row of rough-hewn beams were set up to dry, and in one of them was stuck a long-shafted tree-feller's axe.

Sepp yawned lazily and smiled up at the blazing sky. Well, the monks had patched up their little nest; but they wouldn't have much lasting joy of their work, if he had anything to do with it. They had made a canopy of tarred planks on the church tower, he saw. Those dry chips over there under the beams would catch hold nicely. The monastery would bear the signs of each visit he had made to it. . . .

Suddenly he exploded with laughter, leaned over the edge of the well and slaked his thirst, ducking his face and splashing the horses because they had muddied the water. The Junker squinted at him in annoyance – what the devil was this crazy man laughing at? He couldn't tolerate such undisciplined and childish behaviour from an otherwise efficient soldier, and he swore as he was in the habit of doing when these paroxysms overcame Sepp: 'Shut your mouth – shut your mouth, damn you!'

But Sepp paid no attention. He patted his horse, asked its forgiveness, kissed it on the muzzle, hummed a song and laughed.

The Junker bit back his anger, drew out a bottle from the pocket of his doublet, took a long swig and put it back in his pocket again without offering it to the other. 'St. Joseph's Chapel?' he asked abruptly.

Sepp paid no attention to the question. He danced round the well singing, his body twisting and turning, his thin limbs gangling and flopping. And laughter answered his laughter. A yellow grinning face poked out through the doorway: it was the mad woman. She shuffled in, wagging her hips, tripping and waving and shrieking with joy. He seized her hands and dragged her along as they leaped and sang.

Junker Rüdiger gazed at them in bewilderment; he felt scared. Could this ruffian be possessed . . . mad? And here he was alone with him. 'St. Joseph's Chapel – where is it?' he stammered. 'We must hurry – St. Joseph's Chapel, you mad dog, you!' he fumed, shaking his fist.

Sepp slung the old woman away from him. He bounded wildly over to the beams, jerked out the axe and raised it. 'This could be useful,' he said, strutting across to the door of the sacristy and breaking it open.

'Wait!' shouted the Junker. 'We must shut the gate.'

Sepp waited, intent, unmoving, leaving to the other man the task of closing the two halves of the door and placing the heavy bar in place. But the laughter continued to bubble in his throat, and occasionally it would spurt out as they strode down the nave. Behind them padded the old woman, barefoot.

The trapdoor in St. Joseph's Chapel was nailed up with a double set of iron nails, and they had to hack away at the tough oak so that the noise boomed and re-echoed through the church, and then force it open with all their strength before they succeeded. But then it burst open and they fell back at the stench of noxious, foul air that met them.

'In Hell's name!' sneezed Sepp, hawking. He pushed the trapdoor to one side and tried to fathom the depth of the blackness. 'There's a ladder. It's probably strong enough,' he reported. 'After you, good sir. . . !'

Junker Rüdiger did not reply. He had with him a small leather bag and from it he produced a tinderbox and a wax taper, which he lit and handed to his companion. 'Hurry!' he commanded angrily. 'You damned ape, by evening we could have all the monks and everybody on our backs. . . .' Sepp laughed unconcernedly and went down. A moment later he shouted up, and the Junker took his leather bag and climbed down after him. The old woman took up her perch on the top rung of the ladder and scratched her legs.

The wax taper was placed on a rack on the wall and threw a streak of light under the low mould-covered roof with its hanging cobwebs and lit up a pile of human bones as high as a man filling the whole of one end of the vault. Sepp stood hacking at the pile with his axe, knocking holes in grim-looking skulls and muttering to himself.

'Is it here?' said the Junker. He was holding on to the ladder and had no great mind to abandon it. 'Have you found anything? Where the devil is it, I'm asking?' But at his first step he slipped in some green slime, fell and swore wildly; and the old woman guffawed and gloated. Sepp continued uninterruptedly with what he was doing. He measured the thickness of the pile, inserted the blade of the axe horizontally into the middle of it, pressing it and manoeuvring it till there was only the end of the shaft left to get hold of. 'Aha!' He shook it and hauled on it, and the bones crunched. 'Aha! Aha!' He hauled harder, and a clattering avalanche of bones tumbled about him. Half the pile collapsed and the taper flickered and nearly went out.

'In God's name!' The Junker staggered away, choking and blinded by the stench and the dust. The old woman slid down the ladder and remained sitting on the lowest rung.

Sepp tramped about on the heap, used the shaft of the axe to bring down the rest of the pile bit by bit; he then began raking and sweeping and scooping, causing the skulls to roll and the splinters to fly.

'Here it is!' he shouted hoarsely and straightened up. 'I can see. . .' His voice faltered; he coughed and waved his arms about. 'Come and help me,' he whispered and waved. And the old woman squirmed and wheezed and waved back, but the Junker was at once by his side. Yes, in the name of Satan, there it was! The shrine! There was the glint of a brass-bound corner. . . .

And they both bent double and scooped and raked, and they dug it out – a long, dark-brown carved coffin with handles. The glass lid was protected by slats which were nailed on. They seized the handles and tried to lift it. It was too heavy; but straining, toiling, groaning, they dragged it free of the heap of bones.

Sepp cut the slats and broke them off and smashed in the glass of the lid and the cross-pieces. And in the uncertain light of the taper came the glint and glitter of St. Valerius, from the diadem round his brow, from eye-sockets and nose and mouth, from the gold and silver on his breast, from the rings and pearls on his fingers.

The monk had not lied. They looked at each other, pale and faint from the break in the tension.

The Junker wanted to speak but could not. He moistened his lips and nodded and prepared his leather bag to take the booty. But Sepp snatched the taper, struck it firmly on the shrine, knelt down and groped with trembling hands among the glittering ornaments covering the breast. His length of chain . . . was it there? He pulled at the chains, making the skeleton shake and creak. And he fumbled with the links, because they might have been welded to another length . . .

'Stop that!' ordered the Junker, consumed with haste. 'We can divide up afterwards. Fill up the bag.'

'My piece of chain . . .' he replied piteously. 'I want it. . . .'

'We'll find it later. . . . We'll divide up later,' said the Junker, as though to a fretful child. 'Fill up the bag!' He stood holding it open, quivering with impatience.

The length of chain was not there. Sepp snatched up a bunch of chains. There were bits of bone in with them, and he flung them all into the bag. He spat in the face of the saint, snapped the head off its neck and handed it to the Junker. 'Strip the jewels off that!' he said, grabbing the bag and pouring in chains, medallions, crosses, hearts and limbs of precious metal, and all the precious sacrificial wealth. . . .

But when the skeleton lay there stripped and bare, he felt totally exhausted. Suddenly he felt a deep compulsion to sleep; and he leant his elbows on the shrine and breathed in deep. Oh no, it wouldn't do to be tired now. They had no time to rest. 'This is worth something, this is,' he said drowsily and shook the bag. 'How much would you get for it?' he said glancing up, more alert. The Junker had drawn his dagger and was busy trying to loosen the diadem which was attached to the brow.

'Don't know,' he growled. 'A lot. . . .'

That it would be a lot was something Sepp knew already. And they were to share as equals – *this* they had sworn on oath. It would be a lot; nor would it be any less, if . . . He set to work on the saint's hands; these he had saved till last. Deftly and carefully he prised off the nails' pearls, tore a patch off the loincloth and wrapped them in it. But some of the rings seemed almost forged on to the fingers. This damned plated ring simply would not detach from the left thumb, so he tipped it too into the bag. Couldn't they sell the relics also? . . . 'Hi, master Jew!' he thought with amusement, 'what about a hundred ducats for the thumb of St. Valerius? He who possesses this enjoys complete immunity and security against the long-fingered mob, though he himself can still charm the crown off the emperor's bald pate as well as the last farthing from the pockets of poor invalids and hungry children. . . .' But the Jew is cunning. He won't make any offer for this most sacred thumb – dare not indeed, for fear of the Pope in Rome. He wants more worldly things, precious stones and gold and silver ornaments, these are the things he wants. And for these things he counts out a hundred ducats, a thousand ducats, and no questions asked of a brave soldier on the matter of where these treasures have come from. And the soldier buys himself a set of the finest clothes it is seemly for a peaceful citizen to wear – for you don't catch *him* remaining a soldier any longer! He wants to enjoy what is his in peace, wants a house and a garden and comfort and regular food and drink and silken sheets with down coverlets and a virtuous virgin to take to wife. And when he walks across the market place in the mornings and meets his respectable fellow citizens, they will greet him and he them, and the burgomaster is not too grand to accompany him home, and his young and beautiful wife will pour out the wine. . . .

Sepp smacked his lips, but the roof of his mouth was dry; and he felt deep in his belly the bad air of the vault. And it was cold; he shivered.

The left hand was now stripped, and he was busily screwing away at the rings on the right. . . . This business about the wife and the burgomaster he hadn't really enjoyed all that much today . . . perhaps it had been told a bit too often . . . what the house was to be like . . . what he would buy. . . .

Strange, he didn't seem to be able to remember what he wanted to buy with the money. All his desires seemed dead in him. It didn't help to summon up for pleasurable inspection that crowd of dreams which his desire had recruited . . . they did not obey him, these dreams.

He would get himself . . . what he wanted was. . . . No, he was bored with his own stories. They had become faded and cloying. He disdained them. The gold was his, half of what was in the bag; and before the month was out he would have bought himself the very things themselves, the *actual* things, everything he had a mind to. And he wouldn't have to compel his dreams to be kind to him. . . .

But if only his length of chain had turned up, he wouldn't have exchanged that for a mint of money. He would have sewn it into the lining of his jacket where nobody would suspect its existence and nobody could steal it, for he would never suffer ill-luck as long as he had it.

It wasn't ever bigger than about so – he spanned it with his fingers on his sleeve. And he stiffened and stood there staring, remembering what he was reluctant to remember – the thing that had driven him on in life, and left him scared of looking back. Constantly he had had this memory at his heels. . . . The corpse of a naked man, stretched on the floor with a broad rust-brown scar across its chest and blood on its grey beard and wide-open eyes. He blinked and shook himself. His father's fate. Hah! that monk, the almoner, he had also lain like that. . . . The length of chain had paid interest . . . bloody, golden, exorbitant interest! Here lay St. Valerius, as poor as the corpse of last year's sinner still hanging on the gallows. And tonight the monastery would burn again, and the monks would be turned out into the highways and byways. . . .

Yes, indeed, that piece of chain had brought him gold and good fortune. Revenge was his, and the gold was his. Soon there would be house and home, and barrels of wine, and a virtuous virgin for a wife. . . .

'There you are, you old crone! You shall have your mite!' he laughed, and flicked the last ring to the old woman, who was sitting there lost in thought, staring and not moving.

'Ugh! The way you cackle!' The Junker was poking away at the jewels in the eye-sockets. He was finished with the diadem and the adornments to the nose and mouth and had put the objects in his pocket. 'Don't make me scratch the stone. Pick up the ring and put it in the bag. And shut up!'

'I will laugh and I will cry when I want to,' replied Sepp truculently. All this abuse, all this ordering about would have to stop. And he would say so. He straightened up. 'Shut up yourself! The agreement was that we should be equals and share equally. . . .'

'It was,' the Junker quietly admitted. He tossed the skull into the shrine and looked at him with narrowed eyes. 'Aren't they fine?' He showed off the stones. 'The sensible thing would be to sell them and share the proceeds – they are a pair,' he said amicably, while his glance idly swept over the vault. 'She doesn't really want the ring, and it might as well go in the bag as lie there in the dirt. . . .'

'Put it in the bag yourself – and don't put it in your pocket!' muttered Sepp angrily. That oily conciliatory tone had brought his rage to boiling point. And they were to complete the share-out before leaving the monastery, he insisted brusquely.

'Yes, yes!' the Junker said soothingly, his voice smooth and good-natured. As long as they had time for it. But they shouldn't fall out over a thing like that. He opened the bag, looked in it, then elaborately emptied his pockets. There didn't seem to be as much there as had at first appeared. 'Might there not be a few bits and pieces left in the coffin?' he asked slowly, and Sepp bent down irritably to look. Bloody mean old devil. . . .

'He's coming to stab you!' squealed the old woman. He threw himself to one side, felt a searing slash across his shoulders, and staggered two or three steps. The axe . . . he remembered. His groping hand found the shaft, and an angled blow found its mark. Junker Rüdiger fell without a sound backwards into the pile of bones, his jaw split wide and blood spurting from his throat. . . .

Sepp felt his back . . . he still did not know what was going on. What had happened? The old woman was howling up in the chapel where she had fled.

The Junker twitched; there was a gurgling in his throat. Now he was dying. 'We were to have shared equally, you crafty braggart!' sneered Sepp. Then he threw the bag over his shoulder and climbed up the ladder.

It was already dark in the church and it would be best to hurry. It was only too true that the enemy could fall upon you at night. He stopped and shifted the bag from one shoulder to the other. It wasn't particularly heavy, but it rubbed against the wound on his shoulder, which was bleeding and painful, with the blood running down his back. He ought to tie a bandage over it – one should never neglect cuts and wounds. If you left them to fester, they could be dangerous . . .

But the man who had luck on his side need scarcely fear misfortune – and he himself had been lucky, damned lucky. The wealth he was carrying was his and his alone, since the Junker had broken the agreement and forfeited his share. The rest of the company had had in ample measure what he had promised them before the expedition: meat and fodder and the peasants' modest possessions – things he had not demanded any part of. And he wouldn't be cheating them out of a farthing by not squandering any of his rightful possessions on these simple bandits. . . .

Oh, how the blood had gushed from that noble-born assassin, he smiled murderously as he glanced into St. Joseph's Chapel. A red light came through the trapdoor: the wax taper stood burning on the shrine. Strange it hadn't gone out while they were fighting. It would have been nasty for him if it had.

In the courtyard the horses were neighing and pawing the flagstones. The animals were weary of waiting, had had no hay for their feed. 'Let's not get restless,' he said to them comfortingly, patting them. 'We'll leave at once, on the dot.' They whinnied.

Carefully he washed his wound and bound it. But then he remained sitting and brooding on the edge of the well. Sepp was thinking of telling the others in the band that they had run into a mob of monks and that Junker Rüdiger had been killed – that lie would not be difficult. It would be more difficult to get clear with the bag unshared; and he was in no state to devise a reliable means of bringing it into safekeeping. In the forests and in the valley there lurked peasants and monks. The one road led across the bridge and there the band had mounted a guard; and he would have to remain in their company for the next few days. . . .

It was so silent and deserted there among the tall empty buildings. Occasionally birds would chirp and chatter up in the window openings as they prepared to rest . . . or one of the horses might snort and scrape its hoof. Sepp racked his brains, brooding till he felt he was going crazy. And the difficulties seemed to him to become worse and worse.

Share he would not! He had no intention of giving up the slightest part of what was his. Anyway, the others would not be content with small measure. Undoubtedly they would want the major share – chains and rings and precious stones. And the one who would be left poor at the end would be him. The fear that he might lose this golden wealth throbbed and reverberated within him, until he trembled in an agony of soul.

Dispirited, he stood up. He hadn't eaten at all that day, nor had he brought provisions with him. He inspected the Junker's saddlebags, but found not a crumb. He must have food; it would soon be dark, and he could not stay here. He would have to make his way to the bridge, and he would keep the bag concealed as best he could for as long as he remained with the gang. And it wouldn't do to set fire to the monastery this time. Sepp was close to tears.

The Junker – that scoundrel – would have quickly dealt with the problem! He was so high and mighty they wouldn't have dared let their fingers stray near *his* bag. If that miserable assassin hadn't broken his oath and their agreement, if only he wasn't lying rotting like fat carrion there in that vault, everything would have gone so smoothly. . . .

'I'll ride to the bridge!' Sepp swore, and went to the gate to remove the bar and fling wide the doors. Then he heard a whining sound like that of a terrified dog and he saw the old woman lying crouched in a corner.

'Don't be afraid of me,' he said softly. 'I won't do you any harm, you old crone!'

'Dear Sepp . . . don't go to the bridge,' she whimpered. 'Those nasty soldiers . . . they'll kill you. . . .'

'I must!' he answered gruffly. 'Get out of the way. . . .'

The heavy doors grated on their hinges; and away past the houses and the ashes of the town he stared across the darkening, grey-yellow plain towards the snow peaks to the south. The air was dead calm and wet with dew.

'Dear kind Sepp . . . don't go by the bridge . . . they'll kill you!' she begged. 'Go by the ford. . . .'

The ford? He gave a start. For there *was* a ford a mile and a half above the bridge, but it was never passable until late summer when the river was at its lowest. 'It's impossible at this time of year,' he muttered.

'They used it last week,' she said. 'They are using it . . . they daren't use the bridge because of the nasty soldiers.'

'Who is using it?' He seized her by the arm and shook her.

'Everybody. . . . My sons used it last week,' she whimpered. He looked sharply at her and let her go. Was it just crazy nonsense, or wasn't it? Her sons were dead . . . died five summers ago. . . . But it could be that the ford was passable; the peasants might have done something to it during the war. It wouldn't take a great deal of work to. . . . Well, he would try. If your luck is in, you rarely run much risk.

And as though in a transport of courage and hope he sprang across to the well, picked up the bag, unhitched the Junker's horse and leaped into the saddle.

'Goodbye, old woman! And thanks!' he shouted and rode through the gate at a trot. And she curtsied and replied: 'Goodbye, Sepp! Greet my sons!'

He laughed and sang as he rode through the dusk, not caring to think of danger or treachery.

The monks strung the dead Junker up on the tall new gallows which the monastery built for itself; and a month later he received a companion when the body of an enemy horseman was washed ashore in a backwater below the ford.

Then ardently praying that they would be able to find the right bones, they collected up St. Valerius from the pile of bones and laid him once again in his shrine and decorated him as richly and with as much glitter as they could with their limited resources.

[Original title: *Den gyldne hevn*. Translated by James McFarlane]

RAGNHILD JØLSEN

Hanna Valmoen

Hanna Valmoen lay with her head under the bedclothes, crying. It was unusual for Hanna Valmoen to cry, she had always been such a cheerful girl. And no one must hear it – not Ottilli, who had always said that *he* no doubt thought himself too good for her; not Isak, who had always believed that she was so proud and sure of herself; not her mother, who was old and had nodded and nodded over her woolcarding or her knitting: 'Many a strange thing has happened in this world, my girl!' Mother who had believed so strongly that something just as strange and wonderful was going to happen to Hanna too. Hanna could clearly remember one particular occasion when her mother had reckoned up, at the same time as she was counting the stitches she was casting on for a sock, she had reckoned up one after the other of the lucky girls she had come across in her lifetime or heard tell of – like that Hansine Bækstua, who had lived in a cottage that was so filthy and disgusting that the walls were crawling with lice, and she herself wasn't much better; but didn't she get a doctor's son, and didn't she finish up as a vicar's wife? And Johanna Topknot, as they called her because of the long tangled mass of hair that hung down behind her – and who couldn't stay on as a baker's girl because people complained that they were always finding hair in their bread – *she* got no less than a schoolteacher. Not to mention Mallena, one-armed Elsa's daughter, who wandered from farm to farm, begging and stealing, see if she didn't get the owner of Ulvengården – and *him* she could even afford to get tired of; for one fine day she ran away with a captain or something like that – anyway he had a broad red stripe down his trousers and a long sword at his side – and if it was true what people said, then she had been married in a snow-white silk dress with yards and yards of train. And if these girls had done so well for themselves, Hansine, Johanna, Mallena, who if it comes to that weren't all that good-looking, nor, as far as the old woman could see, was there anything attractive about them, but on the contrary were as full of faults as an old ruin of fungus –

why shouldn't Hanna, who was such a fine girl, well-built, clean, neatly dressed, the sort of girl people turned to look at when she went to church – why should *she* not get anyone she wanted? Yes, that Hanna, have you ever seen such a girl, just look at the bundles of firewood she gathered in the forest – even Isak couldn't carry a heavier load; she was flushed and perhaps a little out of breath when she let the bundle of sticks fall, but that was all – she made nothing of it. A girl like that, why shouldn't *she* do well for herself? And if *he* – well, why shouldn't something come of it, if he was fond of her – and that he certainly was. And she came from a decent family, who'd always kept themselves respectable – her father had been a tenant farmer, who had tilled the soil of Sittgården in the sweat of his brow and struggled down with many a load of rough-hewn logs over the trackless ridges, until one day the cold took him and laid him in the cemetery. Then her mother was left in poverty with six children aged from fourteen to three. But she had never gone on the parish – she'd struggled through with spinning, berry-picking, and earning a little extra here and there, just as doggedly as Lars with his logs. And then there was the estate!

Now old mother Valmoen could lie in her bed and have a good rest, all the toil had made her old and sent her early into her second childhood; but she had raised her children, the three eldest had places of their own now, and the three youngest, who still lived at home at Valmoen, were all hard-working – Isak and Ottilli earned good money on the farm, and Hanna stayed home and helped around the house; for old mother Valmoen wouldn't know what to do without her little girl, Hanna had always been her mother's pet, and kind and good she was too – it was like one wall missing when Hanna wasn't in the cottage, old mother Valmoen used to say.

Now and again Hanna Valmoen lifted her head from under the covers and looked across at her mother's bed; she was so very fond of the smooth white head which lay there – so deeply fond of this mother of hers – they'd had such a happy, cosy time together as they pottered around doing things in the house all day long, talking about this and that. And she was completely different to talk to than the other girls or Ottilli, who usually just pooh-poohed anything Hanna said. Of course they talked about nothing else but boy-friends, the other girls and Ottilli; but the way they talked about it, it was almost as if it didn't mean anything to them; sometimes it was just as if they went out with boys because they thought it was the thing to do – in order to count for anything, you had to have a boy-friend, and nobody wanted to be left out. So many of them went out on the hills with a boy because it was fun; but many others did it to be like the others. And then all that business about rings, which they all made such a fuss about! Some of them had friendship rings, the ones with two hands made of silver; some had rings of French gold, which made your finger black; some had wide, smooth rings of real gold, and the girls who had that sort were always showing them off by scratching their faces the whole time. Hanna Valmoen had a ring too; but that one was made of straw – *he* had been sitting and winding a straw round his finger once, and when he tossed the straw ring away it fell into her lap, and she had kept it – and there was no doubt that she had for a long time been just as fond of that straw ring as any other girl of her gold ring, and to this very day she still kept it in her chest of drawers. And she couldn't for the life of her see why it was necessary to walk about scratching your nose with a gold ring on your finger.

The only thing that really mattered, that was surely the happiness you felt inside – if *that* was great, then it didn't matter if the ring was made of straw; and if *that* was small, then it made no difference if the ring was made of gold. But then she wasn't like the others – it wasn't, as they said, that she was too stuck-up to be friends with them; she just felt that she didn't belong with them. And then they must have found out from Ottilli about *him*; she could see it when she met them as she went to do her shopping at the grocer's, how they nudged each other, and she could often hear them sneering when they'd gone past. But they could do that as much as they liked, Hanna had had so much else to think about, and it was as if nothing could affect her as long as he . . . but now it had all changed, now all the misery came back to her, and she had to cry and cry, whether she thought about her mother, who was so nice, or the girls, who were so nasty, or the straw ring; but most of all when she thought of *him*, who was so good-looking, and whom she – and it was no wonder – was fonder of than all the other girls put together were of their boy-friends, him she had been thinking about every minute of the day, but who had come driving up Sittgårdsbakken that very afternoon together with a fine lady with a long pale blue veil – dear God! – now he had surely forgotten Hanna Valmoen! Hadn't she been thinking so much about him coming, and hadn't she just happened to be standing down by the gate with the cow, just as they came, the two of them. She could have gone back, hidden herself in the bushes when she heard his voice from down the hillside, but she didn't think of it. Side by side they sat in a one-horse carriage, a fine one with large yellow wheels and a glossy long-legged horse pulling it; she was just laughing at something he had said, and she was fair and had red roses in her cheeks; he sat as he usually did, straight and strong as a pine tree, and he held the reins in one hand and a long whip in the other; then he said something else and laughed at it himself – and then he caught sight of *her* by the gate. Then he cracked his long whip, so that the horse started into a gallop, and so they disappeared between the trees. And *she*, how she had been waiting for him, and how she had set her heart on him; oh, he had seemed to her to be the most wonderful man in the whole world, long before he had taken any notice of her, when he came on visits to Sittgården. It was as if he had always had restless blood – he had always been a bit wild and reckless, they said, and it didn't make him any better being down there in France year in and year out; but he was the sort of man that no one could really get cross with – and Hanna Valmoen could understand that well enough – and so well-built, and so strong! She could remember the story of how there once were two men down at the headland with boat-hooks, struggling and pulling for all they were worth to drag a great log up on to a sledge. Then *he* came past, and he pushed the men to one side and pulled the heavy, water-logged tree trunk up on his own, just as if it were nothing at all. Hanna Valmoen just had to think about him, think and cry, even if she cried herself to death! But the strange thing was that as she went over it all in her thoughts, as she had done so often before, counted up on her fingers, both in days and in hours, when he had looked at her, when he had spoken to her, when he had met her, and what happened the day before, and what happened the day after – she got so excited that she almost forgot her sorrow for a while. Oh yes, the first time he had looked at her, it was such a fine summer's day – she was over at the estate helping in the barn, because the milkmaid was ill. He was standing out in the middle of the farmyard just as she came past with her arms full of green fodder; he stood there with one hand on his hip smoking something; his clothes were all white, and she felt hot with embarrassment, because she thought perhaps there was something funny about her, and she thought she would never get across the farmyard and down to the barn, because she could feel him following her with his eyes the whole time. When she got to the passage into the barn she was in such a state that she was shaking all over, so she had to go into the haystore and sit down. A moment later someone came, and when she looked up she saw him standing in his white clothes in the aisle; but he couldn't see her, for she was sitting in the dark. 'There was such a pretty girl went in here,' he said. 'Where are you – are you hiding?' He stood for a minute, waiting for an answer. But she couldn't answer, her heart was beating so violently. Then he twirled his small, fair moustache, and then he went. Afterwards she was very sorry that she hadn't answered despite her trembling and her thumping heart – it would have been such fun to hear what he would have said next; but she had done the right thing, her mother said, when Hanna came home and told her about it. So she tried to be satisfied with that, though *that* was not easy. But then came the great dance. Holm had put up a large, open dance-hall right out on the hill, and the hall was decorated with greenery and flags. The band of the Shooting Club itself played for the dancing; they sat on a dais at one end of the hall, and the newly polished horns shone like gold, and all the red flags glowed too, and all the coloured lights, which hung in long rows up under the roof and amongst the garlands of heather. It all looked so gay! Out on the floor they swung round in the dance, enjoying themselves thoroughly, polkas and barn dances one after the other, and those who didn't know the steps stamped along in their own fashion. Along the posts of the walls there were fastened benches for the girls who were not dancing; but it was mostly the older women who sat there; for the girls were just as keen as the boys to go outside and get some fresh air between dances – and besides, they already knew their way around these hills so well.

As for Hanna, she had been sitting on the benches amongst the older women; she didn't really think she could leave her mother on her own that evening any more than any other time. It was fun just sitting and watching, anyway. And just then along came Holm with a whole company of fine folk, both the merchant from town, with his thick white hair and his pale eyes, and fat older ladies in brown silk dresses and slim young ladies with bands round their waists, and both the older ladies and the younger ones had broad bottoms. And last in the company was he. They all laughed and were in such frightfully good humour. The young ladies all stood in a ring round him the whole time, and when he wanted he could make them laugh so that they squirmed and fluttered their handkerchiefs. But all at once he grew quiet, and stood looking around in all directions, and suddenly he walked abruptly away from the young ladies, straight across the floor over to her and held out his hand: 'Will you dance with me?' he said. So they danced. There was a man who could dance! He didn't hold her loosely – no, firm as a rock – and how he could lead. He didn't go bumping into other people; he swung his partner in the dance better than the doctor swung his fast sleigh. *He* didn't bump your knees, and he didn't trample your toes to pieces. And he could dance backwards too, But she could feel after a while that she was growing heavy and dizzy. 'Are you tired?' he said, and he laughed and danced a little further towards the place where she had been sitting. 'Hup, my lass!' and he lifted her up in the air as he let her go. Holm had spun round towards him, frowning; they said that Holm was not a man who liked anyone – and least of all a member of his own family – making fun of his workers. Fun! Hanna didn't think that he'd been making fun of her in the slightest – he hadn't done anything other than what any lively lad could have thought of doing. But just because he was of fine folk and she was of common folk, they had to say that he was laughing at her; and mother agreed with her too, the other girls were only jealous, she said. Ah yes, that was how things were then! And Hanna's dizziness remained for the whole evening and the night too, after that dance. The boys were flocking round for a while, asking her to dance; but she said no; she just couldn't. And then they laughed, because they got cross: 'No, you're too fine for us now,' they said. 'If he's danced you giddy already, you'd better watch out,' said one with a nasty look in his eyes. But it was true that that dance had been too much for her. As she sat there beside her mother, everything seemed suddenly so very small, she saw the hall and all the people far, far away, and she felt that in a way she was not there herself any longer, and the horn music she could hear now right in her ears, now far off in the roar of the waterfall. And she was surprised when everything went quiet. But then she saw through the mist that something was being offered round on large trays; she saw Holm standing up on the dais with a glass in his hand, saying something – how small he looked too! She saw that he wiped his eyes once, and when he had finished and got down from the dais they all began to shout hurrah – and then she saw that they were chairing Holm in triumph. But while all this was happening, *he* and the young ladies were not there. They must have left almost straight away in order to carry on the party at home.

And then towards midnight Hanna and her mother made their way slowly home; they didn't see a sign of Ottilli, she didn't come home until well on into the next day – there'd been such wild goings-on during the night, Hanna heard later, that people had never seen the like. And yet there was a nice, steady boy who said to her once when she met him: 'You'd have done better to come with us, Hanna, than keep to yourself.' At the time she had puzzled over what the boy could have meant by that, and it was quite a while before she had worked it out. He meant that she would do better to stay and have a merry time with her own people, rather than go and set her heart on one who would only make her unhappy. Oh, everyone had to live in their own way! But it could be that the boy was right after all. . . .

A few days later, as she was standing outside the cottage doing some washing, she again had the feeling that someone was looking at her: it was *him*, with his gun slung on his back. 'Did I frighten you again?' he asked. 'I wonder if you could tell me the short cut to Kroktjernet, please? There's a grebe up there I want to take a shot at!' She started pointing and explaining, and her mother came out too to help. 'No,' he said at last and laughed, 'I can't make head or tail of all that. I shall have to ask you to set me on my way!' He said it very politely. 'Yes,' replied Hanna, and dried her hands and arms. 'Put your shawl on, child,' said her mother, 'you're shivering.' So they set off up the wooded hillside, he and she. 'Did you enjoy the dance, then?' he asked. 'Yes, it was fun,' she answered. 'I heard that you were one of the wildest who carried on through the night,' he said. She clapped her hands together: 'But for heaven's sake, how can they say that – I went home with mother, I did!' She heard him laughing behind her. Soon after that they had to climb up over more uneven ground. 'The going's a bit rough here,' she said. 'But it's the right way!' Then it happened, as she climbed up in front on to a large, green stone, and he was following a little behind, that he suddenly threw his arms around her, those arms that she knew so well from the dance, those arms which held so firmly. And she smelt again the same fine smell of him. 'Now I've caught you, you little runaway!' he said.

After that time they often met in the forest, mostly in the evenings, but also in the middle of a sunny day; and now it was a bit difficult to separate one occasion from the other – it seemed to her just the same as at the dance, with the roar of the waterfall and the mist, and horn-blowers far off in the roar of the waterfall. And he, he had been good and kind – oh no, just as often he had been nasty and horrible! He had asked her if she could swim. That made her laugh; for how could she have learnt that! 'Are you mad, girl,' he said, 'you'll drown one day if you carry on like that! In with you and learn!' She put up a struggle, of course. She begged him not to, and when that did no good, she got cross and shook him by the collar – couldn't he let her be, horrible thing that he was! He thought that was great fun. But if he was strong, then so was she, and it ended with them both falling in. She must have nearly drowned then – dear God, if only it had happened! It seemed to her already as if they were drifting down through something soft and good. But then he pulled her up again, and afterwards they went and lay on a grassy hillside and dried their clothes in the sun. 'I almost thought you were going to drown me for fun,' she had said. Then he looked at her with warmth in his eyes. '*I* drown *you*, Hanna?' was all he said. And she felt how much she loved him – so much that her whole breast ached. 'If only you would,' she said, 'if only you would!' 'I shall drown you and pull you up again every single day,' he laughed. 'No, don't pull me up again!' 'What a funny thing you are,' he said. 'Don't you like being alive?' And then he pulled her towards him and kissed her. Oh yes, she liked being alive. But dear God, dear God, that was how it was then! Now he came along with a young lady with a pale blue veil – and he hardly looked at Hanna Valmoen, just cracked his whip. Why had he bothered with her then, if it was just in order to leave her again; and what had she done to him, that made him crack his whip when he saw her? She was on a lawful errand, and she certainly would never, as God was her witness, cross his path on purpose. But he shouldn't have crossed hers first either! And he should never have been so nice – for nice indeed he was: once he had fastened a large red silken scarf around her neck, and many a time he had had chocolates in splendid boxes in his pocket for her – that must be the sort of thing that young ladies liked! Hanna thought it was far too fine to eat, and she never touched a box until it happened that she was given another one. But if he had been nice, then *she* surely didn't need to be grateful for that; after all, she had given him something too, her whole heart and so much else that she had no more to give. God help those who are poor! And then he'd cracked his whip, the brute! That fine lady ought to know what he was really like! But no doubt he didn't behave to her like he did to Hanna, no doubt he was always on his best behaviour then. But what she ought to do was take her knife in her hand and go up and find him at the farm, that cruel, heartless man, behaving like that.

But as Hanna Valmoen was lying there thinking and crying – and it had got late into the night – she lifted her head from under the covers and listened, holding her breath; she thought she had heard a long whistle out in the darkness. There it was again. Then Hanna Valmoen got up, threw some clothes on and felt her way towards the door. Her mother woke up and sat up in bed:

'Are you going out, Hanna?'

'You mustn't be cross, I can't help it – I've got to go, mother.'

[Original title: *Hanna Valmoen*. Translated by Janet Garton]

OLAV DUUN

The Chapel

It was in the fishermen's shanty, one day when there was no fishing because of the weather.

The men were discussing religious matters. They had been at it the whole of that stormy day. It was somehow in the air that year. A man would realize that he had a certain view which he would express and then defend it to the last. They became heated, many of them, for they knew they were right. But one in the group sat there growing more and more astonished. He kept silent, but he forgot his work. He was not from the same village as the others.

When finally they all grew weary, one of them asked *him* what he thought about things. He shook his head, for all this was beyond his comprehension. The others had settled down to work again now, mending their nets or preparing their lines. They hadn't any time for further talk. Just then he laughed; and when the others looked at him, he straightened up and said: 'Even though it isn't everybody who is saved by faith, I know somebody who was. And she found everlasting bliss as well. Or good fortune, anyway. More than others, indeed! For she had so much more faith. If she is dead now, she must certainly have gone where she wished to go. That's my belief. And that's my view of belief.'

He was not minded to say more. But it was now growing dusk; one by one they laid down their work, and one of them demanded that he should explain his words. So he told this story.

Well, it was back home in the parish of Vaagøy, which is where I come from. It wasn't all that long ago it happened, and I can vouch for the truth of it. It's Olea I'm thinking of – she didn't have any other name. Olea is not a particularly remarkable person. But she *was* a person, I tell you that for sure. That's my religious view, as you call it here.

Olea was the poorest person in Vaagøy. I don't know where you'd find anybody poorer. She owned nothing and she earned nothing.

And if she had earned anything, she'd have drunk it up in coffee, even though she had no coffee kettle of her own.

'Ask her what she lives on!' the women would say. She lives on the belief that she *will* earn some money. And when things get too bad, then you get old Hansen feeling he'd better give her something to eat himself. So she won't starve, they said. When they talked about how she would manage, Olea used to say: 'One thing I do know. As long as I go on living, I'll be penniless. So what am I to do!'

She was clever; so clever that she scared Hansen and the priest as well. She had both reading and reckoning. And what didn't she remember! But she wasn't any the better for that. And so stupid too, you could have wept. For there she was, the poor creature, wanting to save up for a trip up north and thinking she would ever make it! She had a sister who lived somewhere in Nordland. And she was so fond of her that the very mention of her name made her go all to pieces. 'I love her more than I do either coffee or bread,' she would say. She had to see her, she claimed. Impossible to go on living otherwise. And if nothing else would help her to good fortune, then surely misfortune would find a way of helping her. The Good Lord didn't usually stand around helpless.

Whereupon misfortune came. The seas rose high and seemed ready to carry away the whole of Vaagøy. There had been times before, one year or another, when they had looked like doing that, but Vaagøy had managed to escape the worst. But this particular time I'm speaking of, it didn't. First it was all quite still, with no waves. All that happened was that the sea rose higher and higher. It found its way into the boat-houses and the wharfs, found its way up into the fields, into people's houses, and the destruction it caused was a sorry sight.

'Where is it all going to end?' people asked wonderingly.

'I could believe it will end up in Nordland with me,' said Olea. 'At my sister's,' she said.

And to those who were complaining, she always said: 'Surely there's more to come. For this is still no real *misfortune*.' But then the misfortune did happen, for the gales took a hand and the waves came dashing in so that the inlet was like the wild open sea. It tore away boat-houses and cottages, it ploughed over the fields till there was only bare rock left. We thought the whole island was being swept away. We'll never forget that night, those of us who were there. . . . Maybe you've heard about it? Nobody thought he would live to see the morrow, and certainly not see any of his possessions again. Apart from Olea.

'I can't believe I'll lose anything,' she said.

The one who suffered most was Hansen. The sea caused several thousand kroners' worth of damage to the goods down in his warehouse. Of course he could also best afford it, you understand.

Hansen was the local store owner in Vaagøy at that time, as you must know. He was in business in a big way. He had getting on for fifty people under him. Nearly everybody in Vaagøy belonged to him. As for Olea, he got her to scrub the warehouse floor and the pigsty and things like that. Further than that he couldn't drag her. She wasn't made that way. She had a mouth on her that put decent people to flight. She said, God help us, everything that came into her mind – and that was *plenty*.

To him she said that night of misfortune: 'Now we are sailing to eternity, both of us. In the same vessel.' And: 'Tonight will make a human being of you too. You'll see. And then you'll find yourself helping me to get where I want to go.'

When the storm was over, and when everything there was to destroy had been destroyed, it was said that Hansen had turned religious. The night of the storm they had seen him on his knees, some people had. And since then he had been a changed man. There was no need to whisper about it either.

'Yes, yes!' people said.

And Olea said: 'So he's finally taken himself in hand. His wife has been God-fearing all her life, twice as God-fearing as other people. And now she's got him down too. All I wonder now is how all this can help *me*.'

It was said he'd got it bad. Or so people claimed. He was much worse than his wife. People hardly knew him again. His wife had always turned to the priest, but for Hansen that wasn't enough. First came *one* priest, then two, and how they preached! And hymns! It helped not a little now after the misfortune.

'He fell like a man,' said Olea. Now you'd see the wife with piety aplenty in the house. Now it was her turn to be taken in hand.

The others of us weren't in the habit of saying things like that. You never knew what might follow if he were to hear it himself. But Olea was Olea.

And then there was the chapel. He could well afford to put it up himself, but the others would be allowed to join in and contribute their bit, no matter how poor they might be. There were bazaars and fêtes.

Olea came along, like all the rest of them. But while they sang and played their guitars as hard as they could go, so that everybody's eyes shone, she broke in with a laugh: 'God preserve us, but what a lot of claptrap this is! Has the great flood taken away all your sense of decency?'

Then why didn't she just gather up her things and go, we wondered? Well, there was a smell of coffee, and this was meant for everybody – like mercy. That's what she'd heard. She drank herself happy. But that didn't improve her. As the evening went on, the things she said became worse and worse. Especially what she said about their singing. She said it so that Hansen himself could hear.

And afterwards she said so many things both to him and about him that if he hadn't been the man of distinction he was, he must surely have felt greatly insulted. He took it mildly.

The day the chapel was consecrated, she said to him in a voice the whole gathering could hear: 'Yes, it's certainly nice of you to do all this. But if the Lord had really *asked* you to build this building, do you know what you would have done? Well, you'd have set yourself out to help the poor. You would have been a friend in need to us. Yes, that's the truth as I see it,' she whined, 'but that's something only you and I know.'

And these words sank right in, went straight to his soul, that much one could see. But then he asked her if she'd ever thought how things would be for her when she went to meet her Maker.

'No,' she replied. 'I haven't even thought how things will go for Him when the two of us meet. As for you,' she said, 'you won't even get that far. You'll be turned away to spend eternity in some chapel or other!'

He took it mildly this time too. He said a lot of nice things to her. People wondered why he bothered.

But then there was something else to wonder at. They needed a person to clean the chapel and light the fire and look after things generally. All the women in Vaagøy wanted the job, both for the sake of the money and for the blessing it would bring. And why should any one person get it in preference to anybody else? They all kept house like nobody's business.

Then Olea knew what she had to do.

She went straight to his office and told him she must be first in line for the job because she was the least well-off of them all. 'I don't go crawling for my fortune,' she said. 'I'm no mongrel dog to behave like that. I'd rather spend my days here playing the pauper for you all. I wouldn't want to be rich, even if I were coarse enough to be so. But you do know I want to go north in the spring, and I don't have a brass farthing. I'm not going to be able to afford it.'

He shook his head. He didn't want to listen to her. Then she became angry and started abusing him. People felt ashamed for having stood there and listened. Eventually she calmed down again and remembered her sister and fell silent. Indeed, tears even came to her eyes, people said.

'I know I am no ornament to this life,' she said. 'But I won't be here for ever. The time will come when I too will shine, strange though that may sound. As for you,' she said, 'you don't know what you are doing. But things will go ill for you if you deny me this. You'll have a millstone round your neck. You must have *read* about that?' she said.

He looked at her. Then he said to her: 'You who are so spiteful about the chapel, you don't *really* want that job?'

'Yes, I do. Because I need it,' she replied. 'The chapel is my salvation. That's what is going to help me to go north next spring. I'm quite ready to be converted, if that's any help,' she said.

He thought about it. Was silent a long time. Then he spoke: 'If you are serious about that, then you shall have your way. But in that case you must sit by the pulpit at the service on Christmas Eve, and turn to face the congregation and sing with the rest of us. You must sing as one of us.'

To begin with, she was absolutely speechless. Then she pleaded with him, asking if she couldn't be let off more lightly. 'Must I really suffer so sinfully,' she wailed. 'I'd rather you gave me a beating!'

No, she wasn't to be let off any more lightly. For it was the hymn singing she had derided the most. And now she was to be made to show the others that she wouldn't do it ever again. She was to show the congregation that she was a new person, someone worthy of working in such a building.

'Yes, very well!' she said. 'I'll do it! But I am a mongrel dog, all the same.'

So it was agreed. But she said to one and all – for she saw that they knew how things were – that she really took this punishment hard. 'Hansen serves out hard justice!' she lamented. 'I dread it as though I were going to be burnt alive. It's like bristles all down my back, I tremble so much!'

She said this outside the door to the chapel the evening she was about to enter.

'If only I'd never been born! Then I wouldn't have had to go through this! But see, I wasn't meant to escape it, and that's why I am here. Well, I'll go in now!' she said.

In she went, straight up to the pulpit, and sat down on the bench that stood there waiting for her. She was to have the bench to herself. There she sat with her face turned towards us. Everybody could see how she suffered. It was almost *too* much. And when they started singing, she joined in. She turned an angry red, but she sang with all her might and main, all the louder the greater she felt the shame, so that she was heard above all the others. And there she sat in torment as the preacher spoke and people wept. What she did inwardly, whether she prayed or cursed, we didn't know. But it was as a sinner she sat there, a sinner in torment, or so it seemed to us. Ah yes, some of us thought. Whilst others doubtless thought that now she knows her place.

Things didn't improve for her in the days that followed. She didn't hide from people. She was in the chapel for every meeting, but she didn't say anything more, and her face said absolutely nothing. She bore her cross as though she were indeed a new person. When things were over, she would take her bucket and begin scrubbing. Before the old year was out, she had earned herself a silver crown, and this she kept safe as though it were gold.

But when the year was up, her job was up too, and with it her earnings. They came and closed the store in Vaagøy. Hansen went bankrupt. When Olea heard that, she stood stockstill. For who was going to pay for cleaning the chapel now? She stood there, then turned and went on her way. And then they heard her proclaim to wind and weather: 'Now may the Lord come. *He* can punish him. Now is the time I can feel respect for Him.'

After that day she avoided people. The injury and shame had consumed her, we believed.

Everything in Vaagøy stopped, like the wheels of a clock when the weights are run down; and the chapel stood there forgotten. Later that winter some people came and pulled it down and left it in a pile down by the sea. There was some excellent timber there. Hansen had been a pretty smart businessman in this matter; the only thing was that it wasn't paid for. In the spring a cargo boat arrived from Nordland and loaded it aboard; it was to be taken up north and made into a store or something equally worldly. That's how things go.

Well then, the last day the boat was tied up there, Hansen came padding along and ran into Olea. She stopped and smiled at him, and then she said: 'Now I have more faith than you have, for the second time. For I *see*, and that is the true faith – that's how I read the scriptures.'

When the ship was about to sail, people saw Olea come along carrying a bundle of clothes and go on board. People were standing about on the quayside, and as the ship cast off she shouted to them: 'See now if it wasn't the chapel that helped me into taking this trip north. Now I'm leaving! And tell me now if there is no justice. I'm so happy I could sing for you again!'

From this they heard she'd got her old manner of speech back again.

Afterwards they learnt that Hansen was also on that same northbound vessel; he was making there to see if he could get any help from his relatives. Olea is supposed to have said to him when they met on board: 'You mustn't be surprised at the two of us sailing on the same journey. We are in a way no longer of this world. We shall be together as far as the kingdom of heaven. This I now see.'

Neither of them came back.

'Well, that was that,' said the man who had been telling the story. He yawned and stood up, and then he lit the lamp. 'One of them came through all right,' he said. 'That is my belief about belief, as I said. I have told it as I know it. You mustn't think too much about it. You might find a moral there that was both perverse and strange.'

[Original title: *Bedehuset.* Translated by James McFarlane]

KRISTOFER UPPDAL

By Akerselva

A clock which struck twelve times announced that the midnight hour had arrived.
    The town lay in semi-darkness. In the distance there stood leafless trees; they stood there like huge trolls, reaching out long arms and clenched fists. Further off the rows of houses stood out like small mountains with long ridge-tops, and the factory chimneys towered into the air like great stone monuments over the domes and peaks of the mountain ridge. There were lights in some of the windows like fires in the caves on the mountainside, where outlaws sat around the flames and ate spit-roasted meat and feasted their eyes on what they had snatched and stolen during the day, while their eyes every now and then darted glances like rifle bullets into the black wool of the night.
    The noise in the streets died down. In the light of the street lamps, which gleamed fitfully in the night like jewels in a dark hairline, you could see now and again a car starting up jerkily – in haste, like a queen of the night who in a light silken dress rustles to a rendezvous. And then the tapping on the cobble-stones of a lonely wanderer – heavy taps in the night like drops of water falling. A couple of serving girls running away from a policeman with such speed that it was quiet when they had gone. And shadows which slip past me – frightened, bowed shadows which glide along homeless as ghosts through the night.

    I was just about to pop into my house – an upturned boat down by Akerselva – when I was kicked in the face by someone who had stolen in there.
    The kick was so hard that I toppled over and fell on my back. Something thick and wet ran down from my face and coloured the night frost dark brown.
    'Bloody hell!'
    When I came to myself again, I collected together the pieces of

what I thought was myself, got up and considered what I should do. I forgot the boats and everything around me.

'Bloody hell,' I said, 'have things come to such a pass that you haven't even got a boat over your head. Such things are too good for you!'

I laughed.

'Christ, you get kicked out by someone who isn't in any better state than you yourself. Christ! This is the brotherhood that idealists write and talk so much about. This is what they call the cruel struggle for survival, life at its roughest. Christ! One tramp can kill another with a clear conscience, just so long as it means he can keep going a night or two longer. Christ! It's a funny thing about life, you're fond of it even if you're walking around with a snake wound round you sucking up your heart's blood. Christ! You're pleased with life anyway, and want to enjoy it as long as you can. Christ!'

I mopped up most of the blood on my face and scraped away the largest shreds of flesh. They must have been wearing well-heeled shoes, the feet that flayed me.

I stared around.

Along the river bank in both directions there lay overturned boats. And in between them black shadows padded and shuffled, small trolls which seemed to come straight up out of the ground, and small trolls which seemed to sink straight back into it. There in front of me there went a wizened little cripple, with only the stump of an arm dangling at his side.

I had been in the town, living in the world of shadows, for such a long time now that I knew more or less exactly who lived under which boat. But new people were arriving all the time, and others leaving; new people arrived who felt no comradeship and who walked around us like vultures, and wandered around and spied. The man who had kicked me must be a newcomer, none of the people who belonged here had such well-heeled shoes.

Again a clock struck, this time one stroke.

I was so tired, so tired. The intoxicating effect of the home-made spirits I had drunk had worn off, and I couldn't get hold of any more drink before morning.

And the whole time the blood kept running from my face and wetting my neck and chest like rain. I was shaking like an aspen leaf.

'That was a good job, girl, we made three hundred kroner tonight,' said a voice from the boat.

Ssh, wasn't he alone, the man who kicked me?
'You butted him good and proper, Kresjan. He soon went to sleep,' said a voice from the boat.
If I fetched the police and let them arrest those two under the boat, then the man who had 'gone to sleep' would get his money back, and I would get the boat back.
'Ouf, I'm freezing. It's no fun being out on an April night like this. Christ! If I can find my way to where the Cod Fisher or the African Chief are lying, perhaps I can ask them for help,' I thought. 'I should think they'd be good enough to let me creep in with them for one night and stretch myself out on the frozen ground. It'd be good to get a roof over my head.'
But it wasn't easy to find your way amongst all the boats, and all the shadows in the darkness. I might get another kick which would finish me off.
And below me lay the river, black and silent, drinking in the yellowy-brown sewage water which came from the town's sanitary system.
And the people who were lying under the boats and I who was standing there – didn't we too come from the town's sewage and run like excrement in a gutter out to the great sea, which conceals everything like a loving mother.
I had lost the desire to do anything. I didn't dare think of work any more. I was as frightened of work as a night-owl is frightened of light and day.
Oh, if only I had some spirits! Oh for a good drink! For one thing I could do was to drink.

It wasn't more than two months since I and my mates came to town with several hundred kroner in our pockets. And then it was beer and wine and whisky and girls. Christ! Night turned into a long day which lasted a week. But when the long day was over, the money was gone too. Vinblad and Elli 'split town', but I and Little-Kalle stayed behind. We pawned our overcoats and the new clothes we had on, and wore leather breeches and jerkins. The money which was intended for the journey we drank up too. For we were so thirsty that there was no way of stilling our thirst.
New construction workers came to the town every day, and it wasn't difficult to pick up a couple of kroner now and then. We

wandered around drunk and had a good time. But then there were fewer and fewer people who gave us anything.

We couldn't find anywhere to stay at nights.

The first few nights we wandered around in the streets, sat down on house steps now and then and dozed, and then up again to get warmed up. So happy we were in the mornings when we scraped together enough pence to afford a bottle of cheap wine mixture. It really warmed your stomach and did you good. And we certainly needed to get warm, wandering around freezing in our thin clothes.

Oh, Little-Kalle, Little-Kalle, how I remember him, that queer fish, the night he went and left me. Oh yes, he got all serious, living in town, did Little-Kalle. He walked along at my side with bent knees and bowed head.

'Dear boy,' he said, 'we're going to get out.'

'Get out?' I took his arm. 'What are you thinking of?'

I knew well what he was thinking of, I had thought the same thought myself, but I had shied away from it like from a muddy hole I didn't dare to cross.

He squeezed my hand.

'We can't go on like this, dear boy! Out and work, use your arms and your body. Tcha!'

And Little-Kalle leapt around, hitting out with his arms.

'Little-Kalle will do all right for himself, he will. The devil he will!'

'Are you going on the road?'

'You come too, dear boy.'

I started. No, I'd never gone on the road.

'Little-Kalle will get hold of food for both of us, Little-Kalle is good friends with the farmers' girls, Little-Kalle will be drinking and dancing with girls for a long time yet.'

It was morning. Over the Eikeberg ridge gold was blossoming where the forest and sky met. Throughout the town a thousand furnaces were lit, which puffed out grey wool from the factory towers, and the wool floated up high into the air like a curtain which soon hid the gold in the east. Houses woke into life, windows opened their eyelids and smiled up at the sky, gates yawned on their hinges and said good morning to the awakening day; there were young and old people who came out with a flask of coffee in their hands and a lunch pack under their arms, dock workers in leather breeches and blue sweaters and with a clay pipe sticking out from a stubbly face, and the girls for the factories; and the trams whirred along, stopped and whirred along and sang their song on one note, mingled with the clanging of bells, now loud like an organ, now softer like the whisper of a sea far away.

Little-Kalle ferreted through his pockets and pulled out a couple of five-øre pieces.

'You'll need these,' he said, 'it'll buy you a dram when the drink store opens.'

'But –'

'No buts, dear boy.'

'Are you going to – ?'

'Yes, I am.'

Little-Kalle took me by the hand. His crooked finger-stump with the deformed nail dug into my palm. Little-Kalle stared into my eyes, there was a gleam of gold in the greenish-yellow ring in his eyes. For a moment I thought about going with him. Then he let go of my hand. He turned round, and like a forest animal he slunk off up Trondheimsvegen, off to go and join our friend Sulis, far away in Nordland.

'Christ!'

The heel of one of his shoes was worn away, and in his baggy trouser seat there were two eyes which looked mockingly at me.

I turned round and walked unsteadily back into the town, and by now the town was already sweating like an active volcano, and the sweat was collecting into large clouds which rose up from the craters of the volcano.

I went past a girl who was hurrying on her way to the office, with hair as yellow as a dandelion and fair-skinned like raspberry down, with the fragrance of raspberries about her. I thought of one who had once given me strawberries and cream and then the salt of life, and who now belonged to another.

All these lively young girls I met were like heavy roses with a poisonous fragrance, which first awoke all my memories and all my longings, and then made me sad and regretful and then tired – sleepy.

I got more and more ragged and scruffy as I wandered around in that big city. I was ashamed of meeting old acquaintances. I sought the company of the most wretched tramps.

The Leech was standing shaking a bottle.

'It's spirit,' he said.
'Can you drink it?' I said.
'It's like champagne, lad.'
And I learnt to mix spirit from polish.

The Lout was standing with a pail full of paraffin and letting camphor from a bottle drip down into it.

'It's a cocktail,' he said.
'Can you drink it?' I asked.
'It's like whisky and soda, lad.'
And I learnt how to mix paraffin with camphor.

The African Chief was sitting with a basket between his legs.

'Good stuff,' he said.
'Can you eat it?' I asked.
'It's like food from Homansby,' he said.
And I got a list of the houses where you could get bread crusts and other waste food.

'Oh, I could do with a bottle of wine,' said the African Chief.
'Let's see what we've got.'
'I've got one øre!'
'I've got seven!'

And so it went round until we'd all put in what we had. And with the bottle of wine between us we sat down by Vaterlandsbrua and had a party.

'Cheers, hurrah, come on boys!'
'Hurrah!'

Christ, what fine fellows we were, and best of all when it came to boasting.

'I can thrash the whole town, I can,' said the African Chief, and waved his arms in the air.

Pretty-Anna gave him a push, so he fell back with his legs in the air.

'That just shows what a fine fellow you are,' giggled the Cod Fisher; 'no, I can get hold of enough food for all the tramps in town, I can,' he continued, 'because I'm so well known in all the fine houses.'

'It must be from the dustbins, then,' said Pretty-Anna, and she got out a basket of food.

'Aha!'

The Cod Fisher grabbed a thick cake crust for himself, and gnawed at the hard rind until his teeth bled.

Pretty-Anna sat down beside me and found some pieces of meat for me. That was how we became sweethearts.

No, I was in a bad way, I would never get out of the sewers again. Those who could help didn't care about me, and those who cared about me pulled me further and further down into the gutter.

Anyway, I didn't want to get out of it any more. I had become afraid of the light, and I didn't like the sunlit day with its gaily dressed people. No, I belonged in the dark and in the sewers.

Then memory awoke in me, the memory of my mother and my home, when I was small. I wanted to cry, but I had no tears.

I saw my own wretchedness, it was as if my own poverty made fun of me and said: 'It just serves you right, you miserable wretch, you couldn't fend for yourself, you were too soft in the head, you kept away from everyone else and buried yourself in the earth like a worm, you poor devil!'

A clock struck three o'clock.

And Akerselva down below grinned up at me. Even the bloody river was poking fun at me. And the black trees which stood there like naked skeletons shook their bones at me, and the river laughed and teased me: 'Why don't you lie down in my embrace! You'll find no better embrace, you'll find no better rest. Come to me, you poor creature who cannot cope with this life.'

I understood that what the river said was the truth, and that her advice was wise. I stood ready to leap in. Stood and shook my fists in hatred at the gods of fate.

'Answer me, gods of fate,' I said. 'Why do you let me go through the torture you call life? I didn't ask to come here, so you didn't need to give me life. Yes, if I'd been asked in advance, I wouldn't have accepted life – this nightmare which torments me night and day; for me it was no joy to come into the world, I own nothing on the earth to which I came.

'Why wasn't I made a packhorse – if I've got to have life – then I wouldn't have a soul to torment me, and I would be many times as strong for working.

'Was it in anger you created me, gods of fate? To quench your thirst for revenge and to enjoy the sufferings of a creature you had created, you gave me a soul which longed for light and for all the beauty I can never reach – and then you thrust me with brutal hands down into a dark hole which is more suitable for a water rat than for a soul which longs to climb.

'Answer me, you owe me an answer, gods!

'What did you want with me?

'Don't you see that the eyes which were shining are growing dim, and that the heart is freezing to ice?

'Is *that* to be the torment, that you created me beautiful, and then gradually took away the beauty so that I am now only a shell?

'Why didn't you let me be a flower by the roadside? Then perhaps the prettiest girl would pick me and kiss me in the moment of my death.

'You could have created me as anything at all, if I could just have avoided being what I am. For I don't want to be evil, but as things are now my heart is shaking with hatred towards everything.

'But perhaps the gods intended me to be Satan.

'Thanks!

'But now I'm going to die soon. Perhaps then I shall become a flower by the wayside and the prettiest girl will pick me, and when she raises me to her lips I shall sit there and sing the most beautiful song anyone on earth has heard, and I shall sit on her lips and sing to all she kisses.

'Thanks,' I said.

Now I had finished, and now the river could take me.

Then my thoughts took another turn. A man and a woman were quarrelling higher up. And I knew that woman's voice from the old days. Dear God, it was the dialect of my own village.

I had to go up and see who it was. The man went his way, but the girl just stared at me wide-eyed.

'Good heavens,' she breathed.

'Is it you, Sølvi,' I said. 'That we should meet like this!'

She held out her hand.

'Heavens, what do you look like! Things have gone downhill with you too, I see!'

'Oh, Sølvi!'

She washed the blood off me, and said: 'You'd better come home with me. I can see you've nowhere to go.'

She was still pretty, even though she looked a bit haggard, and her clothes were not very neat. Her eyes had lost that beautiful blue light which I had liked so much about her when we had last been together.

I thought about the time we had been working at the same place. Then I was sixteen years old and she was nineteen. In the evenings I helped her in the cow-barn. She was always so happy and so full of life, Sølvi, she hummed and sang.

As she sat there on the milking-stool with her sleeves rolled up, milking, I felt like getting hold of her and sinking my teeth into her. Pressing myself against those large round breasts. Clinging on to those red lips in a kiss which never ended. Staring into those large blue eyes which dreamt only of sinning and of what was fun.

If I tried to get hold of her, she danced away across the floor of the barn. She was so happy and so young at heart that she trembled.

Once when we were making bundles of hay together in the hay loft in the barn, I tickled her. She laughed until she sank down beside me. I carried on tickling her regardless, and she became so strange and quiet. I who was at the age when I was starting to dream about love and such things, I had so many strange thoughts as I lay there and tickled her. But I didn't believe anything bad about Sølvi. She was just so extraordinarily full of life, that was all. If someone had told me then that Sølvi was going to end up as a prostitute in Christiania, I would have found it completely beyond belief.

While I was walking along at her side, I remembered so many things.

Like that time I heard her scream in the barn. And when I ran over to see what it was, it was that Per Trøa who wasn't quite right in the head, he'd forced her down on to a pile of hay and he was kneeling beside her struggling and fighting with her. He let her go when I came. And Sølvi leapt up and got hold of me and kissed me. Tears were shining in her eyes. Then straight after she pushed me away and slapped me in the face with the flat of her hand, so that it burnt like fire after the blow. Then she ran off, but turned round and came back and held out her hand to me and thanked me for helping her. She stepped back a couple of feet, and the words blossomed from her lips:

'You will always be my friend, you will!'

In a way I was in love with Sølvi then. And if I had been a few years older, she would have been mine.

She often teased me: 'If you don't get anyone else you can have me.'

Yes, if I had been older then, that troll would have had to keep her word. Troll! Yes, she was a great troll, full of mischief as she was.

But Sølvi did not become mine, not one single time did she become mine. She became a girl everyone could call their own.

When I didn't say anything as I was walking along there beside her, she said: 'You must think it's strange that I've turned out like this. Perhaps it is strange. I don't understand it myself. I was working at a factory and earning five or six kroner a week, and I couldn't manage on that, so I began to walk the streets in the evenings. I'm not going to work at the factory for six kroner a week. But if I was paid enough to be able to manage, then I should work all right.'

We had now got to where she lived in a little attic room up in Rodeløkka.

She looked after me as if I were a little child. I got better day by day.

At night time she was usually away. It was then that she earned the money we needed to live.

But gradually, as I got better and started to think again, and the ice around my heart melted, I became jealous of the men who had her at night. For there awoke something inside me which told me that I was fond of her. And these feelings which had awoken became stronger and stronger.

In the end I could bear it no longer. I said: 'Will you come with me, and be *mine, only mine*, and we'll go to a building site and I'll start work and you'll be my wife? Will you?' I asked. 'If you'll do that, perhaps we'll make something of our lives.'

She put her arms round my neck. I saw tears in her eyes.

It was the ice disappearing. And a new spring coming.

[Original title: *Ved Akerselva*. Translated by Janet Garton]

JOHAN FALKBERGET

Approaching death

It was close to midnight. Bør Enason from away up in the mountains stood in the old doctor's surgery, shivering in his leather trousers.

It was a cold and starry winter's night. The frost left silver-grey ice patterns on the windows. And outside the snow gusted between the walls of the houses.

Inside the old doctor's place it was warm and cosy. The pine-logs crackled on the fire and the trumpeting angel on the side of the great cast-iron stove was glowing red. Normally this angel was one of the blackest. The gleam of the home-made tallow candle over on the desk flickered in the darkness. The portrait of a long-since-departed colonel hung there between glistening crossed swords. In their time these swords had honourably served the dear departed hero. Now the old warrior had moved on to a heaven in whose realm no swords were needed, so he could just as well afford to leave them behind here on earth. Yes, the old doctor would jest about this when he wasn't himself feeling off colour.

Bør Enason dared not sit down. No, he didn't think that was altogether advisable. These benches were so terribly splendid, upholstered in pink and such like; and there was a possibility he might leave reindeer hair from his coat all over the seats. The old doctor could be quite nasty when he was worked up. And this mustn't happen tonight. Besides, Bør Enason was in a hurry. Klaetta, his girl, was lying there up at Sotaa nearing her end.

He again slapped his leather trousers.

It was by no means certain that he would see Klaetta alive again. She was at the end of her struggles, it seemed.

The tears welled up within him.

It would mean that this lovely girl would not be a spring bride, as it had been intended. Not here below. In the hereafter. . . .

Somebody, it seemed, was destined to lie on the funeral straw up there in the mountains this winter. It never failed when the church bells could be heard up north in the mountains. For then somebody was near to death! And this time it seemed it was Klaetta who was near to death.

The old doctor was busy preparing a bottle of medicine for her. He was an extraordinarily capable healer. What miracles this man had performed! He had snatched people back from black eternity itself. Indeed he had.

The old doctor wasn't very keen on being disturbed so late at night unless it was a matter of life and death – and in this case it certainly seemed to be. . . . As an officer of the crown he had a great responsibility. Quickly he glanced across at the portrait in the crossed swords of his dear departed grandfather as he thoughtfully mixed the potion. These mountain Lapps needed strong medicine if any result was to be achieved.

'Is she your sweetheart, Bør Enason?' he asked. Pity the Lapp lad was so unforthcoming.

The doctor went to look for something in a drawer.

Bør Enason leant forward, fingering his belt.

'Pretty nigh on being!' he replied.

The old doctor added some pungent drops to the bottle. They fell slowly. Then prepared a stopper and inserted it. He went to a lot of trouble to warn the Lapp lad about the contents. The dose must not be exceeded, for dear life's sake.

'So let us hope it will save your girl!' he added.

'Let's hope so!'

Bør Enason quickly put the bottle in his coat pocket. He took out a leather bag which was attached to his waistcoat by a length of plaited woman's hair – and he threw a fistful of chinking silver on the table.

'That's far too much!' said the doctor, and handed him back a goodly number of silver coins.

'It's your due!' replied Bør Enason. Already he was standing with his hand on the frosted door-latch.

'Take these back then!' said the old doctor. 'You might have need of them when you get married,' he said, trying to comfort him. His voice was gentle.

Bør Enason shrank against the door-frame. 'I won't be needing anything for that.' He stood looking down.

A strange silence fell over the old doctor's surgery. The moonlight gleamed bright on the frosted window-panes, and the walls of the room cracked loudly in the intense cold of the night.

The old doctor fell deep in thought. He remembered so much.

One winter's night when the horseman on the fallow steed also rode away with his wife on the saddle before him. Ah yes, that night. . . .

'Well, you'd better hurry and be off now, my lad!' The old doctor peered good-naturedly over his spectacles.

The Lapp lad drove his reindeer through the moonlight and the silvery frost up the narrow valley and into the mountains. The bare heights lay there desolate and the driving snow stung fiercely. Before the sun next set behind Sotaa Hill he must be back with the medicine. It was pneumonia Klaetta had. And now she had reached her seventh day. The day of death.

He made ground quickly going up into the mountains. The reindeer had been rested. The sledge went bobbing across the tufty mountain brushwood, the iron runner on its base scraping and squealing as it sped along. And Bør Enason calculated from the position of the Seven Stars that he would reach the area of Sotaa Hill about midday next day. He shook the reins and shouted. It echoed and re-echoed shrilly in the still mountain air.

In the grey light of the early morning he had already reached Wolf Mountain. And the sun glinted red up among the peaks. Daybreak came. The moon hung low over the mountains to the north. The night stars grew dim and the morning light spread fitfully over the bare mountain wilderness.

From Wolf Mountain home was a half-day's journey with reindeer by traditional reckoning.

It was then that Bør Enason's reindeer began to tire. And Bør Enason saw with terror that the animal was becoming unsteady in its gait. Weariness seemed to overtake it with remarkable speed.

He stood up in the sledge and yelled at the reindeer. And he beat it savagely with the reins. The animal leapt forward with every blow that fell on its back. Then slackened again to a weary trot.

Bør Enason burst into tears. He yelled and beat the animal like a madman. And as the day grew lighter, his yelling turned to lamentation. But there was no one to answer. Only the steep rock faces all round echoed his words cold and hollow like the cry of a mountain owl.

This was the seventh day and Klaetta was lying there battling. The day of death. . . .

Before daylight died away behind Sotaa Hill she would be lying there cold and burnt out in her cottage. And the warmth of the hearth-stone would be cold and burnt out. And the sun would have set. . . .

'Dear God, run!' he shouted to the reindeer. 'You know it's a matter of life or death for Klaetta now. In God's name! She must not die and leave us. *Must* not, do you hear. . . .'

He continued talking to it like this as it stiffened and its legs gave way beneath it. And it lay there trembling with eyes blazing in the sunlight.

Bør Enason stumbled out of the sledge. He threw himself down on his knees beside the animal and began gently patting its neck.

'Oh, don't you remember all that lovely salt you used to get from Klaetta when you were just a miserable little calf!'

The animal raised its head. Its shining eyes reflected the warm yellow of the morning sunlight. It tried to get up, but sank helplessly back again with a groan.

'In God's name . . .'

Bør Enason pulled and tugged at its horns. But it was not the slightest use.

For a moment he stood there staring, his brown eyes filled with tears. His lips trembled with grief and pain. Suddenly he pulled his knife out of its sheath and he braced one knee against the animal's neck.

He would kill the miserable beast!

But as he stood there he felt its poor body cringe in terror. And he grew strangely weak. Weeping uncontrollably, he bent over it. His girl had given so much time to looking after this young bull. She had been so unbelievably kind to it. In his fancy he saw her standing over by the silvery willow trees up in the mountains on a sunlit summer night feeding it salt from her hand. The birch forest stood there, its leaves thirsty for dew; and the sounds of the river hung like some hushed song over the valley in the beautiful summer night.

'My, how can you forget Klaetta!' He clung fast to the reindeer . . .

And the sun climbed up among the peaks. . . . Then, abruptly, Bør Enason started up. Again he braced his knee against the animal and the blade of his knife glinted in the sunlight. The mortally weary animal gave a low bellow and tried to rise. But already the blood was welling out of the wound on to the knife handle – and it no longer had any strength. Was capable of nothing but dying. . . .

Bør Enason pulled out the knife. He placed his mouth over the wound and drank the warm reindeer blood. All his sense of weakness had left him. He straightened himself and stared up into the mountains. Drinking this red drink up here in the mountain wilderness, he became raving wild. . . . Before the sun set behind Sotaa Hill, he would have arrived back, come what may. Again, in his savage thirst, he placed his mouth against the wound and sucked. And he was aware of the reindeer's last dying convulsions. Now the bull stood ready. . . .

His face pale, he sprang up. He snatched his skis from the sledge and put them on — and he set his course across the tufty heather and stormed on towards Wolf Mountain.

Mile after mile; uphill, grimly, heavily, determinedly; downhill, with fine snow flying from his ski pole. Today it was a long way to Sotaa Hill. The mountains seemed to have become tougher than they had ever been before. The sweat ran from his matted hair. On, on, despite the heavy going. . . . He somehow had the feeling that somebody else was also making his urgent way up into these mountains. And the thing was to get there first.

The day moved on. And the sun stood low in the sky. . . .

Bør Enason sank quickly to his knees and drank the cold water of a spring. A yellow streak shone through the birch scrub above the spring.

He rushed on his way again, as the stars came to light about him in the winter evening.

But all at once he stopped and listened. And a pain struck him like the blow of a knife:

'Death!'

He heard the church-bells ringing in the mountains to the north. The sound hung heavily in the air. It was the symbol of the presence of death. . . .

Bør Enason stood still in the evening dusk up there in the mountain wilderness and leant in silent sorrow over his ski pole.

[Original title: *Fegd*. Translated by James McFarlane]

CORA SANDEL

Cousin Thea

She was a worry to our family from the start.

My first real sense of this was probably when, as a schoolgirl of eight or nine and thanks to a well-developed talent for listening and snooping, I suddenly realized what it was *this* time that the grown-ups were talking about in low voices and in veiled terms, and with sighs.

Cousin Thea wanted to be a midwife.

All honour to midwives, but in many families this still represented a break with all decency. They were a splendid class of people, of course, and wholly indispensable: but one assumed without question that they would be recruited from other levels of society. A teacher was something a young girl might be, or an office girl – particularly a teacher. A doctor, if she was extra clever and wanted to give up any idea of house and home, husband and children. But midwife – no.

It built up into a painful business, not least for me personally, at school and so on. At night I begged God not to let Thea become a midwife; and in other respects I was as sour to her as I dared be.

She didn't ever become one. She was an eighteen- or nineteen-year-old girl and had the whole family ranged against her. So that unhappy project was stifled at birth.

Later there was some kind of story about Thea and a young man. A betrothal of that unpleasant, half-scandalous kind which was not uncommon at that time. He was beneath her in class and was not invited to uncle's house. My aunt spent a lot of time in our house during that period, dabbing her eyes and sighing, escorted by Thea's sisters, two splendid girls, well brought up, clever and a joy to all. If I came in, the conversation took on a markedly off-hand tone – something which made my ears veritably sprout new growth under my tightly drawn hair with its parting and its pigtails. Now they had been talking about Thea again. They continued talking about other things, other things altogether. But if only I hung on, a good deal of what was worrying them would leak out. In clipped, low-voiced phrases, cunningly blended in with other remarks. In this way they thought they kept me out of things. But nobody keeps an alert child out of things. Soon I knew that Thea had been seen with some person on lonely roads far outside the town; that scenes had occurred at uncle's office; and that Thea was what was called man-crazy. An outrageous thing to be.

If I was alone with Thea, I wouldn't answer her. That would serve her right. Not that she said all that much. I remember her sitting and sewing away, silent, with bent head. From time to time I myself had to think up something that would make her ask some question or other. And then of course I didn't answer.

That business too died away. Doubtless what happened was that uncle got the person concerned to leave the town. Thea went into service at a parsonage. After a time she came home again. Thereupon there began a daily commotion every time the post was expected. It concerned letters which weren't to fall into Thea's hands.

If only they had simply been from the parson. That would have been something in itself, of course – married man that he was. Yet it would have been understandable. But they were from a small-holder, a mere peasant, and him with a wife and children too. That was terrible. It was beyond the pale. During this period, both at home and at uncle's, I was constantly being asked in an off-hand way if I had seen her putting anything into the post box? I hadn't?

Once I did see her. Saw Thea stop by the box attached to one of the houses on the edge of town, look round in all directions and quickly slip something in. I rushed home, waited till I had more or less got my breath back, and very casually mentioned what I had observed. Confused silence. Until it occurred to somebody that of course it must be that urgent letter which people were afraid Thea might have forgotten about. Now would I please run over to uncle's and tell him it was in the post. Hurry.

As I swung round the corner, Thea was walking slowly from the opposite direction, a long way off, easily recognizable by her rather ungainly walk which was also one of my aunt's worries. I increased my speed. The advantage of being of an age when it was usual to run along the street was on my side.

When Thea arrived I was ensconced with cakes and lemonade. Without saying anything, she walked across the room, obviously intending to go upstairs. My heart thumped with excitement, but my voice was loud and natural as I said: 'I've told them you didn't forget the letter – that you did post it. I saw you.'

Backed by the general opinion, I sat there and said this, and at the same time felt an inexplicable inner disquiet, a curious distaste. Thea momentarily stopped. 'Ah yes,' she said. Then she walked on. Immediately afterwards, my aunt got up and followed her. It was all so exciting that it hurt. On the other hand – when Thea was so impossible and made us all a laughing stock!

But the reverberations of that never reached me. I know nothing about it.

There were three daughters in the house. Several young men came visiting there. They looked in in the afternoon and 'stayed' to supper. They played and sang, looked at albums, told stories. Or amused themselves in the garden with boccia and croquet, depending on the season. It meant a lot to me to be present. I had a great talent for getting myself forgotten in a corner. Later in the evening goodies and fruit appeared on the table. In the days which followed people would tease each other about this and that. Thea was always quiet and silent. My aunt said to her in a low voice: 'Smile a little, talk a little, be like the others.' But no.

She was one of those who became merry on the wrong occasions. In the barn that Midsummer Eve, for example, when she danced with the farm hand, she grew quite hilarious. The idea was to show friendliness to the people. One wasn't intended to enjoy oneself so inordinately. On the contrary. But Thea grew flushed with dancing, beamed and laughed. My aunt had to go across and take her by the arm and whisper a few words. Then she grew quiet.

She was also a little fanciful in her dress, when the general opinion did not prevail against her. She liked to wear a square neckline, while all the others went about with tall whalebone neckbands right up to the ears. God knows, it is said to be artistic and emancipated. She had a nice figure, with a nice chin and neck, but all the same. . . . It didn't look ladylike.

One of those who visited the family was called Brig. He was my pet aversion because he had clammy hands. To avoid greeting him I would run away and hide. Everybody found they had jobs to do, in different parts of the house, when Brig was there. Sooner or later, Thea and he would always find themselves alone together in the sitting room, on the croquet lawn, on the veranda. Then it was a matter of remaining invisible somewhere within earshot. For imagine if Brig *proposed* to Thea!

I wasn't entirely alone in keeping watch. I clashed with several of the others. 'Hush!' they would say to me. 'What are you doing here? Haven't you any homework to do?'

In my mind's eye, I can see Thea, sitting and endlessly sewing. Or suddenly occupied in weeding a flower-bed, or picking withered leaves from a bush. I can hear the cold, clear tones with which she answered Brig, without looking at him.

I took careful note which croquet mallets he used. Or which of the little objects on the table he sat and handled. Then I could avoid picking them up for some time afterwards. But I fully agreed with my aunt and the others that it would be a blessing if he and Thea were to make a match. Brig was also wealthy, sole heir to Brig Farm and Brig Quay and Brigstead.

Thea never got married, irrespective of whether Brig in some unobserved moment actually brought himself to propose or not. She was presumably too peculiar, impossible. I remember her once saying in a loud and angry voice as she stood in the middle of the sitting room floor and not seeing that I was in the offing: 'Give me what is mine and I shall leave and go away. I am not like any of you, and never will be. I'll never bring you anything but sorrow.'

'Be silent!' said my aunt. She sat there with a red patch on both cheeks. And there was silence.

Her sisters married, found excellent husbands and had little ones every other year. Thea remained on at home, helped a little in the house, which was only natural, but wasn't exactly very much cheer. They daren't let her loose in the world, being the way she was. She could have gone to the Training College if she had wanted. It was in the same town. But Thea said she hadn't the brains. Doubtless that wasn't original, yet strangely enough was probably right. Finally, and thanks to his position, my uncle arranged a small post for her in the bank. There she in fact stayed for some time and busied herself with various things at a desk. We could see her from the street. Everybody said it was for the old people's sake that she was allowed to stay there.

Then came the worrying day when Thea was left alone in the world. My aunt died. After that, uncle didn't hold out for very long either. His last words were: 'Look after Thea.'

And certainly they tried to look after her. The sisters, both of them, were willing to take her in. All she had to do was choose. They also offered a little paid work. The little ones continued to arrive; she could make herself useful, didn't need to accept charity. They thought it out so nicely and kindly. Just as long as Thea didn't run off into the world and cause a scandal, they were prepared to do anything.

But Thea did something nobody was prepared for. With her inheritance she bought herself a little house with a garden on the outskirts of the town, opened a shop there, and crowned it all by taking in a child. Dear God!

Her business was of the kind that single women often go in for, and which rarely develops into an enterprise of any size. Sewing materials and similar trifles, a counter in one of the rooms, and a few shelves with boxes on them. A sewing machine and a tailor's dummy. It seemed she was going to take in sewing, too. But what she sewed in the first instance were fanciful dresses with low necks for herself. They were no advertisement.

Of course it happened that other ladies also started little shops. One started a teashop with cakes and sweets which went quite well. But then they were widows. And wept to anybody who would listen to them. They didn't behave as though it was the most natural thing in the world. Thea on the other hand did. And she certainly gained nothing by this.

Nobody actually needed to frequent her shop, poorly stocked as it was, and so far out of the way. The sisters were kind and did come all the same from time to time, though they weren't really allowed to by their husbands. For in the course of time there were a lot of things about Thea.

One was the child, a boy of four or five years old. He wasn't Thea's own, we knew that. But people said he was. She had put him in a children's home when he was born, they said, and taken him back again when she suddenly got her inheritance and could buy a house. The way people put two and two together. And marvel at it. To take in a child as a spinster – that really did start the gossip. Not least when a so-called 'old flame' shows up at the same time and comes and goes in the house.

To begin with nobody knew who he was. A mysterious person who arrived driving a buggy. From a pretty long way off, to judge by the sweating horse and dusty mudguards. And stayed at Thea's for some hours once or twice a week. If it rained, he unhitched the horse and put it in the woodshed. He brought hay for it with him in a sack. That he intended to stay a while wasn't difficult to see.

For a time there was a considerable jump in Thea's business. But little was established beyond the fact that the man would sit in there, smoking and chatting with the boy on his knee while Thea sewed. Well – they clearly weren't so stupid, the two of them, as to allow themselves to be taken by surprise.

He was married, you could see from the ring he wore. He could of course have been a widower, but he wasn't. Soon everybody knew that it was Thea's old flame, the peasant she had once been in correspondence with, with wife and still young children, a farm twenty or thirty miles from the town, fairly recently arrived in the district, didn't get on with his wife who was several years older than he was. Here was the boy's father, people were in no doubt about that. Strapping fellow, moreover.

The sisters went to see Thea. The brothers-in-law went. If she wouldn't think of the living, surely she must think of the dead. 'From now on I think of myself,' said Thea. 'That is my right.'

She had become quite impossible to deal with.

Nobody's roses were like Thea's, nobody's garden so luxuriant and rich. On a tiny little bit of ground all sorts of things grew and flourished. If it was glycinium on the walls, she had it. And a bed of rhododendrons. Her laburnum was a sight to see every single year, her lilac hedge almost nothing but clusters of blossom. And Thea's jasmine was whiter and bigger and had more fragrance after rain than anybody else's in town. There was something incredible about Thea's garden, something oriental.

How did that happen? Well, her old flame came driving over with both manure and soil at the first sign of spring. And helped her and the boy to dig and to cut, to water and to tend, as if the whole lot was his.

Anyway, who knows what it was? The inheritance was tied up in the house. In the long run, the shop wasn't enough to keep body and soul together. A reel of cotton here, a book of pins there to people who weren't very particular and hadn't the time to go looking far, a greetings card or a thimble – that was about the total turnover.

But the boy went to the town's high school. He was called Olsen. Some kind of attempt to disguise the truth, it was said, for her old flame was called Pedersen. He was said to be a clever lad; and he was well looked after. *Too* well. When it came to the dentist, he went twice a year. Yes, and one summer they went away, Thea and he, shut the shop for three weeks and came back home all nice and brown. There was no end to it. And was it right to bring a pauper boy up to such ways? Seeing that the old flame had now passed on?

It was utterly embarrassing the way Thea herself flourished. In this as in everything else she overstepped the mark. You saw it in her walk and in her glance, in her whole bearing, which from a woman's point of view wasn't decent, and didn't befit a lady. As for the men, so help me, they were quite shaken and turned round to look. Now and then one of the sister's husbands would forget himself and be heard to say thoughtlessly 'My God!' That was a far from fortunate remark. His attempts to explain that of course it wasn't meant *that* way were no better.

To tell the truth, Thea became the slightly mysterious donna of this small town, of whom all things are thinkable, about whom anything can be hinted. Every small town has one. Ours had Thea. That old thing, thirty odd, nearly forty, looking like that and behaving in that way. Just as well her parents have passed on.

She had her good sides, despite all the irresponsibility. The time the estate was being divided up, for example, Thea wasn't in the least greedy for any of the lovely old things but simply said of one thing after another: 'You take it. You value it more than I do.' And that was nice. Perhaps also somewhat indifferent. She probably didn't have very much sense for such things.

Yet it was said to look very nice in her little rooms.

When the change occurred isn't easy to say. It must have happened gradually. One day it was evident to everybody.

By then the old flame had really passed on. These things happen. Thea went about as usual. Everything continued looking as it was before: herself and the boy and the garden and the house.

But then one day there was a change.

It began with people saying: 'Terribly thin she's got.' They went on to say: 'Terrible cough she's got. It really isn't very nice to go there any longer.'

For she did have a little circle of regular customers of the kind who can't be bothered to get changed and go looking very far.

The time came when the shop was closed in the mornings. The

boy looked after it in the afternoon, while at the same time doing his homework. He would come out of the inner room with a faraway look in his eyes from the things he had been studying. But he was a good lad and knew where the thimbles were and the cards and the sewing thread and also what they cost. About Thea he said thank you but she was a little tired and was lying down resting.

Then the time came when Thea was taken to hospital. For observation.

The sisters went there. They didn't feel they had any choice. They took flowers and things, sat by the bed and pretended nothing was wrong, mainly for the sake of the old people who lay in their graves. When it became clear what was wrong with Thea, and that she'd allowed it to go too far, they reproached her in sisterly fashion. She should have been more careful, she should have known, etc.

Then Thea would answer roughly as follows: 'I did feel a little tired . . . I did have a bit of pain . . . I knew I had a temperature . . . but I didn't have time to go and lie down. Couldn't afford it either.'

The end came relatively quickly.

She lay there coughing, hollow-cheeked, hollow at the temples, her voice hoarser every day.

The tall, large-limbed lad went visiting her, a stranger to us, with features we couldn't recognize as being from anyone, and a way with him which wasn't ours. He sat and stroked Thea's hand, told her how he was coping at home, how things were with the cat and with the cactus and with the roses. And that he'd halved the order for milk and cream and that he was managing fine, both in the shop and with other things.

Thea lay there and told him what he was to say to this creditor and that one and that one. It became apparent that she had left things in great disorder. She must have been uneasy about the boy, brought up as he was to having the best of everything. Everybody went in fear of her asking them to look after him. But no, not a word.

They comforted each other in their own way, Thea and he. She might say, for example: 'I wore myself out that day for you. . . . That's when you got a taste for that kind of well-being. . . .'

'Yes. Thank you,' said the boy and stroked her hand.

'I managed to subdue that need in you. Now you won't grow into the kind of person who is simply content to . . .'

'You may be sure of that,' said the boy.

Such were the things the sisters had to sit and listen to. For towards the end it was as though she didn't pay any attention to them. Only him.

It wasn't the place to contradict her. She was lying on her deathbed. But it wasn't easy to keep silent. Out of a pauper child she had made a studious young gentleman who now stood alone in the world. If only she'd made him a decent working lad.

But neither he nor Thea appeared to grasp the irresponsibility in that. Quite the reverse.

It transpired that Thea had long lived as though in a sieve, had poured things from one hole into another, had taken a little loan here and a little loan there – from men, naturally – and pretended and lied and talked them round, so that each and every one of them thought he was the only one. A masterly performance in a small town where everybody knows everything. The whole time she had reasoned thus: 'That took care of his school fees . . . his suit . . . that treat . . . so far so good.'

The house was mortgaged right up to the chimney. But the boy is said to have grown into a clever man, strangely enough.

[Original title: *Kusine Tea*. Translated by James McFarlane]

OSKAR BRAATEN

Going home

I

It is lunch break at the factory.
    Some of the girls have thrown themselves down on the floor with bundles under their heads. They are going to try and have a nap.
    Others – some of the youngest – are running about noisy and boisterous and playing in the gangways between the machines. Or they steal in to the stockroom to the boys. And you can hear excited shrieks and shouts from in there.
    Over by one of the windows a young girl is standing alone. She looks around to see if anyone is nearby. Then she quietly opens the window and pokes her head out.
    And she drinks in the fresh spring air.
    Oh, what lovely weather it is today! The sun is burning hot as on a summer's day, and the sky is blue and clear.
    The girl lays her hands on the brick wall outside. Lets them be baked by the sun. The brick wall is so warm and good.
    Down below Akerselva glides past, grey and dirty after passing the factories, but eager and ready for work. It still has many a heavy job to do on the way down before it can rest. There are many factories further down river.
    The two trees down in the 'garden' belonging to the factory manager have got green buds on their dry branches. And a few thin wisps of grass have pushed up bravely around the roots.
    But this is not all that the girl sees. She sees far, far further.
    The picture of a narrow valley appears to her, the picture of a little grey cottage which is lying baking in the sun. And the picture of a rushing river, a little clearer than Akerselva, and the picture of a green forest with trees that are a little more well nourished than those standing down below.
    She tries to hold fast the picture of this cottage. She tries to go inside and look round in the room, tries to greet dear faces and

well-known things, but it is so difficult. The excited laughter of the girls from the inner room forces its way in between the pictures, pushes out the cottage and the forest and the river and the green meadows. And the girl wakes up and realizes that she is staring out over dirty rooftops.

Then she shuts the window again and goes back to her machine. It must be coming up to two o'clock.

She does her work that afternoon as usual. Stops the machine and puts it right when the threads break. Takes the full spools off and puts empty ones on, when that needs doing. It all functions as it should. But there is an air of indifference about her work. She is not *there*. All her thoughts are far away from anything to do with spinning and cotton thread.

Lina, who is working at the next machine, keeps an eye on her. A couple of times she says something to her, but gets no reply.

Then Lina finds a moment to leave her machine and comes over to her: 'What's up with you today, Helga? You're so strange!' But Helga does not reply.

Then Lina puts her hand on her arm: 'Is it spring that's got into you, lass? Have you got an attack of *that* again? Don't you let it get you down, Helga! What have you got to do with spring and sunshine? Does it make any difference to you whether it's summer or winter? Aren't you just as safe and secure in here whether the snow is blowing through the streets or the sun is burning the paving stones? What have you got to do with the sun? Get your chin up, lass, and think of something cheerful!'

But these wise words have no effect. Helga's face does not clear. She just turns a little, looking down: 'I'm going back home again!' she says.

A little smile crosses Lina's face: 'Oh, yes?' she says. 'You are, are you? Yes, yes, my girl. You go. But be quick – before it's too late!'

Helga looks at her: 'What do you mean?'

Lina is not smiling any longer: 'I went home once as well, you see. Went home to the country every single spring. When the days became lighter, and the air mild, and the sun rose higher in the sky, then I got ready to go! And I went! Oh yes – my thoughts went. I myself never got any further than here to the mill. And that's what'll happen to you too. You've set off every spring of the three years you've been in town. You "went" last year, you're "going" this year. And no doubt you'll "go" next year, and the spring after, and many, many times after that. But you'll stay here nevertheless. You'll grow more and more fixed here every day and every year. And one day, far off in the future, when many years have passed and your hair is grey, *then* spring can come! *Then* you'll not be going anywhere! He! he! Because then you won't see the sun or the summer! And *then* you'll be safe!'

Helga looks sharply at her: 'That's not what's going to happen to me!' she says. 'Never in a thousand years! I *am* going home! I'll be off in a few weeks. I'll live ever so cheaply, I'll save money every single day. And by the time summer's really here, I'll be far away! – I can't stand living here in the town! I've *got* to go home!'

'Yes, yes,' says Lina. 'You just go, my lass! But just keep an eye on your work. A thread's just snapped down there.'

II

It is a fine summer evening a couple of months later. A boy and a girl are dragging their steps along the street. They are both in a bad mood, and saying nothing.

They walk a long way up the road. Turn off and cross a ploughed field. Then they come to a meadow with green grass and sit down on the ground.

There are people around on all sides. Folk are out getting a bit of fresh air after the hot day.

A little way away some fellows are lying playing cards and swearing. On the other side there are some young girls sitting, laughing and shouting in their enjoyment of life. And from a hill a good way off comes the bewitching music of an accordion.

But the two sit silent.

He lets his eye travel down towards the town, towards the river and the factories.

She has found some flowers, and is sitting playing with them in her lap. Just now and then she raises her eyes to his face. He is so strange this evening. Must have something on his mind.

Time passes, and it grows late. And the girl becomes restless: 'We'd better be going home!' she says. 'I get so tired in the mornings.'

He looks down: 'Oh, there's no need to be in such a hurry!' he says. 'You've often been out later than this.'

Then he turns to her and his voice becomes warm: 'Have you thought about it then, Helga? Will you do what I asked?'

She sits nibbling at a straw. Does not answer.

He goes on: 'Or perhaps you daren't? Perhaps you're afraid I'll plague the life out of you?'

She looks into his eyes for the first time this evening: 'Oh, you know perfectly well it's not *that*, Edvart. You'd be good to me, I know you would! But I just *can't*, you must see that!'

He smiles scornfully: 'You can't, you say! No, no! Well, there's nothing to be done then. There must be others you care for. And I don't want to stand in the way of Hurrah-Nils or of Swedish Petter!'

He tries to get up, but Helga holds him back: 'Don't go yet!' she begs. 'Don't say awful things like that! You know I'm not interested in those other boys. But I don't *want* to get married to anyone here in town, I've told you that. Next spring I'm going home to stay. I'm not coming back to town any more – I just can't live here!'

He looks thoughtfully at her: 'Is there someone waiting for you at home, perhaps?'

She does not answer at once. His words give her something to think about. She seeks out memories of the old days. And amongst them is the memory of a fair-haired boy back home. Someone who had filled her thoughts many years ago.

She lets go of the arm she is holding: 'What if there is? Have I got to account to anyone?'

He gets up, and now there is no one holding him back: 'No,' he says, 'no you haven't. You can do as you like.'

She gets up too, and they go slowly back the same way they came.

Down on the street he stops: 'But why didn't you go this spring?' he asks. 'You've been talking about it for so long.'

Her voice falters a little: 'Oh, there were so many problems,' she says. 'I need a bit of time to sort myself out. Now I'm going to save money all year, so that I can get myself some nice clothes next spring. I don't want to come home without a stitch on my back.'

A glimmer of hope appears on his face: 'Are you sure that there aren't going to be a few problems next spring too?' he asks.

She smiles confidently: 'No, what could happen?' she asks in wonder. 'I can't see what can possibly stop me, when I *want* to go home!' Her voice is clear and certain.

But winter follows summer. And dreams often sleep through the wintertime. They can wake up every now and then, just enough to make your blood run a little faster, but they soon go to sleep again. They are not very happy in the cold.

The winter evenings often seemed long to Helga. And her little room seemed so cramped. She had to get out and see people.

That winter she spent a lot of time with Edvart. And they had a good time together. Edvart was a good, steady fellow, and she was very fond of him. Went to sleep at night with him in her thoughts, and was happy at the thought of him in the morning. That's the way things are: you have to have someone to think of.

But as time went on after Christmas, the happiness grew less. And Helga lost the fresh roses which had bloomed in her cheeks despite the factory air and the late nights.

And as spring drew nearer, and her thoughts began to travel far off to the country, it often happened that she lay awake throughout the long nights with a feeling of utter hopelessness.

Lina's eyes followed her during the day at the factory. And one afternoon, when she had not been able to get any answer out of Helga, she came over to her: 'You're going to be setting off soon now, then?' she asked.

Helga fitted a new spool: 'Setting off?' she asked. 'Good heavens, you can see what state I'm in, Lina! I can't go home like *this*. I'll have to wait till a bit later. There's no great rush. The summer is long.'

Lina turned away as she smiled.

That autumn they were married, Helga and Edvart.

III

The years pass.

Helga and Edvart struggle through. It is tough going often enough, but they are loyal to each other and pull together, and in that way you can do a great deal.

Helga stayed home from work the first few years after they were married. But when the eldest daughter was old enough to be able to look after the younger children, she went back to work.

They were not too badly off for money now, she and her husband. They had furnished the house quite nicely, and they were not that short of clothes either.

But Helga had still not settled down in the town. The same

longing came over her every single spring. And while she was in this mood, she was fed up with her husband, her children and the factory, and went off and brooded on her own. And Edvart sometimes had to be quite sharp with her to bring her to her senses.

One spring, the longing was stronger than ever and lasted longer.

Edvart tried both being angry and being gentle, but nothing made any difference. In the end he just let her alone, while he tried to think of what to do. And after he had thought for a few days, he found a solution.

She *should* go home again, there where she so dearly longed to be, and where everything was so wonderful. But she should not go alone. He and she and the children, all of them should move back to the village she came from. They would both keep on at the factory and work as hard as they could. And they would not buy anything more for the house after this, but just save and save. Every week they would put a few kroner in the bank, and be as frugal with food and drink as possible. And in a few years, when they had scraped together a few hundred, they would go to where she longed to be and buy a little piece of earth.

He lay and explained this plan to her one night after the children had gone to sleep. And Helga listened with her mouth open. Edvart's voice was so warm and friendly this evening, and his eyes were full of dreams. And everything he said was so well worked out, and was put so clearly and straightforwardly, that she felt a deep sense of security and wellbeing. And when he finally stroked her cheek and asked her if she did not think it would work, she answered in a voice full of emotion: 'Of course it'll work, Edvart! What on earth could prevent it?' And she felt under the covers for his hand: 'Thank you for thinking of it, Edvart!' she said. 'Thank you so much, my dear!'

But one day not long after Edvart is lying ill in bed. He has been coughing for years, and been pale and weak. It is only the constant work and worry which has kept him going. But now he is lying in bed. Growing weaker each day. And one day the doctor says that he will never get up again.

This is a hard blow for him, and his former courage deserts him.

One evening Helga is sitting by his bed. He is silent this evening. Lying thinking about something. And he stares at his wife for a long time. 'Dear God!' he sighs.

She bends over to comfort him. 'You mustn't take it like that,' she says. 'It'll all work out in the end. We must leave it in the hands of God.'

He coughs. 'It doesn't matter about *me*,' he says. And a look of utter hopelessness appears in his eyes. 'But you and the children, Helga? What's going to become of you?'

For a while she cannot think of any answer to this. Cannot find words with any meaning. She searches for thoughts which have given hope earlier. But it is a long time before she finds them. It is mostly dark, heavy thoughts which come into her mind today.

Then she hears a sigh from the bed, and remembers where she is. And she makes herself sound confident and smiles to her husband: 'Edvart dear, there's no need to worry about *us*. If there's no other way out I'll take the children with me and go off home. I've got lots of friends there, and they're bound to help us. I won't be able to go on living in this town any longer anyway, after this.'

She thought she saw something like a sad smile pass over the pale face. But she was not certain about it.

IV

Many years have now passed since Edvart was laid in the grave. Many wearisome years.

Helga is still working at the mill.

There are great changes there now. New machines and new people. When the old machines could not work any longer, they were carried out and broken up and sold as scrap. And the people were sent to a large green meadow at the northern end of the town and buried there.

Lina went that way a long time ago. Now her daughter has taken over the machine after her mother.

Helga's neck has become a little bowed recently. And her hair has become very grey. For there are many heavy burdens to bear in this troublesome world. One after the other of her children has passed away. They had weak chests, all of them. Only her eldest daughter is still alive. She works at the mill with her mother.

One spring evening Helga and her daughter are sitting together in their room. It has been a fine day, with signs of summer to come.

After a while Helga says: 'I was just thinking, my dear. We've been working away here for so many years without a break. It would do us good to have a bit of time off. I've often thought of making the trip home to my village and saying hello to old acquaintances. But something has always happened to stop me. How about you and me making the trip this summer? It would do us both good.'

The daughter turns away. Does not want her mother to see her smiling. And Helga sees nothing. Just carries on: 'You would enjoy seeing what life's like in the country, you as well – you've never been out of the town. It's a different sort of life there, you know! You'll soon see the difference. Goodness, I can't get it into my head how people can live for years on end here in this dreadful town. *I could never get used to it!*'

Now her daughter does smile, and forgets to turn away. And now Helga notices it.

She stares helplessly at her daughter. Then she runs her hand over her forehead: 'Ah, yes! The things I say! Dearie me!'

But then she pulls herself up in her chair and her voice grows stronger: 'Yes, yes, you can laugh, my girl! But I am going anyway, you'll see! And if you don't want to come, I can go alone! I've been that way before, I have, so I'm not frightened. There's no need to laugh at me, because I mean it. Before the green leaves are on the trees, I'll be off! Now you know!'

Helga was not telling a lie.

That spring she did leave.

Though if the truth be told, she did not go all that far. She did not travel up through the country on shining rails.

No. It was a quiet, short journey through the streets.

She did not end up in a beautiful valley with a clear stream and green birch forests. But there was *some* similarity, nevertheless. For it was not all that far from a river where she was either. Akerselva ran quite close by. And there are a few birch trees growing in Nordre Cemetery too.

[Original title: *Heimreisa*. Translated by Janet Garton]

ARTHUR OMRE

Curried eel

Borten changed his clothes, putting on a pair of old trousers and an old jersey, and chuckling a little. He tested the paraffin lamp, pumped it up, lit it, then turned it out again. It wasn't working quite right. The coffee pot was bubbling away out in the kitchen; the coffee smelled good. He glanced at the clock, then took his time over laying the table in the living room. He sat down, ate well, and lingered over his coffee. It was still early. He lit his pipe and began mending the lamp. Fine, fine, he grunted.

There was a loud ring at the front door. Borten put the lamp on the table and went out. A shortish man in a cape was standing there – shortish and stout. Borten was also fleshy, but tall. In his old trousers and jersey he looked like a real old salt.

'What can I do for you?' Borten asked. He grunted as he spoke.

'Can you spare me a few minutes?' the man replied in a high treble voice.

'Come in,' said Borten. He opened the living-room door and followed the man in. He offered the man a chair and sat down expectantly at the table.

'My name is Hammer,' said the man, putting the stress on Hammer.

'Ah yes, indeed,' said Borten, a little taken aback. He stood up and said: 'Pleased to meet you, Herr Hammer.'

'Are you sure?' said Hammer.

'My dear sir, what do you mean?' Borten asked stiffly.

'I mean you weren't very pleased to hear that my name was *Hammer*. That's what I mean,' said Hammer with emphasis.

'Now just you listen to me, Hammer . . .'

'You have a bad conscience,' said Hammer.

'But, my dear man, for what reason? You mustn't go round saying things like that!'

'Allow me to say precisely what I want to say,' said Hammer. 'And at this particular moment I want to tell you the truth and nothing but the truth. Please note that, Herr Borten.'

'To be frank, Herr Hammer . . .'

'To be frank, you have been having an affair with my wife,' said Hammer in a high treble.

'Rubbish . . . what rubbish . . .'

'He! he! he!' Hammer laughed loudly. 'Just what she said too. "Rubbish, what rubbish." She got that from you. She's never used that phrase before. I'll bet you use it every day.'

'Rubbish,' said Borten. 'I've no desire to sit here listening to such nonsense. Be off with you now, or else . . .'

'Or else?' said Hammer mildly, ingratiatingly.

'Or else I'll throw you out.'

'Ha! ha! Yes, that's good, Herr Borten.'

Borten stood up.

'Sit down!' shouted Hammer.

Borten sat down. 'You must be stark staring mad. Or drunk,' said Borten.

'Transparently sane and extremely sober,' Hammer replied. 'Now listen to me! My wife has been out to our place in the country every Saturday for the past six weeks. She has returned every Monday. I couldn't work out why on earth she needed so much time to get the place in order. We came out yesterday to spend the summer here as usual. I made enquiries of a certain lady who lives over on the other side. It wasn't difficult to get information. She told me that my wife had spent every Saturday evening and – I'll have you notice – every Saturday night here with you, Herr Borten. In there.'

Hammer pointed with his revolver to the bedroom.

'Rubbish . . . what rubbish!' said Borten.

'I have proof,' said Hammer. 'Incontrovertible proof. I have the evidence of several witnesses who have followed my wife, who have seen and heard everything. . . . I have it all in writing. You know how people are out in a place like this . . . they are easily shocked. . . . He! he! he! You have been careless, very careless. Here, read one of the depositions. There's no point in destroying the paper. I have several. And I can get this one replaced. Here you are, Herr Borten.'

Borten read the document, then put it down. Hammer put it in his breast pocket. 'Apart from that,' he said, 'apart from that, my wife has confessed. I have it in writing. I have a feeling . . . hm . . . I have a feeling she likes you better than me.'

'So what do you want?' asked Borten, withdrawn.

'This is what I want,' said Hammer. He brought out a typewritten sheet of paper, placed it on the table together with a fountain pen.

'I'm not signing anything!' said Borten.

'Sign it!' said Hammer.

Borten looked at him for a moment, took the fountain pen and signed it.

'Thank you!' said Hammer. 'Thank you very much, Herr Borten. I draw your attention to the fact that unless you marry my wife two months after the divorce at the latest, you will lose your excellent job. I can also do you quite considerable damage in other ways. You are not a rich man . . . not even what I would call well off. Nor are you any longer young. You have a good position and your job is an easy one . . . much too easy, in fact. If you marry my wife, you can keep it. I owned a good part of the company before. Now I've got sixty per cent of the shares. Make your own enquiries.'

'All right,' said Borten weakly. 'But . . . are you really so anxious to get rid of her?'

'I don't like being led by the nose,' said Hammer. 'I am a man of honour. You must be that too. You must accept the consequences. You must do the decent thing by a woman.'

Borten nervously moved the lamp.

'Leave that lamp alone,' said Hammer. 'You weren't thinking of throwing it? I shall go. Sit quietly at the table until I'm out of the house. Keep your hands in your lap.'

Borten shifted his hands off the table.

'What do you use that lamp for? In the out-house?' Hammer asked.

'No, I've got electricity out there, too. I use it when I go out spearing fish.'

'Trout?'

'Sometimes sea-trout. Mostly eel.'

'On the far side?'

'Well . . . a bit further north on the far side. It's also good inside the bay. But they've got their eyes on you there, that loose-tongued lot. They're quite ready to spear their fish illegally themselves . . . but they report anybody else.'

'Yes, I'll say!' said Hammer. 'Six years ago, just here. . . . But what about a bit further north? Wouldn't you say?'

'A few places, if you know where. Great . . .'

'I know a place on the south side. I caught some huge beauties there,' said Hammer.

'All right. But the big ones aren't always best. Medium-sized.'

'You may be right, Borten. Do you fry them?'

'Fry!' cried Borten outraged.

'I said fry,' said Hammer, in his treble voice. 'Now, let me tell you. First, salt them overnight. Then, cut them in pieces five centimetres long, split them, wash them well in warm water, soak them in red wine – preferably Burgundy – for six or seven hours, and then cook them in a hot frying pan with plenty of butter. Pepper, but nothing else. Try that! I'll bet . . .'

'I'll stick to them boiled with masses of curry,' said Borten. 'The usual Danish way.'

'Dill?'

'Ye-e-s. . . . I don't often use dill, but . . .'

'Oh, but yes. . . . Lovely in curry. Had you thought of going out this evening?'

'Yes. It's a bit early yet.'

Hammer drew back the curtain and looked out. 'Damn!' he said. 'I've got my own boat ready but nobody to row for me. There's one lad I can rely on in the town. Difficult. . . . Have you got a lad?'

'I use Nilsen. He's a bit surly.'

'Now if only I had some suitable clothes. I can row.'

'Clothes? Good Lord, we're not short of those. Bit big, perhaps, but . . . we can turn them up. And I've got boots . . . good boots. Gumboots . . . we'll manage. . . .'

'Really? You mean that, Borten?'

Borten fetched the clothes. Hammer changed in the kitchen; he laid the revolver on the kitchen bench, then afterwards put it in his right-hand jacket pocket. . . . To have it 'handy', thought Borten. He's frightened I might turn on him. No, there's nothing to be done about it. Bloody fool that I was! Get married again? Huh! . . . And to Mrs Hammer? Huh! . . . Not too bad, all in all . . . but she does nag . . . a terrible nag. . . .

'A spot of coffee, Hammer?'

'Thanks!' said Hammer. 'Could do with a drop. Missed my coffee today . . . was a bit . . . ah . . . worked up. He! he! he!' He took a cup

from the kitchen, sat down, drank a full cup, black, then leapt up.
'Ready when you are, Borten. Shall we say the south side?'
'No, the north,' said Borten.
'Let's toss for it,' said Hammer. He took out a coin.
It came down 'north'. Borten grinned happily. 'I'll row there,' he said. 'And back as well. I like rowing. I've got strong arms. Rowing's good for you.'
Hammer glanced at him. 'You're a fair hulk,' he said. 'I can take a spell, too. I like rowing. I'm starting to put it on a bit. Too fond of food. He! he! he! We'll take half an hour each with the spear, eh? Half an hour goes quickly.'
'All too quickly,' said Borten. 'Half an hour each seems all right.'
He went over to the corner cupboard and filled up a hip flask.
'Old Løiten?' said Hammer. 'I was just thinking about that myself. It's good to have a drop or two with you. I drink Old Løiten myself. I'll bring a bottle over next time.'
They lumbered out, a bit heavy both of them. Borten was tall and heavier than Hammer. Hammer looking a bit comical in clothes too big for him, an old windcheater over his jacket; short, broad, shapeless. Both in fishing caps. Fishermen. Borten fetched the spear from the back of the shed. Hammer was carrying the unlit lamp; he trudged down the path, walked slowly down to the jetty, looked round, said nothing. They stepped cautiously down into the boat and Borten rowed silently out, with sailcloth round the oars where they fitted into the rowlocks. Weather good. A slight breeze. Fine conditions for spearing fish. They met nobody in the inlet, came round to the north side, let the boat drift and listened.
'Fine!' said Hammer.
Borten lit the lamp. It burned well. He hung it on a hook on the front of the bow and fitted an iron plate over it so that the light went down into the water.
'One thing,' said Borten. 'We split the fine if it should come to that, eh?'
'Naturally,' said Hammer. 'Naturally, Borten. It's a hundred crowns the first time. I don't mind accepting the charge myself. Means nothing to me. This is worth a cool thousand any day . . . at least. . . .'
'Row a bit closer to land,' said Borten. 'There . . . steady . . . gently . . . now follow the shore line inwards.'
Borten's bulk loomed large at the front of the boat; with his spear

he stood there bent over in an attitude of attack, staring down into the water.

'Ha!' he said. He thrust the spear in quickly and swiftly drew it out again. A large eel was wriggling on the forked end, wrapping itself round the wooden shaft.

'Well, I'll be . . .' said Hammer.

'Ssh!' whispered Borten. 'Keep her going gently . . . steady . . . that's it. . . . Ha!' he said, making a thrust.

Five hours later Borten and Hammer were carrying a tub between them up the path to the house.

'Heavy?' said Borten.

'Pretty heavy,' said Hammer. 'Bit too much water.'

'That's all right,' said Borten. 'We'll skin them tomorrow morning.'

They set the tub down in the shed and locked up after them.

'Puh!' said Hammer. 'What about some coffee and a sandwich, Borten?' He changed in the kitchen. 'Nice place, Borten. Nicer than mine. Bit neglected. Nice as it is.'

'I like it that way,' said Borten. 'I don't like things painted. Prefer the wood as it is. I slap a bit of oil on the floorboards now and then, but otherwise I just leave things. I don't like smart houses in the forest. I like it as it is. I fish . . . see to the boat . . . cut down a few trees. Damned shame one can't spend half the year out here.'

'You're here pretty often, Borten. . . . H'm, why don't you call me Johan.'

'My name's Peter,' said Borten, responding.

'Seems only natural,' said Hammer. 'We're sort of relatives. He! he! he! . . . Brothers-in-law. . . .'

'Ha! ha! ha!' growled Borten, chuckling. He put the kettle on and got a good blaze going in the stove. Went into the living room and lit a fire in the hearth. It crackled and burnt merrily. Whereupon Hammer placed the revolver on the kitchen table.

'It's not loaded,' said Hammer.

'Couldn't be certain,' said Borten.

'Frightened?'

'I can't deny I . . .'

'I've never fired a shot,' said Hammer. 'I daren't shoot. I don't like the noise.'

They sat drinking coffee and eating bread and jam until one in the morning. They had worked up quite an appetite.

'You'll stay over till tomorrow? You've got a long way,' said Borten. 'There's plenty of room here. Good bed. . . .'

'I know,' said Hammer. 'He! he! he! I wonder if I might take another slice. Good jam, very good jam.' He took a large slice.

'There'll be eel for dinner tomorrow,' said Borten. 'You'll be staying?'

'Don't be silly!' said Hammer. 'Of course I'm staying. Have you got any curry powder?'

'Naturally,' said Borten. 'Masses of curry powder. . . .'

'No need to worry about all these documents and things,' said Hammer.

'No?'

Hammer went over to the fire, took the documents from his breast pocket and threw them into the flames. 'You must forgive me,' he said. 'Let me tell you straight. I had certain ulterior motives. He! he! he! Nancy is of a rather amorous disposition.'

'I know that,' said Borten.

'You aren't exactly her first lover,' said Hammer.

'I know that,' said Borten.

'She likes having a new one every spring, but she always comes back to me.'

'I know that,' said Borten.

'I felt I was getting a bit tired of it all,' said Hammer. 'This time I really thought I'd let her go her own way. It would suit me very well, I thought. So I kept a close eye on you both. Had a pretty good hold over you. He! he! he!'

'You had,' said Borten. 'Still have, if it comes to that. . . .'

'Forget it,' said Hammer. 'Forget it. I don't mean you any harm. You're too nice a fellow for that. It doesn't make any difference to me. I'm used to her. Know how to manage her. She would miss me . . . and pretty badly, too. She'll behave herself now for a good long while. You might as well have her the rest of the time. No bother. Forget it. . . .'

'Thanks,' growled Borten. 'I'm beginning to feel sleepy. Looking forward to tomorrow's dinner. We'll take a couple of medium-sized ones with nice firm flesh . . . lots of curry. . . .'

'You can say that again. . . .'

Borten and Hammer retired to their beds. Quietly, securely, Borten fell asleep.

'We'll try the south side tomorrow evening,' said Hammer

sleepily. 'There'll be a good few left over for smoking, too.'
'Trout?' mumbled Borten, half-asleep.
'No, eel,' said Hammer. Then he fell asleep.

[Original title: *Ål i karri*. Translated by James McFarlane]

ARNULF ØVERLAND

Missing, presumed dead

Frau Hempel was busy clearing the kitchen table when there was a ring at the door. She was still not fully dressed; but Etti had already left, so she had to go and answer the door herself.

A man was standing outside, wearing a cap and a grey overcoat. He had a duffel bag under his arm. He said nothing, just stood there looking at her; he cleared his throat a little but said nothing.

She was about to slam the door shut again – she had nothing to give away. Anyway, she didn't like people coming ringing the doorbell, particularly not when she was alone in the house.

Then he took a step towards her and held the door.

'Lisa!' he said.

Did he know her? Frau Hempel stared into the worn and weather-beaten face. It resembled something she had dreamt. The voice also resembled. . . . Then she gave a cry. She let go the door, stepped back, groped her way down the passage into the sitting room and sat down.

The man followed her.

'It's me!' he said.

'You're alive?' she whispered. Terror welled up in her breast.

'Yes,' he said.

'We thought you were dead!'

'No. I was taken prisoner.'

'You were on the missing list. Then we heard nothing more from you. Not a word. Why didn't you write?'

'There was no post. We tried a few times to send letters, and they said they would send them, but. . . . After that we had no paper.'

'Was it Russia you were?'

'Yes, Siberia.'

'The whole time? Wasn't it in 1915 you were posted missing?'

'Yes.'

'And now it's 1930. Fifteen years!'

'Yes.'

'But why haven't you come before this? The war was over in 1918!'

'In 1918? So it was! We were in prison camp near Krasnoyarsk for three years. Then along came Koltshak. We fought with him against the Bolsheviks. Then we got taken prisoner again. That was in 1919. After that we were put on building roads . . . and working on the land.'

'So you weren't in prison camp the whole time?'

'No, the last few years we were free.'

'Couldn't you have come home then?'

'And walk half-way round the world? No.'

She looked at him. This was her husband, returned. A grey ageing man who resembled Georg's father. Once she had been married to him – was indeed still married to him!

She looked at him. She was no longer afraid. She was not frightened of this impoverished old man. But she did not know what she was going to do about him. He stood there in front of her, his bag still under his arm; but she could not bring herself to ask him to sit down – for in a way he was of course in his own home.

Somebody went past on the stairs outside. She had forgotten to shut the doors behind her. She now felt a little weak at the knees.

'Won't you put your bag down?' she said.

'Yes.' He went over to the door and put it down. There was also a chair there. He sat down. He placed his cap on top of the bag. He was rather tired. He had walked all the way from the Schlesischer Bahnhof.

'Have you had any breakfast? Would you like me to make you a sandwich?' she asked.

'Yes, please.'

She went out and put on the coffee pot.

A short while after she came in again, in her outdoor things, coat and hat. 'It's all there ready for you. I have to go now. I'll be back this evening.'

'Are you going?'

'Yes, I have to go to the shop.'

'The shop?'

'Yes. At the workshops!'

'Yes, of course. You've still got them?'

'Yes.'

'And you can manage to run them?'

'Yes, of course I can. How else would we live?'
'That's right. But you must have taught yourself something about them?'
'Yes, I have. And of course I've got Nolte. Yes, Nolte is the watchmaker. And I serve in the shop.'
'Yes, of course.'
'Well, I have to go now. Lord, it's after nine o'clock! Goodbye then!'

He went out into the kitchen and had something to eat. Then he went back into the sitting room. Here he could sit and make himself at home – here back home again. It was strange. But he had not thought it would be like this.

In some ways the room was still the same: the old sofa and the table and the old chairs were still there. Apart from these there were some new and unfamiliar things: a fine new mirror between the windows and a large oak sideboard with glass doors and silver fittings. This was not his. It was fine. But it was not his.

Then what about his wife – what about her? A little older – yes, of course she was. But she wasn't all that old. Let's see: in 1914 she had been twenty-five. So she's forty. But she was still reasonably good-looking. A bit fat – but heavens above!

A spasm of fear ran through him – just enough to make him tell himself that he *had* come back again. But he *had* thought it would have been different.

Granted, he had arrived unexpectedly. And it had certainly been a long time. Doubtless he had also changed a great deal, so that it wasn't easy to recognize him again. Then there was the fact that she had believed him dead. But then, after a moment's surprise, shouldn't she have recognized him? And then they should surely have embraced each other, and then there should have been a solemn moment: the father home from the war!

And precisely because she had believed him to be dead, surely she should have been doubly pleased to find that he was alive. There should have been a solemn and festive occasion with him sitting at his own table with his wife and children. Really, there should have been some sort of celebration.

And she'd been in such a hurry that he hadn't even had time to ask after Etti! She must be a big girl now. Good Lord, she must be . . . must be very nearly eighteen!

Surely it wasn't her he'd met on the stairs? That young lady who had passed him wearing light-coloured silk stockings and a fur coat? A whiff of whose perfume he had caught as he pressed himself against the wall when she went past? Impossible!

Perhaps he could find a photograph of her? A few photographs hung over the sofa. Yes, this young girl in the confirmation dress must be Etti. She was beautiful. Strange that this mature lady should be his daughter.

And there he was himself, on the middle of the wall, in uniform. This was the picture he had had taken the day he had been called up. Now with black crêpe round the frame, and artificial flowers, and his Iron Cross! Loved and missed!

He sat down to wait. That was something he had learnt to do. He had learnt how to wait!

A long time passed. He had been out in the kitchen again and buttered himself a few more slices of bread. He still had a little tobacco left.

At six o'clock Lisa arrived back and began making the dinner. At seven o'clock Etti arrived.

She gave a cry of surprise when she saw him. Her mother came in.

'It's your father,' she said.

The daughter looked at them uncomprehendingly.

'It's your father come back from the war!'

'What war?'

'*The* war, child. The Great War!'

'Oh, but . . .'

'He's been a prisoner in Siberia.'

'But you always said . . .'

'Yes, that's what we thought!'

'Etti!' he said, and held out his arms to her.

'Hello!' she said. She remained standing, looking at him. That she had a father, that he'd come home – these were things she heard her mother say; and surely *she* must know. But take it all in – that was a different matter. For instance, was he now going to live with them? This man?

The mother went out into the kitchen again. The two of them were left alone in the room. It became painful.

'Just a moment!' said Etti and disappeared. She came in again with a tablecloth and plates and laid the table.

They ate in silence. After dinner Etti went out; she had arranged to meet somebody. The other two remained sitting.

'So you've come back home again,' she said.
That was true enough. He had nothing to say to that.
'What had you thought of doing now?'
'I suppose I might . . . start in the workshop again?'
'There isn't much doing,' she said. 'There isn't work for more than two people. And Nolte of course has a share in the business. He's a partner.'

He said nothing to this either. He said nothing about it being his workshop. For that had been long ago. Nor was it certain that he would be up to it now, either – he probably hadn't the hands for intricate work like that. Perhaps he'd better start looking for something else.

'What do you think I ought to do?' he said.
'God knows. There's nothing but unemployment and high prices around here. Everybody's out of a job. And the cost of living is so high, so awfully high, that Etti and I can barely manage. So if you can't find a job, I don't know . . .'

Frau Hempel took out some mending and began working on it. Nine o'clock came. She began to yawn.

'I'd better make you up a bed,' she said.

She went into the bedroom and returned with a blanket and some sheets and a pillow and started to make up the sofa.

'Am I sleeping here?' he asked.
'Well? Etti and I are sleeping in the bedroom, aren't we?'

[Original title: *Den savnede*. Translated by James McFarlane]

SIGURD HOEL

The Murderer

One day there was a new man at the breakfast table.

He was much bigger than the others. Not a lot taller perhaps; but he was so broad. He sat at the end of the table, and Anders, who was sitting still on a stool by the wall, saw him from behind. His back was nearly as broad as the table top.

The others talked and told stories. The new man did not say much.

It was the first day of the harvest, and Anders turned the grindstone after the mid-morning rest. Afterwards he asked Embret what sort of a fellow that man was.

Embret just stood there for a while, seeing that his scythe was ready for cutting. Then he said casually: 'Who, Martin? That's just Martin, that is.'

He banged a little at the pegs which held the leather strap around the handle of the scythe. Then he said: 'Some people call him the murderer.'

'The murderer? Why murderer?'

But Embret clearly thought he had said enough.

'Murderer? Oh, it's only something folks say.'

With that he closed up behind his beard and his long nose. He hung the handle of the scythe over his shoulder and followed the others down to the field. But it was easy to see from his whole gait and the bend of his knees that something or other was upsetting him considerably.

For the rest of the day, Anders thought of nothing else but this murderer. When the farmhands came in to eat, he watched him furtively. When they went back to the fields he followed; at a safe distance, but still he followed. He was afraid of this new man, but he had to watch him; he had never seen a murderer before.

Actually he did not look so very dangerous. Yes, he was big; but so quiet and withdrawn. Hardly ever said a word, and when he did speak, it was in such a quiet, pleasant voice. When he sat down or got up he was so careful, almost as if he were frightened of breaking something. It was true that most things did look small and fragile when placed next to him.

In the harvesting team he went last. First went Embret, who belonged to the farm, and then came Nils from Kleiva, light and quick as a squirrel. And then came Martin.

They were cutting the thick clover meadow. It was easy to see when you looked at both Embret and Nils that it was heavy going. But you could not see it when you looked at Martin. He looked as if he were just strolling along behind.

If the mower who was last in line was the best, it was easy for him to force the pace and exhaust those in front of him, if he wanted to. All he had to do was to move up close behind them. Embret was a good mower, everyone said that, and he had forced the pace often enough, he had told the tale himself many times.

Martin did not try to do that. He just strolled along quietly a good way behind Nils. His scythe seemed to move of itself through the thick clover. Sshh! and then sshh! again.

But he cut a much broader swath than the others.

Anders stood some way off and watched.

Perhaps it was not so strange that the whetstone slapped in such an affronted fashion against the seat of Embret's trousers.

The next day, when Anders was alone with Nils, he asked him more about it.

Nils started, and looked round quickly over both shoulders. He often did that before he said anything; he looked like a squirrel peering round both sides of a tree trunk. Then he said: 'Murderer? No, it's only a nickname he's been given, that.'

He looked round quickly twice more: 'But he is a criminal, you know, or so they say. He's been in prison, you know.' With that he darted away.

Anders kept away from the field the next day. Perhaps this Martin was dangerous after all.

Then it was evening. Anders was standing out in the yard and enjoying himself throwing stones over the roof of the barn. He was not really allowed to, for there were fields just behind the barn. That was why he had such a funny tickling sensation in his tummy every time he threw one.

Then Martin came lumbering along. 'Throwing stones, are you?' he said. Then he picked up a big stone. 'Look, this is the way to throw stones!' He threw the big stone – and Anders stood and stared. The stone flew off, further and further, until it vanished into the air, so far away that Anders could not even think that far.

From that moment Anders knew. Criminal or murderer or prison, it made no difference. He just wanted to be with Martin, and learn to throw stones just as far as he did.

That he never did learn. But otherwise he learnt a great number of things from Martin in the time that followed. He learnt to recognize new birds by their call and to imitate them, so that they became curious and answered and came nearer. He learnt to work out north and south in a forest when the sky was clouded over. He learnt to tell from the ants and gnats whether it was going to rain, and from the rowan tree and the birch whether it was going to be a wet autumn. You could tell by the turning of the weather in August whether it was going to be a hard winter (though that was a more reliable sign in the old days).

Martin was full of such old signs and omens, and he liked to talk about them, but preferably when there were no grown-ups listening. He was happiest together with children, was Martin. He was a bit simple, the other grown-ups said. Anders and the other children could not see that, but perhaps that was because they were not grown up yet. He never mocked them, and never bragged or told tall stories. Perhaps that was what the grown-ups meant.

He certainly was the friendliest man in the world. And the strongest. Anders was constantly at his heels.

Nevertheless, he was a little bit frightened of him deep down inside. The friendliest man he knew was a criminal and had been in prison. Something dangerous was lurking there.

One day, many years later, Anders was allowed to go off eastwards into the forest with Martin to gather cloudberries. Martin knew his way so well around the forest to the east.

They had found quite a lot of cloudberries; Anders could not carry any more, at any rate. Now it was getting on into the afternoon, and it was time to start back.

Martin was thinking about something as he walked along. He was very quiet, and that was unusual when there were just the two of them.

Suddenly he said: 'You know, I've just thought – we're quite close to Dompen now. That's where I come from, you know. We might just as well have a look in. . . .'

They had not been walking long when they came to flatter ground. And suddenly they were not in thick forest any more but in more open woodland, where there were only Christmas trees growing.

Martin walked round and retraced his steps a few times; it was as if he was not quite sure where he was.

Then suddenly they came to a small clearing in the wood.

It was the site of a small farm they were standing on. You could still see a little of the foundations, and in the middle there was a small heap of bricks and stones. That was where the chimney stack had been. There were brambles growing over it now.

Martin stood still for some time and looked at it. Quietly, as always. He did not say anything, just looked as if he were thinking about something.

Then it was as if he suddenly remembered Anders was there. 'Just wait here a minute, Anders,' he said. 'I just want to have a bit of a look round.'

He went off, and was gone for quite a while. When he came back, he was if anything even more quiet than usual.

Then they walked on along a cow-track. They went past a couple of big stone cairns, half-hidden by small fir trees and brambles. A little later they arrived at another small farm site.

'Now this place, this was Langlia,' said Martin.

More cairns, and then another site. That was Nordbråten. Then there was nothing more, thick forest took over again. The other deserted farms lay on the other side of the bog.

Martin said nothing on the way home. And Anders did not ask. He knew the whole story by now, as it was told by people in the village.

Martin was a good-natured fellow all right. But it was pure chance that he had not become a murderer, so people said.

He had been the tenant farmer at Dompen. It was deep in the forest, and a pretty miserable place it was; the soil was mostly stones and the buildings were almost falling down. But he had always lived there, as had his father before him, and *his* father before him. They had worked for the owner for so many days every year as rent for the farm.

But then it happened that the forest was sold to a large company. And one day the order went forth, as they say, that all the tenant farms in the forest should be turned back into forest. They had calculated in town that they would make a better profit by doing that.

The other tenants gave up without a fight. Most of them ended up in America.

But as for Martin, he must have been a bit stupid and a bit slow to understand, and he got a bit awkward about it, as good-natured people can now and then. At any rate he did not understand why he should have to leave his farm. He had always worked the allotted number of days for the owner, as had his father before him, and *his* father before him. And he had just cleared a new potato patch, and you would never believe the number of stones there had been in it. And he had got himself a wife and child too. He simply stayed there. He was sent a warning, and then another warning. But he could not really grasp what was going on. He stayed there.

So out came the bailiff, one day in late autumn, with braid on his cap and the required witnesses and everything according to the rules, and formally and legally evicted Martin and his wife and child and cow and goat and two sheep, and put the seal of the law on the door, or whatever it is called. It looked as if Martin finally understood that they meant business; in any case, he did not protest – in fact he did not say anything at all. The bailiff went back down to the village again as quickly as possible – he was perhaps not all that proud of what he had had to do.

A week later it was rumoured in the village that Martin had simply moved back into the house and barn again as if nothing had happened.

Now things were beginning to get serious. The bailiff had to go up there again and read out the law to Martin, and perform a legal eviction all over again. And the same day the head forester, the company's representative in the village, went into the forest with men and horses and pulled down the old farmhouse. Whether or not Martin had thought of moving back in again this time was never known for sure; he was standing outside with his wife and child and cow and goat and sheep when the men arrived. The head forester went and told him off, and got a bit hot under the collar about it – he knew that people were laughing at him a bit on account of this episode.

Martin did not have much to say in reply. Not a single word actually, if the truth be told. He and his wife and son stood and listened until the head forester had finished. Then they went and sat on the fence a little way off and watched the men pulling down the farmhouse and the barn. The head forester uttered a final few words of warning – and then he returned to the village.

But he had forgotten one thing – to pull down the potato store.

Old-fashioned potato stores like this one often lie a little way away from the house – that was no doubt why he had forgotten it. The cellar itself is sunk in the ground, as it ought to be. On the surface of the ground there is only the store-loft, or vault, as it is called, with a normal thatched roof over it. From the outside one of these potato stores looks like a house whose walls have sunk into the ground right up to the eaves.

Towards Christmas a rumour reached the village that Martin was living in the potato store, or rather in the vault, with his family and his animals. He had patched up the holes in the cracked walls with moss, and built a sort of fireplace in one corner.

There was nothing for it – the bailiff would have to go up there again and evict him. He was getting cross now, the bailiff – it was about time this nonsense came to an end. It was a long way up to the farm, and it was cold, and it was snowing – the bailiff cursed and swore.

So did the head forester who came up just afterwards to pull down the potato store. He was beside himself with rage. It was no secret that people in the village thought this was a huge joke. Whatever he felt about this business to start with, it had reached the point where it had become a matter of honour for the head forester now. You could not let people get away with anything, after all. . . . He poured out his wrath over Martin and his wife and child. They stood still in the deep snow, all three, and looked at him. The animals had gone. They had been taken in payment of debts. It is expensive to be evicted so often. Although it is said that they had eaten one of the sheep themselves.

It looked as if the head forester had won this time. Martin went away. Some said that he was living in an old log cabin deep in the forest, but nobody knew anything for sure.

Then came the spring. And with it a new rumour: Martin had moved back with his wife and child to his farm again! They were living in a lean-to built of fir branches which they had erected over the potato store. And they were busy setting potatoes as though nothing had happened!

A large expedition set out. The bailiff and the bailiff's clerk and witnesses and the head forester and horses and men with tools and rifles. You had to be prepared for anything – it was obvious that the fellow was off his head.

They found the family and the lean-to and the potato patch with the newly sown potatoes. They pulled down the lean-to – and pulled down the fence around the farm while they were about it, so that job was done too, and threw all the rails from the fence on to a heap and set fire to them, and threw the fir branches from the lean-to on top, and let the whole thing go up in smoke. Then they dug up all the potatoes again and collected them in a sack and confiscated them, just to be sure. The law must run its course.

The law did not meet any opposition this time either. Martin just stood there and watched, with his great fists hanging passively by his sides, looking as if he would stand there for ever thinking about it. Pale and thin he looked, and pale and thin were his wife and child too. They had not had too good a time of it that winter, wherever they had been living. . . .

That evening the head forester was sitting with a group of loggers down by the river. He was sitting with the head logger, and had been drinking a little, and was boasting about what he had done earlier that day. He no doubt did not feel any too sure, either of himself or of those who were sitting listening, and that was probably why he exaggerated so much. That Martin was a broken man now, he said. He had stood up there, as meek as a lad who'd had a thrashing, lean and skinny and with no strength left. . . .

Suddenly Martin was standing there. He did not say anything, but got hold of the head forester almost absent-mindedly and lifted him up from the log he had been sitting on, and laid him across his knees. Then he smacked him on the bottom a few times with the flat of his hand, as you would smack a naughty child. They were pretty loud smacks, according to those who had been watching; but it was not exactly dangerous.

But then it must have happened that he got more worked up as he hit him. Or perhaps it was because the head forester yelled so much – he screamed like a stuck pig, they said. Whatever the reason, Martin picked up the head forester and laid him down on his back and put his knee in a few times, until six or eight loggers came and lifted him off.

The head forester had to be carried inside, and the doctor was brought. All the ribs in his body were broken. He hovered between life and death, as they say, for many weeks. But he recovered – otherwise Martin Dompen would not have got off with six months.

Well, there it is. Then time drifted over the story, as it drifts over everything. The murderer – it was only in jest they called Martin by that name. It was the head forester who had used it in all seriousness, at the trial.

When he got out of prison he managed to get the lease of another forest farm, where he felt at home, so people said – it was a long and arduous trek into the forest, and the soil was poor and stony, and the buildings were almost as old and decrepit as they had been at the former place. But it was mostly the wife and son who looked after the new farm. He himself was mostly out working down in the village – so perhaps he did not feel so much at home as all that after all. He was not a fast worker, he got hold of tools so slowly and carefully that it was as if he was afraid that they would break when he touched them. It was quite a sight to see him lift an iron harrow. It was otherwise reckoned to be quite a feat for one man to lift one; but he got hold of it and lifted it up as carefully as if it were made of gossamer, and he was afraid it would come to pieces in his hands.

He was just the same with a hoe, an axe, or a spade. He was just the same with the horses he was in charge of. He handled them as gently as if they had been small children. And indeed most horses did look very small beside him.

They say that he has been like that ever since the head forester just came to pieces in his hands. It had given him a kind of shock – it was as if he had realized that there was no point in setting up any resistance against people as weak as that.

[Original title: *Morderen*. Translated by Janet Garton]

TARJEI VESAAS

It snows and snows

It snows and snows over the plains – in a boundless wasteland. Not one living tree. A house stands here, just one, it grows smaller hour by hour, and will be buried by the snow.

The drifts around the house are growing. Silently and lightly stars drop down on to the roof. No weight at all – but at the last the roof-beams will crack under the crushing load.

It is day, though gloomy with the heavy grey tones in the air. They do not change, there is no pause in the fall any more. As it snows now, it will keep on snowing.

It is through this that the lonely dark river flows.

A wide black curve is just visible a little way off. It is so flat here that no sound can be heard, although the powerful current is running swiftly. Dark and swift it passes by, and is gone in the white flurry. Nothing sticks up out of it to create resistance and rushing noise. The darkly flowing depths have no idea of what resistance is. The snow falls into it, but cannot be seen, cannot settle, carried away in an instant by the sucking force.

It snows and snows.

Inside this house it is not silent at all: music is playing, unceasingly. Competing with the snowfall outside. More and more music is demanded, as though in defiance or terror – or both these things mixed together.

'Play!' comes the shout, in a hoarse voice.

So it plays a fraction louder.

The defiant shout comes from a room which looks out over the wide curve of the river. Far inside the house, but out towards the river. There sits a man alone. He is fighting for his life against the stars which drift down and settle on his roof. He feels the weight of each one, for it is him it affects, every tiny weight which is added to it.

So it is only the tinkling snow-stars and him now. And then the curve. Those three. Everything else the scissors have cut through.

Or it is left behind, overcome, or lost – in any case it is not here. Now it is the falling ice-cold stars. They are more beautiful than any human being can conceive, and they settle more gently than the smallest leaf, sprinkle down to wipe him out. He can feel their fine, dangerous weight, and that there is no end to them.

'Play!' he calls out in command, and the room plays. The music is himself – it is the only thing that helps in a battle with the stars. But to make the music he has to take piece by piece of what he has in himself to protect himself with.

'These are terrible stars,' he thinks.

The stars are settling in deep layers up there, and listening to him below, he feels.

'Play!' he shouts, and sacrifices a new piece of his innermost self. And all the music which can possibly be found, plays. Not for a moment can it stop the stars, but it is his weapon nevertheless. It *is* a power he has.

He looks closely at the wall in front of him. Has the roof begun to slip down? No, not yet. But it will soon enough. It is a question of time.

Yet that does not seem to be the most important. There is something else he must look at and look at.

That curve.

'Yes, I see it,' he says, as though someone had asked him to pay attention. It is the ever-gliding curve, and he stands at the window as if trapped.

The dark curve flows on. He stares at it, entranced. The unclear surface glides through the snowfall, and has no end, does not stop, does not start. The man who is looking at it feels his eyes glued to it.

The river curves this way, he tries to say next, under the pressure of need and loneliness. It is a memory from *before* – now it is almost just a trick of the tongue.

'Oh no,' he says quickly, 'no longer now.' The curve does not change a hair's breadth. The curve flows swiftly by.

'We are listening!' say the stars on the roof, monotonous and meaningless. But they *are* death.

At once he must tear himself away from the river curve, and fight for his life.

'Play!' he shouts, although it had not stopped, but on the contrary played with all its strength.

The house is riven by sounds, stands there in the wasteland like a little forgotten musical box.

Then it came.
The wall slipped down with a sudden jerk. The lonely one saw it with whitening eyes, they opened wide.
The stars out there have become enough, now the beams were giving way, just a little bit.
'We're listening,' say the small stars, and they listen intently. In the meantime more and more drift down.
Then the call comes louder from the innermost room. He *is* the music and the demand for the music – he just does not know how this has happened. They are wrestling together. On one side the call: 'Play! Play!'
'We're playing all the time,' answers the music.
'Not enough. Play more!'
'We're playing and playing,' answers the music bewildered, 'but we have not got the notes any longer.'
But on this side he does not listen: 'Why aren't you playing as you should?'
He gets the answer: 'The scissors have been out cutting.'
Of course. The scissors. Startled, he thinks of the scissors. Does not know what it is.
In the meantime it is snowing. The stars settle, light as nothing at all. We are listening, they say, paralysingly monotonous. Drawing, listening. Everything goes in to him in the room, everything which can crush, grind to pieces, and suck up. The strengthening strings which went through here are cut off, one by one. Where are the hidden scissors? He does not know. What he knows is strictly limited. But he holds out.
'Play!' he commands, with the power of his powerlessness.
'We're playing so that the house is fit to burst,' answers the music.
Outside flows the dark river curve. The man stares out at it, out from his house under the snow. He can never go with it. Now the room has shrunk further under the weight, the roof has come closer. The stars are sucking the marrow out of him with their listening. He feels that it is happening.
'Something must start to happen!' he thinks.
But the scissors cut it before it is thought. All the thousand strings

he had, where are they! The scissors stand outside the door and cut. He is rummaging amongst cut-off ends.

'I don't want to,' he thinks.

He begins to call out names which might have meant the greatest joy and the greatest sorrow.

'Cut off,' comes the reply. A little flat click which means cut off, cut off.

There were many important things once! I must get through to them!

'Cut off,' is the reply.

Happenings, great and small, innumerable: cut off. They *were* just brief happenings, that is all, something which passed, and had disappeared in a short while – like the rain which evaporates from a raised forehead.

He takes another piece of himself for more music. Does not know any longer what is the music and what is *him*. The scissors have been busy. Skeins of strings wave in the windless air.

'Play!' he calls.

'We are doing,' answers the poor music.

The roof drops down further with small jerks.

'Listen!' he says.

The music does not want to listen. Plays for its life.

He bursts the walls with music – it does not help. He takes a new piece of his precious time, and throws it into an insatiable darkness. The cold masses of stars listen, empty and deadly, to him down below the whole time, and want to suck him dry with their blind pumps. Although it is the river curve out there that he is staring at.

Lonely and boundless – and yet hardly room to move. It does not snow any heavier, because it cannot, *but it can seem so*, and the current carries it swiftly away and is as before. The playing house is a little box in the drifts, as if forgotten by some giant-sized child.

Then it grows dark and the day is over. There is little time to act.

Towards midnight the music nevertheless sounds louder – however he has managed that. Perhaps the darkness just makes it sound like that.

It is silent on the roof, while the slow fall goes on. The stars listen so intensely that it hurts, is that not enough? The music plays loudly and wildly, so that no sound from the soundlessness can force its way to the heart of the ill-fated one. Of the earth-born and stubborn one.

'It is the scissors,' he thinks. 'If I could just slip past them,' he thinks obstinately.

He is smaller now, and shrinking. It is going into the music. But he remains standing. It is just that he cannot see the mighty curve any longer. *It* is still flowing, in the darkness, but his eyes do not have strength enough to reach it.

The room buckles beneath the weight of the snow. Is squashed together. He has little room – even though he is so much smaller himself. He holds his breath and listens to the stars he is battling against. He and they listen to each other like a trembling battle of strength with no movement.

'Play!' he calls, and grows less.

'What is it?' he calls too, out into the snowy night. But there is no reply to *that*.

Must be *past* midnight now. It is snowing, in blind drifts. The house is playing. It stands there, tiny, but he has still some reserves left, it is as if nothing can break him. The roof sinks down, the walls come inwards towards him.

The scissors and all they have cut are far off now. *Now* he has enough with the battle.

What else is there?

Not a living soul knows.

He can hardly move at all, but still.

It snows and snows over the unyielding will. Pours out of floodgates which are never emptied. All is formless darkness by the great curve. The drifts deepen swiftly. The house stands and plays, and must not stop being a house.

[Original title: *Det snør og snør*. Translated by Janet Garton]

AKSEL SANDEMOSE

The Rat

They were three days out at sea when the cook discovered there was a rat on board. Lack of drinking water had made it wild and reckless; regularly it was seen sitting on one of the water tanks licking up any drops which had been spilled. It was a peculiar animal with a very pointed snout, almost like a fish, and blue-black down the whole of its back. When it leapt off the water tank, it would give a great thump with its tail like a beaver.

The rat became the sole topic of conversation and the object of much love-hate. It prompted long discussions about shipwreck, plague, and the workings of the rat mind; and also daily eruptions of fury, for desperation drove it to make the strangest kinds of raids. The man they called 'the Parson' found all his cigarettes ruined; and it gnawed holes in the skipper's patent-leather shoes. If any night the beast managed to get into the galley, it devastated everything. A price of five kroner was put on the head of the invader, with drinks all round the day it was caught. But for a long time none of the organized hunts was successful. It was a highly talented rat. One morning it sat on the table drinking coffee from the skipper's cup. After this he carried a revolver and raised the reward to ten kroner plus a whole bottle of spirits. The coffee cup and its contents he dropped overboard, controlling his feelings with difficulty. He was the only one who otherwise didn't talk about the rat; but his eyes swept the deck in a way different from before.

Above them stretched the dome of a clear and still wintry sky. On every side was the desolate sea, stretching thousands of miles. In the middle of it lay the *Fulton*, a little world in that endless space. The last six people in the world were frantically hunting a rat.

They began to think of it as a very remarkable rat, something unique in natural history. It could both laugh and talk; it could read men's thoughts and its droppings were rounded pellets with red specks on them. Bjarne maintained it was a male, but that provoked the cook who said it was a female which any time might produce a litter of young – any child could see that. How else did you explain those red specks?

Bjarne looked rather confused; then, bridling, asked whether the cook had never heard of stomach ulcers? Just wait, the beast would die of its own accord! Or perhaps the specks came from the fact that it was actually a plague carrier. What do you mean, damn it – that female droppings necessarily must have red specks on them?

The Lapp did not answer, but he sneered as though to say he knew more about these things than Bjarne.

The mate mixed some whisky and water and left it on deck in a bowl. He wanted to get the rat drunk. But the animal just sat and laughed at the bowl; and when the skipper came along with his revolver, the rat was gone like the wind. The mate kept watch on it a whole morning, during which time nobody was allowed to hunt it. But it didn't touch the drink; it only sat there, its shiny coal-black eyes blinking, and disappeared like a flash if anybody approached. It had long ago discovered that nobody could get at it under the galley, and it spent a lot of its time there. But it had other impenetrable places. The whole vessel was carefully searched, but nobody understood where it could be living.

When the mate came on deck after dinner, he immediately went to look at the bowl. 'Hey! It's drunk it!' he shouted excitedly. But there was no drunk rat to be seen, and the mate became dubious. He squinted across at Goldie who was at the wheel, but the big man only yawned and looked up at the sails. The mate heard laughter from the deckhouse and angrily went below with the empty bowl. He didn't ever try again to make the rat drunk.

The rat was the very pivot about which the world turned. It was the great name which is remembered when the age is forgotten. It was the Flying Dutchman, or Terje Vigen, Caesar or a nigger who is to be lynched. Indeed it was much more – it was the expression of the unifying social idea, was itself that very idea. It was the wife you wish to divorce, the girl you cannot have, as well as the one you don't want. It was lodged in your heart, and wouldn't let itself be caught.

And this is how the entry ran in Claes Winckel's diary: 'Last night the rat was in the deckhouse and bit Bjarne Vik on the cheek while he was asleep. It was a nasty wound.'

The attack caused turmoil. Bjarne leapt out of his bunk and smote both the cook and the Parson about the head just to be sure. It developed into a real brawl before the two victims had a chance to protest their innocence, whereupon the cook then set about Bjarne.

Thereafter there were enough rat stories to fill a library: rats that ate small children or buried their dead with elaborate funeral rites, rats that walked along telephone wires, and others that ate nails – nails by the pound. They polished up everything they knew about the Black Death and plague rats, about Siamese twin rats and rats without hind legs. But the rat on the *Fulton* was incomparably the rarest of rats, on this they were all agreed – biting grown men on the face! Bjarne threw out the suggestion that it wasn't really a rat at all. What then? Well, he didn't know – had anybody heard tell of kangaroos? Nonsense, said the Parson, shrinking back in terror. 'A kangaroo is a kind of bear,' the cook believed, '– with a long tail.' Bjarne then wondered if it might be a dwarf kangaroo.

'It's a female rat full of baby rats,' the cook declared.

At which Bjarne insisted that in any case it was a male.

Everybody slept uneasily once the rat had displayed its evil disposition. That very same day Bjarne was bitten a second time, this time on the nose. He completely lost his temper and rushed aft in his shirt-tails. 'Look at this, cap'n! What kind of a bloody ship is this – where you get eaten alive by rats and lice!'

The skipper looked at him icily, and gradually Bjarne's voice sank to a low muttering. He shambled up forward again. For the rest of his off-duty watch he sat there with a length of plank in his hand, glowering like a fanatic. The rat did not show up.

'Something's got to be done, Mr Mate,' said the skipper. 'That rat is mad, rabid.'

Immediately after that Goldie came into the deckhouse and said: 'Now it's all clear. The rat is mad. It's got rabies, rat madness.'

Bjarne turned white.

The mate didn't know what to do. They had already tried mass hunts, and the rat was at all events not so crazy as to allow himself to be caught. He racked his brains over the problem.

Then the skipper took over the wheel from the Parson, and said: 'Mr Mate! Get all hands to go and find out how the rat gets into the hold. That's where it is when it's not around.'

They searched every inch of the vessel, up and down. But this they had done before, and they found no holes this time either. And there sat the rat in the middle of the main hatch!

Bjarne grew red with fury. They surrounded the enemy, armed

with brooms and poles. The skipper simply abandoned the wheel and came with his bare fists. Pssh! There was no rat there.

Of what significance is it whence a boat comes or whither it is bound when there is a rat to dance attendance on? The rat was their life's mission, was their life's dread; it was all spirits, good and evil. It gave them the illusion that life had a meaning. What meaning could life possibly have had if there had been no rat? They regarded it with the same suppressed disgust as adults bring to the drinking of milk – but what meaning has life without milk? They swore they'd pursue the rat till they'd caught it – even if this meant they were eternally doomed to sail round Iceland until Judgement Day in the hunt for a rat. But they also thought – obscurely, as people do when their minds are unhinged: 'What shall we do after Judgement Day if we can't go chasing around after the rat in the kingdom of heaven?'

They speculated about traps, discussed traps endlessly. They dreamed about traps of the most diabolical construction, and brushed up on everything they had heard about mediaeval torture. Bjarne pointed to his wounds, and his eyes bulged like glistening cherries: 'It bit me! Has it bitten any of you, by any chance? I'm only asking. Has it bitten any of you?'

'Puh!' said the cook. 'It's only that it has a nose for trash and gonorrhoea.'

Bjarne executed a noisy war dance. 'Sheer envy, you stinking Chink!'

Goldie realized that Bjarne really had a feeling that some kind of honour had been vouchsafed him because, when the next time the rat attacked the Parson – who woke up with a roar during the dog watch – he was so jealous he almost forgot to say anything. The Parson struck out in all directions, screaming and carrying on enough to bring the entire vessel into uproar. All his knuckles were bleeding from the wild blows he struck against the inside of his bunk. The rat had taken a bite out of his lower lip. Almost immediately it started swelling near the wound, and his lower face turned discoloured. That same morning he was lying delirious, saying things he should really have kept to himself. One man sat by him the whole time, mostly to watch out for the rat.

The skipper did what he could for the sick man, and looked very grim. This had to be put a stop to. You couldn't have things like this happening aboard the *Fulton*, a three-masted schooner. Was this some kind of circus, and he a clown?

He summoned the crew and made a speech: 'As you know, there is a rat on board. There's something wrong with this rat. It bites people. And now the Par . . . Johannes Hansen, that is – now *Johannes* is lying there sick. I have offered a reward. It's large enough for a mangy parson. I don't understand why you all put up with the creature anyway. Therefore: the rat must be dead within twenty-four hours.'

He threw the mate a glance as though to suggest he suspected him of having brought the animal on board with him; then he went down to his cabin. The mate also thought he ought to make a speech; he was just rehearsing it to himself when there came a roaring sound and great commotion from the cabin – and there up the stairway came the rat like a spectre. Goldie got as far as raising a foot to kick it. The rat was gone.

The skipper followed slowly behind. His eyes wandered from one to the other and finally stopped at Bjarne Vik: 'You take eight hours rat watch! After that the cook will relieve you. You'll keep changing like that without regard to normal duty until the rat is caught.'

Bjarne, swaggering, began systematically. Of course he was the right man. He wasn't the sort to take to his bed because of a paltry bite or two.

First he got hold of some lengths of boarding and carefully nailed them firmly round the skirting of the galley. Now the little monster couldn't hide himself there. Then he assured himself that the rat was not in the deckhouse and hermetically sealed it. Goldie snarled and shouted that he and the Parson were being suffocated. Bjarne persuaded him to keep quiet; and he took the cook's oath that the rat was not in the cabin. Then with the skipper's permission he shut that up too. Then he started at the furthest part of the deck with a solid rope end in his hand, turning everything over and looking suspiciously out along the boom. After this he jumped down and was about to continue along when the mate yelled: 'Here it comes!'

Bjarne saw the rat running from the stern and he rushed towards it. With an elegant leap the rat sprang on to the ship's rail and was already past Bjarne. The latter now performed a trick which had brought him much acclaim on many occasions – he did as the rat had done and chased it along the rail. The ship rolled – it was an impossible achievement! The cook in his confusion let go the wheel, and the mate stood there as stiff as a post: 'Good God Almighty!'

Bjarne was a real artiste in this matter, this the mate knew. But this exploit left him speechless. Bjarne took several big bounds and managed not only to get safely down but also to bend and send the rope whistling after the fugitive. He also found time for an oath.

The first time the rat was too quick, but the second time the rope thwacked against the rail where it was running, perhaps even in part hit it. At all events the rat fell overboard. A cry of delight stuck in the mate's throat, for Bjarne went in headfirst after it.

As ill luck would have it, the cook had just had to give the ship its helm. It took several precious moments before it could be luffed again, and then it would not put about either. By the time this had taken place, Bjarne was a good way astern.

The skipper and Goldie came on deck; a couple of lifebuoys were thrown out. The skipper shouted: 'Can you see the buoy?'

Bjarne's answer was indistinct, but he kept making for the buoy. Then they saw that the rat was sitting on his head. It was digging its claws into the sailor's hair and raising its head as though sniffing for something.

'If only I had a rifle now . . .' said the mate.

With one look the skipper cut him down to size; and in his confusion he turned to attend to the sails. They drew nearer to the swimmer who had set course for the ship where they stood ready with buoys and lines. They talked more about the rat than about Bjarne; it obviously was feeling greatly uncertain, and looked round nervously in search of some more inviting craft.

The skipper was at the helm and calculated the moment precisely. The sails hung slack as Bjarne came under the bows. He seized a buoy which was fastened to a line, and said brokenly: 'You . . .'

They heard the entreaty; they heard the sob in his voice, and they worked fast with no superfluous words. The cold water had nearly finished him; and they all knew how mortal terror strikes when rescue is near. Goldie leant bodily out through a bilge port; the mate hitched a line round one of his legs and made it fast to a ring on the main hatch. Meanwhile the skipper hung over the rail and, just to make sure, harpooned Bjarne with a boat hook. As the ship heeled over, Goldie managed to get a rope round his comrade, at which point a very wet rat ran across Goldie's back and vanished God knows where.

The skipper concluded his written report thus: 'I thus now have two men in their bunks, and the rat is as lively as ever. Moreover it has become much cleverer, as rats do after hot pursuit. It now has illusions of grandeur, and makes fun of us. It ought to end its days in some maritime museum.'

Bjarne lay wrapped in blankets up to his nose, staring silently into space. The Parson rambled on deliriously, saying his prayers and cursing. Goldie came below with a mug: 'Here's some grog for you from the skipper. This damn well ought to set you on your feet again!'

They shared the grog.

'The sight of you swimming around with a rat on your head,' sniggered Goldie. 'By all the saints, if that wasn't the most damn-fool thing I've ever seen!'

'What about you! Why didn't you catch it?'

'Catch it? With my teeth, I suppose you mean?' Goldie replied. 'I had enough to do hanging on to you, especially after you fainted and just hung there like a sack. I suppose I should have taken a bite at it? But the skipper and the mates were idiots to let it get away. And there's the Parson there has got rat-madness. Though I reckon he was already a bit rabid even before. Pretty soon he'll be rushing around biting us all, you watch! I don't trust anything to do with this ship any more!'

Half an hour later Bjarne came up on deck. He was staggering and was very red in the face. He tottered aft in his bare feet with a blanket round him like a toga.

'We'll grab him,' whispered the skipper. 'He's out of his mind!'

Then Bjarne stretched out a bare arm. In his hand he was clutching a gaping rat. The skipper said softly: 'If you let that thing go again, I'll have you drowned for sure!'

Bjarne lifted the rat up to his face and looked at it with hate. Its eyes stood out like blisters. 'So you wanted to bite me?' he said. 'And ride on my head? Well, see now if you can't find yourself a better head!'

He flung the rat overboard. It spread out its legs in an effort to fly, but couldn't manage it.

There was only a light breeze. They hung over the stern and watched the rat swimming after the *Fulton*. It wanted to join them.

Slowly the gap increased. The rat was swimming like a mad thing; this they saw clearly when it was lifted up by the swell.

It was nearly sunset, and the men grew silent as they stood there watching the rat. Each man had his own thoughts, and they did not look at each other.

Goldie was the first to tear himself free. He left before the rat was out of sight. . . . Aye, that's how we swim our own brief lives, towards a shore that sinks in the sea.

He had a feeling that some day the rat would climb aboard to safety again . . . some day. . . .

Bjarne could no longer see the rat. He looked with feverish eyes at the skipper, who read in those eyes ten kroner and a bottle of spirits.

But a gap now separated high from low. The skipper turned and went below.

'You can tell Bjarne,' he said later to the mate, 'that he'll be credited with ten kroner and that he can draw one bottle from you our first Saturday night in Eskefjord.'

The mate made a mental note of this. That was the way for a captain to speak.

[Original title: *Rotten*. Translated by James McFarlane]

JOHAN BORGEN

In the grass

'Oh, look at that cloud!' she said, half sitting up in the grass and pointing. 'It looks exactly like a lion!'
'Exactly,' he said.
'You're not looking at it. There! It looks exactly like a rearing lion!'
He said: 'It's horses that rear. Lions don't rear.'
'*This* one does. You're not even looking at it!'
'I am,' he said, getting up into a sitting position as well. 'It's a cumulus.'
'A what?'
'A cumulus. It's a cumulus cloud.'
'It looks exactly like a rearing lion. No, not there, silly. *There!* No, it's starting to look like a camel now.'
'Exactly like a camel. It looks like two camels.'
'Two camels? But it's only got one head!'
'It looks like two camels with one head. Can't you see the humps? Four humps.'
'But you're looking at the wrong cloud! No, not there! *There!*'
'Oh yes, that one. Yes, it does look like a camel, doesn't it?'
'Not any more. Now it looks like. . . . Look, there's a tower!'
'Yes indeed, a tower. Right on top of the camel's back.'
'Can you really see it?' she said, and looked into his eyes. The sky was reflected in his green irises. 'Now it looks like one of those . . .'
'Cumulus?' he said, and returned her look. 'It doesn't *look like* a cumulus, it *is* a cumulus.'
'Hm,' she said, and lay down again, still looking into his eyes. 'What does that mean anyway, that it is and doesn't look like? It must surely be because it looks like something that it's been called after it.'
'You are clever,' he said. 'I love you.'
'Because I'm so clever?'
'Regardless. Cumulus means hill-cloud. It looks like hills growing up out of one another.'

'There you are. I knew it was because it looked like something. Besides, it doesn't matter what it looks like. Hill-cloud? Cumulus is much prettier. What was that other word you knew?'

'Oh, I don't know. I know so many words.'

'Yes.'

'What do you mean?'

'You know so many words. I wish I knew many words.'

'You know lots of words, darling. Now you know cumulus too. About clouds that look like camels and rearing lions.'

'Lions don't rear. Anyway it doesn't matter.'

'What doesn't matter?'

'What that cloud looked like. Now I can't even see it.'

'It's disintegrated. Can't you see? It's all disintegrated.'

'I'm not looking at it. I don't want to know about things that disintegrate. What was that other word?'

'What other word, darling?'

'The other one, the one you said yesterday. You must know which one I mean?'

'I don't know what you mean. What was it about?'

'I've no idea. It was such a lovely word. No, put your arm like that.'

'Like that?'

'Just like that. How can you remember all these words?'

'But my love, that's what my work's all about. It's not the words I remember.'

'Don't you remember the words?'

'Yes, dear, I do remember the words too, but not specially the words. What they stand for.'

'Stand for?'

'Yes, or mean if you like. I remember words because they mean certain things.'

'How difficult.' She half sat up again, frowning with the effort of remembering. 'Now I know!' she cried. 'Chiroterium!'

'Chiroterium?'

'Yes, of course. Chiroterium. You said it yesterday.'

'What about?'

'*You* should know that! You said chiroterium about something or other.'

'Chiroterium? It means the fossilized footprints of land animals.'

'There you are, you see? That must have been what you said it about, then! Chiroterium, you said. It was down in the hollow amongst all those stones.'

'Oh, now I remember,' he said, pleased. 'But that wasn't yesterday. It must have been at least a week ago.'

'It was yesterday.'

'But darling, that was right over on the other side of the fjord. We haven't been there for several days.'

'Five days.'

'All right, five days then. Yes, you're right, it was Friday.'

'There you are. And you said it was at least a week ago. It was me that was right.'

'You said yesterday, my love.'

'Well all right, Friday then. It's not that important. Didn't you say chiroterium, then?'

'Yes, yes, if you say so. I *think* they were fossilized footprints. Strange.'

'Why is it so strange?'

'That they should be just there. I mean there where we were.'

'It's not so strange as all that. I'm sure you see things like that everywhere. Do you know what coccidiosis is?'

'Coccidiosis? Just a minute. . . .'

'An epidemic disease found in rabbits and ptarmigan.'

'That's right!' he said in amazement. 'How did you know that?'

'Oh, I know a lot of things, I do. It was you who didn't know that. And anyway you can't know whether it was right when you didn't know it.'

'How right you are. Now I know it, anyway.'

'Just like me. Now I know that cumulus means camel.'

He struggled not to say it, but he said it: 'Cumulus doesn't exactly mean camel,' he said.

'Yes, but you just said it. You said it about that cloud.'

'I said it about that cloud that *you* thought *looked* like a camel – that it was called cumulus. Something that towers up and up so that it grows. You know we have the word cumulative. In elections and things like that.'

'Elections?'

'Yes, parliamentary elections and suchlike. You can have a cumulative system of voting.'

'If you aren't lying here talking about politics! Parliamentary elections when I'm talking about camels!'

'You were talking about clouds.'

'All right, about clouds then. And then you talk about parliamentary elections.'

'I was talking about cumulative and cumulus.'

'And I about epidemic diseases in rabbits. He's right, you know, Ibsen.'

'Ibsen?'

'Yes, Ibsen. Isn't he the one who writes about people always being alone?'

'Yes – is it? Does Ibsen say that?'

'Of course he does. That just when you think you're really close to someone, then whoops. . . .'

'That's absolutely right. I didn't know that you . . .'

'There you are, you see. I know a lot of things that you don't know. But it's quite likely it was someone else.'

'But my dearest, if it was someone else, then it wasn't Ibsen.'

'Good heavens, how you argue about things. I think you must have got out of bed the wrong side.'

He laughed. 'You know very well how I got out of bed. You were tossing and turning so much in your sleep that I fell on the floor.'

'That's just what I said. Anyway, it was Ibsen who wrote that poem, "What a funny-shaped cloud".'

'"What a funny-shaped cloud, why it looks like a horse. . . ."'

'That's right. It was in our reading book.'

'It's from *Peer Gynt*.'

'It was in our reading book. It was called "What a funny-shaped cloud".'

'From *Peer Gynt*. That bit where Peer is lying in the grass looking up into the sky. It characterizes him as a daydreamer.'

'Oh.'

'He escapes into dreams always, the whole time.'

'Hm.'

'Why do you say "Hm"?'

'That's a shame.'

'What's a shame, my love?'

'When you say that about that poem in our reading book. It was so fine in the reading book. And now you say it's from *Peer Gynt*.'

'Yes, but it is from *Peer Gynt*, my sweet.'

'I know. That's what's such a shame. It was in our reading book. It

was so lovely. I had a dress with a flounced skirt and smocking on it and lace edging round the neck.'
   'You must have been terribly sweet.'
   'Do you think I'm old now?'
   'But darling . . .'
   'Since you think I was so sweet then!'
   'But darling, I didn't know you then.'
   'How can you know that, then? I used to bite my nails.'
   'Did you bite your nails?'
   'Down to the quick. It used to bleed, and then I got ink on it. Nobody said that was sweet.'
   'And you read *Peer Gynt* too?'
   'I read "What a funny-shaped cloud". It was so lovely.'
   'It *is* a fine poem.'
   'That's what I said. And then you say it characterizes something or other. I think Peer Gynt was all right, I do.'
   'When he ran off with the bride?'
   'Yes, then as well. And then he left her, right in the middle of the mountain.'
   'Did you think that was such a fine act? What if I . . .'
   'First he raped her and then he went and left her.'
   'Did he rape her? It doesn't say anything about that.'
   'Of course it does. He raped her, and then he told her to go to the devil.'
   'And you think that was all right.'
   'At least he didn't tell her that that cloud looked like a cumulus.'
   '*Is* a cumulus. Doesn't look like.'
   'All right, *is* then. He didn't say that.'
   He sat up again. He picked a blade of grass and chewed it. 'Do you mean that I'm a pedant?' he asked quietly.
   'Darling,' she said and sat up too. 'I was only talking about Ibsen, you know, Ibsen and things like that. You're not the only one who knows everything. What is a pendant anyway?'
   '*Pe*dant, not *pen*.'
   'All right, what is a pendant then?'
   'P-e-d-a-n-t. Oh blast. It's people like me, I suppose. Boring.'
   'You're not boring at all. Just a little . . .'
   'Pedantic?'
   'Yes, pendantic. Just a little. My dearest pendant.'
   He sighed in her embrace. Then he didn't sigh any longer. He

whispered: 'Would you like me to be a little bit more – Peer Gynt?'
  'Perhaps!'
  'Like. . . . Perhaps she asked him to?'
  'Perhaps she did. I think she did ask him.'
  'Then it wasn't rape.'
  'Yes it was.'
  'Come! Come, my love!'
  'Here in the grass?'
  'Come!'
  'My lion! My rearing lion!'

                [Original title: *I gresset*. Translated by Janet Garton]

TORBORG NEDREAAS

Red reflections

The double doors to the street were still standing wide open, and they had not collected everything from the pavement. A broken kitchen lamp lay at the very edge of the pavement, and an ironing board and some kitchen utensils which were strung together stood against the wall of the house, together with a large wickerwork basket, which was held together by a piece of rope wound round it. A small Christmas tree in a pot stood beside it. The garland of Norwegian flags had come loose and was lying in the dirt of the muddy pavement, and a shiny paper angel, much too big for that little tree, was swinging to and fro in the wind. The windows gaped open, curtainless, in the apartment where Evelyn and her folks had lived.

Herdis had a dry, empty feeling inside her. She leant against the wall, just as she had done the previous night to watch the eviction, and saw it all again. Once before she had watched while someone was evicted, but that was a long time ago and it was different then. In those days there was a great commotion when people were evicted; they had stood round and jeered at the police and yelled 'Ya-ha, ya-ha' and made a row.

But now it was done in silence. The kids would stand around not knowing what to do, watching as all the things gradually piled up on the pavement; some would help to load the hand-cart, but without looking at the people they were helping. The women from round about would stand silently against the house walls, and disappear like shadows when they had seen enough. Such evictions were not an uncommon occurrence any longer.

Demonstrations and disturbances in the streets were not uncommon either. Wild-cat strikes and protests against inflation blew up like sporadic hailstorms in various parts of the town; the kids from the back streets regarded it as a chance to have a bit of free fun, and trudged along, silent and hungry, after the workers down to the shipyards, looking forward to some brass-band music and perhaps a few scuffles if the police were waiting for them in Solheimsviken. But nothing more came of it. The storms passed over, a grey stillness descended on the area again. Even the steadily growing number of evictions aroused no excitement.

Herdis wandered homewards with her eyes on the pavement and her music case bumping against her thin legs. Jenny disappeared into her room the moment she had opened the door for her. As Herdis hung up her coat in the hall she noticed that her mother's and father's coats were both there. She listened – there was no sound from the living rooms. Neither were there any lights on. She warmed her hands by the stove in the dining room without putting the light on, and between the curtains through into the drawing room, which were drawn back, she could see the faint glimmer of the Christmas tree in the dark.

The night before, a small Christmas tree in a pot had been carried out from Evelyn's folks' and put down on the pavement, with garlands of Norwegian flags which had come loose and hung down into the mud on the pavement. She stood and let herself feel what it was like to be *home*, in warm, comfortable, and pleasant rooms. The piano keys smiled in a friendly way in the gaslight which shone through the window. Quietly, as if she were afraid of waking someone, she went into the drawing room and climbed into a chair, where she curled up. She hardly dared to breathe for fear of disturbing the almost painful stream of sensations which crowded in upon her.

From the bedroom she could hear her parents talking to each other. For a moment she listened – thank goodness. They were talking quietly, normally. Then she saw it in her mind's eye, one thing after another. Things were lifted and moved and carried out and down the stairs and left in the street. The piano. It stood freezing in the street, it was raining on it. The palms of her hands began to sweat, she took deep breaths. Things like that *did* happen to some people. It was difficult to believe when you were sitting in a good warm room. It was difficult to believe any of it when you were comfortably off yourself, difficult to believe it completely even if you knew it. You could not believe things until you felt them so deeply that you experienced them yourself. Herdis felt as if she were missing something when she was not able to grasp the experience, the times when she was passively contented or passively discontented, because she could not get hold of and be a part of the experiences of people she knew and people she did not know. Even though the experience itself filled her only with unease and fear.

She was continually preoccupied with the thought of war. But when she tried to imagine what it was like, she could not manage it. She discovered that she did not believe that people shot each other down, that human blood was shed. She could not manage to feel what it was like to have lost an arm or a leg, however much it said about it in the papers. And she knew that all the others were like her, that she was like all the others – they ate and drank, worried about inflation, wished for things and clothes and sweets, laughed and lived and slept. She and all the others were made in such a way that little children could be crushed and towns burnt down in other countries, without it becoming unbearable.

For what was war? It meant for example that Olsens the bakers were not Olsens the bakers any longer; he was now called Harder the shipowner, and needed two floors of Olsen's corner for his family, so that Elsi had her own room in English style and gave large parties.

War was strikes and discontent and the fact that the children from the back streets were skinnier and more ragged than before.

War was bread and dripping and hoarding away stores in the attic. The respectable little families down in Sølverstad did without their breakfast eggs and cakes with their coffee, and scraped together enough to be able to buy a silk dress and a second-hand top hat, so that they could make a good impression on the more fortunate, who would one day arrive with riding horses and cars and champagne lunches. They hoarded flour and goat's cheese, so as to make sure of not going hungry when times got even worse.

War, that was about little things. War meant that the rats grew fat and dangerous.

Herdis realized that she was sitting bolt upright, in a most uncomfortable position, and gripping the arms of the chair tightly. The voices from the bedroom disturbed her, they were burning in the walls and made her skin shivery with anxiety.

Suddenly her lips grew cold; her father's voice was raised, loud and ominous, in the other room. Mother's low laughter flared up through father's hoarse, grating shouts – Herdis was up out of her chair in a flash and into the dining room where she switched on the light. Suddenly she was afraid of the dark.

The light frightened her even more. Something terrible was happening at this moment, something in the little house was being destroyed. The door to the entrance hall was standing half open. The bedroom door was jerked open, father rushed through the hall, mother was trying to hold him back. She was still laughing her little breathless laugh, her blouse was torn at the shoulder.

Everything happened in a sudden rush, just like the comic films Herdis sometimes saw at the cinema: father had a bunch of ten-kroner notes in his hand, he tore at them and crumpled them and threw them into the stove. The flames were devouring them hungrily even before father had shut the stove door.

Herdis could not feel her own body any longer. It was like in her dreams – she herself did not exist, while terrible things were happening around her. She felt as if she were falling into the stove together with the notes and being burnt up with them. Money, money – just what they never had enough of! She heard his hurt, cracked voice but did not understand what he was shouting; the walls were burning, her home was burning. She heard mother say: 'You're mad.'

Herdis had hardly had time to take in the unbelievable thing father was doing with the money, when something even worse happened, something which was worst of all, now something happened which was unbearable. Father threw himself down on the chaise-longue and burst into tears. They were terrible tears. Herdis never knew that men could cry. He sat hunched over, with his hands over his eyes, and sobbed aloud; it sounded like bitter laughter, a shuddering, tearing laughter, his shoulders heaved and his mouth twisted bitterly.

Mother stood rubbing her shoulder, where there was a blue mark. Her little laugh had become so helpless. She called his name softly and gently. Then he leapt up – 'Go, just go! *He* can give you everything you want' – he sank down again in uncontrollable, shameless sobbing.

Herdis was unable to move a muscle, and just as in her dreams there was no one who noticed her presence. She saw herself throw herself down in front of her father and cling to him, kiss him and tell him she loved him. But she stood quite still. She shut her eyes and stood and died.

As so often before, it passed over again. But yet it was not like before. The passionate atmosphere of reconciliation which she feared and hated because it made her lonely was not there this time. Her parents were polite to each other, even respectful. Herdis longed for them to kiss each other and embrace and forget her – sooner that.

Every now and then mother had a little cry on her own, but straight afterwards she sat down at the piano and sang operetta melodies with her soft and sparkling voice, her eyes dreamy with happiness.

Herdis froze between them. She froze all the time at home now, unless she had an exciting book to read. She wished she had a sister, and pretended to herself that the little girls she knew were her sisters – preferably those who were in some kind of difficulty – Evelyn who had had all her teeth pulled out and had moved to the slums, Julia who had gone to a cheerless children's home, Christi whom she had lied to when she said she had lost the magic glass. Her parents often had long, low-voiced conversations out of her hearing. She escaped into dreams of desperate, pleading hope.

The hope grew into a fearful joy when her mother one day asked if she would like to go to the cinema with her. It was a long time since she had been out with mother, and the cinema was an event and an occasion. She jumped up and down beside her mother with her hand under her arm, and felt a warm glow of affection and possessiveness. All the splintered anxiety she had felt recently was pushed so far to the back of her mind that she really felt a sudden desire for cakes as they walked past a café window. She asked cautiously whether they might go to the café after the cinema – mother was so warm and affectionate that it made her daring. And when the answer was a wholehearted yes, she became completely happy, and thought that everything was going to be all right again, absolutely all right. She would ask if they could buy some cakes to take home for father too. If she had had money herself – yes, if she had had any money herself – it was quite unbelievable that anyone could put money in the stove and burn it, however angry they were with it —

When mother had bought the cinema tickets, Herdis suddenly saw that she was standing crying.

'But mummy – you've got tears on your cheeks —'

'It's so windy out. Oh dear, my eyes can't stand all that wind.'

Mother was just going to shut her handbag, but she opened it again and took out a five-kroner note which she gave to Herdis. Herdis was struck dumb, she did not dare to believe straight away that it was true, she had never owned, never dreamt of owning so much money. Mother closed her hand over the note. It took some time to convince Herdis that she was allowed to spend it just as she wished.

The auditorium had gone dark. Then the green light streamed on to the screen, there was a sound like pouring rain in the auditorium, and a lady began to play a cheerful march on the untuned piano. Herdis felt her mother's arm hugging her warmly. Mother said: 'You must enjoy yourself with it. Just be happy and glad and make sure you enjoy yourself.' Then she paused for a moment, holding her breath.

'I'm going to leave,' she said, in a hoarse voice. 'Your father and I are going to separate.'

And then the film began. Herdis did not see any of it. She tried dizzily to think about the five-kroner note, about everything she could buy with it. It all hurt too much.

Mother's eyes were red from crying behind her veil when they came out of the cinema. Herdis heard her talking – now she had to be a good, sensible little girl, she was so big and clever. She must try to understand Mummy.

The wind had increased; the gas-lights, which had just been lit, guttered. To Herdis it felt as if the ground was blowing away from under her. Everything was blowing away, mother and father were blowing away, and her home, everything. She clung desperately to her mother's arm, she shrieked and begged and cried – they *mustn't* separate, it wasn't true – she made herself wretched, worked herself into hysteria, big girl that she was. Mother's voice was calm and mild and terrible: 'It has to be like this.'

Herdis calmed down, she just froze. They forgot that they were going to the café, they let themselves be borne by the wind through the park, mother talked. Herdis would understand when she was older. Mother had fallen in love with someone else.

Herdis could feel the five-kroner note inside her mitten, like something wicked and shameful. She wanted to give it back to her mother, wanted to get rid of it, but was torn by a miserable desire to keep it instead. She had a vague feeling that she would perhaps regret it if she surrendered all the possibilities it offered. And she felt unhappy and wretched because she was incapable of giving it back again.

The feeling of homelessness was even worse at home than it was outside. The wind had turned into a storm, the window fasteners rattled. Inside Herdis's head some of the phrases from the merry tunes played at the cinema churned round and round, making her unbearably miserable. And her parents stifled her with a wall of friendliness.

Suddenly father leapt out on to the balcony. From below there came shouts and the sound of fire bells being rung, salvoes of galloping horses' hoofs echoed through the streets.

'*The whole town is on fire!*'

Father shouted down to someone and was told that the fire had begun somewhere in Strandgaten. Mother's face went white. Father said: 'I think I'll go down and see.' He went out into the hall and came back with his hat and coat.

'I suppose you'll being going *there*. But – someone must stay at home with the child.' There was a mixture of bitter scorn and questioning hope, and sorrow in his voice and glance. But the little flicker of hope which it contained leapt like a spark over to Herdis, it rushed through her mind – if mummy stays at home with me, everything will be all right again. Mother looked down and said in a voice that was only a whisper: 'Jenny is at home.'

A little later the front door shut after father, and a cold grey mist descended on Herdis.

Jenny came in from the balcony with her hair blown into a storm by the wind. 'It's blowing away up Småstranen now, the wind's blowing it down to the market and Veiten. I can't understand what kind of lass you are, that don't want to go up to Sydneshaugen and have a look.'

Herdis shook her head. She persuaded Jenny to go, she was not afraid of being left on her own. Sølverstad was not in any immediate danger. A red glow as if from a feverish sunset lay over the houses and pavements, while the storm tore at the slates and the window fastenings and howled round the corners.

Herdis was glad to be alone. She could see down in the street that people here and there were moving things out, getting ready to flee. Herdis stood and watched them without seeing anything, she stood bowed under the weight of her own pain. She had not known that sorrow could hurt so much, the pain raged and flamed within her. Now she knew that the man her mother – the one who –

He lived in Strandgaten. Strandgaten was on fire.

Dear God, let his house burn down. Let him be burned in it.

She ran frightened out of the dining room. When God looked

down to see who it was who had whispered those terrible words, he would find the room empty. Restlessly she went into the bedroom and looked out of the window into the back yard. There was a humming from all the iron steps as if from a large double-bass when the wind came sweeping down over the sloping roofs; doors and windows creaked and groaned. Over the roofs the sky was quite red; every now and then a handful of sparks spurted over the chimney pots like fireworks, scattered like stars and went out. From the town came a noise of muffled thuds and a continual hiss of flames and fire hoses. The red light was reflected dimly in the dark bedroom. She wished Jenny had been there after all. Just there in the flat. Not that she could talk to her, she had nothing to say. Her own sick pain was lashed by a new, frightened excitement which seared and soothed at the same time. Now it was all burning up, now the flames were devouring everything which hurt her. It was an exhausting and agonizing feeling, but with flashes of exhilaration too, like forcing one's way through a storm or being out alone in a thunderstorm. A driving whirl of disjointed thoughts piled up inside her and urged her into a feverish intoxication of emotion.

The bedroom was oppressive. She ran up to the loft. It was cold up there, but she put a box under the sloping window and put her head out through the open window to cool her face. Now she could hear the noise of the fire clearly. There was a thundering and a crashing and a scraping of heavy metal plates; far away someone screamed. All this about her father and mother had suddenly become unreal, just as unreal as the fiery sky, as the flickering red light on the floor of the loft, as the fire which swept across the town. A wordless thought sprang up like a spurt of flames within her and caught the soreness in her like the stinging lash of a whip – Strandgaten. Mother – if mother was in the middle of the blaze, if she – Herdis curled up and clutched herself as if the whiplash had struck her right in the stomach. Fear suffocated her. 'Mummy,' she moaned softly between her teeth.

All at once the pain parted with a violent surge, thoughts of her mother were smothered by the picture – *this* was a fear she was sharing with many, many people, maybe at this precise moment. The crashing, the hissing, and all the indeterminate gusts of sound from the burning town were suddenly very close to her, as if it were something in her which released them. Mothers went in fear for their children, children went in fear for their mothers, she felt their cries in her hammering temples, a dark and angry terror overcame her like a heavy giddiness, she felt as if she were going to be sick.

This was what it was like in war. The fear which threatened to crush her to pieces was the fear of living people here and now and the whole time, only much worse, and much more real. She had managed to get down from the box, and sat crouched in the corner with clenched fists; she sat and held her hands clasped tightly around a new knowledge, and felt that it was a terrible and agonizing treasure she had found.

Exhaustion made her feel calmer and cooler, though the thoughts did not cease piling up inside her head. One of the little girls in the street had vanished one evening a few years earlier; Herdis saw her as she ran round the corner, and she saw her now and wanted to shout to her and run after her and take her with her. It was only now that she realized how crazy it was that a living little girl should stop there and not exist any more. And the world was full of little girls who were full of mischief and did not want to go home and go to bed at night; in the countries where there was war there were also lots of them, and many many were just left lying there, burnt or smashed, and did not get any further.

Her thoughts came in pictures rather than words, and the pictures told a story like a brutal film. 'Mummy,' she whimpered involuntarily. She remembered where her mother was, and began to cry. But the thoughts raged hatefully on, and her crying stopped bitterly.

Julia. She did not know where that children's home was. She longed for Julia. Julia, Julia. She had never been really nice to Julia. She hardly ever saw her any more.

She crept up on to the box again and clung to the window post. Shreds of sooty material were blowing about, floating between the sparks in the red, angry sky. It could be burning money. Ten-kroner notes. A splintering sound pierced through the noise from the town, the sound of glass smashing. And with the feeling that something was gripping her heart and squeezing it until she felt she would burst, she suddenly saw father again, relived it all over again – he sat hunched over on the chaise-longue in the dining room whilst the reflection of the flames danced around the room and the fire tore at the walls – no, no – it was *now* it was burning. He just sobbed loudly and brokenly —

'Mummy,' it came out as a whispered cry. She tried to make

herself cry, but could not find any release from the pressure inside herself, no tears would come.

Suddenly she started to hunt urgently for something in an old doll's pram with three wheels and a ragged hood, which was standing there. She had hidden some things there.

She found the prism, and looked at it. Since Christi had come home she had not looked into it. Since the time she had told Christi that she had lost it she had not dared to look into it for fear of being found out. She stood feeling it with cold, clammy fingers. She put it to her eye and looked up.

She saw nothing. The red sky was splintered, pierced through by green flashes, there was yellow and there was mauve light which moved and changed, but it was all meaningless. *She saw nothing.* Feverishly she moved around, turned the piece of glass between her fingers so that new colours and forms sprang to life, but the experience was a dead one, and only made her feel disturbed. Her hand shook as she lowered the piece of glass. She half-closed her eyes as if she wanted to hold fast to what she had seen before with her eyelids, to relive the fairy tale of the magic glass, without the magic glass. *To see.*

She saw only her own racing thoughts. Mother and father are going to separate. Living people kill other living people. Mummy is going to leave me, mummy is going to go away. There was only a name on a list which was left, there was only the name of Nikolai left when his boat was torpedoed. Mummy, mummy – I never want to see that man. The town is burning down tonight, *the whole town is burning.*

She opened her eyes, reality was pressing down on her with a desperate weight; it hit her between the eyes with crushing force. Mummy, mummy, help me.

She wished suddenly that Jenny had come back, that Jenny was down there waiting for her, she could not bear being so completely alone any longer.

Jenny had not come. No one had come. They had forgotten her, all of them. And the magic glass was not a magic glass any longer, she had to manage with her own eyes. She was filled with a bitter calm. Everything was bad, everything was pain, wherever she turned she found only pain. She took the five-kroner note out of the pocket of her pinafore in order to look at it and find a little comfort in all the brilliant possibilities it offered.

It looked back at her. It looked evilly at her. Payment for having the ground cut away from under her feet —

A cold terror ran down her spine when she had opened the door of the stove and dropped it in. Now it was curling up. First it went black, then it flamed up. Then there was no five-kroner note any longer. She tried with all the force of her will not to think of everything you could get for five kroner. But she failed. The corners of her mouth drooped, trembling, as she thought of it all with a great and lonely sorrow. And everything was still painful, still just as painful.

But yet she felt, falteringly, a kind of ground beneath her feet again.

[Original title: *Røde reflekser*. Translated by Janet Garton]

NILS JOHAN RUD

You are no older than you were

She woke to the sound of her daughter busy in the bathroom. They had overslept. Weariness hung over her like a fog, yet at the same time a wakeful alertness was on its way, born of a purely physical irritation: they had kept her awake too long last night.

'Birgit!'

There was no answer to her shout; presumably it couldn't be heard there under the shower. Strange that the girl could take all this time over her shower when she was so late in getting up.

'Birgit!'

No, there was no answer. She lay there trying to pull herself together and wake up. The agitation from last night was there again, in her nerves. A pain in the ear-drums from listening. How shamelessly she had listened.

The water stopped running. The sounds grew more muted: a thin friendly gurgling.

'Birgit!'

'Yes, mother.'

'Can you see to your own breakfast? I've a headache. I'll try to sleep it off.'

Her daughter was already on the go, back and forth in the corridor between the bedrooms, putting on her clothes, collecting up books and lecture notes. You could hear everything; it was penetrating. Everything made a noise, every item of clothing, every piece of paper.

'Things went on till pretty late last night, Birgit.'

'Yes, they did. And I overslept.'

'Did they leave together?'

'What did you say, mother?'

'When did the boys leave?'

'I didn't look at the time.'

She must have fallen asleep before they went, but she had a kind of recollection of footsteps on the stairs. Did they leave together?

'I'm sorry if you couldn't get to sleep, mother. Try and catch up now! I must be off. Bye! bye!'

The daughter clattered down the stairs. The mother settled herself more comfortably, drew the blanket over her face, and murmured as though praying for rest: 'You are no older than you were. You are no older than you were. You are no older than you were.'

But it was a prayer that brought her painfully awake. She got up and took her shower, allowing the streaming water to cool her naked body, first with a kind of mild Gulf Stream and following it with a freezing cold torrent.

After this she felt renewed, free of her misused night and ready for the unused day. She decided to set about cleaning up in her daughter's room – where it was presumably most needed.

The presumption was correct: an empty wine bottle and three dirty glasses; ashtrays full; bed unmade.

The sight of it provoked her curiosity, sharpened her exploring eyes. Simultaneously a warning note sounded within her: You've no business here! Your daughter usually does her own tidying up. When she has the time. She is no longer a child.

It could be put off. Best to put it off. In case a tidied room might be mistaken for a ransacked room.

Well, she was just taking a look, a quick look. Enjoying her prerogative as a housewife of looking into one of the rooms in the house. And staying there a little too long.

What made her pause was a little envelope. A tiny packet. It was lying in one of the ashtrays.

She was no longer all that familiar with packets of that kind, but she knew well enough what they contained – knowledge which went back a number of years now.

The packet was empty. Carefully, cautiously, she placed it back among the cigarette ends and quickly went out of the room, as though afraid of having left traces.

Her irritation lasted the whole morning. Angrily she cleaned and tidied most of the house. Apart from her daughter's room. Scoured it yard by yard, with pure and righteous intent. Preparing for the show-down. Rehearsing her mother's duty, her moral responsibility.

Her anger persisted until the place was clean and things made tidy, so that she could think. But thinking made her feel so alone in the house, as though in fear.

So she went out to town – a suburb. To the shops. Essential purchases. Soon done; and she had no time for a chat when she met people she knew. She felt herself blushing when people greeted her – neighbours whom she had no reason at all to blush for. This caused her renewed anger, but different. Her anger became altogether different.

The hours passed without her really being prepared for the show-down. She laid the table for dinner. She was at it again: listening. A throbbing pain in the tenderest of her nerve cells.

When the daughter returned and let herself in, the mother knew suddenly how to meet the situation: You mustn't give her the slightest suspicion of what you know.

They ate together as usual. Talked about everyday things. Until there was a natural occasion to say: 'I cleaned up most of the house today. But I didn't manage to get your room done.'

'Don't see why you should. I'll do it myself.'

And, lightly: 'It's nice that you bring your friends back home, Birgit. I know Anders already, of course. But what about the new boy. What did you say he was called?'

'Per. Per Jonsen.'

'Nice boys. Young men, I suppose I should say.'

'That's right, mother, you should. They're both a year or two older than me.'

They looked each other in the eye, mother and daughter, openly, confidently.

'Well, you must invite them again, Birgit. Whenever you like.'

'Silly it went on so late. I hope it didn't keep you awake.'

'Not at all!'

'We kept the record-player turned pretty low.'

The daughter sat there somewhat restless. 'Why don't we wash up straightaway!'

'There's not much. I can see to it myself. Why don't you tidy up your own room! The way you had to go rushing out this morning, I can imagine what it must be looking like! And only getting an hour's sleep! You must be tired.'

They went their separate ways. The daughter to her dirty wine glasses and her full ashtrays. The mother to her kitchen, and deeper into her inward thoughts. Into a memory that was almost like new, and so liberated from time past that it seemed as though it might have happened last night.

Some time I'll tell you about it, Birgit. When we know so much about each other that we dare face up to it. When this thing which only one of us knows is no longer a matter of fear or shame. Yet I hadn't realized that this fear was something I had kept concealed for close on twenty years. And what more do I know of it now? What was there in it that was more than fear? What of it was shame?

That evening, too, I was meant to be on watch. I had gone along as chaperon for my elder sister. At that time, that was something expected in our circles. That when young people stayed the night anywhere, there had to be at least three of them. When sexually mature friends went off on holiday.

I was there on account of my sister and her friend. I was so much younger than both of them. It was a kind of safeguard for them to have under the same roof a sister who was below the age of consent. Yes, when we women reach sixteen it is called 'the age of consent', a legal concept.

I cannot think that I was fully conscious of my status. But had I reached sixteen?

I was not entirely ignorant. My curiosity had become pretty physical. Parents know remarkably little about when this occurs. When it concerns their own children, anyway. But I hadn't imagined that my sister required protection from her friend. This much about myself I can remember.

The cottage we were staying in had only one room, in which there was a fireplace. There was only one bed, but it was wide. At a pinch, all three of us could have found room there. But we said that only as a joke. And we teased each other about this before we turned in.

As we had arranged, he crept into a sleeping bay right close to the fireplace. My sister and I shared the bed. I lay on the outside, as seeming most suitable.

It's astonishing how clearly I remember it all. Though I fancy it's only rarely been through my mind since. Then only fleetingly, and with a feeling of fun – this secret I've never betrayed to anyone. Strange that only now it takes on the aspect of fear.

They waited a long time. The fire in the hearth went out. The moon shone grey into the room through the small window-frames.

Then he came, a form so clearly of flesh and blood that I felt the warmth of him.

They were so certain I was asleep. Cautiously she drew the covers aside on her side to make an opening for him as he climbed over me and lay down.

I did not dare move hand or foot; my breathing sounded strangulated – they were to hear it and take it for deep sleep.

The fact that they then waited so long – that also seemed unbearable. The way they so slowly drew the covers over themselves, so cautiously embraced.

Till their breathing so conjoined that I seemed to move in rhythm with them, dazed and sickened.

They were quick. It couldn't have lasted all that long, though what took place between them was not *my* excitement – and even though every sign, every sound, and every movement induced a participation from my own body, all I felt was fear in case I might be disclosed as a witness.

I had had my eyes shut. I saw nothing of what happened while he was with her. Nor did I see anything of him as he made his retreat over me; I was aware of him only as a smell of nakedness.

She fell asleep the moment she had rearranged the covers. That was a new shock to my senses: that she went and fell asleep while he was still standing there by the hearth raking the ashes.

It was then that I opened my eyes and looked at him. A little flickering flame flared up from the ashes and I caught a glimpse of his manhood. He straightened up, then he was lost in the darkness. And I saw only the glowing embers.

Now I knew more about that terror of mine. Suddenly I also knew that I lay there unfulfilled – and is that the shame of it?

And now this was what she had been waiting for, waiting a whole week: for them to return, both of them together, or just the one of them. As though the days had been preparing her for it; as though they were wanting to come to her.

They both came. She herself happened to answer the door, bade them welcome. This meant then that she knew them both, Anders and Per.

'Is Birgit at home?'

'Just go right on up!'

Thereupon the hours passed; the record-player; the voices; the laughter. The time came when she herself ought to retire, go to bed – she who stood outside. They were after all adult people –

sufficiently adult that a mother's worries were no longer any concern.

The music, in so far as she could hear it, was turned down; a subdued disquiet reached her in the sitting room. A signal that they now acknowledged it was bedtime for the lady of the house.

This merely left her more tense than ever, sitting there in the best chair under the reading lamp. What had she got out of it, sitting there and concentrating her attention on a book? Concentrating on a glass of wine, listening to it every time she placed her mouth to it, listening every time for the red sound she tried to make by running her moistened finger round the edge of it. But never did she succeed in making this red sound audible.

So rarely did it happen that she sat alone with a glass. And with a small fire in the hearth, expecting nobody.

They were right. It was now time to retire. A signal only too meaningful for someone who was so sensitive to sounds, as when the daughter turned down the record-player.

She shut her book, turned out the lamp. There was sufficient light coming through the mesh of the fireguard to cast a dark glow which brought things in the room closer, more palpable, like living things. The chair she had been sitting in breathed at her back. Bottle and glasses standing there on the table; the last log in the fireplace was burning itself out.

Their presence became stronger, came closer and ever closer as she climbed the stairs, stealthily and quietly, as their voices penetrated down the corridor, her daughter's so distinct that it could be heard apart from the others'.

Quickly she undressed and stood there in her nightdress, winding up the alarm clock; she had turned back the blanket – then abruptly changed her mind, tense and wakeful.

Up there the sounds had become so penetrating, the others' presence altogether too near – only the few steps from the one bedroom to the other. She was forced to listen, compelled to listen.

She threw a wrap round herself in her thin nightdress and went down again, quickly and warily, until she had once again shut herself in the sitting room. She poured out a drink, half-emptied the glass, and sank down relaxed in the best chair.

It was her plain right to know when guests left. At least to be able to hear them leave, to hear when one or the other left – the most sensible arrangement was if night visitors left together.

The sitting room around her was alive; everything was awake; chairs and sofa opened up to her, suddenly hospitable, exclusive to her. She sat down briefly here, briefly there, sensing the warmth of the room, her body exulting in it, breathing the pungent aroma of the firewood, the resin and the tannin. She put on more wood, stood close to the fire, lightly dressed as she was, saw the flames reflected in the wine in the glass in her hand, listened as all the summers came crackling out of the burning hardwood logs.

And all the sounds became hers and hers alone, with all things from outside and from above driven out. Once again she opened her book under the reading lamp.

The peace lasted until it became a strain to attend to the black on white on a book's printed page, until the vein in her neck throbbed, until her throat constricted and she had to drink to quench her thirst.

Then she put out the light to free herself of the book's welter of words, words so strange that there was no recognizing any of them.

The room regained its darkness, a darkness like wine, a red translucent glow over all things, objects she knew, sharing time and place with them, because all down the years they had been hers.

Then there were steps on the stairs, steps she had been listening for, cautiously one foot after the other through the night-time house. She counted them, matched them, as sounds, as feet, as they drew nearer, and they were of one person alone.

And it was as though they had been her own, as simultaneously step by step she moved barefoot towards the door. Till she stood there with her hand on the latch, till she opened the door and surprised him just as he reached the final step.

'You leaving, Anders!'

They stood face to face. She had on the instant frightened something out of the expression on his face. Had it merely been weariness? Now it was unreadable.

'It's late,' he said.

'Why aren't you two leaving together? I don't like you leaving alone,' she said.

He turned, reluctant, embarrassed, wishing to go. But her hand rested on his arm, willing something to which she had not yet given her authority. The hand derived its grip from a desire which was autonomous. This hand terrified her, but filled her increasingly with its blind intent.

'It's cold out here in the passage. Come in and join me for a while, Anders. I must talk to you.'

She drew him into the firelight glow beside her, and it seemed to her that a flame sprang to life in him as soon as he was within the room and she had shut the door, a glow in that young face, restless as the flame in the hearth.

'Have a seat. I'll get you a glass.'

She motioned him to the sofa; he sat down as though commanded. She brought out a second glass, then filled them both. The glasses remained there untouched.

Then she sat down beside him, sensed he had grown aware of her, of how flimsily she was dressed, how open.

'I don't want you to be the first to leave. It makes me feel so ashamed.'

He made no answer.

'You were also the first to leave the last time you were both here.'

'What's wrong with that?'

He drew back. Without his having moved, she felt that he drew back.

'It makes me feel so alone.'

'I don't understand.'

'You do understand, Anders. Please stay here till he's gone.'

'Is it all right? I'm thinking of *you*.'

She felt a thrill of pleasure at the note of intimacy in his reply, his readiness to respond.

'Won't you have some wine? Please do!'

His hand holding the glass trembled. Hers was quite steady.

After they had drunk, they sat silent, listening. It had grown so quiet in the house. And they understood each other, understood that they were both listening for the same thing. She thought: now, together, we feel ashamed.

The realization came like an arousal. She sensed him being drawn towards her, gauging her, hot, knowing of her desire, drinking deep from his glass and watching her, dark in the darkness. They saw each other only as dim shapes. She took hold of him with both hands, wanting to know how it felt to hold that dim shape. Far, far away the record-player started up again. A third breath . . . a fourth, she thought . . . no, the fifth, a tormented gasp suppressed to try to keep down the sound.

'Do you think I am shameless?'

'What has that to do with me?'

'I want to be shameless. My deepest desire is to be shameless.'

He answered her hands with his. Hard hands which would misunderstand her, but she was in no state to explain herself. And his own frustration had been too recent for him to understand hers. So there was nothing else for it but let him misunderstand what it is to be without shame.

As he pulled her wrap down over her shoulders, she freed her arms and lay there outstretched. Then, brutally, he threw himself upon her.

'No, no! I want it to be enjoyable.'

But he took her viciously, joylessly, without even properly undressing, falling upon her still half-clad, violently, vengefully, entering quickly into her desire.

As soon as it was over, he wanted to put his clothes straight and go. Without having uttered a word to her – either tender or hard.

'No, you must wait here with me. That's what it was for!' And her hand had regained its composure, that alien hand that was the wilful agent of her desires; it forced him to sit down again; it also filled the glasses.

His face had taken on its merely boyish look again; and this he knew and he felt sorry.

'There wasn't much in it for you,' he said. It was intended scornfully, but she heard how helpless it was. Without feeling pity, she heard it.

'There wasn't much in it for you either,' she said. 'But it was my fault. And it's kind of you not to leave me. That's enough for me now.'

Together they sat there, waiting, listening. Brought close to each other by their listening. The darkness in the room was merciful, with only the glow from the hearth to indicate the direction of the door.

Slowly her body began to tremble; now it was only by their drawn breath that they spoke to each other, so empty were they of intelligible words.

Breathing thus, holding their wine glasses, they sat together till they heard footsteps on the stairs, till they heard the front door shut, till the tension fell away and he stood up, and there was no desire in her hand to restrain him.

It was then that he was allowed to leave. They exchanged neither thanks nor farewells.

The house grew quiet; there was nothing to listen for. Slowly in the silence she went upstairs, stood in the corridor until her body screamed for some sound.

And with something re-found, in her anger she walked across to her daughter's door. Close up against it: 'Birgit!'

She opened it uninvited. Cool night air came to meet her from a window opened wide, bringing in a gust of rain weather, letting out a smell of tobacco; there was a rustle of the moving curtains.

'Birgit!'

There was no answer but that of sleep, the calm, life-embracing sound of deep sleep. And from deep within herself, suppressed, through her lips:

'Birgit! Aren't you ashamed of yourself?'

[Original title: *Du er ikke eldre enn du var*. Translated by James McFarlane]

TOROLF ELSTER

In a small room

'You've a smudge on your cheek,' she said. 'No, the other one. A bit higher up. . . . Now it's gone. I'm incorrigible, you see,' she laughed.

He smiled and for the first time looked straight at her. 'Or else you have to know . . . ten times, a hundred times in the course of a single evening. . . . Is my nose shiny? Is my hair tidy?'

'Then . . .' he began thinking again. But her eyes looked past him as though the tiny room stretched endlessly behind him. She whispered in her warm, husky voice: 'I interrupted you. I just happened to think how nice it is to think about . . . well, even about things like little smudges on one's cheek all these years.'

She turned her head and looked into his face. He sat without answering, his elbows on the table; but he smiled back, a little shyly, a little evasively, as her eyes lit up with amusement.

'Can you tell me why nobody has written about the poetry of stairwells? You know, I never see one of those dark miserable stairwells with worn treads and bad smells and peeling paint and sinister troglodytes who grunt angrily at anybody standing on the stairs but what it gives me a stab of pleasure. If only people knew!'

'Oh, yes.' He hesitated; his eyes grew dull. 'Well, I don't know. When suddenly one's father . . .'

He sounded so sombre she had to laugh. 'And he lays into you while I stand there listening, and you think it's all terribly embarrassing, and it's all I can do to stop myself laughing. You were so sweet, caught there red-handed. . . .'

He sat there silent. He reached out for the cigarette packet, then suddenly pushed it away and put his hands flat on the table. He searched for words.

'*You* . . .' he said without looking at her.

Quickly she placed her hand on his. 'Don't say it. There's no need to say it. Yes, when I look back,' she continued slowly and firmly, as if he had not said anything, 'there's nothing I like better than to think of those evenings we went walking the streets on the outskirts of the town and had no money and nowhere to go. The fact that we had none, was as if . . . well, as if actually we had everything, wasn't it? Those little streets we never realized existed and which somehow became *ours*. And we ran and read the name-plates and laughed at the names and laughed at the people passing by. . . .'

'And you got me to climb over into the gardens and steal roses for you!'

'You know, I'd actually forgotten that. But now I think you did it more to show off than to please me. To convince yourself you didn't give a damn for anything.'

'It was stupid of me,' he said, and the shadow fell across his face again. 'But it's too late now to try putting those roses back again,' he added, lightly.

'You wouldn't have the heart! I was as proud as could be that you were so daring. Yes, what a lot of funny things there were! Do you remember those frightful evenings we spent with your family – they put me in mind of half-chewed, stretched-out chewing gum. I still shudder at them.' She drew her dust-coat round her with a pretended shudder. 'And you didn't make things any easier! You certainly didn't!'

He raised his hands as though to defend himself, half in jest, half in earnest. 'Don't talk about it, please! It's not a very nice thing to talk about,' he added, with that twist to his mouth she knew so well. 'Anything that wasn't . . . well, that wasn't *you* in those years just seemed awful. I've thought a lot about those times. You could be pretty foul yourself sometimes, worse than you think. Now and then I couldn't help feeling rather bitter about you – *you* were so easy, so sure of yourself, with everything cut and dried. I . . . I never dared feel sure of you . . . I couldn't *quite* bring myself to believe. . . . You were so self-possessed, so terribly . . . matter of fact, so . . .'

'Smug?' she suggested.

'No, but it was unthinkable that you could ever . . . be impressed.'

Her face was naked for a moment, as though she hadn't heard. She stared at the wall, shook her head slightly to herself. Her jaw muscles tensed. It was as though she was gathering herself. Then she turned her head and looked composedly into his eyes.

'Actually, you were everything I longed for. All those things I'd never had. You got me to feel it was *allowed* to dream. To me, *you* were the rich one, I the poor one.'

She rose and stood for a moment beside the tiny square window. The morning sun caught her brown hair. 'Sure of myself, you said. All those evenings I sat staring at the telephone. Circled round it, trying to hypnotize it. But nothing would make that telephone ring. And I would look at the clock, and find that only five minutes had gone since the last time I'd looked at it. So I thought I might try going out to the bathroom to see if I could trick the telephone into ringing while I wasn't there. And my heart would jump if a car stopped. . . .'

'And then I did ring?'

'Sometimes,' she said earnestly. 'But sometimes you didn't ring. God damn you, I'd feel like saying. Then of course I wouldn't be able to get to sleep, stupid creature that I was. So I would put something on and walk out into the black night. I can never walk along John Collett Allee without thinking of those nights. Have you ever tried doing that – walking the streets like that alone at night feeling desperate? Oh, I was furious with you – for being able to make me feel so stupid!'

He looked up at her with a sudden smile which seemed somehow to draw them both out of that oppressive half-light. 'And on other nights there was *I* walking the streets somewhere else perhaps, because *you* hadn't rung. I couldn't keep on endlessly ringing you, because I thought you'd think this chap never leaves me in peace!'

'There were *some* times I probably thought that too. I had to have a bit of peace so that I could think over . . . this business of the two of us. There was so much I was uncertain about. About myself of course, mostly. And everything was so different from what I had imagined. Dreamt. So much more complicated, as it were!' She wrinkled her brow, making an effort. 'It was a relationship involving two people. It was a responsibility. It was a test. Something you couldn't push off on to other people.'

'Of course, before that you had . . .'

'That was different. That was something quite mad. I hardly grasped what was going on. I was just a child. He was twenty years older. It *was* in a way a fantastic experience – but in a totally *different* way. I'm sure I wasn't really fond of him, actually. It was like being flung out into space. Basically not very nice, on the whole. I've never

wanted to think about it – that shows something was wrong. . . .'
Her eyes grew darker. 'Obviously my fault. . . .'

'And then . . . he killed himself?'

'Then he killed himself. It wasn't on my account. Not on anybody's account. Just a feeling of depression that never went away. He wasn't capable of being happy. I wasn't happy either, at that time.' She looked down at the bright pattern of the window so as not to see how his hands trembled. Then, after a short while, she continued in a low voice. 'It wasn't until I met you that I understood what it was to be happy. That to be fond of somebody really means being *happy*. That being together means being happy. *That* is something . . . I'll never forget.'

He looked at the face which of all the faces in the world he knew best, at the pallid, half-open lips, as though in that grey light he wished to explore what was there within. As if he was trying to see her through five years of mist. He blinked his eyes, cleared his throat. 'And as for *me* . . . I'll never forget. . . .' The words stuck fast; he gripped the edge of the table as though to prevent the table from suddenly flying away.

'Exactly! Why should we forget!' she said quickly and eagerly. 'So long as we take with us everything worth remembering, then surely we can cope with whatever comes along. Every little thing like that. It's not just something that happens and that's the end of it. It's like . . . a kind of pillar holding up your whole life. That was rather well put, wasn't it?'

He sat for a while thinking about it. She looked tensely at him, a little stiff-necked as though her head was held fast in a vice. For a moment he was quite thrown; then he grasped what she had been saying, and it was as though it all broke out in a chaos of thoughts. 'Strange how even the most hellish things . . . when they are linked with something it's nice to think about . . . stop being hellish. Even the fact that one has been stupid doesn't matter then. Heavens, I remember at the start, before there was really anything between us, you seemed to be cooling off. I thought you were trying to avoid me. You *were*, in fact. And I often saw you together with that other fellow, you know, the one who . . . yes. I could well understand you must have thought me stupid and boring and . . . well . . . a bit plebeian. But I *wouldn't* believe it. I'm sure I haven't told you before, but when the clock got round to three I would take up my position outside your office, round the corner so that you wouldn't see me when you came out. And then I tried to make it seem that I was running into you by chance. I had thought out exactly what I was going to say, all rather nonchalant. . . . Then one day it clicked. "Morning!" I said. "Morning!" you said. Then we both went our various ways. Of course it wouldn't have done, you know, to have set up chance encounters like that very often. And in the evenings I would walk past the house in Josephinesgate, on the off-chance that . . . maybe you'd be going in or coming out. . . . And one evening that other fellow came out. I remember I almost crawled home. I just wanted to hide myself away for ever, for I felt he'd seen me and recognized me and of course realized. Did he *say* anything?'

He had also grown quite animated. She sat looking at him, listening and responding to the poignant throb in his voice. It released something within her, and from her throat came a little happy laugh. 'Oh no, he didn't say anything. But don't you think I sensed what was going on?'

'Oh, many's the time I was furious with you!' He said the words a little breathlessly, as though he felt a sudden compulsion to confess. 'Just when I thought things were going fine, suddenly – at a party, or wherever it was – suddenly you would go off and make eyes at some other stupid fool who happened to be there. I couldn't understand it. It seemed like a kind of treachery to me. As for *me* . . . I only had thoughts for you. I didn't understand *then* that you had so much to give it was impossible for one man to take it all.'

'That sounds terribly flattering, but it doesn't hold water,' she laughed. 'Rather it was that I was always unsure of myself. Time and time again I needed to recover my self-confidence by feeling that other men admired me. New men. No sooner had an affair begun to last than I began to feel unsure of it. A sense of *security* – that only came gradually. And it was you I got it from. But you know. . . .'

They glanced at each other. They both grimaced, happily. She was about to say something, teasingly, when he abruptly ran his fingers through his hair. His face became like a reflection in disturbed water. Abruptly he stood up, causing the chair to scrape against the floor. He walked up and down, his hands in his pockets, without looking at her.

Her eyes . . . pale . . . nervously followed the tall, stooping figure, restlessly shrugging its shoulders as though he were speaking to himself. 'Why don't you sit down! Don't keep pacing up and down like a lion in a cage. . . .' Abruptly she stopped.

'A lion, yes!' That curt laugh which on occasion had terrified her. He sat down again, suddenly and gloomily serious. He pushed the squat wooden chair across to her. Looked at her till his eyes seemed almost to cling to her. She placed her hand on his knee, stroked it lightly. He placed his hand over hers. Drew breath. 'You know. . . ?'
'Yes?'
'When . . . when I . . . after that business . . . was it . . .'
Gently she shook her head. 'No . . . but you understand . . . I couldn't *then* exactly. . . .' She was silent for a moment, drew a quick breath, then looked up at him; the slight tenseness about the mouth was gone. 'But that was so terribly long ago. I can hardly remember it any more. I only remember all those things from *before* . . . it's been such a short time since.' She gripped his hand tightly. 'There are so many things I've wanted to ask you not to be angry with me about. I *mean* it. I've been far, far too preoccupied with myself many times. Never once thought that you might also have problems. You know, nothing about me ever seems to have been quite in order,' she continued, almost pleading. 'Just remember that I've never had a proper home. Never lived anywhere for any length of time. On the move all round Europe. Never had any time to make friends. I hardly knew what it was to play. Except in my thoughts. I can scarcely remember my mother. And my father was so distant, so dour. He never joked. Just wanted me to read grown-up books. Apart from that he more or less let me do as I liked. If I did something wrong he just looked at me. But sometimes he could have a fit of temper. It would nearly scare me out of my wits.'

She opened her handbag, put a cigarette in her mouth, but remained sitting staring at the burning match until it went out. She put the cigarette down on the table. 'You know . . . no, I'm sure I've never talked about it . . . after the suicide, when everything came out about him and me, I seriously thought of taking my own life. There was of course a frightful scandal, in our circles, and my stepmother virtually drove me out of the house. . . . People only had to look at me . . . I couldn't bear it! Thank God it was as if I was in a daze, so I didn't see everything. Sat all day in my room staring at the wall. I think I was a bit mad. And that's made me always a little afraid of myself, deep within. But you never understood that.'

He smiled gravely, protectively. 'Oh, I think there were many times when I understood how things were with you.'

She nodded quickly, eagerly. 'Yes, of course you understood.

You almost never said anything, but I *felt* you understood. Those times when I'd been hysterical and impossible. That you were really prepared to put up with me! That's more than I can understand.'

He looked at her as though studying whether she meant it. 'Put up with you! Me! I felt it was difficult enough holding on to you! I can tell you I was in fact mortally afraid of losing you.' Again, his face took on an expression of wry, bitter humour. 'I managed to fool you pretty well, didn't I?'

She shook her head and answered almost angrily. 'No! Not the way you think. But in other ways. . . . You've no idea how I used to wonder what you looked like deep down inside. Sometimes it was just curiosity. Sometimes it seemed a matter of life and death. And then they say it's woman who is the Sphinx!

'But there were some times,' she continued in a far-away voice, 'when I had no such misgivings. And it's all *those* times I remember now . . . as if they were yesterday. There were some days . . . maybe I'd just looked in on you in your office . . . you might have been busy and were pressed for time and I had to leave . . . when the streets seemed radiant with sheer happiness as never before. Just because I knew that you were there, sitting there in *that* office, at *that* desk, with *that* mop of hair. If only you knew all the streets . . . all the houses I came to love because that was where I walked after I'd been with you.'

She looked up at him – expectantly. He ran his hand over his hair, somewhat confused. It had thinned a little. He looked away from her; his voice became uncertain again. 'There is so much I should have said. . . . It's just that I'm a bit confused. It's as though I can't quite . . .'

But then he stopped and shrugged his shoulders as though trying to throw something off. His face had that slightly arrogant, slightly apologetic expression she knew so well. 'I'm sure you must think I was stupid sometimes?'

'Well yes, I do. I think *some* times you were stupid. That you were clumsy and childish and so on when I wanted you to be firm and strong. Because I myself felt so clumsy and childish and so on. Sometimes I thought you were stupider than all the other boys. For *them* I could of course take as they were. But you I always had to be comparing with some crazy ideal or other.'

He nodded slowly several times. 'And yet . . . you were right, all the same. But even *you* didn't understand *how* weak I was. And you also succeeded in getting me to forget it. You did! Every time I came away humiliated from some encounter or other I'd had with this harsh world and I was a little frightened of meeting you in case you might see how little I was . . . no sooner had I caught sight of you and your little red hat than the whole thing was forgotten. Perhaps if you'd understood . . .'

She snorted. 'That? Things like that of course I understood. I mean things that could be understood. You are no weaker than other people. But perhaps you were just a tiny bit afraid that I might discover . . . *some* weaknesses. And that was rather stupid of you. You seemed as if you were always on your guard.'

'Do you think that's so strange?' he asked vehemently. 'I just couldn't believe that anybody could accept me as I was. At home there was only one rule: that I should be kept in my place. That was the way I felt it was, at all events. The boy must be taught humility! Finally I came to think that everything I did was wrong. But nobody had to notice it. Rather I had to be in on everything.'

'Yes,' she said to herself in a low voice, pondering, as though trying to make some calculation come out right. 'It was easy to exploit you.' Then she repudiated the thought. 'Easy for me, I mean. I am ashamed when I think about it.'

He did not answer. Sat fumbling with a matchstick in the ashtray. Slowly she stretched out a hand to smooth away the wrinkles on his brow with her fingertips. Stroked his hand till it stopped trembling. Their eyes met.

'Isn't it stupid of us to sit here like this? As though we'd somehow been nasty to each other! It's clear that being in love can never be something you can take for granted. Yet all the same we feel so sure of it. Uncertain and yet at the same time certain. . . . Oh, I'm just rambling on. . . . But can anybody claim that we didn't have a good time together? Answer me that!'

'Yes, we had a good time,' he answered, and suddenly raised his head, looked her fixedly in the eyes as though it was a kind of test.

She calmly returned his look, then she bent forward over the table towards him. The colour had returned to her cheeks, and there was a light in her eyes. 'This summer I went back up to our old haunts,' she said. 'And, you know . . . as I walked past those fields, those that are so full of cow parsley, it was as though you were there still. In the air. As though the fence and the grey houses and the stream running down the hillside and the birch trees were *us* . . . a part of us. And always will be. And I walked deep into the forest. It was as if I could still see the footprints of our shoes in the moss. I sat on that rock . . . you remember that big flat rock where those wild raspberries were? And I was twenty years old again. And everything was ours . . . drawn and painted with our joys and our small sorrows. And I felt so strongly that we must never . . . we must never betray those things that *were*. That we must never forget how one person could make another happy. Isn't that right?'

She reached out her hand in the air searching for the words, finding them one by one, and seeming to hand them to him. 'When you are in love with somebody, it's as though every separate little thing contributes to some precious overall pattern. We became richer and richer, and it is the one treasure which moth and rust do not corrupt. The *little* things. Like undressing and feeling that somebody is watching. Looking at you, at your long white legs, at the operation scar on your belly. And *liking* looking at you. And each time being a little shy of each other . . . because each time is new. Our souls as naked as our bodies . . . being as one and yet at the same time two. That's the real point, you know. That you are in fact a *different* person from me. Why indeed should I want to try to analyse you . . . expose and explain your innermost being? Why should I make you less exciting?'

'Exciting? You thought I was exciting?' he burst out in astonishment.

'For me you'll always be the most exciting thing that's ever happened to me. Yes, even the first time. . . . You were so apprehensive.' She laughed suddenly. Many a time he had thought it sounded like beer being poured into a glass. 'So unsure if you would do it right. But then I was so unsure myself, so it wasn't really very easy for me.'

He turned on his chair, bringing his face quite close to hers.

'Do I remember! I'll never forget! Specially not the first time.' His voice had suddenly become very deep. 'I could hardly believe you were real. Giving yourself. And at the same time giving me a strength I never believed I had. And when you were naked and I forgot to . . . to. . . . For you were like . . .'

He was so close to her that he felt her faint cool breath on his face.

'Say it!'

The words came with some embarrassment. 'I can still remember

'... in that dark, sad room, you remember ... thinking how true it was, this saying about being at one with nature. That you were like being out in the fields on a warm summer's day. Or like lying and looking up into the warm clear sky. Like feeling grass under your feet, like hearing the wind in the treetops.' He stopped, somewhat embarrassed. But the words came flooding. 'And I saw tears in your eyes and you said it was just because you were happy. ...'

'That was beautifully said,' she whispered. 'And as I lay ... as I did so many many times with shut eyes, *feeling* those dark blue eyes of yours as though a light from them were shining right through my skin. ...' Her hand resting on the table suddenly clenched. 'Oh, I cannot ... cannot ...'

Particles of dust danced in the slanting sunlight.

She grew silent, stared vacantly at the bare green-painted wall, moved her hands down to her handbag. She opened her mouth a few times but no words came. It was as if one could see her thoughts running over long overgrown paths within her head. Then a teasing smile lit up her face as though her thoughts had reached a clearing in the forest.

'Do you remember how furious you were many a time when the last tram had gone and you had to footslog half the night to see me home? You claimed I did it on purpose. And I did do it on purpose ... sometimes ... once at any rate. ... We never talked so well together as we did walking home at night like that. Then there was always the chance, wasn't there, we'd hit upon some good idea or other.' She laughed. 'You remember the time we took that short-cut through the woods and it was so muddy ...?'

'And I tried to carry you ...'

'And we fell over in the mud ...'

'And you ...'

'I couldn't help myself.' His eyes grew distant. Already he was accompanying her thoughts on their wanderings. 'Those nights ... light summer nights when I lay with my arm about you and my hand could feel how your heart was beating. ... And those evenings we sat on the veranda and we had the whole house to ourselves and some of your father's French vermouth. And it never became really dark, and we looked out over the fjord in that greying light, hardly ever speaking, but we just had a feeling that everything ... absolutely everything we dreamed of ... would happen some time. ...'

'And it *did* happen,' she said quickly. 'Just thinking it meant that it had happened. If then it *actually* happened, it was just some later, indifferent copy of the first time. What we dream is what lasts. Yes, those rare evenings! And you sat and talked so earnestly. And I had difficulty in fully understanding you, but simply had that nice feeling that everything you were saying and thinking was for me.'

He nodded. 'In a way that's what I did too at that time. But there were many old and bad thoughts as well. Later on there were of course rather more of *that* kind.'

But his thoughts had already moved on. They sat silent for a while as though listening to something, a distant murmuring. Her voice cut into the murmuring. 'That summer, yes! The last summer before . . . before the war. That was the time we nearly capsized, do you remember? That is perhaps the one thing I am least likely to forget. How terribly dangerous it was. Yet with you sitting there so confidently at the helm it never once occurred to me to be frightened. Even though I did think we were about to drown.'

'That was precisely the moment when I was determined you should feel secure,' he said, and she remarked his old proud sense of self-respect. 'Had it been anybody else . . .'

'What do we care about others!'

'No, what do we care about others,' he laughed eagerly. There was life in his eyes now. 'Do you remember . . . it was that same summer . . . when the two of us were there among the sand-dunes and thought nobody could see us . . . and there was somebody standing there with his eyes on stalks, and we thought nothing of it. Not a thing!' He stretched. 'Strange all the things you start remembering when once you start. It's true what you said . . . about treasures where moth and rust do not corrupt. And what's even finer,' he said almost excitedly, with trembling lips, 'you can take it with you! You . . .' he began abruptly, but broke off. 'You must go now.'

He rose quickly. She also rose, stood for a moment, walked over to him, took both his hands, looked at them, ran her fingers over them. They did not tremble. Then she looked up at him with a faint smile.

'Bye-bye then,' he said, 'I nearly said – for now.'

'Say . . . for now . . . Knut.'

He answered with a brief laugh. 'As the two blind men said on the shore – see you again soon!'

She quickly stroked his cheek. 'You're right. It's strange how much you remember when once you start. And even if we don't think about it, we feel it's there.'

He merely nodded. Stood there till the door shut. Then he lay down on his bed, his hands folded behind his head.

When she came out, they saw she was as pale as a corpse. 'It's nothing,' she said. 'Just let me sit down for a moment.' They reached her just in time to catch her as she fell.

Later she lay at home on her own bed. Completely exhausted. She twisted and turned in restless sleep, as the evening papers were coming out with the report that the death sentence upon Knut Vik, torturer and informer, had been carried out.

[Original title: *I et lite rom*. Translated by James McFarlane]

AGNAR MYKLE

Raisins of degradation

'Is that *The Princess?*' asks his little brother.

High on the hillside behind the town, in the unquiet darkness of the night, a still quite young man and a quite small boy stand looking out over the harbour and the fjord. In an effort to get really high up, they have struck off the road and made up the slope where the snowdrifts lie rock-hard, covered with a thin layer of powdered snow. They have to dig the heels of their boots into the bank of snow to keep a foothold.

'Yes,' says the quite young man. He recognizes it by its sound. He knows all the boats by their sound.

Both of them are wearing mittens on their hands. Hand-knitted Trøndelag mittens, good protection against the cold. But the wind goes through them as though they were made of fly netting. Through the thick mittens he feels the young boy gripping his finger with all the excitement of childhood. And the boy sniffles, for it is bitterly cold. Sixteen degrees of frost, and snow.

Yes, there are boats tied up down there. Tonight they sing a peculiarly triumphant song. Have they some message? The young man does not know.

These boats are the only friends he has in the world. Night after night, year after year he has been coming down to the quayside to watch the boats coming in. But he never wants to watch them when they cast off and leave. The boats are his friends; nobody can take these boats away from him; they are his boats. For him a boat coming in was a symbol of life and fable, an attempt to capture the wonder of the moment of arrival.

Though actually it isn't really the boats he goes to look at. What he generally does is join the group of waiting people – right in the middle of them, for it is where the crush is greatest that he is at one and the same time both most lively and most passive, both active and anonymous, both close to and distant from the mystery he has come to experience. One never experiences loneliness so intensely and so completely as in the midst of a jabbering, jostling crowd which is standing in the darkness of the night on a quayside waiting for a boat.

When he has finished his evening's homework, he sometimes goes to the cinema. But more often he takes a walk down to the quayside. Always, in this town, there will be some boat coming in. Some of the boats have come from afar and have small tugs to assist them; others have only been across to the other side of the fjord and are returning with farm workers, commercial travellers, boy scouts, lay preachers, and townsfolk who have had a day out in the country. Now and again he will take the tram down; he has his own corner on the rear platform in beside the black brake-wheel. There he can stand with the brake lever between his knees and turn his back on the other passengers and be alone with himself, for it is good to prepare one's mind for the meeting with the boats. Other times he will walk to save the twenty øre. When one's mother has to cope with all the household expenses on her own, it isn't always very nice to ask for money.

What was it she had said that evening, out in the kitchen while the young man stood at the mirror over the washbasin trying to shave without bleeding too much? What was it she had said as she stood over the ironing board, turning her thin, rounded back to him?

'It's going to be grown-ups only round at Mrs. Bye's tonight, so I don't think I ought to take Svein along. Otherwise I'd have taken him, you know.'

Well, he did like to see his mother having an evening out and seeing something of her friends. It wasn't so often she had the chance.

But then she had said something that hurt, something that cut into his soul, something he could not forget.

'And since you are not going anywhere tonight, you won't mind staying at home and looking after Svein, will you?'

That's what she had said.

'*And since you are not going anywhere tonight . . .*'

He feels the cold going right through him in the darkness of the night; a longing welled up in him, a longing to be alone with his hopeless solitude. But his brother is at his side, stumbling along and gripping his hand.

'Listen to those hooters!' says Svein, his lower lip hanging wet. 'How do they do that? I can see the mate pulls a string. But what actually happens?'

'Just try for once in a while to stop asking questions – you're driving me mad!' the young man says.

Nursemaid, that's what he is. Yes, nursemaid is the word for it. On an evening like this, when people the world over meet one another in warm and joyous friendship, when an outstretched hand finds a hand, and soul finds soul – on an evening like this he has to be nursemaid. On an evening like this all he can do is stand there in that white, rock-hard snowdrift with this wild longing of his, looking down on his boats.

'But just listen to that little one,' says his brother. 'Listen to the noise it's making!'

Down there they lie, his friends the boats. Nobody can take the boats from him. And suddenly it is as if, despite the distance, he is again down there on the great quayside, stomping up and down while he waits for the boat – his friend the boat – to come gliding in through the night darkness.

Once again, as a thousand times before, he feels the shining freight-train rails and the round cobblestones under his feet. Even when snow is lying on the quayside he can feel the round cobblestones under his feet.

He remembers the sound of the squealing railway engines and their unlubricated springs, the sound of the winches and the shouted commands, the piercing motor-car horns and the bicycle bells, the sound of barrels rolling and bales that hit the quayside with a dull thud, the bellowing of the cattle and the rattling of the chains holding them, the whistle of a thin tow-rope through the air, the infinitely sad and offended gulls.

He knows all the warehouses down on the quay. And he knows all the shipping agents and all the dock workers by sight. But they don't know him.

But the quayside is not simply something to see and hear and feel under one's feet. He could walk there blind and deaf and still know that he was on the quayside. For it is the smell – the smell of the quay and the wharf and the ship's side which will always live in his nostrils and remind him of the hopeless loneliness and the nameless degradation of youth in the midst of a jabbering, jostling crowd of people.

In summer it is the smell of brackish water, greasy oily brackish water with strange shifting patterns of colour, and the smell of the sheds sweating in the baking sun.

In winter it is the smell of snow and fish and salt sea air and fresh, glistening, steaming horse-droppings.

But always the persistent smell of tar and fish oil, of fish boxes and herring barrels, of coffee sacks and animal carcasses, of syrup kegs and apple cases and molasses and tarred paper, the smell of untreated calfskin and the sour, salt whiff of rolls of rusting wire-netting, the resinous smell from the stacks of unplaned timber, the stench of coagulated blood and rotting cabbage, and the strange bitter scent of raspberry canes and young apple trees and small slender silver firs standing propped up against the wall of the warehouse with their roots wrapped in sacking as though their feet had frostbite.

But overriding all other smells is the smell from within the boats! Dear God, when the cook opened the door of the galley! Then the hot smell of the ship came pouring out: the smell of salt meat and pork and peas, of coffee and boiled halibut, of fried coalfish and roast veal, of boiled potatoes and creamed beans, the smell of fried onions and burning coal, the smell of sweaty faces and slimy washing-up water, the stench of burnt stewed fruit and freshly stewed prunes and disinfectant saltpetre, the stink of the slop pails being emptied over the side. This is the most marvellous smell in the world, so warm, so animal warm. And before it reaches your nostrils it has swept across the deck, crept under the warm bellies of the cattle on the gangway, glided past the open doors and fondled the hot-water pipes on the ceiling, and it has absorbed into itself the smell of discarded crumpled sheets and greasy pillows, the smell of human bodies and people's clothes, the smell of lavatories always out of order, the smell of unwashed stockings and unemptied cardboard boxes in small metal containers on the edge of the quay, the smell of dirty workclothes and polished brass, the smell of beer and cheap brandy, and the hot smell of oil and coaldust from the engine-room. Altogether, when it reaches your nose, it is the world's most fabulous, most marvellous smell, for it is so warm, so humanly warm. Thousands of human destinies lie in that smell. If one were a poet, one would only have to sneeze once: it would be a hymn of praise about people who have suffered and people who have wept, people who have barked orders and people who have grumbled at them, brave men and cowardly men, those who have watched and those who have slept, those who have worked and those who have idled in deckchairs, those who were good sailors and those who were so seasick they had to be tied to their bunks, men and women who have slapped and tickled and whored in the narrow bunks.

Up to a point he could manage with the smell. He could be content to stand and watch for the cook to open the door to the galley, and then take a deep breath.

'Listen!' Svein says. 'That was *The Princess* again! How it can hoot!'

They kick a new foothold in the rock-hard snowdrift to prevent themselves being frozen hard to the spot.

The crowd always becomes animated as the boat comes in. The thing is to pay attention and calculate precisely where to stand to be right opposite the gangway.

Some of the people are doubtless there to collect goods which have come by the boat. But most of them, the majority, are standing there waiting for somebody to arrive, one of *them*: a father, a mother, a husband, a wife, a son, a daughter, a brother, a loved one, a friend. They stand there in the darkness of the night, all set, with smiles and greetings ready; there they stand in the darkness on the quayside under the piercing electric bulb high up in the air, waiting for somebody they can call their own. The young man is the only one to whom nobody is coming.

The boat glides slowly and hesitantly in to the quayside. Slowly and heavily, with the engines in reverse. And the propeller makes strange dark, ice-green, sucking whirls in the still, smooth water, and a warm yellow light comes from the portholes down by the waterline. The harbour water places its wet furrowed cheek against the edge of the quay and sighs.

Then he is carried forward, jostled along by the crowd. Lonely and nameless, he is pushed right up to the gangway. With long experience one can generally calculate correctly. And now they begin to swarm up, all the people from inside the boat.

Then he stands there like a being from another planet, staring at the faces of the people as they pass in review down the gangway. The old country-wife with the grey hair and the black straw hat with the long hatpin in it. Then the man in the sports jacket and knee breeches carrying a little sleeping child. Then the fat woman with the glasses, the brown fur coat, and the dilapidated basket. Then the girl with the yellow hair, the pale lips, and the sour little eyes. Then the boy with the big teeth and snub nose. Then the lean, stoop-shouldered fisherman with his black, greasy, peaked cap. Then the woman with the asters. Then the boy with the rucksack and the milk can. Then the woman with the uniform hat and the guitar. Then the two laughing girls who have to walk arm in arm, even down a gangway.

And as they go past the young man, as they stumble and sway down the gangway trying to find the right place to tread and clinging to the bent zinc tubing of the railing, he is filled with an abysmal sorrow and despair.

Have you not come? Weren't you on it?

Some of the people look in astonishment into the pale despairing face. Is sorrow and terror written so clearly in his eyes?

The woman with the asters smiles as she walks past him. And inside his overcoat pockets he stretches out his hands towards the fresh, sparkling, dew-drenched, blue-violet, red-violet, white and rust-red flowers she clasps in her embrace. But they were not for him. They were for a woman behind him.

The young girl with the black hair, the bright eyes, the red lips, the warm oval face – she also smiles as she passes him. And in his coat pockets he stretches out his hands towards her. He wants to place his hands round her neck, gently round her neck, gently beneath her thick hair, till his finger-tips meet at the nape of her neck. That is how he wishes to meet her, soul against soul, lips against lips. Only those who thirst for love know precisely, down to the smallest detail, how a meeting between a man and a woman must be. But the smile was not for him. She was not for him. She was for a young man in a check overcoat standing at the rear of the crowd beside a motor car, one foot on the running board and a cigarette in the corner of his mouth.

The fisherman with the greasy peaked cap holds out an envelope as he comes down the gangway. A letter? *The letter?* The letter which is to open the door, the letter which is to open the world, the letter with the ticket and the word in it? Is this the letter? For far far away, beyond the fjord, beyond the mountains, there must be another world, a world with a sun and a woman and a friend, a world with white coral reefs round a blue lagoon. Is this the letter?

'Look there!' shouts Svein. 'And there! A green one! A-a-h, look!'

The letter was not for him. It was for the ship's agent behind him. There are never letters for him.

All around him and his little brother the rockets sped up towards the black night sky, and the boats howled their hoarse New Year serenade. Oh, come, my boats!

'Is it twelve o'clock now?' Svein asks.

He nods. He cannot speak.

It probably wasn't a letter anyway. Probably just some grubby note, scribbled in pencil, for fifteen heads of winter cabbage. Winter cabbage!

'Well, happy New Year, then!' says Svein, pressing his big brother's mitten. And then he adds, shy and proud at one and the same time: 'Mother said I had to remember to say that!'

Oh, Mother has good reason to be proud of her youngest boy!

Yes, this is New Year. New Year's Eve. This is the moment when friendship and warmth and love and anticipation are kindled in people's minds over the whole planet Earth. This is the moment when they feel a breath from the inscrutable timelessness of space, when they hear the fateful ticking of the world's clock. They catch a sudden sense of eternity, and shudder at the smallness of their own apportioned part. The heavy metallic vibrations of the sound of the church bells cause their hands momentarily to tremble and spill champagne on the carpet. For a second they are silent and serious and pass judgement upon themselves and try to think of some good resolution. If one was on the spot at that moment, one could well get their signature to a declaration that they would never again lie, never steal, never oppress or go to war. But then somebody clears his throat, whereupon they kiss each other and excitedly wish each other a happy New Year. Then they drink to each other and swill the cold and loathsome sense of the turning world down their throats. This is the moment when people become friends; flushed with warmth and handshaking and togetherness and champagne, their eyes grow large.

And from some little way up behind the boys, from the big, well-lighted, imposing shipowner's residence, comes the delicate, high-pitched, ringing sound that is made when one flicks the rim of an expensive sand-blasted wineglass cautiously with one's finger. The young man has never seen a sand-blasted glass. All he knows is exactly what the sound is like. Tonight he can hear the sound. No sound on earth is so full of human warmth, abundance, and friendliness as the sound of a finger flicked on a sand-blasted glass.

The rockets sputtered only intermittently now. And like some final flourish a big one comes sailing up from down on the quay. He sees its faint light like some goddess's javelin throw, up into the air, higher, higher, until it reaches the top of its arc and coughs a burst of red and green and blue and yellow and violet and silver. And the fragments sink slowly like glittering confetti down towards the black fjord. A little patrol boat gives a hoot, then checks itself. And suddenly it is quiet.

And as though he had read his brother's thoughts, little Svein says: 'Do you think anybody's ever tried riding on a rocket?'

'Nonsense!' he replies.

But even though the rockets and the church bells and the ships' hooters are finished, there are lights in the town. Lights shine from thousands of houses, from thousands of windows, and behind the windows are people. Happy people, people in festive mood, sociable people who laugh and dance and hold hands. There are beautiful young women, with soft white skins and pearl necklaces and long gleaming hair. Their full lips glow from kisses from strong, clean-shaven men. Love shines out of their eyes; love and warmth shine out of their windows. The warmth of love from a thousand people, from a thousand eyes, from a thousand clasped hands, from a thousand lighted windows rises up towards him in the biting cold of the winter night like a flapping carpet, like some marvellous oriental carpet. Like a carpet with a thousand needles in it.

'But – are you *crying*?' says Svein, and the little boy nearly slips down off the snowdrift in his urgent childish concern to look his brother in the face.

'Nonsense!' he says. 'It's the snow.' The night cold makes the eyes run, the nose run, and he dries them on his mitten.

Then suddenly they both realize how cold it is in reality. The snow howls between the drifts, up the hillside, up to where they stand and stretch to see out across the town, straining their eyes to see. They pull the collars of their coats up round their faces and blow warm air into their mittens. Then they begn to shuffle downwards while the snow crackles beneath their feet. The night sky above them is clear, and the air is clean. There are lights in all the windows of all the houses; there is a buzz of music and laughter. At one place the curtains are drawn back and he can see them up there dancing under strange Chinese lanterns and with curious hats on their heads. From the window hangs a narrow ribbon, a paper streamer that flaps in the wind. As though he were stealing the very apple from the tree of life itself he wades through the snow to the wall of the house, tears the paper streamer loose and rolls it up in his hand.

'I'm looking forward to it,' says Svein.

'To what?' he asks in astonishment, hurt and angry.

'Don't you remember Mother saying she'd leave something nice out for us? So we could enjoy ourselves?'

And he tries to subdue the strange bitter laughter that rises up in him, whilst Svein looks at him unhappily and uncomprehendingly.

A big mirror stands in the entrance. It is there for Mother's customers to use. But it doesn't really wear out the mirror if he occasionally takes a look in it on his own account.

And suddenly he freezes. The shabby dark-blue hat with the turned-down brim, the pale face with its pimples and its razor cuts, the cheap garish scarf – where in that picture of a nineteen-year-old schoolboy was he to find a single cue for faith, courage, determination, hope, confidence? He goes chill at the sight of his image in the mirror, and at a certain thought: a hurtful, numbing thought that again rises up within him. He is glad that Mother is out.

For *if* she had stayed at home this evening, she would either have said: 'Don't be too late tonight if you go out.'

— And then he would have been compelled to think the thought that when he did go out, it was only to walk, by himself in desperate loneliness, around the streets, looking in his loneliness in the lighted and frosted shop windows, and finally to stand in infinite loneliness in the middle of the crowd down at the quay. —

Or she would have asked: 'Aren't you going out anywhere tonight?'

And then he would have been forced to remember those hurtful killing moments at school, full of blank but controlled despair, when his classmates put their heads together and talked in low, intense voices about the parties they are going to, the clothes they will wear, the alcohol they will drink, the girls they will seduce. He would be forced to recall his despair, his friendlessness, his total loneliness. He might perhaps have been able to lie to his mother and say he was going to a party, and then walk the streets until two o'clock. But to himself, within himself, he would be forced to shape a sentence of abysmal despair, of black degradation and total dejection, a sentence which could not be formulated other than: 'No, Mother, nobody in this whole wide world has invited me out tonight.'

And to avoid being held at this, to turn away from the loathsome picture of endless hopelessness, to employ again the old desperate device of seeking some crack or unevenness in the rock face of the world to cling to, he tears the garish scarf from round his neck as though it was choking him; and his bitter delight at the fact that his mother is out and cannot force him into a corner of self-exposure – this delight he gives vent to in a shout that fills this brown, gloomy entrance: '*Svein!*'

'Yes!' comes a voice from within the sitting room. And he goes in, quickly, without taking off his overcoat. He slings his hat and his scarf on to the little table in the entrance which has doubtless at some time been a man's smoking table.

There is the boy, still wearing his overcoat and his black knitted cap and standing by the sideboard chewing.

'Look!' he says with his mouth full. 'Nuts! And raisins!'

Was he for a moment kindly disposed towards his brother? Was he for a moment ready to try to build a shaky bridge over to the warmth and the shining joyful eyes of the little boy? He no longer knows. All he knows is that the raisins in the bowl his brother is handing him are too much. It is too much.

'You don't seem very pleased,' says Svein, 'that Mother has been so kind.'

What in the name of all eternity is he to answer? What will a ten-year-old boy understand of his sorrow and his hunger? This boy for whom a story of cowboys and Indians gives great delight, who needs only a new toy motor car to have him whooping for joy, and who is in ecstasies over a bowl of raisins? What is he to say to him for an answer?

And at once he feels the hurt and the torment rising up in him. He doesn't want them to, but they come all the same. It is like a dam bursting. What is it he wants? A boat, a flower, a friend, a girl, warm hair, a letter about warmth and friendship and love! All life's grapes, life's firm, plump, dew-wet, bloom-covered grapes – these are what he wishes to reach out and grasp. And then he gets offered raisins!

Like a signboard hanging on the senseless mad rush of his youth, on its thirst, its hunger, its sorrow, its degradation, and his unbearable loneliness are these brown, wrinkled, dried-out little things in the bowl, sitting there and looking at him, darkly, stickily, mockingly. Raisins of degradation!

He snatches the bowl from the boy and slings it against the wall. Raisins and bits of blue china rain down on the household's one source of income: the electric sewing machine in the corner.

When Svein looks at him, greatly taken aback, it is as though all the threads of life and its disappointments converge in that grey, chewing face of the boy in front of him. And with his eyes shut, he hits him with all his strength over the ear.

He notes with amazement that the boy does not cry and he opens his eyes to look at him. The impress of the boy's head, his ear, enclosed in the soft wool of his knitted cap, is burnt on the flat of his hand.

The boy hangs on. His astonishment is doubtless greater than his pain. But his lips tremble, and a half-chewed raisin falls out of his mouth as he says: 'That . . . that wasn't very nice of you. I haven't done anything to you.'

There was no need to tell him that. But to add to it all, the boy continues with a mature earnestness which is both cutting and disturbing: 'I don't think that was the way Mother wanted us to begin the New Year.'

His mouth is taut, his lips pursed, and his child's blue eyes slowly fill. Then the boy turns and goes.

He has no idea how long he has been standing out in the kitchen. It might have been five minutes, it might have been an hour. He has stood staring the whole time at the gas ring. There are blue flowers on the piece of oil-cloth the ring stands on. By the side of it stands the pot for putting spent matches in.

And finally the despair within him subsides; the river is empty; the mind relaxes.

It is dark inside the bedroom. Little Svein is sleeping in one of the double beds. Mother usually sleeps in the other.

'Are you asleep?' he asks in the darkness. Only the dark and the cold answer him.

He tiptoes closer; now he can see his brother. He sleeps where he usually sleeps. But it seems he hasn't managed to undress properly, for his black jersey is visible above the bed-covers.

The young man stands watching him and listening: a little boy, lying there with his hair flattened down over his forehead and breathing peacefully and steadily into his pillow. But occasionally he pauses in his breathing and hiccups. Children who have cried themselves to sleep tend to sleep in this fashion.

The young man would have asked him for forgiveness. But the boy is asleep.

And the young man falls on his knees by the bedside of his only friend – the only person in the world he can call his friend and who will be proud to claim his friendship. Now, in the darkness and the silence he can do this; and he moistens his brother's pillow with the tears of the night and loneliness.

And the old year is over; and tonight the miracle happened with the New Year. And the young man's clenched hand opens over the crocheted bedcover, and from his hand a paper streamer unrolls and falls to the ground.

A thin, narrow, red paper streamer, a little roll of paper, which for all people all over the world has its own warm significance, but especially for young men who live so far to the north that summer and companionship are the exception, and winter's darkness and loneliness the rule.

[Original title: *Skjenselens korinter*. Translated by James McFarlane]

SOLVEIG CHRISTOV

The Glory of Mankind

The chaplain stopped the car down on the road, for a chaplain should come to people on foot. Especially an army chaplain. On the other hand, it would be difficult for him to make all his calls without a car. He had many calls to make.

In the course of the war he had sat by the bedside of hundreds of dying men, and most of the dying had asked him to take a greeting or a message to those dear ones who would be left behind.

Now one would expect a chaplain to be a man of his word. But he went further than that, he thought it was of great importance that these messages and greetings were delivered. He believed it was God's own voice which spoke through the dying as they stood before their chaplain on the great threshold.

It had grown into a whole notebook full of names, greetings, and messages. The chaplain had almost got through it, he had got up to T.

Tams . . .

The day was hot, his uniform was hot, and the chaplain stopped and mopped his brow. He thought of grief.

He knew grief in all its forms and gradations. Wild, noisy grief; dry, frozen grief; introverted, sighing grief. And he enjoyed the fine little thrill of excitement which always went through him before he had discovered exactly what kind of grief was present in the people he visited. Not until he had discovered that could he determine the strategic points at which he could aim his consolation.

It happened at times that the grief had grown old with the passing of the years. But he always succeeded in polishing it so bright again that it was a tribute to the fallen, and to God, who did not let a sparrow fall to the ground without his notice.

The chaplain usually ended his visits with prayers and songs. He prayed for peace on earth and he sang of the glory of heaven. The chaplain was a good singer. Before God had called him to his service, he had wanted to become a singer. But he was not bitter because he had had to offer up the singer within him on the altar of God. On the contrary, he invariably enjoyed the gasp of amazement that went through people in house and cottage when he lifted up his voice.

This Miss Hassel had been difficult to find. She had moved from the place where the dying man had said that she lived, and it had been pure detective work to trace her. Finally he had got her address from a down-and-out pianist. The pianist had asked him to give his warmest regards to Berti.

But she was not called Berti, she was called Berta, Berta Hassel. Her dead fiancé was called Herman, Herman Tams. The message he had been asked to give consisted of just one short sentence.

The chaplain arrived in the yard. The houses around it were old and decrepit, but the yard nevertheless gave an impression of well-being. A fair-haired boy was standing by the wall of the barn, sharpening a knife on a grindstone.

'Hello, young fellow,' said the chaplain, 'is this where Berta Hassel lives?'

'Yes,' said the boy, 'this is where Berti lives. She's out in the fields, but Auntie's inside.'

'Thank you,' said the chaplain, 'and who may you be?'

The chaplain never lost an opportunity to inform himself of relevant facts; it was an important source of his strength.

'Can't you see that,' said the boy. 'I'm the helper.'

'Of course, now I can see that,' said the chaplain. He went across the yard and knocked on the front door. A thin, grey-haired woman opened it. She became visibly nervous when he said who he was and for what reason he had come. She called to the boy at the grindstone and told him to run and fetch Berti. Say she was to be quick, there was a visitor for her.

'It's all right,' he said soothingly, 'there's not such a great hurry.' She blinked nervously and asked him to come in. He was surprised by the interior of the house. Three sunny rooms one after the other, and there were many bookshelves, rugs, and paintings. Also a piano. He was pleased to see the latter, as he liked to accompany himself when he sang.

'Well, this is a nice place,' he said, soothing again.

'Oh – yes,' she said.

'I can see you're fond of reading.'

'They're my niece's books,' she said. 'Berti moved out here when the university closed.'

'But you are the one who plays,' he said.

'No, Berti's the one who plays. Well, she only plays in the winter, she hasn't time during the rest of the year. She grows vegetables. You see, we had very little food. But in the autumn she'll be starting her studies again. It'll be very lonely for me.'

The sun streamed in through the windows, and the chaplain now saw that the furniture and rugs were old and worn. But he also realized what it was which gave these rooms such a particular charm. It was all the flowers. There were flowers everywhere, flowers, foliage, and grasses, all mixed together in a strangely carefree way. It looked as if a whole meadow had been gathered.

'I hope I haven't come at an inconvenient time,' said the chaplain.

She looked at him uncomprehendingly.

'This isn't a special occasion,' he said, 'all these flowers . . .'

'Oh no,' she said, 'there aren't any special occasions, hardly anybody comes here. But Berti says that the flowers are free in the summer. She really has an eye for . . . for . . .'

'Beauty,' he said.

'Yes,' she said, 'just so, just so, vicar.'

She took a deep breath and continued: 'But I would like to tell you one thing, vicar, and that is that my niece is a very good person. . . .'

The chaplain was surprised, it sounded as though the aunt thought it necessary to defend her niece. Or to prepare him, to warn him perhaps?

'When my husband died, I was left here comfortably off. I leased out most of the land. When my niece came, she began to grow vegetables on the little bit of land I had left. And believe me, vicar, it's an absolute marvel to see how she made it grow and bear fruit. Load after load went from here to the town, and she didn't make a penny profit. In fact she sometimes sold at a loss. I sometimes used to reproach her for that, because she's not well off at all, but she said: "People must have food." Now can you understand that she is a good person?'

'It is more blessed to give than to receive,' he said.

'That is what my niece thinks too. But she has not learnt it from . . . from the scriptures.'

The aunt looked at him.

'I understand,' he said.

The aunt breathed a sigh of relief, she stopped twisting her fingers together and her gaze became grey and calm. She looked like a person who has done her duty and found peace.

'Perhaps you will take a cup of tea with my niece, vicar. . . .'

'Yes thank you, if it is not too much trouble. . . .'

'No, not at all. Excuse me a moment, I'll put the water on to boil. I'm sure my niece will be here soon. . . .'

She went.

The chaplain wandered around the room, he leafed through the music lying on the piano and discovered that Beethoven was Miss Hassel's favourite composer. He turned over a book that lay on a chair, Wergeland's poems. Fancy that. . . .

But nowhere could he see a photograph of the dead fiancé. There were no photographs at all, even the lid of the piano was clear apart from a bowl of water-lilies. It was true that there was a painted portrait hanging in the dining room, but that was of a fat white-haired gentleman who must have ceased to be available for active service long before the portrait was painted. The chaplain assumed that it was the aunt's deceased husband.

He found it rather odd that there was no photograph of the dead man. Photographs like that normally stood in a place of honour in the houses he had visited up to now, whether the family's grief was new or old. They were often decorated with black ribbons or flowers, and such photographs had often been a great help to him.

The chaplain heard footsteps, but it was only the little boy who appeared in the doorway.

'She's just coming,' he said, 'she's just washing the worst of the muck off.'

The boy disappeared again, and the chaplain found himself staring at the door expectantly. When she finally arrived, she was just about the opposite of everything he had imagined. She was the smallest and thinnest woman he had seen, and she was nearly all eyes, eyes of a clear blue which were shadowed by the deep, dark hollows they lay in. Her black hair was cut in a boyish style, and he could not help noticing her tiny sun-burnt ears. They were so perfect they looked almost indecent. She was wearing a newly ironed blue shirt and a pair of faded trousers of khaki material.

She said: 'I am Berta Hassel, did you want me?'

Her voice was unexpectedly deep and melodious, definitely too large for the rest of that little person. It seemed as if she did not want to shake his hand, but just as it was becoming embarrassing, she held hers out after all. She withdrew it again quickly.

The chaplain became a little uncertain.

'I was with your fiancé, Herman Tams, when he died,' he said.

'Had he . . . had he asked for you?'

'Yes, and he asked me to give you his love.'

'Thank you,' she said and turned away.

At that moment her aunt came in with a tea trolley. She looked at her niece's averted face, then looked at the chaplain and nodded slightly.

'I should think you'd like a cup of tea,' she said a little loudly. 'It's a good thing I baked some rolls today.'

'Don't you want some tea, Auntie?'

'I've already had some,' said her aunt, 'but please help yourselves.'

The aunt went.

Berta Hassel poured out the tea, put a teaspoon of honey in each cup, stirred them both and gave him one. Then she put both hands round her own cup, lifted it to her mouth and drank with pleasure.

Not a glimmer of grief had she shown.

'Drink,' she said, 'it's good.'

The chaplain drank, he felt a sweet shock on his tastebuds and said: 'Delicious, pure nectar.'

'Dried clover and dock leaves,' she said, 'and honey from my own bees. At least the war has given me this drink.'

The chaplain remembered his errand, and put his cup down.

'Take a roll,' she said quickly. He took a roll. It was still too early to give her the message.

She poured herself another cup; and as she poured, she said: 'Herman died more than five years ago. Why didn't you come before?'

'Your fiancé fell at Tenden bridge,' he said. 'As you know, it was at the beginning of the war. After Tenden I followed the troops northwards until we had to cross the border to Sweden, and from there I travelled to England and Scotland. So you will understand that I could not come before.'

'No, of course,' she said.

'Your fiancé was very courageous at Tenden bridge,' he said. It was a sentence which normally made a good impression on relatives.

'You mean he *killed* a lot of people?'

'I mean he showed courage and bravery.'

'No doubt that means that he *killed* a lot of people,' she said. 'Isn't that what being courageous in war means?'

She pronounced the word *killed* in a deliberately brutal way. As if she wanted to make her dead lover into a murderer.

The chaplain said: 'We had to lose the battle of Tenden bridge despite our soldiers' eagerness to fight. We were short of everything, equipment, ammunition – in short, we were unprepared for war. It must never happen again.'

'That we are unprepared for war?'

'Yes, but if men would open their hearts to God . . .'

'How did you find me,' she interrupted, 'Herman couldn't have known that I would end up here.'

He explained about the trouble he had gone to in order to find her, explained about the pianist who had finally helped him. And who had also sent his regards.

Then she smiled and turned fully towards him.

'Arve,' she said in a warm voice. 'And how was he, what was he like?'

'I don't know,' said the chaplain.

'But he wasn't drunk?'

'No, he wasn't drunk.'

– But in all probability he had recently been drunk, thought the chaplain. Or had the intention of soon becoming so again.

He said nothing about this.

'Then,' she said, 'then perhaps he'll manage to get over it. You see, he lost something very precious during the war.'

He heard a little tremor in her voice as she spoke the last sentence. It was the first time she had shown any sign of possessing feelings. And these feelings emerged not because of her dead fiancé, but because of a down-and-out pianist.

'Many people lost things in the war,' he said.

'That's true,' she said. 'But Arve . . .'

She was silent. The chaplain did not ask what Arve had lost. The chaplain had driven a hundred kilometres to bring a message from a dead man, not a living one.

'I was pleased that he could give me your address,' he said, 'so that I could fulfil your fiancé's last wish, and bring you his love and a message.'

'A message? A message as well, chaplain?'

The chaplain thought he could hear an undertone of mockery in the deep voice.

'Yes,' he said, 'a message.'

The chaplain could remember it clearly, but he closed his mouth firmly on the short sentence and thought of God's mysterious ways. Perhaps Herman Tams had been spared worse things than death.

She got up and began to walk up and down the room, she stared at his closed mouth and said: 'I shall tell you something, chaplain. I was totally opposed to my fiancé going to the war.'

'Were you opposed to him doing his duty?'

'His duty to whom?'

'To God and his country.'

She waved her arms impatiently.

'He had a greater duty, he had his duty towards mankind. God and country are ideas created by man; if you don't agree with that, you must at least agree that without man these ideas could not be understood. Therefore man comes first. We, Herman and I, we knew how glorious man is. You perhaps know that Herman and I studied medicine together, and at more or less the same time we were seized by the great fear, the fear that one or more of these thousand processes which happen silently in man, might stop. It is a fairly common fear, but it gripped us hard. When we recovered from it, we both knew that man is glorious. Nothing of what man has built up around himself can compare with man himself. Therefore we must regard every single human being as a sacred object.

'When the war came, I told him he couldn't go. I said, "You can't kill, you can't destroy a human being." '

The chaplain looked at the piano; there would not be any singing.

'The flesh is the dwelling place of the soul,' he said.

'Oh, let us not forget the soul,' she said, 'it helps us amongst other things to see the glory of man. But Herman said: "What good will it do if I alone protest against the destruction of man. I'll be regarded as a coward, a traitor. If I survive, I want to live in this country, work here and be respected." "Respected by blindness, stupidity, and ignorance," I said. We talked all night, but the image of man as a sacred object perished within him. It was too deeply undermined in advance, in part by you, chaplain.'

'By me?'

'If you had stood in the place allotted to you by God, then Herman would not have stood so alone, then perhaps he would have had courage enough.'

'I stand in the place God has given me, Miss Hassel. It is not the easiest, but I do not complain.'

'You should have stood in the streets, in the market places, and everywhere you should have shouted out what God commanded you to shout: "Thou shalt not kill." '

'My child,' he said mildly, 'God has never said that you shall not defend yourself when you are confronted by an insane murderer.'

'No,' she said, 'he has not done that. But he has said that you shall not kill.'

'What would you do, Berta Hassel, if an insane murderer forced his way into your house and was going to kill you and your sleeping children?'

'My children?'

'Supposing you had children. . . .'

'I would of course try to disarm him, if necessary kill him. His glorious nature is sick, and therefore he must be protected from himself.'

'Quite right,' said the chaplain, 'that was what we did too, we tried to drive away the murderer from the little country which is our home.'

He felt a little sorry for her, she had such a high forehead, she ought to have been too clever to let herself be driven into a corner like that, by the irrefutable argument.

She went to the window and opened it. A large, chunky bumble bee fell into the room, the chaplain did not like the sound of the humming wings. When she turned round, he saw that she did not in any way feel that she had been defeated. Her eyes were narrowed to two slits, there was a yellow glint in them, and for some reason it made him think of mousetraps in dark cellar passages.

'Chaplain,' she said, 'we spoke of the Christian church whose faith you profess and whose servant you also are. Do you think that all your millions of fellow Christians in Germany were insane murderers? Do you think that the priests who invoked God's blessing on the German weapons were insane murderers, do you think that your colleagues, the army chaplains in the German army, were insane murderers?'

'The German community was deceived,' said the chaplain, 'they were deceived into believing that they were fighting a defensive war. . . .'

'Well,' she said. 'That is what happens when you put your trust in words which God has not spoken. If on the other hand the Christian church listened to what God *has* said, what he said quite emphatically and wrote with his own finger upon the stone, then your church could not let itself be deceived by these two ideas, defence and attack, because they would mean the same, and that is the breaking of God's commandment. And if you remember, chaplain, the first Christians turned the other cheek, they let themselves be thrown to wild animals, they let themselves be burned like torches, without lifting a finger. But they conquered, your church conquered solely on the basis of God's commandment, chaplain.'

The bumble bee had hidden itself in a large bunch of daisies which stood on a low table beside him. The chaplain became nervous at the close proximity of the enormous bee.

'The Christian church emerged into the light of day, and churches with spires and bells were built. But what did you do with the commandments, chaplain? You dipped them in dough and fried them in lard. You have made doughnuts out of God's commandments, and now you roll the doughnuts from one to the other just as you think fit, and you get fat on your fingers. . . .'

The chaplain was a little startled by this image of doughnuts. They had been his favourite food while he was studying, a modest luxury, doughnuts with cold milk. But one day he found a razor-blade in a swelling doughnut, and since that day he had abandoned that particular pleasure.

'You forget that God is love,' he said, 'that there is forgiveness for a sinner who repents.'

'In other words, your God has set his demands on his own creation so high that those demands cannot be fulfilled. He cannot have done it in ignorance of mankind, he must have done it on purpose, so that he can enjoy the pleasure of dispensing forgiveness continually. In that way you make your God into a power-seeking tyrant, chaplain.'

'God sent his only begotten son so that all those who believe in him shall not perish, but have everlasting life.'

At that moment the door was opened, and the little boy put his head round it.

'Berti,' he said, 'I'm going to bathe.'

'What?'

'I'm going to bathe. . . .'

'Go and bathe. . . .'

When the door was closed she looked at him, it seemed almost as if she was ashamed.

'Here I am talking and talking,' she muttered, 'when you've come all that long way. . . .'

'It often does you good to get it off your chest,' said the chaplain mildly. But he no longer had any hope of seeing grief awaken in this misguided, hardened soul.

'What I meant to say,' she said, 'is that I still disagree with my dead fiancé. It is no argument for him that he also let his own glory be destroyed. I still think that man should not be destroyed.'

She stuck two fingers up into the air as if she was taking an oath, and then she sat down in the chair.

'Tell me the message,' she said. She curled up and put her head on her knees, then she clasped her hands around her ankles.

The chaplain could see her ribs through her blouse, and could count the knobs of her backbone, they lay like pearls on a string downwards from her neck. It was a most peculiar position in which to receive a message. The chaplain stood up, he had forgotten the message.

'Your fiancé asked me to tell you this . . .' he said in a clear voice. He leafed through the notebook and found Herman Tams, fallen at Tenden bridge.

'My . . .' he began. Then his voice failed. He was a sorely tried chaplain to begin with, and now he felt as though he had a cork in his throat. He was aware of the woman in the chair, realized suddenly that this position of hers was a kind of defensive position. She sensed an attack in the dead man's message, and it was her firm intention to repulse this attack. She was a fortress with breastworks and embrasures of bone and sinew, and the whole fortress trembled with an intense determination to defend.

But she was also in anguish, in great anguish.

He tried in vain to make his voice work, the sentence danced in front of his eyes with thin, bloodshot letters. The enormous bumble bee hurled itself like a mad thing against a closed window at the other end of the room.

'Oh, God,' cried his soul, 'your will be done. . . .'

Then it happened, the cork came loose and all his pent-up voice was released:

'My love, you were right, you are right.'

The sentence resounded through the room, the dead man's message had been spoken. The chaplain put the notebook in his breast pocket and mopped his forehead. Berta Hassel had not moved, but a change had nevertheless come over the blue bundle in the chair.

It was not a fortress any longer.

A strange silence began to fill the room. It came from her and spread like rings on a clear grey lake. When it reached him, he noticed also something else. Grief had come. He could not be mistaken, for he was familiar with grief. But the nature of this grief was unknown to him. It had the completely unfathomable element in it, that it made him, the chaplain, superfluous.

He did not understand it, but the realization that this was how it was forced itself upon him, forced him out of the door, swept him down the road.

The last little bit back to the car he was almost running. The car was as hot as a baker's oven, he wound all the windows down and took off his uniform jacket, he noticed that he stank of sweat.

'The glory of mankind,' he thought bitterly, 'the glory of mankind?'

[Original title: *Menneskets herlighet*. Translated by Janet Garton]

JENS BJØRNEBOE

Life and the youth

In Alexandria there lived a youth who was converted to the Christian faith. After his christening he felt a great longing, and he went to his teacher and said: 'I believe that there is great pain and great suffering on earth, and I do not know it, so I wish to go out into the world in order to know all suffering and all pain. Before I know of all the evil which happens I cannot begin to live a life in truth. All that I feel, think, and say will be a lie as long as I do not know all the pain in the world.'

His teacher, who had educated him in the faith and in the mysteries, looked at him and said: 'My son, in this as in all else which concerns your heart, you must choose for yourself. And what you say is true; no one can live in truth before he knows pain and the evil which is its cause. Yet I must warn you: the journey you are to undertake may be more dangerous than you know. You are young; your faith has not yet been tried; the truth may be too heavy a burden for your shoulders. Rather stay here, devote yourself to study, live a life of piety and work, and do not seek out suffering.'

The youth answered: 'Father, this has come to me with a force greater than that of thought. I must go out and seek it.'

'Then go,' answered the teacher, 'I shall pray that the angels of God may go with you. But you know not what you are doing!'

The youth bade farewell to his family and friends, took a staff in his hand and set forth. It was to be a very long journey.

After a few hours' walking, the road led past the edge of a desert. Here the youth left the road and went into the desert, far from everything, and fasted for three days and three nights. Then he made a vow: never would he think of himself and of his own life, but always keep his eyes on the truth of others' suffering, and try to feel the pain of others as his own.

Then he prayed: 'Oh, Lord, thou creator of the earth and of all things! Thou who hast created the sun and all life which lives in the water, on the earth and in the air – thou hast created me, who am no more than a worm in thy sight! Let me know all the suffering on earth, let me feel all the sorrow of the world, and let me never forget what I have seen!'

And when he turned, there was a desert hare sitting behind him, and he realized that the Lord had heard his prayer. Then he arose and walked on. But his way led past a man of God who lived alone in the desert, and the man of God called after him, so that the youth turned and knelt before him and said: 'Speak, your son is listening!'

And the hermit replied: 'I see by your face that God has set his mark upon you. What do you desire?'

The youth was moved and said: 'I wish to know the pain of the world, I wish to know it completely, so that I then may walk in truth and not in a lie.'

'Do you also wish to know the greatest pain?' asked the hermit.

'Yes,' replied the youth. 'Also the greatest.'

'You know not what you speak of,' said the man of God, 'but your wish shall be fulfilled. But on the day it is fulfilled, then you must think of me and remember what I say: do you see the plant which stands beside this spring?'

'I see it.'

'It would not live for one day, if the angels of the Lord did not support it. Will you remember that?'

'I shall remember.'

The youth returned to his road, and after a while he found a dog lying by the edge of the road. Men had left it lying there, because it was sick, and could not keep up with the animals and people who had gone on. It was in great pain, and was moving its head from side to side, and it did not understand why it was in pain. And it was whining. And the youth picked up a stone to kill it, but he was not used to killing, so he struck it many times, first on one side of the head and then on the other, and the dog tried to crawl away from him as he struck it, but it had not the strength. At last it lay still and whined no more. And the youth went on, but his hands were shaking. For he had been sheltered from much in his childhood.

He walked on and came to the great towns, and he saw the sufferings of all mankind; he saw the mothers' pain as they gave birth, and he saw the mothers' pain over their dead children. He saw children being sold as slaves to the great glass factories, where they could not live for more than a few years because of the heat from the ovens. He saw these children sleeping in chains at night; he saw them stop growing, and saw how death became visible in their faces. He saw men's sufferings in war, and that of prisoners when they were cast into chains, or when they were blinded with irons. He saw men being flayed alive as punishment for their misdeeds, or torn into small pieces with pincers. He saw the pain of the lonely, the rejected, the outcast – and he was ashamed of all the suffering which did not affect him. And he thought that the whole world was like a woman in labour; and that only in the greatest pain could a higher race of men be born. For that was his belief.

Yet he still had much to see; and it took him many years, and when the day came that he had seen all the pain in the world, he was no longer a youth, but a man with a furrowed face, and all that he had seen lay within him like a stone. He felt a deep sorrow over what he had seen, but he said to himself: 'Now you have seen all suffering; you have seen that the world is like a woman in childbirth, who shall bring forth a higher race of men. Go now out into the desert and speak to God; perhaps he will answer you! Then you can begin a life in truth, for now you have seen the truth.'

But when he turned his back upon men, at once he became anxious about what was happening in the towns; for perhaps new pain and suffering had come upon mankind? For what he had seen he could not forget, and his thoughts dwelt continually on what men were now doing to each other, for he knew that their hearts were hard. And he turned and went back to the town.

In the town he saw that men were behaving towards each other as before, but worse; the evil in the world was increasing and was like a swarm of flies in summertime around a dead animal. And he saw that the new man was not born, but that each pain engendered a thousand new pains, and that each injustice fathered new injustice, and that the evil amongst men was stronger than the good. And each time something evil happened, he followed its tracks and saw how it engendered greater evil, and he saw that evil surrounded the earth like a black cloud, and that it blotted out the sun. And he saw into men's breasts, and their hearts could not forget the pain and the injustice which was done to them, and their hearts became harder and harder. And in the town market-place he cried out to God and said: 'Show me a man who can forget the pain and the injustice which is done to him! Just one man!'

But God did not reply, and the man thought that in this way the higher race of men will not be born, and he was filled with sorrow and felt that he had a great grief to bear. And he thought: 'If I cannot forget the injustice which is done to *others,* how can I expect others to forget the injustice which is done to *themselves?*' And he looked about him in the world and saw that all was pain, and that the suffering was without end. And he wept.

The next day he sought new pain and new injustice in the world, and he felt that now he saw more truly and more clearly, because he no longer believed that the world was like a woman in childbirth, and that a new race of men would be born. Day after day he saw new suffering, and he never forgot any of what he had seen. Not even at night did he find oblivion in sleep, but he awoke and cried out after bad dreams. And he cried to God and said: 'What have I done, that I should be granted this knowledge: that the suffering is without end!'

But God did not reply. Again he went out into the desert in order to be alone and to speak with the Lord, but after he had walked for half a day he felt that he was fleeing from the sight of the sufferings which afflicted mankind, and he turned, saying: 'Never shall I flee from what happens on this earth!' Again he saw new pain; he went to places of execution and saw men having their eyes gouged out and their intestines torn apart, and he said to himself: 'This is what life on earth is like, this is how the Lord has created us, that we do this to each other. Why are our hearts so hard?'

Then the day came that he no longer desired to go out into the desert. And he understood that he could no longer leave what he saw, but that he was bound to it, and that he had no eyes for anything other than suffering. Everything else was but a dream or a mirage. If he saw a child playing and laughing, then he saw at the same time in his mind all the pain he had seen in his life, and he no longer saw the smile on the child's face, but he saw it bowed down in tears over future pain. Then he understood that his youthful wish had been fulfilled; he knew that he had seen the pain of the world, and that he would never be able to forget it. Now he himself belonged to what he had seen, and he cried to God: 'Lord, I have seen all the pain of the earth; I must bear the sorrow of the whole world, and I can forget nothing! I am like a dead dog at the edge of the road. Grant now that thy servant be released from this life. He has seen enough, and a life in truth he cannot bear to live!' But the Lord did not reply. And he cried again: 'Lord, why dost thou not let men perish by their own evil? Is there no limit set to their actions?' But he turned his back on the Lord and went out amongst men, and he saw that there was no limit to their actions. Everyone could commit all the evil he wished, and there was no limit at all to the evil of kings and men of power. He saw warriors pull out the tongues of the defeated, make them into slaves, and rip open pregnant women with knives. And never did the angels of the Lord intervene and put a stop to their actions. Then he said to himself, 'I was right! Suffering is without end. Men treat each other like mad wolves, and the pain is never at an end. Of all the things on earth, death is the only good thing. I have seen the truth, and I have become the prisoner of the truth!'

And he cried to the Lord: 'Now let me die, and let me forget what I have seen!' And he threw himself to the ground and foamed at the mouth and screamed out like one possessed, and cried: 'Let me forget! Let me forget! The pain I have within me is greater than all the pain I have seen, for I carry it all within me at once!'

But the Lord did not allow him to forget. And he went out into the desert and lived there like a wild animal. He fasted and scourged himself with thorny branches and cut himself on sharp stones, but he forgot nothing, not a whit did he forget of what he had seen. He sat on the rocks of the desert and howled, and wild animals were afraid of him and went far off to avoid him. And he howled at the Lord like a wolf, and he said: 'Let me forget! Let me forget!' And he rolled in the sand and threw stones in the air. But he could not forget. Then he screamed at the Lord and said: 'I spoke to thee when I was a child and knew not what I said. Is thy heart as hard as the hearts of men?'

And he was like a man possessed, and his hair and beard and nails were never cut, and he was without clothes in the desert. And he felt as though burning coals lay in his breast after all the things he had seen. And he wept. And he said to himself: 'Can any pain be greater than this?'

One morning he fell into deep thought, such that he remained in thought the whole day, and he said to himself the whole time: 'Can it be possible that any pain is greater than this? Can it be possible that I still have not met the greatest pain?' And after three days he arose and went back to men to discover the final pain. And when he met mankind again, he thought: 'Who am I that I would chastise them?' But he was like an animal to look at, with burning eyes, and men threw stones and unmentionable things after him, and he took no notice. For he wished to find the greatest pain, and he went to the temple of Moloch, and to the temple of Baal, where the priests placed children in the red-hot hands of the idols, while they cried out:

'Truly, Baal-Zebub is just! Truly, Moloch is great! See, he is eating flesh!'

And he heard the screams of small children, and he thought: 'This pain is terrible, but the pain of innocent children is not greater than that of sinners.'

And he cried out with a loud voice: 'Lord, why dost thou not sweep away with thy left hand all this abomination?'

But the Lord did not answer, and he said to himself: 'Does it make no difference which god I cry out to? Can no one answer?'

And all the pain and all the evil he had seen arose within him, and he said to himself: 'There is no god, and all this pain is meaningless. Never will the lamentation of mankind reach the ear of God. Everything under the heavens is without meaning, and the new race of men will never emerge.' And he wept, but he did not cry out, and he understood that he had met the final pain, and he returned to the desert and lived in his cave.

And he spoke to the beasts of prey and the vultures and the scorpions and snakes of the desert, and said: 'There are no limits to evil. Suffering is without end, and pain has no meaning.'

And to himself he said: 'Truly, scales have fallen from my eyes, and now I live in truth. Now I have felt the final pain, and I am still alive. Now I will go to men and be as one of them, for I will no longer endure the pain of all, but only my own. For all pain is meaningless.'

But he could no longer raise himself up because of his sorrow, for he was filled with the pain of mankind, and it was like carrying a heavy block of stone. And he crawled on hands and knees over to the spring, for he was thirsty, but he remained lying by the spring without the strength to drink, and he thought: 'Truly, this is death!' And he laughed aloud. Then he said to himself: 'Today I have laughed like a young man!' And he fainted and lay unconscious for a long time, and when he awoke he drank from the spring, and he saw that beside the spring there was a young plant, which looked as fresh as if it had rained on it. Then he remembered the man of God whom he had promised in his youth to remember on the day he had seen the greatest pain. And he said to himself: 'Truly, in this spring and in this plant there is no evil!'

And he cried to God: 'Praise and glory be to thee, that I have seen the running water and the green plant!'

And the Lord sent two ravens to him from heaven, and they

brought him bread. He ate of the bread and drank of the spring, for he had not tasted food for many days.

The next day he arose and went to his native town. But his eyes were like those of an old man as he stood before his teacher. And his teacher was very old.

'My son, have you now seen all the pain of the world?' asked the old man.

'All the pain of the world,' answered the man.

'Also the final pain?'

'Also the final pain.'

'Has the Lord spoken to you from the heavens, since you stand before me again?'

'Yes, he sent me two ravens with bread.'

Then the old man stood up: 'Now let me see if you can smile,' he said.

And the man smiled, like a young man.

[Original title: *Ynglingen og livet*. Translated by Janet Garton]

KJELL ASKILDSEN

Encounter

The trees, the loose sand where the path was most trampled even though people rarely walked there, the dike with its bridge across – a fine bridge, three rotting planks.

'And then?'

'He struck. I only saw his polished shoes. He's always had polished shoes. And a little of his trouser legs. I didn't want to scream, but in the end I had to. He didn't let up until I began to weep.'

Still a few yards of path, pine needles, smooth under the soles of one's shoes, then the beach, sand and sea, unchanged. Like the time he . . . like the time I . . . I?

'Did you think you had forgotten?'

'Not forgotten, perhaps. But time and distance and the fact that he sent for me. After all I'm no longer what I was. At least I supposed so.'

'And he?'

'Everything here is as it was before. I mean the stage settings are the same. And their demand for some appropriate course of action cannot be resisted.'

It was ebb-tide. The sand was hard. They followed the line of the shore. A tree root washed ashore and half buried, an empty bottle, a dead jellyfish transfixed by a stick, the smell of seaweed and undergrowth, the low sky. It will soon start to rain, not a breath of air.

'So you are leaving again?'

'Yes.'

He did not hear what she was asking. Suddenly he saw the brown curtaining, but surely it had hung between the two rooms, it was not there but on the balcony outside the bedroom, the blinds almost wholly down, the strip of light at the bottom, their legs and the voices, the rain on the back of his shirt. . . . 'But I tell you I've never . . .' 'That's what you say! . . .' The abrupt movement, his knobbly knees, her face a few inches from the floor, not a cry, I could have prevented it, I could have knocked on the window pane, I wanted to, it is not true that I didn't want to, and anyway how was I to know that things were not as they should have been, with walls and shelves full of God, with atonement behind the locked closet door, the galoshes and the umbrellas. . . .

The pavilion, the dog roses, the clearing, the first raindrops (now you'll get wet, that doesn't matter, your dress, that doesn't matter, here take this jacket, how warm it is, won't you be cold?), the raindrops on the back of his shirt. What was I doing on the balcony, in the rain?

'It wasn't only me he would beat,' he said. 'Mother also.'

'Why?'

'I don't know.'

Why? 'But I tell you I've never.' Was that all I heard? Had I run away, jumped down from the balcony before it was over? I couldn't see what she was feeling, her head hung down, it wasn't possible to read her expression, but she wasn't weeping, not while I was looking, I couldn't possibly have seen everything.

'What was she like, in fact?'

'Mother? Kind, I should say. She often wept. She never gossiped, not as far as I know, and when Father let me out of the closet she was never around, I don't know where she was, but she was never in the sitting room or in the kitchen. Did you know her?'

'By sight, yes. I remember she blushed easily.'

'That's right. I'd forgotten that.'

It was very noticeable. Not easily overlooked.

'I remember once . . .' he said. 'She was sitting sewing. I think I wasn't well, and it happened I was allowed to sleep on the divan in the dining room. We didn't say anything. Neither of us had said anything for a long time. Then suddenly she blushed. I lay there looking at her. I couldn't take my eyes off her. And whether it was then or some other time, I asked her why Father never blushed, but she didn't answer.'

The houses, the street alongside the park with the ancient lime trees, the gentle rain, cool against the back of his shirt, the house with the big veranda, the pear trees lining the road (aren't you coming in, actually I should, perhaps you'd rather come for coffee, gladly, thanks for the loan, you must be freezing you are all wet on your back, shall we say about five, thanks for the trip), the door that slammed behind her, the way home . . . home?

He let himself in. He heard his father clattering about with the pans.

'Is that you, Gabriel?'

'Yes.'

There was a smell of fish. He went up and changed his shirt. The window stood open towards the quiet street, the low houses. His glance moved over GOD IS LOVE in a black frame over the bed. He took it down. Now you are being childish, no I'm not. He put it into the low cupboard at the foot of the bed.

'Are you coming, Gabriel?'

He took his time. His father had sat down. He waited. He clasped his hands and bowed his head. Gabriel looked out of the window.

'You'll have to take pot-luck.'

They sat facing each other.

'This tastes good.'

'You have to learn to turn your hand to anything when you live on your own.'

It didn't taste nice. There was too little salt in the fish. There was no salt cellar on the table. And he doesn't dare, and I don't dare, such is he, such am I, there is nothing here for me to do.

'It's good to have you back here again, lad. It's been empty since your mother passed away.'

He did not reply. The kitchen clock ticked and the tap dripped. It's my turn to say something, what shall I say?

'Did she suffer any pain?'

'No. But she'd have liked to say goodbye to you. She wanted to ask your forgiveness.'

'What for?'

'Everybody has something or other to ask forgiveness for.'

'Really?'

'God . . .'

'I'd like you to keep God out of it.'

'I won't. I can't.'

'Then let's not talk about it.'

Silence.

'Have you been to see her grave?'

'Not yet.'

'Maybe you would like to take a few fresh flowers along from the garden. Are you going there this afternoon?'

'I'm meeting Bodil.'

'Who's that?'
'Bodil Karin.'
'Oh, yes.'
'Thanks for the meal.'
The father bent his head and clasped his hands and moved his lips, but noiselessly.
'You're welcome.'
Up the stairs, the room, I contradicted him, the darker patch where GOD IS LOVE had hung, perhaps he'll come up and see it, it wasn't raining any longer, a slit of sunlight fell across the mirror, then we can sit on the veranda, steps on the stairs, I can't reach to hang it in place again, I won't open the door.

He didn't come, he went into the bedroom. Gabriel sat down on the bed and felt his heart hammering. I've become the same again, he thought. I can wriggle, I can take a picture down from the wall, but I am back in the net again. I am a little sinner again, just like that other time.

That other time. The window stood open, the curtain moved gently against the pale night sky, they couldn't stop caressing each other, the bed-cover had fallen on the floor, the naked flesh, the chirp of the grasshoppers through the window, the faint rustling of the leaves, the calm breathing – are you cold, no are you, no – the soft darkness, his hands quietly moving now that there was no hurry and so much to hold fast to, all the quiet-spoken words, their meaning less important than their euphony – listen to the trees, listen to the grasshoppers, how quiet it is – long thoughts on new unfamiliar roads, big happy words that looked not for an answer but for an echo, the blond hair on the pillow, the scents, the July evening and her – I'm so happy I could weep – and then: the rattle of the door, the steps, the voices, the instantaneous guilt, seconds of panic, she: lock the door, the steps on the stairs, the door handle, father: why have you locked the door Gabriel. I have a visitor. I think it's about time we all went to bed. The shame at the fact that his father had not knocked, the fear and the feeling of guilt, strong enough already then but even stronger when he came back after having seen her home, it had grown late, his father in the darkness in the sitting room: I want to talk to you Gabriel. Silence. I saw that it was a girl, who was she. No answer. It was dark in your room and the door was locked, who was she. I won't tell you. But I know who it was. I only asked so as to give you a chance of not hiding anything from me, but since you won't say anything I can only believe the worst and it's my duty to tell her father. If you do that. I will do it. That's rotten. Be careful what you say, Gabriel. It's rotten rotten.

There was sun in the mirror. He went down the stairs and out of the house, the road was wet and hard after the rain. He rang.

'Mother's out. Make yourself at home. Will you have coffee or tea?'

'Either. Can I sit on the veranda?'

'Of course.'

He went out and sat down in a basket chair. She pottered about. She hummed a tune. A feeling of peace came over him, a sense of mental and physical well-being which he had doubtless experienced before, but very rarely.

'You must enjoy being here.'

'You think so?'

'With this veranda and this garden.'

'It has to be looked after, and anyway the summer is short. You must have forgotten what it's like here in winter.'

Tea with lemon, cheese and biscuits, the distant sound of a chain-saw.

'If you only knew how often I've walked past the fence here and dreamt how fine it must be to have a garden like this.'

'You used to have a fine garden yourselves.'

'There wasn't a single place anywhere in it that couldn't be seen from the house. I couldn't hide myself away, either in the garden or in the house, apart from the cellar.'

'Didn't you have a room of your own then?'

'Yes, but I wasn't allowed to lock the door. I wasn't to have any secrets from them, and they came in any time they fancied and without knocking. I had a desk with drawers you could lock but I wasn't allowed to hide the key. True I can't remember them actually forbidding me, but then it wasn't necessary. Those secrets I did have I hid in other places. I remember once I forgot my diary, a little yellow notebook which was easy to hide. I left it lying on the bedside table. I must have been about fifteen or sixteen, and I'd written on the outside of the book that it was mine and it wasn't to be opened by anybody but me. Mother hadn't merely opened it, she'd written in pencil at the top of one of the pages: God sees all.'

'What was it in fact that made you leave home?'

'I don't know. I don't remember. I know that must sound strange, for it's not all *that* long ago, but I really don't remember. Sometimes I think it was when I saw my father strike my mother. But that can't be right. It must have been much later.'

'How strange.'

'Yes. There's so much I don't remember. There are things I don't know if I've really lived them or only dreamt them, and these are things not very long ago in time. Other things I can remember very clearly, but I'm not always able to say when they occurred. Whether it was when I was eight or ten or fifteen. But the most remarkable thing of all is perhaps that at certain times in my life I must have dreamt the same thing night after night, to the point where I began to doubt whether it really was a dream, or whether I might equally well have lived it. For a while I believed for instance that I'd taken my matriculation examination, that I hadn't done the written examination in English, not because I wasn't able. It wasn't a bad dream; on the contrary it was good. I turned up for the examination, but then I just sat there looking at the others. I knew it wasn't necessary to write any answer; that it was a wholly unnecessary exercise, that I might just as well take a walk in the forest. So I got up and went. I know it must sound strange; but for a time – I have the feeling it must have been several months – I half believed that I'd really gone out of the examination room, though in fact I knew better than that. If only I could explain. . . .'

'I understand,' she said. She got up. 'I'll be back in a minute.' He no longer felt any sense of well-being. I must ask my father. He's the only one who can tell me, if he can. If he will.

'I must go,' he said.

'Already?'

'I must talk to my father. Can I phone you?'

'Certainly.'

He left straightaway, as though to keep his decision warm. I must do it now. Now or never. I am frightened without any reason. As a child I had reason enough, because he would hit me. Now I'm frightened because of how things used to be. He can't do anything to me; I am the one who can do something to him. Maybe. All he can do is tell me. I'm not afraid of the truth.

'Is that you, Gabriel?'

'Yes.'

'Are you back already? Would you like some coffee?'

'No, thank you.'

He sat down at the round table in the smallest room. The sun had moved far to the west and was sending shafts of light in through the north windows, right across to the brown curtaining.

'I want to ask you something.'

'Ask away.'

'This isn't meant to go dragging things up again. But why – and I'm asking because I don't know, and it sounds strange – why did I leave home? I mean, what happened that made me leave home?'

'Let's not go dragging all that up again. Let bygones be bygones.'

'No. I've got to know.'

'I have tried to understand how it could have happened, in what way I failed. For you mustn't think I've put all the blame on you.'

'Let's not talk about blame. What do you think?'

'Perhaps I was too fond of you.'

'Is that the way you see things?'

'Perhaps I was too attached to you.'

'You wanted me to be like you.'

'Are you accusing me?'

'I didn't want to be like you. Maybe I did when I was quite little, I don't remember. But not later. I called you Abraham.'

'Abraham?'

'And I was Isaac. As far back as I can remember I've been afraid of you. Not merely because you punished me. . . .'

'I never punished you without good reason.'

'That is something I also believed once, because I always felt guilty. Because I wasn't old enough to distinguish between guilt and guilty feelings.'

'There's no difference between those two things.'

'Yes, there is. Why was mother always blushing?'

'Let your mother rest in peace.'

'She is resting in peace. Why did you punish her?'

'Punish her?'

'You struck her.'

'When?'

'I don't know. I saw you. Was it because she was too kind to me?'

'Gabriel! Was it this that brought you here?'

'No, no! I shouldn't have come.'

'You should have come in a different frame of mind.'

'Just tell me why I left.'

'That's something your conscience ought to be able to tell you.'

'What do you mean?'
'You didn't leave empty-handed.'
'I know that.'
'Your mother never really got over that.'
Gabriel stood up.
'I see I'm not getting anywhere. You are carrying on where you left off. You are playing on my guilt feelings, and hiding behind God. You never punished me without good reason, you said. What reason? What reasons? The same reasons that made the Inquisition wipe out all those who opposed the authority of the church. You believe you were too fond of me? Measure your love by the number of hours I was shut in the clothes closet!'
'Do you really think I did that with a light heart?'
'I don't know. But you did it with a clear conscience.'
'Yes. Can you say the same about your own actions?'
'No. But the executioners from the concentration camps can say the same about theirs. Does that absolve them from guilt?'
'That's enough, Gabriel. You've said more than I would have accepted from anybody but you. Some day you will understand that you have done me a wrong. I am now an old man, and I may not live long enough to see it, but one day you'll realize. . . .'
'Be quiet!'
'I'll say what I like in my own house!'
'Then wait until I've gone!'
The entrance hall, the stairs up, I tremble, the room, at least I managed to tell him, the case, any way he didn't win, what does 'win' mean, ultimately we all lose, short-term victories are long-term defeats, but it wasn't to conquer that I came but for once not to be conquered, I won't hang it in place again, it shall be my final greeting, GOD IS LOVE in a little room, that was that, it wasn't a long visit, so long as now he doesn't, down the stairs, but I can't just go without saying goodbye, yes I can, because I am afraid? This will not be a flight but a parting, shall I knock or just walk in? I knock, I'm not at home here any more, he doesn't reply, so I'll go, he must have heard me, unless he's gone out into the garden.
He opened the door. His father was sitting in the high-backed chair and looked at him.
'I've come to say goodbye.'
'You are leaving?'
'Yes.'

'I hadn't thought it would be like this.'
'Nor I.'
'I wish I understood you.'
He did not answer.
'I was glad when you wrote to say you were coming.'
'I'm sorry it ended like this.'
'Are you?'
'What do you mean?'
'Are you really sorry?'
'I said so, didn't I? I didn't want to fight with you. I didn't even want to prove you wrong. Tell me one thing, Father. Suppose I hadn't been your son, suppose I were only an acquaintance of yours, and you knew the same about me as you know now, would you have looked forward to meeting me, to having me living under your roof?'
'Naturally it wouldn't have been the same.'
'No. And if you'd only been one of my fellow creatures and not my father, I wouldn't have come to visit you. But doesn't that mean that it's only convention that binds us together? We are father and son, so we're naturally expected to show devotion to each other. If we don't, we get guilt feelings. But why? Are there any reasonable grounds for believing that devotion is biologically determined? We don't demand of ourselves that we should show devotion towards a neighbour or a colleague? I don't know if you understand what I mean.'
'Yes, I do. So that's the way you see things. A convention. May God forgive you those words, Gabriel. Some day you'll surely realize how mistaken you are.'
'That's what you've always said. As far back as I can remember you've prophesied a day when. . . . How different things might have been if you hadn't believed in God.'
'Or if you had believed in Him.'
'Yes. As things are, we are condemned to torment each other.'
'Don't blame God for that.'
'Not God. The idea of a God, the stubborn myth of a power which justifies actions and attitudes which the future will call inhuman. You believe that God is the object of a faith, but that's not true. God is the faith in God, and therefore God will die. He is dying day by day.'
'You are crazy.'

'No, I'm just the representative of a future which refuses to accept its inheritance, which refuses to carry God on its back.'
'Now you must go.'
'Yes.'
He walked to the door. He placed his hand on the doorknob. Then he turned and cast a final glance at his father sitting motionless in the high-backed chair, his eyes shut and his hands clutching the worn arms of the chair.

[Original title: *Møte*. Translated by James McFarlane]

BJØRG VIK

Liv

She sees that he is wearing his dirty green shirt as he is on his way out to fill the car up and buy tobacco, it is as if something rips inside her, she stops short between the bathroom and the kitchen and snaps at him:
'You're not going in that shirt?'
After he has gone, after the harsh voices, there is just the silence and the children creep around her and look past her, scared. She searches in the cupboard for something to give them, finds a packet of biscuits and carries on washing clothes in the bathroom. Straightens her back, runs her hand through her hair and catches sight of her face in the misted mirror: hard, taut, her eyes black and burnt-out, like stones.

The dial shows a quarter to six when the alarm rings. She stretches out a hand.
Hands.
The thought is simultaneous with the action: it is just our hands, it is our hands they want.
She stumbles out to the bathroom, one step at a time, it is like climbing a ladder, do not look down or the dizziness will come, do not look forwards or backwards, or the exhaustion will come. She gets dressed while Sven is in the bathroom, looks out the boys' clothes, puts the alarm clock in their room, makes the bed, drinks coffee, makes packed lunches, writes notes: the boys are to wash the stairs or shake the rugs, fetch in the washing if it rains, milk, bread, potatoes, remember to clean shoes, lock up bicycles.
At twenty past six they drive out between the blocks of houses, she half asleep and shivering in the front seat. That fine feeling of alertness from those first years, cold pure morning air, the newspaper boys, the first workers' buses, she does not feel it any longer. She looks listlessly at the trees along the road, the foliage is new and fresh, in the gardens there stand tulips, the grass has already been cut.

A thin haze in the morning light, it will clear, the day is getting itself ready, for others, not for her or Sven. His heavy hands on the steering wheel, hands, that is what they want. She rolls the window down, feels the air blowing on her skin, takes a breath:

Liv Nilsen, you're thirty-two, there's nothing wrong with you, you're fine.

They park in the narrow back street behind the factory, in the slow stream moving towards the cloakrooms they separate, the door is locked behind them, not that it really matters, but just the knowledge that they are locked in like animals. It makes them so small, so passive.

She puts on an apron and changes her shoes, fastens her locker, laughter from the young girls, the bodies around her, some words in passing, a smile, a greeting, she has long thought that it is a kind of comfort they give each other. They spread out to the machines and the benches in the great pottery-turning hall, the extractor fan is already going. The morning light is thrusting against the dusty windows, mingling with the light from the strip lighting on the ceiling, it does not matter what the weather is like, it does not reach them through the dirty window panes. All is as usual, the cement floor, the bare walls, the machines, the trolleys, the drying shelves.

The spindles turn, the hands do their work, she knows this job. When you polish a couple of thousand plates a day, you know the job. She has four spindles in front of her, the humming from those four spindles and from the others, the sound of the roller machines and the automatic plate machines and the intense sucking noise from the fan make it difficult to talk. She polishes one plate after another with the grinding disc and the sponge, two and a half thousand it must be by quarter to four. Now and then a plate goes into the reject bin, now and then she shifts her weight from one foot over to the other, now and then she straightens her back, tries to relax the tension in her shoulders.

She ought to think about something. It is as if the repetition in the work produces repetitions in her head, it is the same small circles she trudges round in, there are spindles in her head too. Around one of them whirr the boys, if only they do all right at school, if only they cycle carefully, if only they don't make a mess at home, don't ruin their clothes, remember to do the shopping. She feels the ache in the pit of her stomach again: if only they could have had a bit more energy with the boys, been a bit more cheerful, thought of things to do. Around the other whirrs the flat, what she has to do at home, what needs repairing, what new things they need, which bills are due. Sven is in this spindle too, he runs into one with the things and the bills, the car and the repairs. Again she feels the ache: poor Sven, eight hours with the trolleys and the kilns in the firing hall, home with her, a young old woman with grey skin and dead hair, aching shoulders, heavy legs, empty, empty, spindles in her head. A long time ago he talked of technical college, of electronics, but once you have gone in through the factory gates there are not many ways out. She cannot see any.

   She stayed at home for a few years when the boys were small, they managed. Sven took extra jobs, house-painting, roofing, demolition, she could not bear to see him wearing himself out day and night. And she never got used to using up all the money he earned and always being short. It was hard to begin at the factory again, she would rather have had a part-time job, she was half dead with tiredness by the time the children were in bed in the evening. Now the tiredness is different, it is a fog she trudges through all day long. And the spindles in her head turn more and more slowly, have less and less to spin round.

   She has set them as close as possible, red and white petunias in one box and pansies and dwarf pinks in the other. Perhaps they will have room for a box of tomato plants. She waters the plants, loosens the earth and pinches out the faded blooms, hears children shouting below on the open trampled stretches of grass between the blocks, sees the cars standing parked, the washing on the lines, the sandpits and bicycles and windows which gleam white in the afternoon sun.

   If they lived in a terraced house or a detached house, then perhaps many things would have been different. When they were saving up for a car they thought that many things would be different. It did not happen, but it was fine to dream about it happening.

   While she is tidying the flower boxes on the balcony, she often thinks about the house, what it would have looked like, how the sun would fall on the newly-mown lawn and the flowers along the wall, they would have deck-chairs and a parasol over the table.

   She tries to catch a glimpse of Stig and Kai down below, it is strange to see them at a distance, to see what they look like together with the others. Now and again she feels a sudden fear: what kind of working life will they have? what kind of world will they live in?

The plates whirr, the hands do their job, the machines hum, the fine dust in the air, the tiredness in her leg muscles, the spring day outside, the trolleys of crockery to and fro on the cement floor. She takes the plates off the plaster moulds, hand, disc, sponge, piles up the plates on the trolley as she finishes with them, she is pushing things into a gaping hole, into insatiable jaws. It is called production, it sounds fine, for her the word has no meaning.

What time is it? Will she make the piece-work rate?

There is no one who asks who she is, what she thinks, how she does the job, that has nothing to do with the matter, they count up the trays of polished plates, she has to polish two and a half thousand every day, that is all that counts.

She has got into the habit of seeing the pile of polished plates in front of her, she has worked out that there are about a hundred plates in a pile one metre high. So a thousand plates are ten metres, she polishes a pile twenty-five metres high every day. After a week her pile has grown, become a plate-tower of one hundred and twenty-five metres. How high is the tower after four weeks? Or after four months, four years, eight years? The Eiffel Tower is three hundred metres high, in three weeks she has polished a pile of plates higher than the Eiffel Tower. How many Eiffel Towers of plates has she built during these years? The thought of the pile makes her head spin, her wrists grow leaden, she tries to think of something else.

Does anyone count what they do in the office, how many letters they write, how many phone calls? Ridiculous thought. They wander in and out of the factory, just as they please, to the shops, to the dentist, they do not need a note in order to be let out and no one deducts it from their wages. There are rumours about the wages of the office staff, some of them are said to get double the amount of the top wage for shop-floor workers, nobody knows for sure, someone heard something. And they know about the villas they live in, the cottages they build, the cars they trade in.

When the female office staff walk through the hall they look after them, notice their clothes, their hair, their hands. Many would like a change of job, would like to get away from piece-work and hourly pay and the same tiring movements, it is said that some of them sell their souls in order to get on to a monthly salary.

Solidarity, says Gun. That is only a word, a word which belongs in songs and party speeches. All they want is to get away from where they are, the majority of them. When you have been walking in a fog long enough, plodding along like a trained animal at the machines long enough and seeing the others plod, then there are not many fine feelings left.

The little yard which separates the two wings, the factory building and the office block, that yard divides the world in two, into two different worlds. It is strange to think that they know so little about each other, that they have so little to say to each other.

She sees Hedvig's back, that round old back over the casting bench, she has been standing there for forty-four years. After the last wage rise she now gets almost ten kroner an hour. After twenty years she got a bonus payment of twenty-five øre an hour, a long-service bonus, they had a good laugh about that. After twenty-five years with the firm she was given the gold pin, when she finishes in a couple of years she will get two or three thousand extra for long and faithful service. And the vase, of course.

Gun says they are too passive, they must get involved, have opinions, come to meetings. She tells them that all the men earn almost fifteen kroner an hour, as if they did not know that.

Go to meetings? Who dares to say anything there? And who listens to what they say? About doing the same job?

Women!

That is what they think. They are not worth as much, they ought to stay at home. Those who have to work are just the ones who have done something stupid, since they cannot be provided for like other decent women. And if they both work, then they should just be pleased about the extra money the wife gets. It is as if they are not necessary here, not in the same way the men are.

And then *they* are to stand up in meetings and believe in themselves and make others believe what they say?

'They must understand one day,' says Gun, 'if we get a decent wage we can share the responsibility.'

'They don't want to share,' says Inger, 'they'd rather work themselves to death. They have to have us to boss about, you see.'

Gun asks why they put up with it. Gun can ask, she is young, not married, no children, she does not know the fog, the tiredness. There is a lot of gossip at the factory about Gun, that she has had an abortion, that she set a higher tempo for piece-work in the grinding shop, that she puts herself forward at works meetings, tries to impress the men.

The hands work. They stand there in stalls like silent cattle, letting themselves be milked.

If only they could have exchanged jobs, not done the same thing the whole time. But they do not understand it, do not know about production, time studies, work processes, no one has explained anything to them. Gun talks about bonuses and co-operative group management, they could share the responsibility, relieve each other, have a change. But they are used to things the way they are now, they are not sure if they dare do anything else. Perhaps the pay would be worse, perhaps they would have to work harder.

On Friday night she has cleaned the whole flat. On Saturday she changes the beds or cleans the windows, she has showered and washed her hair, in the afternoon she has to clean out the kitchen cupboards or bake. If they are going out for a trip on Sunday she has to prepare Sunday dinner as well. She knows that she cleans the windows more often than other people, washes clothes more often, and that Gun says she is wasting time and wearing herself out. But Gun does not know what it is like, what it looks like inside her.

She walks around the room, she has put red petunias in a bowl on the table, the sofa cover is worn, she should have taken that course in soft furnishings. Or the one in English or democracy at work or consumer training. She smiles, all these clever people who want to make you different, and who only make you smaller and even more stupid because you can never join in with any of it.

She gets changed, tries to put on some make-up, make her hair look nice. Today no one shall see that she stands at a machine eight hours a day, today she shall look like the others. The others, that is those with shining, brightly polished façades, well dressed, sunburnt, those with tulips in their gardens, a daily help and holidays abroad. They are well dressed in a different way from her, something casual about the expensive clothes, as if it's not all that important anyway. She has the feeling that they are making fun of it all, that they can afford to make fun of it too. And that she is stupid for paying so much attention to how she looks, and how Sven and the boys look, and the flat and the stairs and the windows.

She tidies up the newspapers, straightens the curtains. Sven is down at the garage washing the car, he will come home and change, and then they are going to town to do the Saturday shopping. She knows the prices and the special offers and knows where to buy things, afterwards they have a cup of coffee in the cafeteria.

It is half-past twelve, the bell rings, time for the lunch break.

She washes her hands and goes to the canteen, sits down at her usual table with Gun and Inger and Agnes. Sven sits together with some of his mates from the firing hall. Voices, laughter, scraping chair legs, people in and out of the door, the queue at the counter. The sunlight white and merciless through the windows, someone draws the curtains.

'You look tired,' says Gun, 'is it your back?'

'My shoulders,' says Liv and tries to relax in the tubular steel chair. Gun fetches coffee, they get out their sandwiches. How many times has she sat here and unwrapped sandwiches together with Gun and Inger and Agnes? Heard them talk about this and that, seen their hands, their faces, laughed together with them, been serious or fed up or miserable together with them.

They talk about the Monday film on television, afterwards Inger talks about the house they are building, about Fredrik and her who toil away on the site every evening, she can hardly get up in the morning. Inger chews her lower lip the whole time, it is something she has started to do recently, a jerky, rabbit-like gnawing. Agnes talks about the caravan they are going to buy, there is a toilet and a utility sink in it, she is going to make curtains.

'There's a meeting tonight,' says Gun, 'you haven't forgotten?'

'It's my washing day,' says Agnes.

'We're going to discuss the arrangement of the work force, the fact that they've managed to place all the women in the lowest paid groups. You must come.'

'We've got to finish concreting the foundations,' says Inger.

'You'll come, Liv?'

'I'll try.'

'You're all hopeless,' says Gun, 'we'll never get anywhere when you just don't bother.'

'They won't listen to us anyway.'

'Well, they certainly won't listen to you when you're at home doing the washing and watching TV.'

'Who's to do the washing then?' asks Agnes. She looks as if she is almost laughing.

'You should share it,' says Gun, 'you don't need to be slaves at home as well. I can't understand why you put up with it!'

Agnes laughs, nudges Inger with her elbow.

'Rolf do the washing? And Fredrik iron blouses and patch trousers?'

'I honestly believe you enjoy it,' says Gun. 'You enjoy toiling and slaving.'

'You're right,' says Liv, 'we are slaves. We put up with everything, that's why nothing will ever change.'

They look at each other, look into each other's grey faces in the harsh spring light, dry hard hands which grasp cigarettes, matches, coffee cups. No one laughs, no one says anything, Gun just sits and looks at them. It is as if she is using the silence now. Liv looks at her, she is not eager and insistent as she usually is. She seems to see a new expression in that young, broad face, a kind of despair. She feels the nearness of these women she has known so long, about whom she knows so much, feels Agnes's and Inger's old tiredness and Gun's new despair; in a way it hurts most to know about that.

She is standing at the spindles again, the familiar sound, the familiar movements, they calm her down, the repetition calms everything down in them. No one can stand and do the same thing, hour after hour, and continue to rage or despair. That is the best thing about it, the dulling effect. She knows that Gun would say it is the worst thing.

But there is that pile of plates. It has become an obsession with her, it rises up as high as a tower, as high as a skyscraper, stands swaying before her, a plate-tower as high as the sky which will one day collapse on top of her. It seems to her that if she could one day *see* that pile of plates she has polished, she would go mad.

She remembers Ida who suddenly went for the drying cupboards and overturned the trolleys, tore down everything around her, she went completely wild and they had to carry her out. Perhaps Ida had seen the pile.

She thinks about the peculiar rabbity chewing that Inger has started on, thinks about Agnes who is going to sew curtains for a caravan, earn money for a caravan. She dips her naked arm into the glaze and glazes one cup after another, she glazes twelve thousand cups a day. Nevertheless she can sit in the canteen and laugh, her laughter is comforting, without that they would perhaps not have been able to keep going.

They watch the Saturday variety show on television, the boys have had a bath, tea has been eaten, the beer drunk. She yawns, feels the ache in her shoulders. On the floor above they are having a party, music and laughter come in waves, in sudden gusts down through the block. Sven is sitting with Kai on his knee, they are laughing at something on the screen. She thinks about Sunday, it will no doubt follow the usual pattern, car trip, coffee in flasks, perhaps a football match or a dog show, home again, parents, brothers and sisters, the usual talk about children and illness and money, about cottages and boats. And home to the Sunday film, put the clothes for Monday's washing in to soak and know that there is a week ahead.

Sven gets the boys to bed while she washes up after the evening meal. There is nothing wrong with you, Liv, she thinks, the works doctor has only just told you that your blood test was fine, no blood-pressure or anything, recommended exercise and vitamin pills. If only she could get a little exercise in her head, in the slow spindles in there.

She says goodnight to the boys, puts her cheek against smooth childish skin, they smell of soap and clean sheets, it is good. In the sitting room Sven has put out small glasses and a little bottle, the fact that he did not get it out while the boys were up makes her feel warm towards him.

'Cheers,' he says and blinks at her with eyes narrowed, almost like the old days. She drinks and wishes that the brandy would make her more lively, so that she is not so tired and lifeless every night, falling asleep with her back to him. It is not that he forces himself upon her, he is just disappointed by it, and the next day becomes a little harder to get through. She thinks of Agnes, who tells her that when they have quarrelled, she and Rolf, they go to separate restaurants. It is almost as if she is boasting about it. We get on well together, thinks Liv, Sven would never think of doing anything like that.

On the floor above one of the children has woken up and is crying, they can hear the persistent crying together with the music and the thumps on the floor. She sees the heavy, thick-set body beside her, and knows how hard it has to work, what his body and her body have to endure every day, and nevertheless their bodies must have enough love left to give away. It is so still inside her, what was it like to feel something, dream of something, long for something?

'Cheers,' she says, and tries to smile as he lights the candle on the table.

At twenty to four they stand pressed up together in the corridors, they have changed, the smell of warm bodies mingles with the smell of colour dyes from the painting shop, the smell of dust and chemicals and skin, for her it all merges into one: the smell of used body. She thinks that it ought to be a fine smell, and does not understand why she finds it so disagreeable.

At a quarter to four they are let out, she manages to do a bit of shopping before they get into the car. Sven also smells of used body, and she knows that she does so herself. She looks at his hands, they look a little more insensitive every day.

With a kind of gentle shock she realizes that the fruit trees have finished blossoming, and she hardly noticed that the blossoms had come at all. She stares through the car window, hedges, trees, bushes, tries to gather in a little of this spring day. If they could have gone for a walk this afternoon, picked lilies of the valley, breathed in the fresh air, taken in the smell of may and leaves and sun. She thinks of the dinner that has to be cooked, the washing up, the fridge which has to be defrosted, the pile of ironing, the winter clothes which have to be put away. Oh heavens, the attic needs clearing out too.

The rest of the day passes at a steady plod, she sees herself doing the same things again and again, things which never make her any different, which never make anything any different. At the same time she is aware of all that she never gets done, books and papers she does not get read, people she never visits, things she never learns. The knowledge sits in this ache in the pit of her stomach, in the painful emptiness there.

Hasn't she just got herself to thank for it all?

That she did not get some higher education, a different job or a different husband? She has often thought that, worried at the thought, reproached herself for not being a different person.

Now she thinks differently: there is something behind it, something she cannot see clearly but can make out the shadow of. That a game is being played with people like her and Sven, that they are being drained and used and have not enough strength left to turn the game in their favour. And that *that* is what the game is about, that is what is happening all day long. And has been happening as long as she can remember, from when she left school, the whole time she lived at home and wished herself somewhere else, wished for something else, other things around her, other clothes, other people. When she went through the factory gates the first day, was it she who chose it? Or was it something which had made her like that, so that she only had that gate to go through?

The pile of ironing is as high as ever, if she leaves the rest till tomorrow then she will not be able to prepare dinner for a couple of days in advance, like she does every Wednesday. Sven has cleared out the waste pipe in the bathroom and helped Stig to mend a puncture on his bike, and then he has driven round to a friend's to help him to get his boat on the water.

She takes out the plug, stands the iron up on one end and lights a cigarette. Her feet are heavy. She thinks about the attic and the meeting at work, she remembers Gun's face in the lunch break.

While she is putting away the clothes, the boys come in and make a noise around her and rummage for slices of bread and cheese in the kitchen. Kai has switched on the television, and when she comes into the sitting room and sees the milk he has spilt on the floor, everything goes dark for her, she screams at him and slaps him hard in the face. In a flash, before she turns away, she registers the cold tearless stare. They are used to it now, used to the hard voice and the hard hands.

The hateful silence from the children settles around her, and when Sven stands there smelling of beer and oil and with varnish stains on his clothes and asks if she is not going to that meeting, she begins to cry.

She cries, and listens frightened to the sound of her own crying, thin sobs with hoarse noises in her throat, an animal's crying. Cries and is aware of the children in the doorway, of Sven's large helpless hands, the spring evening outside and the meeting she will not get to, and the thought takes shape inside her, becomes a scream inside her: who are they, what do they look like, the people who have made her life like this?

[Original title: *Liv*. Translated by Janet Garton]

DAG SOLSTAD

At the theatre

I had really given up hope of finding anything new in it now. To tell the truth I had begun to be bored by it. Not in such a way that I yawned, but I had reached that point of despair which is aversion. I knew that the next stage was apathy. That's why I am pleased that I discovered it – in spite of everything. Don't think that I am talking about a new interpretation, something which can stimulate my intellectual fantasy, and nothing more. I am talking about a new dimension. And I am very confused. Frightened in a way. Yes, frightened. But also relieved. Hope has been revived. But this sounds unclear, let me begin at the beginning, let me begin with myself.

I am a theatre-goer. Every evening I go to the little theatre on the edge of the town centre to see the same play being performed. How many years I have been doing this I do not know, but I can hardly remember having lived in any other way. Sometimes it has occurred to me that my passion for the theatre is of such a kind that the term theatre-goer seems strangely pale. Theatre-lover would be better. Though that does not fit either, I am not so much a theatre-lover, it is more mania than love which has driven me here. Perhaps a completely new word, theatromane, would fit best. For you see, I am dependent on this play in a particular way which is difficult to explain. Even now, when I know it inside out and can predict in advance even the tone of voice in which the lines will be spoken, and know exactly how far the hero has to stand from the orchestra pit at any given time, I would feel it to be an irredeemable act of betrayal if I stayed away for an evening. Why? I do not know. It is perhaps just a habit, but when a habit has become so fixed it does not explain anything.

Let me say a little about the play. Unfortunately I cannot go into details, I would just like to indicate that it is a continuous battle. Man against man. Unending. The characters change constantly, it can be a dwarf, an officer, a hotel manager, a porter, a passing gentleman in a black suit, etc. But one person is present in all the scenes, and that is the hero of the play. He is involved in all the battles, in fact where he is there is always a battle. A couple of times he is alone on stage, but his solitude is only apparent. Even the monologue he delivers reveals that new battles are on the way, or that the battle is continuing – in the monologue. Never a rest, never a refuge, never a chance to repose in beauty – but such is, I suppose, the nature of the theatre.

Throughout two acts these battles are fought, man against man, or man's battle against man for objects, on towards the final conclusion, an anticlimax where the hero stands wordlessly and looks back at the stage with a face empty of joy and stares out over the auditorium as if he is waiting for an applause which does not come – for I never applaud.

I sit in the stalls. There is no one in front of me, and no one beside me. But up in the circle I have occasionally been aware of the presence of others. I have never turned round, but sometimes I have heard coughing, the rustling of sweet papers, and quite often I have heard laughter. Since it is a serious play which is being performed, where there is not as far as I can judge a single moment which is conducive to laughter, I have deduced from this that it must be groups of schoolchildren who come here now and then to be educated in the noble art of going to the theatre. But on occasion it has sounded as if there were grown-ups laughing too, but that might have been the teachers, who, in order to try to disguise the fact that they are bad pedagogues, have shared in the laughter in order to give the impression that it is actually the right place to laugh. They no doubt thought they would get me to join in, but I'm too much of an old hand to be made a fool of in the theatre, and especially with this play, which I know inside out. But to be quite honest, I must admit that the laughter has at times seemed to me to be ironic. I have heard grown-ups laugh openly. Ironically. I have heard young people laugh. Maliciously. This has almost ruined the performance. The actors are disturbed, they pause for half a second or so, the rhythm of the scene is broken. But fortunately it has never caused any change in the actual style of the performance.

Not until last night. But that was not caused by any intervention from the circle up there in the dark. It was towards the end of the first act. I had been sitting and enjoying the dialogue, admiring the way in which the actors were fired by their roles, even though they had been saying the same lines, making the same movements since time immemorial. It struck me that it was recognition which had come to seem important to me recently. Of course I had been bored by the play, felt indifferent to it, but to be able to recognize something is a valuable thing. In a way I had never quite been able to accept the end, or the harrowing action. There had been too much conflict in my view. Not that I have anything against conflict in itself, but the outcome of a conflict is a victory and a defeat. I had enjoyed the victory, that I will say. But not the defeat. That pained me. It made me in the early days – when I had still not reconciled myself to the irrevocable – want to leap up on to the stage and ask: 'But can't you see? He's finished. Don't you understand? How can you behave as if nothing was wrong?'

But that was long ago. Now I had accepted the whole play. I knew that what happened happened, and what happened happened again and again. I had become the perfect theatre-goer or theatromane. Involvement had disappeared, it is true. But I had found something else in its place: security, a feeling of substance. I had achieved uninvolved involvement. I was involved in every single scene, without any results or consequences having any effect on me. I was not worried about how things were going to turn out. Because I knew that. I tried to feel what it was like to be each one of the characters – without going so far as to hope that the one I knew was going to lose should win, because that was an impossibility. I enjoyed the play as it was, the regularity of it. It could give me an indescribable feeling of pleasure to watch the actions of the hero just before he hit out at some poor wretch, how they were the same from one time to the next, how he knew his role perfectly, with what somnambulistic certainty he moved, yet without leaving any doubt about the fact that he put all of his ardent blood into the role every time. It was a brilliant acting performance – and the others supported him. In short: a perfect production.

There was only one thing I missed: what it was I cannot express exactly. Perhaps I get somewhere near to it when I say that I missed the specifically human element. In myself. You see, as the years passed I had the same feeling which I assume that experimental psychologists have when they sit there in their white coats and with gloves on their hands and watch the behaviour of their rats in the labyrinths. Not the first time they are going to try out their hypothesis, but when they are going to verify it for the 88th or 94th time. Then I think the psychologists must have the same good feeling which I had, the same pride in observing the operation of a law. But this predictability became a straitjacket, it sometimes made me feel a desire to get up, go out into the evening and wander along the cheerful streets, stand outside cafés and listen to the dance music coming from inside. But I did not do it, because deep inside, this predictability had become an obsession with me. It was for this reason that I paid particular attention to the laughter from the circle, felt sensitive about irony and sarcasm, coarseness. Because it gave rise to a fear of a break in the perfectionism. Ask a pedant, a perfectionist, what the greatest evil is. He will answer: irregularity. Without any doubt, irregularity.

But then last night something happened. Something which I have not been able to forget. Something which has made me confused. It was towards the end of the first act. It was while the hero was tormenting the hunchbacked dwarf. I saw it in the dwarf's face. The new dimension. The threat. The rebellion. I saw hatred gleam in his eyes. But it was not that. Hatred had always gleamed in his eyes. It was part of the role. Made the role moving, if I may say so. Neither was it the fact that the dwarf's hump suddenly became visible, seemed to grow. *That* was a plastic trick which I had long admired. But something new had entered. A defiance. Not against being tormented, for that defiance had also been there the whole time, that pride in the midst of degradation which had given the dwarf's role monumental power. But a new defiance, a new monumentality had appeared. A hesitation. I saw it just in that little tenth of a second as the dwarf was about to bow his head and the hump to grow and the lighting technician to let the light gather into a cone, which illuminated the hump like a halo. *He hesitated.* It was as if he did not want to. Did not want to bow his head, did not want to let himself be stared at on the stage like a degraded saint. I saw it. I am in no doubt about it. I jerked back in my seat. But then he returned to his role, bowed his head, let himself be tormented. But I who had been watching the scene for years, I saw that something new had entered. Despair about having to play this role. That everything is decided. That he could do nothing, that he could not do anything else, break out of the play, cry out, answer back, anything at all. Despair about all the countless possibilities which he was not allowed to make use of.

Then he just stood there. While the shaft of light encircled his head like a halo until the curtain fell.

That evening I had not noticed whether anyone was sitting in the circle. In the interval I listened more tensely than ever. Silence. I felt an amazingly strong desire to turn round and peer up at the circle under the roof, and also – entirely without reason – to turn round and see if anyone was sitting on the seats just behind me even though I had never noticed any noise coming from there. I even felt a desire to get up and go up to the circle and sit there during the next act, whether there was anyone sitting there or not. I had to force myself to remain seated sunk in deep thought as is my custom. But I listened. Silence. I knew that behind me the auditorium lay in darkness – they never put the lights up during the interval – heavy columns, garlands, carvings, and high up, but not far away, the circle where perhaps someone was sitting, perhaps no one was sitting, all lying in darkness just behind me. Just over my head there was a closed box, and now I wondered whether anyone was sitting there. In the early days when I was here it had often happened that I glanced up there, but the curtain was always closed. I had been preoccupied with whether anyone was sitting hidden in the darkness there, but I never heard any noise or applause from up there. Now I glanced up there again. I could just make out the heavy curtains which screened it off forbiddingly just over my head. As before. Silence. Stillness. I got out an old programme and tore it into tiny pieces.

For a long time the last act went according to plan. Despite my previous excitement, I soon calmed down again. I amused myself by saying the lines in my head before they were spoken on stage – habit had even taught me to pronounce them with the same diction as the speakers – and nodded in satisfaction when everything was obviously functioning normally. The same sequence of pauses between speeches as before, the same pitch, the actors stood at the same distance from each other, everything happened exactly as before.

The change happened suddenly. I can point exactly to where and when it happened. It was while the hero was standing alone on stage delivering an important monologue. Then a voice could be heard – it must have come from backstage, it must have been someone who was hidden in the wings – asking in an everyday tone of voice for a glass of water. But it must have been there right from the beginning, because when I heard the voice it did not come like a sudden rush of sound, but like a confirmation of something I had known for a long time. The whole thing must have shifted imperceptibly until it suddenly came to a point where a confrontation was unavoidable.

But I did not have time to ponder it, for suddenly all the actors appeared on stage. They must have followed a momentary impulse, for some were dressed in their costumes, while others were half naked and yet others changed into suits. The hero carried on as though nothing had happened. But one of them pushed him to one side. I saw his face, one half was made up, the other was obscenely white. It was as if he had two faces, one for the stage and one which was nakedly unborn and therefore frightening. He seized a vase of flowers, poured out the water which ran in a thin trickle across the stage floor and down into the orchestra pit, at the same time as he scattered the flowers to the winds. Then the others began to sing obscene songs. The hero went on with his monologue, but his voice was drowned. Then they stopped, and I heard the hero's voice. It had now become unreal, like a gramophone record which had been played so many times that no one could be bothered to listen any more. It was as if a pattern had got tangled, like a beautiful carpet where the threads were finely interwoven, and which now, before my helplessly fixed gaze, had whirled up and come away from its backing – which disintegrated into nothingness – and floated like flurrying coloured snowflakes over the stage. Or like figures engraved in a sheet of bronze, where the lines had suddenly risen from the hollows in the bronze and taken on a life of their own.

And after that things happened quickly. The half-naked actors drew back to the left side of the stage, behind the curtain, those in costume went to the right together with those who were dressed. Only one remained on the stage together with the hero, the one who had thrown the flowers, the one with the conflicting face. He was dressed in a light summer suit. From the sides faces appeared from behind the curtain, made-up faces, naked faces. They stared at me. I heard them laughing and fighting for the best places. Once one of them pointed at me.

The hero spoke his lines, finished his monologue and began on the first sentence of a dialogue. He stopped and waited for the reply. It did not come. The hero waited for the usual number of seconds and then continued. The man in the light suit threw back his head and laughed. The unborn face was turned towards me. Completely smooth, when he laughed the skin did not wrinkle, I could not see that he was laughing. I could only hear it.

He went over to the hero and placed his hand on his shoulder. The hero ignored him, spoke his lines – it was actually comical, I felt like laughing, but at the same time something told me that this was dangerous. The man in the light suit gave the hero a gentle push. The hero's face was drawn, he looked hurt, for a moment I felt sympathy for him. The orchestra began to play feverishly, and I heard someone wrestling with the curtain. Suddenly I realized that this was reality.

Even though it was a very gentle push, he swayed. I was amazed at how weak he was. He tried to stay on his feet, for a moment it looked as though he were going to manage it, but then the man in the light suit hit him on the shoulder and he fell against a tree in the background. It was pale brown like trees in children's water-colour paintings. I wanted to get up. I saw as if through a fever, a nightmare, that the curtain in front of the box was moving. I heard the doors to the foyer being opened. Was it someone going? Was it someone coming? He tried to get up, managed to get so far, but then sank down like a punctured bicycle wheel. The tree split. I saw that it was part of the set, it was cardboard. The light brown part curled over, I saw the back of it, colourless cardboard. At the same moment daylight became visible. It came from the back of the stage, through a window high up on the wall which I had formerly believed to be part of the scenery, and shone through the cardboard and into my eyes. I heard applause behind me, it started quite suddenly. The man in the light suit moved to one side, as if to let me see the fallen figure better. The cardboard bulged. Stronger light, intense light. He lay motionless. The applause roared out behind me, it sounded as if the whole circle was full of people watching, of small badly-behaved children and delighted teachers. And some could not stay up in the circle, they had to come closer, and now they were sitting just behind my back making a row.

And then the actor in the light suit, the one with the double face, raised his hands and clapped. He bowed to the hero and clapped. And in his mouth he had a flower and I thought I could see clearly that flowers were also springing out of the unborn skin of his face.

Then I got up. I had lost. But they clapped. Why were they clapping? I don't know, I don't know. If anyone asks me, I cannot answer whether it was in derision or in enthusiasm. I looked for the dwarf. He was not there. But I heard the champagne corks popping in the back room under the stage and I imagined to myself that it was the dwarf who was down in the dressing room drinking champagne. Out in the foyer I heard them open the outer door. The wind came in. It was cold. But no one left the theatre.

After a while a carpenter appeared and carried off the scenery.

Later, through the salvoes of clapping, I heard hammering. And I ask: is the scenery being repaired or destroyed?

Now a day has passed. It is evening again. Theatre time is approaching. A dark suit is lying on the chair in front of me. But I hesitate. The theatre is an uncertain place now. And I would like to stay at home and drink tea. But I must go. That is where necessity lies now. But I can decide not to go. Nevertheless the necessity is there. On the stage anything can happen. Who will win tonight? Am I excited? I am frightened. But fear is also necessary. I can run away from fear. But fear is necessary.

[Original title: *I teater*. Translated by Janet Garton]

Brief Biographies

Compiled by James McFarlane and Janet Garton

Tryggve ANDERSEN (1866–1920) was probably the most accomplished short-story writer of his generation in Norway, though too scrupulous a stylist and too self-critical an artist to achieve more than a quantitatively modest output. A characteristically 'nineties' figure, a neo-romantic who found himself greatly attracted by some of the larger figures of German Romanticism, especially Novalis and E. T. A. Hoffmann (to say nothing of his also being an Egyptologist manqué), he took 'honesty' as the keyword of his authorship, rigorously excising anything that seemed to approach falsity of tone or spuriousness of effect. His was a severely disciplined style, unsentimental, with nothing 'merely' confessional or self-revelatory. His best-known work, *I Cancelliraadens dage* (1897), set in the Napoleonic age, was more a cycle of short stories than the novel it proclaimed itself to be. 'Gilded revenge' ('Den gyldne hevn') was one of a collection of stories published in 1904 under the title of *Gamle Folk*.

Kjell ASKILDSEN (b. 1929) made his debut in the fifties with a volume of short stories (the main impact of which at the time was to shock local opinion by its sexual explicitness) and two rather impenetrable novels that had the critics making comparisons with Kafka. But he has subsequently established himself as much more a characteristically 'sixties' man, with his second volume of short stories, *Kulisser* (1966) – from which the present story, 'Encounter' ('Møte'), is taken – showing much more assurance and independence of style, and his novel *Omgivelser* (1960) offering a technically sophisticated statement that not only do we all live and act under the press of our individual contexts (including our fellow creatures) but we are inescapably also essential elements in the determining contexts of the lives of others. The result was that this novel offered a kind of up-dated version of the *Wahlverwandtschaften* theme. His novel of 1974, *Kjære, kjære Oluf*, examines some of the more unexpected side-effects of women's liberation.

Jens BJØRNEBOE (1920–76) was not only a novelist, dramatist, and poet but also one of the leading polemicists of his day, a controversial figure who deliberately set out to antagonize the Establishment. There are two main themes in his work: firstly, an attack on all forms of unacceptable authoritarianism; secondly, an obsessive preoccupation with the problem of evil, both with reference to concrete political and social situations (as in his novel about the Second World War, *Før hanen galer*, 1952), and in a more abstract and metaphysical sense, as in the trilogy *Frihetens øyeblikk* (1966), *Kruttårnet* (1969), and *Stillheten* (1973), his best-known work. A man of wide-ranging talents, Bjørneboe tried his hand at many genres, ranging from classical sonnets to Brecht-inspired social dramas, though in fact the short story was not a form in which he was particularly active. 'Life and the youth' ('Ynglingen og livet') was first printed in *Ordet*, no. 1, 1960, and later incorporated with a few slight changes as a chapter of *Stillheten*.

Bjørnstjerne BJØRNSON (1832–1910), Ibsen's great contemporary and rival, a man of extraordinarily varied gifts and interests who gave in prodigal fashion the wealth of his astonishing talents: as author, journalist, public speaker, editor, theatre director, and a score of other things besides. His writings are the enduring elements of a life that was devoted to causes: national, political, social, literary, educational, linguistic, theatrical. As a lyric poet, he reached heights of sublimity unapproached by any other writer in Norway; as a dramatist, he initiated some of the most important developments in European drama in the nineteenth century; as a prolific novelist, it has been said of his work that 'his victories were resounding, his mistakes tremendous'. His shorter narrative pieces, especially his so-called 'Peasant Tales' of the late 1850s and 1860s, were uniquely important in the development of the genre in Norway; particularly arresting was the terse and understated nature of the conversational exchanges, the simple reticence of the characters, which more than anything held the narrative taut. The piece included here, 'The Father' ('Fadren'), was first published in 1860.

Johan BORGEN (1902–79), a writer of elegant and witty, often satirical, prose in many genres: novels, short stories, essays, and journalism. A persistent theme of his work is the existential problem of identity, of creating one's own personality in a world which seems to offer so many conflicting possibilities. This theme is illustrated most fully by the character of Wilfred Sagan in the *Lillelord* trilogy (3 vols, 1955, 1956, and 1957): a gifted man capable of fulfilment in several directions, he cannot commit himself wholeheartedly to any, but postpones the choice until that in itself becomes a choice. Disintegration of personality and its laborious rebuilding, often through flashbacks to early memories, recurs in many of his novels of the post-war period. Many of his short stories have become Norwegian classics, with their ability to capture a dramatic conflict or evoke a mood or a scene in a few lines. The best-known of several collections is *Noveller i utvalg 1936–1961* (1961), from which this present story, 'In the grass' ('I gresset'), is taken.

Oskar BRAATEN (1881–1939), novelist and dramatist, who from his original working-class background in the poor East End of Oslo worked his way up to a career as a bookseller and author. He was the first Norwegian to write about the hard and poverty-stricken lives of the industrial workers of Oslo; but he is less concerned with political and social reform than with a warm and sympathetic portrayal of the workers' struggles, their solidarity and their courage. He gives a particularly affectionate picture of the women workers and their everyday heroism, as in his best-known plays *Ungen* (1911) and *Den store barnedåpen* (1925), and in many short stories. 'Going home' ('Heimreisa') is taken from the collection *Mens hjulene står* (1916).

Solveig CHRISTOV (b. 1918) has written novels, short stories, and plays, mostly in a markedly realistic style, with a certain emphasis on psychological studies of sexual conflict, as in *Syv dager og syv netter* (1955) and *Elskerens hjemkomst* (1961). Other of her novels are symbolic and allegorical studies of the human dilemma. She came relatively late to the short-story form, and her first collection, *Jegeren og viltet* (from which this present story, 'The Glory of Mankind' ('Menneskets herlighet'), is taken), did not appear until 1962, by which time she had already published eight novels and two plays. Many would claim that, despite this, her best work is possibly to be found in the shorter narrative form.

Olav DUUN (1876–1939), novelist and short-story writer, was in one sense a deeply committed regional author: the geographical setting of his works is almost always the craggy coastal district running north from Trondheim; and he wrote in a *Nynorsk* which was powerfully influenced by the dialect of that region. On the other hand, along with this there went a very modern sensitivity and a sophistication of mind which gives his work a universality of meaning and a cultural currency far beyond its regional constraints. It was once said of him by a distinguished Danish contemporary that, by comparison, André Gide could seem a trifle provincial. His chief work, *Juvikfolke* (1918–23), a six-volume novel cycle, has been published in English translation as *The People of Juvik* (1930–5). Two other of his novels are also translated: *Det gode samvite* (1916, as *Good Conscience*, 1928) and *Menneske og maktene* (1938, *as Floodtide of Fate*, 1960). Duun is without doubt one of the most important novelists writing in Norwegian this century. The story with which he is represented here – 'The Chapel' ('Bedehuset') – was first published in 1930.

Torolf ELSTER (b. 1911) belongs to the third generation of a family of writers, both his father and his grandfather having made their marks as authors during the late nineteenth and early twentieth centuries. The background to many of his own novels – as indeed of the short story 'In a small room' ('I et lite rom') included here and taken from the published collection *Klovnen* (1953) – is often the larger international political scene of which he has remained all his life an informed observer: the Hitler era, the Czech crisis, the war years and after have all directly served his narrative purposes. His characteristic skill lies then in the way in which he brings the interpersonally political into fictional relationship with the individually psychological, whereby both are illuminated.

Johan FALKBERGET (1879–1967), novelist and short-story writer, had his roots deep in the mining community of Røros. Although still a young man when his first novel was published in 1907, he had already spent twenty years working as a miner. It is this close contact with the life of the community that gives all his work its powerful sense of locality – the valleys and the mountains of Rondane. At the same time, his novels have a strongly defined historical dimension, and the sense of the past is vividly conveyed. His most important works are the novels (or novel cycles) *Den fjerde nattevakt* (1923, translated as *The Fourth Night Watch*, 1968), the three volumes of *Christianus Sextus* (1927–35), and the four volumes of *Nattens brød* (1940–59). 'Approaching death' ('Fegd') was first published in 1910 in the collection *Vargfjeldet*, and later in a heavily revised form (which forms the basis for the present translation) in *Runer på fjellvegen* in 1945.

Arne GARBORG (1851–1924) was possessed of a restless questing spirit and a penetrating and analytical mind that delighted in the examination of those social and moral problems that faced the Norway of his day: the religious conflicts that attended the clash of positivism, pietism, and other sectarian movements; the so-called 'morality debates' that centred on the notorious Christiania Bohême; and the threat to traditional rural life styles from the encroachment of urbanization. Though he was unusually versatile – a novelist of power, an occasional dramatist, a lyric poet of haunting quality, and a critic and essayist – he only rarely attempted the short-story form. Two of his novels of the nineties have been translated: *Fred* (1892, as *Peace*, 1930) and *Den burtkomne Faderen* (1899, as *The Lost Father*, 1930). He became in time one of the leaders of the *Nynorsk* movement, and was one of the first to display its poetic capabilities. 'Dying' ('Døy') was written in 1891 and published in *Fjell-luft og andre småstykke* (1903).

Knut HAMSUN (1859–1952), without doubt by international standards the best-known and most widely read author writing in Norwegian in this century, and probably – as many would claim, though others would vehemently, for essentially extrinsic and indeed political reasons, dispute – the greatest. Author of a score or so of major novels (all of which have been translated into English as well as into other world languages), of several plays and of a modest measure of lyric poetry, and Nobel Prize-winner in 1920, he has delighted generations of readers by his sovereign command over the narrative medium and by the exuberance of his inventiveness, just as he has also exasperated others by the particular social and political values implicit in his novels. He turned only comparatively rarely to the short-story form, though it might be argued that some of his medium-length fiction – such as the early *Hunger* (1890) or *Pan* (1894) – might properly be classed as Novellen rather than novels; the sureness and delicacy of touch he does show in these shorter works makes one regret that he did not attempt the genre more often. The present story, 'Slaves of love' ('Kjærlighedens slaver'), was published in 1903 in the collection entitled *Kratskog*.

Sigurd HOEL (1890–1960), novelist, essayist, and critic, was a left-wing radical who in his youth was a member of the influential group of young intellectuals associated with the periodical *Mot Dag*, together with Arnulf Øverland and Helge Krog. He campaigned in his writing for political and social reform, including greater equality for women (as in *En Dag i Oktober*, 1931, translated as *One Day in October*, 1933) and a more liberal upbringing and education of children, of whom there are in his work many sympathetic portraits, particularly of the sensitive Anders in *Veien til verdens ende* (1933). He pointed an accusing finger at the repressive patriarchal society which he saw as the root cause of Nazism, an evil of which he was aware early in the 1930s, and to which he returned again and again in his novels (for example, *Møte ved milepelen*, 1947, trs. *Meeting at the Milestone*, 1951, and *Stevnemøte med glemte år*, 1954). Influenced by Freud and Wilhelm Reich, his novels and stories contain many fine psychological studies of the growth of an individual mind and how it can become stunted, how repression and puritanical intolerance can generate a fear of life and of love. 'The Murderer' ('Morderen') was published in *Prinsessen på Glassberget* (1939).

Ragnhild JØLSEN (1875–1908) was born into an ancient landowning family living in patriarchal splendour at Enebakk, east of Oslo. When she was a child her father went bankrupt as a result of unwise speculations and was forced to sell the family estate. The region, the family tradition and its financial failure provide the background to nearly all she has written: mostly Gothic-romantic novels shot through with macabre decay and decadent eroticism. Often these works have a fiercely independent and unconventional central female character, similar to herself. But her acute observation of the estate workers, their miserable living conditions, and the impact of industrialization also bore fruit in short stories in a more realistic vein, including 'Hanna Valmoen', collected in *Brukshistorier* (1907), widely considered to be her best achievement. After her travels abroad (notably to Italy, where she met Hans E. Kinck, who admired her writing and helped with much good advice) she returned home to live in a small house on the Enebakk estate. But she found it hard to settle to a quiet life and died of an overdose of sleeping drugs at the age of 33.

Alexander KIELLAND (1849–1906) combined in his novels a stern radicalism of outlook – 'You must read the *whole* of Stuart Mill', he commanded his sister in 1880 – with a deft and elegantly ironical style that derived much from his wide reading of European authors: Kierkegaard, Dickens, Heine, Strindberg, and a number of contemporary French novelists. Several of his novels exist in English translation, including what is probably his masterpiece *Garman og Worse* (1880, trs. *Garman and Worse*, 1885) and its sequel *Skipper Worse* (1882, trs. 1885). He also published two volumes of short stories (in 1879 and 1891, many of them translated into English); it was the kind of narrative writing he found most congenial, appealing both to his sense of controlled form and to his delight in giving pointed expression to his views on contemporary social and moral abuses. 'At the ball' ('Balstemning') is taken from the collection of 1879, entitled *Novelletter*.

Hans KINCK (1865–1926) was a close contemporary of Knut Hamsun, and (many would claim) a writer of comparable stature, though in terms of literary quality in many ways his polar opposite. His was a mind tormented by the larger problems of existence, but sustained by the conviction that, in the unending struggle to comprehend life with its seemingly unpredictable crises and catastrophes, writing was an indispensable forensic tool. He was a prolific writer, not only of novels and short stories – of which he published eleven volumes between 1895 and his death in 1926 – but also of poetic and prose drama. Only one of his novels has been translated into English, and that by no means his best: *Ungt Folk* (1893, as *Young People*, 1929). His most impressive works are probably his poetic drama *Driftekaren* (1908) and his three-volume novel *Sneskavlen brast* (1918–19). 'White anemones' ('Hvidsymre i utslaatten') is taken from the collection *Flaggermusvinger* (1895).

Jonas LIE (1833–1908) is traditionally associated with Ibsen, Bjørnson, and Kielland as one of the 'Big Four' of nineteenth-century Norwegian literature, a novelist whose popularity during his own lifetime was that of a great innovator: the man who wrote the first novels of the sea, the first novels of commercial life, the first truly realistic accounts of northern Norway in modern times. But to concentrate on this is to overlook one of the more important sources of Lie's narrative power: a chthonic fantasy, a delight in the mysterious and the irrational that lies at the centre of his work, however much the staider realism of some of his other and often more highly esteemed novels seems to belie it. This quality is immediately evident in the story included in this anthology, 'Isaac and the priest of Brönö' ('Isak og Brønøpræsten'), taken from his collection of shorter narrative pieces *Trold* (1891, translated as *Weird Tales from Northern Seas*, 1893).

Agnar MYKLE (b. 1915). The story 'Raisins of degradation' ('Skjenselens korinter') is taken from the collection *Taustigen*, published in 1948.

Torborg NEDREAAS (b. 1906), a novelist and short-story writer, whose books contain many sensitive portraits of people living lonely, isolated lives and longing for warmth and affection. She has also written politically committed literature, in the form of an anti-NATO novel. She is, however, best known for the series of books about the girl Herdis: *Trylleglasset* (1950), *Musikk fra en blå brønn* (1960), and *Ved neste nymåne* (1971). *Trylleglasset* (from which the present story, 'Red reflections' ('Røde reflekser'), is taken) consists of a series of chapters composed like short stories, set in the writer's native Bergen; in it she gives an account of the early life of the thoughtful and impressionable girl, torn by the conflict between her parents but finding inner reserves of strength to combat her despair.

Sigbjørn OBSTFELDER (1866–1900), poet and short-story writer, was perhaps the most internationally attuned of Norway's 'nineties' generation of writers, with close affinities to Walt Whitman, to Baudelaire, and to Jens Peter Jacobsen, and occupying a position very much in the mainstream of what was to become European Modernism. His mind, endlessly searching for enlightenment and reassurance about life's larger mysteries and about his own role in existence, was greatly vulnerable to self-doubt, much tormented by a sense of alienation. His lyric poetry, on which his reputation mainly rests, held a precarious equilibrium between sentiment and sentimentality, between sobriety and ecstasy, between the chaste and the erotic, between the worldly and the cosmic. His prose, not only in his short stories but also in his astonishing semi-fictive, semi-confessional *En præsts dagbog* (1900), is assertively 'lyrical'. 'The Plain' ('Sletten') was one of two short stories published under the title of *To novelletter* in 1895.

Arthur OMRE (1887–1967) began his writing career with a flurry of novels in the late 1930s, publishing his first book at the age of 47. In these works, and in the later post-war period, he examined (with a measure of first-hand experience to guide him) the world of criminality, the mentality of prison life, the anguish of escape and flight, the tensions of being on the run. Only after the war did it become apparent that the form best suited to his narrative talents was the short story. In his clipped, compacted – as some have said, 'hard-boiled' – style, immediate in its precise observation yet oblique in its meaning, laconically ironic, there was a distinctly American influence: he always enjoyed it when people compared him with Hemingway. 'Curried eel' ('Ål i karri') is one of his more light-hearted pieces taken from the volume entitled *Stort sett pent vær* (1948).

Arnulf ØVERLAND (1889–1968) was primarily a lyric poet, indeed one of Norway's leading poets of the twentieth century. But he was active in other genres, too; and alongside volumes of essays, speeches, and articles, he also in the course of his career brought out three collections of short stories: *Den haarde fred* (1916), *Deilig er jorden* (1923), and *Gud plantet en have* (1931), from which the present story, 'Missing, presumed dead' ('Den savnede'), is taken. In his prose, as in his poetry, there is a spare precision, a willed strength, and a direct and uncompromising honesty. His entire career as an author was marked by a passionate and courageous commitment to those values and aspects of life in which he had faith – a courage which incurred the wrath of the Nazi occupying authorities and led to his incarceration in Sachsenhausen concentration camp from 1942 to 1945.

Nils Johan RUD (b. 1908) may be credited with contributing as much to the development of the short story in Norway by his editorship of the periodical *Magasinet* as he did as a practitioner of the art itself. His forty years in the editorial chair gave both guidance and encouragement to the genre. He is himself a prolific writer, whose six novels published in the thirties established him as an author wholly absorbed by the problematic relationship that exists between nature and human nature. His first published volume of short stories, *Fri jord*, did not come out until 1945; and this he followed by what most people would claim as his major work, a novel trilogy (1947–9) about the brutalizing impact of war upon human nature. Since then he has published a good round dozen or more fictional works, including at least a further six volumes of short stories. The present story, 'You are no older than you were' ('Du er ikke eldre enn du var'), first appeared in 1972.

Cora SANDEL (the pen-name of Sara Cecilia Margareta Gjørwel Fabricius, 1880–1974) is a novelist and short-story writer of international distinction, best known outside Norway probably for her brilliantly observed *Alberte* trilogy: *Alberte og Jacob* (1926, translated as *Alberta and Jacob*, 1962), *Alberte og friheten* (1931, trs. *Alberta and Freedom*, 1963), and *Bare Alberte* (1939, trs. *Alberta alone*, 1965). A comparative latecomer to authorship, she published her first book at the age of 46 after a chequered and often hand-to-mouth existence, fifteen years of which were spent in Paris in a vain endeavour to establish herself as a painter. In her novels she shows a consummate skill in her capacity to portray women: their dreams, frustrations, sufferings and (rare) triumphs in what is for them often a hostile or unsympathetic or indifferent world, and in conditions and among conventions that stifle or impede fulfilment. Her contempt for the ways of small-town society is total; her repudiation of the tyranny of the conventional 'woman's role' is entire; and her sense of fellow-feeling for the lonely, the vulnerable, the hypersensitive is profound. Other of her works which have been translated into English include *Kranes konditori* (1945, as *Krane's café*, 1967) and *Kjøp ikke Dondi* (1958, as *The Leech*, 1960). 'Cousin Thea' ('Kusine Tea') was published in the collection of short stories entitled *Mange takk, doktor* (1935).

Aksel SANDEMOSE (1899–1965), novelist and essayist, was born in Denmark and his first books were written and published in that country. In 1929, however, after an early and restless career which included some years at sea and a period spent working in Canada, he returned to Scandinavia, settled in Norway, and thereafter wrote in Norwegian. His work shows an almost obsessive preoccupation with those deeper sources of human conduct that run to extremes, those mysterious and irrational impulses that result in explosive violence and even murder. *En flyktning krysser sitt spor* (1933, translated as *A Fugitive Crosses his Tracks*, 1936) explores the mind of a murderer in what is a technically virtuoso composition, interweaving association, symbol, and myth into a narrative of extraordinary density. This was followed in 1936 by another complexly wrought work, *Vi pynter oss med horn* (trs. *Horns for our adornment*, 1939), from which the present story of 'The Rat' ('Rotten') is taken. In the post-war years his output of novels and stories, articles, 'epistles', travel commentaries and other works was prolific and qualitatively impressive.

Amalie SKRAM (1846–1905) was a controversial writer whose novels provoked much criticism during her lifetime for their 'unfeminine' outspokenness, especially on the theme of female sexuality. She attempted to portray the harsh reality of life as she saw it without any softening; her central characters are often women whose ability to love and be loved has been destroyed by their repressive milieu and upbringing. Although she was not a programmatically Naturalist writer, she had much in common with the movement: a basic conviction that the darker forces in life were usually predominant, and that there was little one could do to escape from the influence of heredity and environment. She is remembered above all for her novel series *Hellemyrsfolket* (1887–98, 4 vols.), an intense and grimly depressing story of a family marked by poverty and alcoholism. 'Karen's Christmas' ('Karens jul') first appeared in the pages of *Politiken* in 1885 and was then reprinted in the collection *Fire fortællinger* (1892).

Dag SOLSTAD (b. 1941) was a member of the group of young writers connected with the magazine *Profil* in the mid-1960s and made his debut with modernistic short stories printed in that magazine. Towards the end of the decade, like many others of his generation, he became convinced of the necessity for political involvement – a conviction which eventually led him to join a Marxist-Leninist group of the Socialist party. In his best work, such as the novel *25.september-plassen* (1974), a study of the development of Norwegian society since 1945 culminating in the Common Market referendum of 1972, told through the fortunes of a working-class family, he combines a political message with a fine sense for significant detail. His most ambitious work to date is a trilogy about the Second World War (with volumes published in 1977, 1978, and 1980), in which he attempts to write the history of the war from the point of view of the working class, which was in his opinion betrayed by those in power. 'At the theatre' ('I teater') was first published in a group anthology (Gruppe 66) in 1966, and was reprinted in *Dag Solstad. Et festskrift til 30-årsdagen, 16 juli 1971*.

Kristofer UPPDAL (1878–1961), poet and novelist, was forced by family circumstances to leave home and start earning his living as a child, becoming first a farm worker and then a miner and construction worker. He took an active part in union work, but at the same time studied and read on his own, until in 1913 he married and decided to try to live by his pen. In his poems and his novels it is above all the life of the migrant construction worker, 'rallaren', which he describes, the tough physical environment and the sense of adventure and of freedom which compensated for the lack of material, bourgeois comforts. His most important work is *Dansen gjenom skuggeheimen* (1910–24), a series of ten novels with varying but connected main characters, through whose colourful lives Uppdal conveys a wide-ranging – and at the same time highly subjective – account of the foundation and growth of the Norwegian Labour movement. 'By Akerselva' ('Ved Akerselva') is from the collection *Ved Akerselva og andre forteljingar* (1910).

Tarjei VESAAS (1897–1970) was a poet, novelist, and short-story writer. A farmer's son from Telemark, Vesaas decided early to become a writer rather than a farmer; but his work remains imbued with a sense of the importance of roots, and of the strength which man can draw from his natural surroundings – as in *Det Store Spelet* (1934, translated as *The Great Cycle*, 1967) in which a rebellious farmer's son matures into an acceptance that the farm is where he belongs. In his novels, as in his poems, Vesaas's language (he wrote in *Nynorsk*) is lyrical, deceptively simple, and full of imagery. He conveys his meaning often in terms of complex central symbols that illustrate man's isolation and his urgent need for contact and communication. There is the dark house in *Huset i mørkret* (1945), representative of the atmosphere of war-time Norway, with its silent threatening corridors of loneliness and the determination which will not be cowed by the nameless terror at the centre; the ice palace in *Is-slottet* (1963, trs. *The Ice Palace*, 1966), in which the frozen waterfall becomes an image of a withdrawal into dangerous solitude and which must be broken through for life to flow once more; or the bridge in *Bruene* (1966, trs. *The Bridges*, 1969) which expresses the possibility for two young people to reach out and help a third who would otherwise perish. 'It snows and snows' ('Det snør og snør') was first published in 1959 in *Ein vakker dag*.

Bjørg VIK (b. 1935) has probably had her greatest successes as a short-story writer, though she has also written novels and plays of distinction. Most of her works are set in her native Oslo and depict the harassed and stressful lives of those living and competing in a consumer society. In her early works there is a tendency to concentrate on the relationships of young married couples, the problems of jealousy and infidelity. More recently her scope has widened to include a greater range of human and social conflicts, from the rivalry of schoolgirls and their training in modelling themselves on an idealistic 'feminine' pattern, to the cautious and fearful lives of ageing spinsters, who seem to disapprove of the world and yet only need some small kindness to be able to respond warmly. Particularly intense and sympathetic are her portrayals in the short stories in *Kvinneakvariet* (1972) – from which the present story, 'Liv', is taken – and *Fortellinger om frihet* (1975) of women in their middle years, desperately trying to fulfil a double role as housewife and wage-earner and feeling that they fail on both counts, and of feminists struggling to create a new role and a new ethos and not quite knowing how to.

F